Despite the Angels

Madeline A Stringer

Published by Moonsong Books.

This book is dedicated to the memory of my Dad,
Richard (Dick) Stringer.

It is also for my husband, George Gogan,
who made me get on with it.

"Our birth is but a sleep and a forgetting:
The soul that rises with us, our life's Star,
hath had elsewhere its setting,
and cometh from afar:
not in entire forgetfulness,
and not in utter nakedness,
But trailing clouds of glory do we come
from God, who is our home"

Intimations of Immortality, William Wordsworth

"A little while, a moment of rest upon the wind,
and another woman shall bear me."

The Prophet, Kahlil Gibran

My name is Jotin

and I am exasperated with this 'guardian angel' job. David will be here to get married in a minute, and it's not in The Plan. He's meant to marry Lucy, not Kathleen. I have been trying to stop him for two months now with no success. It's a crazy system, putting these humans here on Earth without telling them the plan and giving them free will. And we have to 'guide' them without an easy means of communication. They think they're on their own and don't listen. As David would say, it is bloody stupid. And he would say, if he only knew. No, if he knew he'd be clinging to me, begging me – "Save me, Jotin, save me!" – and I would. Of course I would. I love the silly creature, have done for millennia, since he was brand new and I had just been promoted. He was one of the first souls to be put into my care, before going into his first earth life. But he has never been very good at hearing me in any of his lives and this time he's woeful.

I wish we were given bodies, then we could grab the silly fools and push them where they needed to go. If I had a body David would be safely in hospital, not on his way to get married. As it is, he felt only a tiny draught as some of my energy punched through his face. I know, I know; I shouldn't have done it, I should respect his energy field, but I mean really – I had tried everything.

I had to get out of the house. I couldn't watch his smug grin a moment longer. That's why I'm here. Hovering in a church garden, if this sad square of grass merits such a title. I should go inside and try to put a stop to this nonsense, but I'm running out of ideas.

The guests are arriving now. The women's smiles are bright and false. The men are, appropriately, wearing black - the colour of mourning in this culture. Here comes David now, still grinning.

I'm not much help to anyone. Spirit guides are supposed to be calm, knowing what we do, but I've been in a human body often enough to make me irrational and furious sometimes. And I'm quite good at using humans' best bad language, which strangely, can soothe my energies a little. It doesn't make me feel less helpless, or less angry at Kathleen. She thinks she's getting what she wants.

Big mistake.

My darling idiot boy is about to waste another of these precious lives.

Chapter 1
Dublin, May 1972

David emerged from the church, his bride on his arm, grinned at his envious pals and looked around the small garden at his friends and relatives gathered in the sunshine. He watched two small nephews, uncomfortably dressed, chasing each other just inside the railings. Then he noticed some flowers. He stared, only realising after a few moments that the flowers were on the T-shirt of a girl standing outside the railings, looking in at the wedding party. She was licking a choc-ice, paying attention to the piece of sliding chocolate, and drinking in the details of the wedding. David smiled at the sight. *Jotin leapt up and down and shouted to the girl's guide -*

"She's too young, I told you. Stop trying to get them together. Get her out of here. I'll talk to you later."

"Nice one, David, hold it!" David smiled vaguely towards the photographer, but he was watching the little girl with the choc-ice, noticing that she was holding the handlebars of her bicycle with one hand and managing her ice cream with the other. There was a loaf of bread in the front basket of her bike. Flowers on shirts, thought David, what is it about flowers?

"Nothing now, David. She's not for you now," said Jotin.

"OK, Lucy, my darling," said Trynor, as he concentrated, his energies pulling at the wheel of Lucy's bike. "Come on, we're not wanted." The bike fell, the bread fell out of the basket, and Lucy turned around to rescue it before the bag of tomatoes could roll all over the path. She hauled the bike upright, got up on the saddle and pedalled away.

David watched the two boys, who were fighting now, before turning to his new wife.

"OK, Kathleen?" he asked, "Not too much for you?" Kathleen smiled at him and shook her head, her glossy hair bouncing under the veil.

"No. Everything is just fine, thanks."

James came over, all Best Man efficiency.

"We really should be moving, if we've to get to the hotel by two." David and Kathleen walked with self-conscious dignity towards the car under a shower of confetti.

Lucy was sitting at the kitchen table, eating a tomato sandwich and breathlessly describing the wedding to her parents and sister.

"The bride had a long white dress with lacy bits and it had a long tail out the back that people stepped on by mistake and there were three ladies in pink dresses down to the ground and little creamy waistcoats and they had bunches of flowers too like the bride and there were two little girls smaller than me -"

"My size?" Alison butted in.

"One was about your size and one was very little, maybe she was three,"

"Oh my goodness," said Lucy's mother, "imagine the trouble of controlling a three year old at a wedding!"

"I think she was being good. She was holding the older girl's hand," said Lucy after some thought, "and there was a big black car waiting for them, with ribbons on it." Her eyes were shining.

"Where was this wedding? I hope you weren't at George-n-John's, it's much too far away." Lucy's father looked stern.

"Of course I wasn't. It was at that church just past the shops. The one we never go into."

"Our Lady of the blessed somethings. And was there a groom at this wedding?"

"I don't know, what is it?"

"The man who is getting married."

"Oh Daddy, of course!" Lucy considered this, "There would have to be, wouldn't there? I think he was just in black."

"You women," said her dad, "see nothing but the clothes."

"Well, when I was busy watching, the bike fell over and I had to rescue it, so I didn't see everything. Can you please take off the trainer wheels? Alison is far too old for them, they're loose anyway - that's how it fell and they get in my way. And it's embarrassing, I'm ten. Actually, I think I need a bigger bike, then we wouldn't have to share. Can I have a bigger bike, Dad, please?"

"Yes, Daddy, get another bike, then I can keep the staylisers on. I'll fall if they're off. It could just be my bike, with staylisers."

"Stabilisers, baby!" Lucy mocked.

10

"I'll think about it. Help Mum with the tidying, both of you. I want to get on with the garden while it's dry."

Jotin was waiting when Trynor arrived. If he had had a body he would have been sitting still, staring into the middle distance. As it was, his energies were just a little flat.

"I told you it wouldn't work. That you were too late, that she is too young for him. Stop trying to get them together now."

"It's only twelve years. That's nothing. Why are you so fussed about it? I'm seven hundred years older than you and we get on fine. And my little Spanish Infanta was only three when she was betrothed; it worked out well."

"Oh, Trynor, that was hundreds of years ago and because her parents were royalty. We just used the fashion of the times and their social surroundings. Times have changed. Did you still not take another life?"

"I did, but I could only be spared a short one. I had to die young, during the second big war. But I got to taste some food. The latkes were wonderful - and strudel! It was almost worth it for the strudel. The hunger later was terrible, it hurt. I certainly know now why humans are so interested in food, when it hurts if you have none. The other children cried."

"Did you not cry?" Jotin was interested; he could remember being in several wars.

"No. I seemed to remember here. I knew there was more than that camp. I think I could hear my guide. When the end came, I held some of the children and told them it would be all right and they were calmer."

"Good for you. So there is some value in spending all your time here!"

"Yes, it seems so. Of course, some of the others were very young souls. Hadn't spent much time anywhere. It is very tough on such babies, to learn so much so suddenly."

"Grows them up fast." Jotin was pensive. After a long time he spoke again. "So what will we do about this problem? Apart from the fact that we've made them different religions, twelve years is too much. I thought you understood that there was no point showing Lucy to him just after he married Kathleen. Husbands do not leave their brand new wives for ten-year-old girls. Or as the

humans would say, not the well behaved new husbands we get to look after 'up here'!" Jotin and Trynor laughed, amused as always by the notion that there was a fiery 'down there' for the sinners. After a while, Trynor spoke again.

"But you've married him off now. What did you do that for?"

"I tried to stop him. I sent him three hunches. When he didn't pay any attention to the first two and explained away the third as pre-wedding jitters, I burnt out the kitchen of the hotel they had booked. But it wasn't enough, because Kathleen had told him that lie. He's too scared not to marry his pregnant girlfriend. They're all so caught up in the nonsense about sin and think it makes a difference if a priest mutters the right words over them. And not always too bothered about being good people, so long as nobody finds out."

"What has he done?"

"No, I don't mean David. Just people in general. Look around at some of them, misbehaving in all sorts of ways, but telling other people how they should behave. The Cretan priestess thought she was doing nothing wrong, but she made our people take that vow and she's still going on about it. At least these days they say 'till death do us part' and we can all start fresh. Maybe that's what we'll have to do, yet again, if my idea doesn't work."

Trynor's energies shifted and eddied as he thought through the situation.

"I'm sorry, Jo. I made a big mess, didn't I? Got distracted by that war in the east. A few of the others I look after were caught up in it, and being in a war myself so recently, it seemed so important-"

"Maybe it was. Maybe even more important than our problem here. Death on a large scale always seems so urgent. It doesn't really matter how soon we get Lucy and David together again, except for all the nagging we have to put up with from their 'baby'; not to mention that Planidi and her wretched vow. Being a priestess in Crete went to her head, I think."

"What is she saying now?"

"Same as ever. That everyone else who took a vow in her sanctuary managed to keep it and that our two are letting her down."

"Four thousand years later."

12

"Yes, she's unusual, all right. Her guide works on her, but she keeps coming back to it. I knew it was a bad idea when she said it. Somehow I just felt it."

"But we want Lucy and David to get together anyway. They have such good energies when they do, remember when they were Alessia and Danthys in Crete? You never know what they or their children might achieve."

"We must get on with it. There is no guarantee that this world will last forever and then where could we send them? It could take millions of years for another planet as good to be ready and what would we do with them, not to mention all the other souls hanging around at Home here, with no lives to go to? The thought is unbearable." Jotin slumped, his usually large energies contracting as he looked forward into a future he did not relish.

"Yes, and them being in different soul groups here makes it worse. They see so little of each other," Trynor was fluttering on the spot, wondering how to cheer his friend, "so what can we do?"

"I do have a 'Plan B' for this life, if you'll work with me and hold off till Lucy is old enough to marry. Kathleen is helping on this one, though she doesn't know it. Her guide told me about the outline plan for Kathleen and it works well for our needs too. So promise me - no more flowery T-shirts for the moment. Let your Lucy be a child, and enjoy it."

"Oh, she does. You know, she still loves her Noah's Ark, even though it's only plastic. Still occasionally makes it new plasticine animals. I'll work on her Dad about the bike. Now, are you going to explain your plan?"

So Jotin did.

Chapter 2
Crete 1598 B.C.E.

Trynor sat in the sun at the palace in Malatos, nearly two day's walk east of Knossos, allowing it to freshen his energies. He watched fondly as Alessia chattered happily to her friend the scribe, who worked next door to Mikolos' gold workshop. They had got into the habit of bringing their lunches to a shady corner of the courtyard, protected from the midday sun.

"There's no point going to sit at the viewpoint with the others," the scribe had explained to Alessia the first time they had lunch together, "when I can't see the sea."

"But I thought-" Alessia started, but she was cut off-

"No I can see it of course, but just as a big blue blur. It is frustrating when everyone else is pointing out the diving birds and the fishing boats. I have never seen a bird fly, they are always too far away. That's why I learnt to write, it was close enough to see. Even so I have to put my nose so close I get clay on the end of it. I could have learnt goldsmithing like you, except for the times where it has to be melted. My hair would have gone up in flames. Cooking is dangerous enough."

"Have you caught fire?" asked Alessia.

"Oh, yes, a few times. I eat mostly raw food, it is safer. And I fall over things I can't see."

"But you can see? You are not like Filos?" Filos was an old blind fisherman, whom the whole town supported because he could predict storms by smelling the air.

"No, I can see perfectly when I come close, like this. Oh, you have the prettiest freckles on your nose!"

"Have I?" Alessia rubbed her nose, suddenly self-conscious. She changed the subject. "Is there a spirit for writing like there is for gold?"

The scribe considered this for a while. "I do not think so. No-one has ever told me so. The marks all have meanings and if you know them you can share information, that's all. Why do you ask?"

"I thought everything had a spirit, I never met anything that

15

didn't. I talked with the spirit of the clay I worked with back home in Tylissos; and on my way here to Malatos I learnt how to talk to the earth spirit. I would be lonely without the spirits to talk to. Are you not lonely?"

"No, I am too busy. I can hear the voices of the other scribes whenever I read the tablets, then I put my voice in the clay for them. I have friends in other towns who I have never met, but we can talk to each other."

Alessia's eyes shone with this new idea. "So your tablets do have spirits, they have yours," she said, taking the scribe's hand, "put in there by you. That is truly magic!"

"Would you like to learn how to do it?"

"No thanks," said Alessia. "I do not need to, I can talk to you for real. And I am busy learning gold. Talking with the spirit of the gold is like talking to the sun spirit, because gold shines like the sun and lasts, too. But the pieces with beads sometimes sparkle like water, so maybe I should learn the water dance too." She fluttered her hands as she spoke.

"Do you know other dances?"

"I learnt the 'earth walk' while I was travelling here from home. I came with the bull dancing troupe, you know, and wanted to learn to dance with the bulls, but Hetrion, their owner, said you have to start that when you start to walk. So he told one of the dancers to teach me the earth walk. It's a slow dance in honour of the earth and if you do it right you can feel the little movements the earth makes when she is restless." She shuddered with the memory of the first time she had been led in that slow sensuous dance and blushed slightly. The listening woman saw the colour change but said nothing. She could always pretend to see less than she did.

"They let me join in when they danced at the Grand Palace at Knossos on the way here." Now Alessia's eyes were shining. "It was worth having to leave home to experience that. Helping to thank the earth's spirit for the Queen!" Alessia grew silent as her own words struck home to her. The scribe put out a hand and stroked her shoulder.

"It is hard, to leave your home. I know, I had to come here to be able to work. No-one needed writing in my village and there was nothing else I could do."

"I could. I was a good potter, my parents' best apprentice," said Alessia. "And I liked working with the clay spirit, it is soft and yielding, a feminine spirit. But then I met Mikolos when he was passing through and he talked of the gold things he creates here. I just felt I had to come, I don't know why."

Trynor smiled to himself. "I know why, my darling girl, it was because I suggested it. You should have known too by now, but Danthys is away selling his bangles at a fair in Sitia. When he returns the story can continue."

"My mother cannot write, but she can make pictures. She gave me one to bring with me, it is my whole family on a clay tablet just like yours, as though they were pushing their faces out through the clay. So I have a little piece of their spirit with me. I miss them, especially Paslona. She is so little and maybe will have forgotten me when she sees me again. I do not know how long that will be," Alessia grew silent. She didn't miss everyone in the village. She had been glad to get away from Niklon. He was a real nuisance, thinking Alessia was interested in him, trying to touch her and assuming she would bring him something gold when she went home because he heard her promising trinkets to her girlfriends. Niklon had shadowed her and she had come away largely because of him. There was something about him she didn't like. She shuddered, *Trynor stretched out his energies to smooth Alessia's, trying to remove the unwanted memory.*

"Not to worry, love. You don't like him because you know him from two hundred years ago, when you beat him in a fight. He wants to get his own back. I managed to persuade his guide Roki that you should not be together in this life and I hope Niklon will get over it without ever needing to spend a life with you. Your Danthys is coming soon. I was talking to Jotin not long ago."

Chapter 3

"Did I not tell you," Trynor had asked Jotin, *"about Alessia going up to see Planidi before she came here?"*

"No, who's Planidi?"

"The local oracle near Tylissos, her home place. Wretched woman, got herself a reputation for reading the stones, so now no one there listens to their guides at all. Alessia didn't trust herself to make up her own mind even though I'd told her what to do. No, it had to be Planidi. It was a lovely evening when she went, just at new moon. That's a good time to ask the Mother Goddess questions, you know."

"Oh really? Why?"

"Because they think it means the Mother Goddess is returning and all will continue well so long as the moon behaves as normal."

"Well, that's probably right, anyway." Jotin laughed and Trynor joined in.

"Yes, of course, but not for the mystical reasons they think." He paused and looked around, *"Where was I?"*

"Going to see an oracle," said Jotin.

"Oh, yes. Lovely night. Thyme scented air, moonlight, the works. Gorgeous, but she didn't pay it any attention, just rushed on up to the top of the little hill. *I would have tripped on the loose stones if I'd had to do it in a body, but* she was young and nimble.

Planidi was waiting in the circular sanctuary making her preparations. She raised a bronze rod towards the waxing moon and held the double-headed axe at its end so that from her viewpoint its points touched those of the moon. She closed her eyes and started an incantation to the Mother, who she assumed watched over her and everybody else on the island. When Alessia arrived Planidi drew a circle in the dust with the end of her rod and motioned the girl into it, where she knelt, her face raised to the crescent of light that showed that the Mother was listening.

"Ask your question now, daughter, while Diktynna's light shines on you. The Mother will always answer those who seek her wisdom in the right way." She put nine polished marble pebbles into

19

Alessia's hands and Alessia raised the Speaking Stones towards the moon, as she recited the old familiar words:

"Mother of all, mother of all your daughters, who guides us and gifts to us all our power, which is your power, help me now." She paused, searching for the best words to use, although she correctly suspected that the 'Mother' already knew what was in her heart. "Help me now to decide should I go? Should I study under Mikolos of Malatos, to craft the precious gold?" She stopped again, wondering if that was enough, "or should I stay and continue to learn from my father? I think I would be better with gold than clay." She stopped, aghast at having given her opinion to the Mother, who she thought knew far more than her. *Of course we do!* Planidi had divined the answers to everything for all of Alessia's sixteen years. "I ask this humbly and that I may play my proper role in harmony with the spirits of the places where I will belong, and for the greater wonder of all children of the mother. I will follow your decision. So be it." She bowed her head.

"Well said. Now throw the stones."

Alessia raised her face and hands to the moonlight and tossed the pebbles up in the air. They fell around her except for one, which fell between her bare breasts and nestled there gleaming. Planidi gasped and her hand flew to her mouth.

"Don't say it" I said. *I was standing just outside the circle, invisible to the living humans, drawn into the proceedings despite my best intentions. "Don't tell my girl anything about stones to the heart, or about the one that fell outside the circle either."* Planidi's head swung round and when she saw the stone lying behind Alessia, outside the circle, her grip on her rod tightened and she raised it towards the moon as though to defend herself.

"Oh, goodness, stop this now," I said, *"There's no need to tell her nonsense. The stones mean nothing, you know that. You're just well tuned in to us. So listen again, please, and stop inventing superstitions. Just tell her to go to Mikolos' studio. She's right, she would be very good with intricate work. Don't let a good skill go to waste. It's a straightforward life for her this time, it's all planned, but she'd be more fulfilled and happy with the gold than with clay."* Planidi said nothing. Her black curls moved a little in the night air and we could all hear the crickets in the valley making the soft air loud.

"Guide of Planidi the Oracle, we need you!" I moved to stand nearer to the motionless woman. As I passed Alessia I murmured to her, "don't worry, we'll get her talking in a moment. Be patient."

As soon as I spoke I could see a deep purple light forming at one side of the sanctuary and moving forwards towards Planidi. "How can I help you, Trynor?"

"Make sure Planidi doesn't dramatise her stones again. Nothing bad will happen to Alessia, it's all arranged. She should go to Malatos, she'd be right at home with gold and there's someone waiting to meet her there."

Planidi's guide stepped towards her and whispered in her ear. Planidi concentrated, her eyes rising towards the moon, as slowly her hands and arms relaxed and she rested the end of the bronze rod on the ground. She leant it against her so that the double axe was over her shoulder and stretched out her arms to Alessia.

"The Mother has spoken, my child. The answer is simple, the stones show us that you should train with Mikolos. You must craft something in honour of the Mother, who will guard and watch over you."

Alessia jumped to her feet, the pebble fell from between her breasts and rolled out of the dust circle, where it lay making a pair with the one which had fallen there earlier. Planidi watched it go and shivered. Alessia raised her arms to the moon and gathered an armful of moonlight to her chest.

"Oh, Great Mother, I give you thanks and honour you. I will walk in your light even though I craft the sun metal. I will use it well." She brought her hands to her forehead and poured out the symbolic moonlight over her upturned face.

Five minutes later Alessia was still standing in the sanctuary deep in thought. She had been pushed gently out of the circle by Planidi, who brushed out the circle in the dust, while reciting the closing prayers and picking up the nine pebbles. The oracle wiped them tenderly on a soft cloth and then put them in a leather pouch hanging from her belt. She turned to leave.

"Come on, Alessia, you have your answer. How can you have a problem now?" Alessia turned a worried face to her.

"How will I tell my parents? Especially Father, he loves the clay so much. And I made a really good pot last week, a vase. I decorated it with dolphins, they have so much movement, swimming and frolicking around it."

"It's easy. You just say that the Mother spoke to you and tells you to use your skills in another medium. Mikolos is well known, your parents will not be afraid for you."

"No, I know that. But they will know that I had this idea myself, the Mother doesn't just stand in your path and say 'GO'. You have to ask her the question. They'll feel rejected that I asked at all."

Planidi paused and looked upwards towards the moon which as the night deepened was beginning to dip down behind the sanctuary on the higher mountain that watched over the village. She wondered how to answer this question. Why indeed do we get ideas, she thought. Where do they come from?

"Sometimes people just have them, Planidi," I could just hear her guide's words. "You were all given free will and imagination. Sometimes there's no mystery at all. But sometimes we suggest and sometimes we support. I'll let you guess which this was. It doesn't matter anyway, it's all for the good and to help Trynor's girl here to learn and grow."

"You were guided by the Mother," said Planidi, "who knows us all better than we know ourselves. Sometimes she speaks to us in our sleep and then we think it is our own idea. Tell your parents that and they will be content." *It is wonderful to find humans who listen to us and hear us clearly, isn't it?*

It was useful that Alessia could hear me a bit when we were leaving Tylissos. She was plodding with a dull ache inside her, forcing herself not to look back, afraid that she would lose her resolve and return to the village. *I really felt for her, but I knew she should come to Malatos, so I danced and shimmered in front of her, calling out to her, pulling her attention forward so she looked ahead and allowed herself to look to the future. And it's nearly starting, a more interesting lunch companion will be here soon, didn't you say?"*

"Yes," said Jotin, "Danthys is on his way back. His father will be pleased, all the fine gold products have been sold."

Alessia jumped to her feet and brushed crumbs off her skirt. "Rasifi is back, I must go. Can I help you back to your workshop?"

"No thank you, dear. I know this yard as well as my own hand. I will just sit for a few moments in the sun." The scribe moved a little, closed her eyes and raised her face to the light.

Alessia trotted back to the gold workshop, where Rasifi, known to the town as 'the goldsmith's wife', but actually the most skilled smith, was settling to her workbench. Alessia was growing very fond of Rasifi, who behaved to her like a foster mother and kept up the pretence that Mikolos was in charge of the workshop. It helped keep their two sons, Taklidon and Kadmos, in control, to let them think their father was the boss. They had accepted Alessia with good grace and apart from playing some practical jokes on her, as is usual with new apprentices, they were treating her as an equal.

Two days later, during the afternoon, there was a delighted roar from the workshop next door and a great deal of laughter. Minutes later Bullneck put his head around the door and said "Come out here and congratulate my son! All his fine bangles sold and orders for more!"

Bullneck was another goldsmith, a huge stocky man whose head seemed to sit right on his chest. He looked more like an oarsman than a fine craft worker, but anyone who assumed that was sadly mistaken. Alessia had been shown some of his work and it was, though she didn't want to admit it, better than Mikolos and Rasifi's. Rasifi led them all out into the bright courtyard where they squinted in the sudden light. Alessia could see an unfamiliar figure just behind Bullneck's shoulder. He was standing facing the sun so the small double axe hanging round his neck on a fine cord glinted and caught Alessia's eye. He had unusually light coloured hair, brown rather than black, and fair skin. He was wearing a short white skirt, pleated at the front, similar to the palace staff at Knossos. She wondered if he was on the staff of the Malatos palace and looked to see if he was wearing any insignia *Trynor was also looking and grinned at his old friend.*

"Hello, Jotin. I told you I'd get her here and here we are! Now get him to look the right way and we're sorted."

"Danthys, my boy, it seems that the apprentice has eyes for you," Bullneck rumbled. Alessia became aware of several pairs of eyes turned her way.

"I'm sorry, I didn't mean to stare. I just wondered if it was livery, I mean if he was a servant, oh no, I mean..." Alessia stopped, her face flaming, and looked at her feet. Rasifi's two boys sniggered and their mother quelled them with a glare. There was a silence so total that Alessia could hear a lamb bleat on the distant hillside. Danthys spoke.

"It's all right. It's my own fault for wearing this. My mother is from Egypt and I visited her family last summer for my temple ceremony. The linen cloth is so cool I prefer it to wool."

"It's expensive. You should save it for special occasions" grumbled Bullneck.

"I think this is a special occasion, father," said Danthys. The silence for a moment was even more profound and Alessia became aware of the sound of the waves against the rocks, or maybe it was the noise inside her own ears. She looked up at Danthys. He was looking at her as though there was no-one else around. He smiled and she felt his smile pulling on the edges of her mouth, so that it too turned up and she found herself grinning at him as though they were old friends. Then there was a sound of retching and everyone looked at Kadmos who had two fingers in his mouth and was pretending to vomit. His brother laughed and was joined by everyone else, except Alessia and Danthys, who just went on smiling at each other, until Bullneck said

"All right, that's enough, my boy, your trip is over. I need to discuss the design of the sacrificial cup with you, or we will have nothing to show to the Queen."

Danthys touched his chest in a farewell gesture, bowed slightly from the hips and turned away. Alessia stood in the doorway looking after him as he walked back to his own workplace and wondered about what had just happened. She wondered why he seemed familiar.

"Because of the linen skirt," said Trynor, "you don't remember, but we planned that you would see his skirt. Linen is so rare here, it was a pretty safe bet. We were right. And of course he has been looking at your necklace."

Alessia put her hand up and felt her pendant. She had made it herself out of a tiny bit of leftover clay, at the end of one of her last days as a potter. There had only just been time to glaze it. It was a tiny eight petalled flower, a copy of one she had seen once on a vase. It was white and showed up in contrast to her skin where it lay on a leather thong between her breasts.

24

Chapter 4

Many times over the next few months Alessia saw Danthys. Sometimes the two families ate together on the shady side of the courtyard, Mikolos and Bullneck sharing memories of past exploits, teasing each other about their failings and including their wives and children in the banter. Alessia got used to being considered one of the family and stopped blushing when attention was focussed on her. Unless it was Danthys. He had only to look her way for her to feel that the whole world was looking at her. Yet she didn't care. Let them look, she thought, what harm? But she was never alone with him. Alessia began to wonder if Danthys was really interested in her, or if his relaxed friendliness was simply because she was part of Mikolos' family. She missed her sisters and because she was so busy working she had not had the opportunity to meet anyone who could become a new friend. Now she was in her new home, watching Rasifi start some of the preparations for the celebrations of the grape harvest and remembering sadly how she and her old friends had wound vine leaves into each others' hair last year. Rasifi noticed that she had gone quiet.

"Your first festival with us – quite an event!" Rasifi came over to Alessia and put a large arm across her shoulders, hugging Alessia to her. "But your first away from your people. It's hard, remembering. But you can use that remembering to make contact with them, of a sort."

"How?" Alessia was puzzled. How could she make contact with people who were so far away?

"Come outside with me." Rasifi led the way out of the house and down the street to where it widened out and they could see the darkening sky, kept brighter by the rising moon.

"It's the grape harvest at your home too, isn't it? And they'll be missing you too, won't they?" said Rasifi, "They'll be thinking of you just as much as you are thinking of them. So look at the moon and ask her to look down on them and send your love to them. They will hear, I'm sure of it." Rasifi raised her arms to the moon and closed her eyes. Alessia copied her and in her mind sent the messages as Rasifi had suggested. As she did she felt a strange happiness steal over her, almost as though her mother had crept in to watch her as she used to do when Alessia was very small. She sighed and opened her eyes. Rasifi was smiling at her.

"Well, did it work? Did they hear you?"

"I can hardly believe it, but I think my mother did," said Alessia slowly. It would be lovely to know, she thought. When I see her next I will ask.

"She heard you, Alessia. I made sure of that. She looked out of the window and saw the moon and thought of you. They haven't forgotten." Trynor stroked Alessia and faded out.

"So now we can concentrate on getting ready for the festival. Come on, we have some cooking to do."

The main celebrants of the grape harvest were, of course, the people who worked with the grapes and who made it into wine. But it was a happy day for everyone and everyone made the most of it, gathering in the late afternoon in the open area between the town and the palace. There would be bull-dancing to ensure a plentiful harvest this year and to keep the vines in good health for the next season. There would be a procession of children, dressed up in colourful costumes, usually with a grape theme, with prizes for the most imaginative. There would be feasting, plenty to drink, bonfires, singing and music-making.

Rasifi told Alessia that she missed her daughter Elena most acutely whenever she had to make herself presentable, as having another's eye to help apply the rouge and kohl was so much more reliable than depending on the images in a mirror.

"I can be quite a sight! Ours is a good smooth mirror, but it is still not as clear as the real thing. It is good to have another female eye in the house. Those men think make-up does itself and make a fuss when I try to be accurate and take my time. I hope you don't mind helping me?" Alessia assured her that it would please her too, to have someone to share the preparations with and told Rasifi about her sisters and friends back at home, how they had used vine-leaves last year. So they sent Kadmos off to find them some leaves, while Alessia helped Rasifi into her long decorated skirt and fastened the apron on top. Rasifi grumbled about her weight as they squeezed her into her bodice and it strained across the shoulders.

"I swear there is more of me tumbling out the front than even the Mother Goddess has need of," she panted, as she surveyed herself in the polished bronze mirror. But at least I do not need any rouge to accentuate my breasts, not like you, dear."

Alessia put on her skirt and bodice and Rasifi pulled on the laces on the bodice for her, so that her breasts would be pulled together to show off her cleavage. Then they got out the rouge and highlighted their lips and nipples, Rasifi using her artist's eye to put just enough between Alessia's breasts.

"Well, if he doesn't notice you now he's not a real man and you'll be better off without him," she said, as she wiped her fingers on a cloth. Alessia pretended not to hear as she took out her kohl and handed it to Rasifi to outline her eyelids for her. Then Kadmos was back with two trailing lengths of vine full of leaves. While the two women wound the leaves through each other's hair, Kadmos watched and gave superfluous advice when anything went wrong. Eventually they were ready and came out into the main room to look over the food they would bring to the celebrations. Mikolos caught hold of Rasifi's hand and spun her round, looking her up and down and grinning widely.

"Not only a wonderful cook and an expert goldsmith, but a beautiful woman too!" He pulled his wife into an embrace. Alessia was surprised to find herself spun around like Rasifi, as Taklidon grabbed her hand.

"And my mother is teaching you beauty as well as gold working!" Taklidon put his hands on Alessia's back and pulled her towards him. She stiffened, bending her forearms in front of her chest and turning her head to one side to avoid his mouth. But she kept her voice light and tried to put laughter into her tone as she said yes, Rasifi had taught her a lot, but that the best dish she had made for the feast was from a recipe of her own mother's and that she hoped he and Kadmos would like it. Taklidon took his hands from her as though he had been stung and strutted out of the room, followed by a peal of laughter from Kadmos. Rasifi, pulling her clothes back into their former neatness, sent Kadmos after Taklidon to bring him back to help carry the food.

"Don't think badly of him for that, Alessia" she whispered. "It's the first time he has shown an interest in a woman. He's just practising. He'll choose better next time." When Taklidon came back in to pick up some of the dishes to go to the picnic site, he would not meet anyone's eye. He looked at Alessia from under half closed lids and muttered under his breath.

"Do not let him upset you, Alessia. He will find another, more suitable. He is not right for you, remember that."

Alessia picked up one small bowl, as did Rasifi; they made Mikolos and the two boys carry the bigger dishes to the picnic site. The palace craftsmen were gathering together and would receive gifts of wine and grape juice from the palace. When they arrived there was already a festive atmosphere. The food was being shared as the groups sat on the ground enjoying the warmth of the late afternoon sun. Other women came to look in their bowls and praise Alessia and Rasifi for their culinary skills and on their beauty. There was much laughter and exchanging of outrageous gossip. Wine jars were handed around and soon the stories became more preposterous, the laughter louder and the mutual praise more extravagant. As the dusk fell, there were cries for 'music, music' and 'dance'.

"Alessia can dance" said Kadmos, through a large mouthful of honey cake. "She does it all the time."

"Come on, then, Alessia!" said someone, "let's see you!"

"I only do the earth walk," Alessia admitted, "It's not the sort of dance you want to see today. It's very gentle."

"A dance is a dance," said another voice. "Come on, start us off." Then the gentle tune Alessia remembered from Hetrion's troupe started up, so she shook out her hair and stood up. She walked to a clear space, stood quietly for a moment to acknowledge the Earth Spirit and then started the slow familiar moves. The others watched her for a few moments, but as she had predicted, this was not the sort of dance they wanted on such a day and the chattering gradually swelled again, as attention slipped away from her. Alessia continued her dance to the earth: to stop would have been the height of disrespect. After a few minutes, she became aware of another dancer, moving with her, following her lead and then, to her delight, taking the lead, allowing her to follow in the half remembered steps she had only partially learned with Hetrion. Together they circled and swayed and as she danced with the earth she was only half aware that the noise of the revellers was becoming distant and the quietness of the night was clearer.

As one they dipped and turned together and Alessia allowed herself to glance up to see if what she hoped was true and yes, it was

Danthys who was dancing with her, leading her further and further away from the party. She caught his eye and grinned, and as he grinned back at her the moment came in the dance for the reminder that the earth is only sleeping. They both made the small quick move and then Danthys did it again and Alessia followed, her breath catching. They circled once more and then Danthys was making a series of the earthquake moves, his lively eyes meeting hers. A laugh bubbled up her throat and burst out. As they made the next circle move, Danthys caught her hand and she spun towards him. His arm was around her and his eyes just above hers as they looked deep within her. She could feel his heart thumping in his chest. He put his hand on her breast.

"I can feel your heart, Alessia. It wasn't such a strenuous dance, was it? Or are you like me, so pleased to be here you can hardly bear it?"

"I can feel yours too, Danthys. And the sweat on you!" Alessia stopped, wondering which out of all the things she could say, would be right. She looked up at him again, so close she could see the little beads of sweat on his lip. She reached up a finger and wiped them off. As she did he pulled her to him and kissed her, hard. He kept one hand on her breast and stroked it as she ran her hands down his bare back and returned his kiss.

"We'll get cold here," said Danthys, at last pulling his mouth away from hers. "Come, up to the workshop." He pulled her hand and broke into a trot towards the palace. Alessia followed willingly, but thinking to herself that it was as well she was willing, as Danthys had not asked her opinion. He didn't need to, she thought, he knows me too well.

Over by the nearest bonfire, just starting now against the chill of the evening, Rasifi leaned over to Mikolos and whispered, indicating the direction of the palace. Mikolos nodded and smiled, put an arm around his wife and took another long drink from his wine cup. The world was turning as it should.

Danthys led Alessia into his father's workshop and lit an oil-lamp. Then he beckoned her over to a corner, where there were several large cushions on the floor. Suddenly shy, Alessia hung back, but Danthys reached out to her and ran his hands through her long curls, dislodging the vine leaves. She put her hand up and stroked his smooth brown hair. Smiling at each other they knelt down onto the soft cushions. Danthys pulled at the laces of Alessia's bodice, but in his haste did it the wrong way and tightened them. Alessia picked at the knots, distracted by Danthys' mouth travelling all over her bare flesh. At last she got the laces undone and also her apron and skirt. Then she turned her attention to the clasp on Danthys' skirt.

"We're definitely not needed now, Trynor," said Jotin. *"They know what to do from here."*

"How do you know? They might not," protested Trynor.

"I remember. I was a man several times. It comes naturally. You really should try it again sometime, it would help you."

"Not me," said Trynor, *"far too uncomfortable, having a body. I've watched. Mostly pain, of various sorts. My one life ended badly, you know. That's how I know what pain is and that I'm not keen on it."*

"There's pleasure too, though. The taste of a fig straight off the tree, the feeling of warm water on your skin, the smell of a tiny baby. You can't imagine. Come on outside, we're in the way."

Later, Alessia sat up on the cushions and stretched. Her legs felt soft and useless and the sweat on her naked body was beginning to cool. Danthys was sleeping, his arms thrown out and his mouth slightly open. He looks lovely, she thought. He is lovely, so gentle but insistent, so funny. She looked around in the dim flickering light. It was much the same as Mikolos' workshop; all the familiar tools were there. She tested her legs and found that they would actually hold her. She got up and started to look around, running her fingers over the familiar shapes, thankful that they were now familiar and that she had not stayed behind in the west and been a potter all her days.

"Do you want to see it?" Danthys voice was slow and soft, "Do you want to see our cup?"

"Oh, Danthys, I shouldn't. It's too near to being finished. It is a contest, after all. What if I told Mikolos what it's like by mistake? It would give him an unfair advantage. Your father might be angry, if he lost like that. I wouldn't like to see him angry."

"You don't need to worry about that. He is almost never angry. That bull neck is just a joke the gods played on him, he's really very gentle."

"I'm glad you didn't get his neck" said Alessia, as she traced a finger up Danthys' long throat and along his jaw. "I suppose you must have an Egyptian neck?"

"Yes, I look like my mother, as you know. But I'm all Cretan inside."

"You can even do the earth walk, how did you learn that?"

"Well, I actually learnt that in Egypt, last year. I think it's the same as the Cretan one?" Alessia's finger had now reached Danthys' mouth and was following the outline of his lips. He darted his face forward and took her finger into his mouth as he pulled her down again onto the cushions.

"Look, before we go back to the celebrations. Tell me what you think of it, at least." Danthys ignored Alessia's protests, opened a heavy box at the back of the shop and lifted out a cloth bundle. He unrolled it and the gold gleamed in the soft light. It was big for a gold cup, plain but well proportioned, with three small handles.

"It's very beautiful," she said, "but it has no decorations on it!"

"My father can't decide how to decorate it. He makes ornaments for it, then melts them down again. He has tried dolphins, axes, a bull, - what has yours got on it?"

Alessia ran her hands over the solid gold, feeling its spirit warm under her fingers. The little handles were too small, she thought, for such a heavy cup.

"I'm not sure if Rasifi has decided," she said, as her hands unconsciously shaped Mikolos and Rasifi's cup in the air. Danthys watched, unable to pull his eyes away from her, even had he wished. His hands began to move in the same shapes. *Jotin was looking in through the doorway and would have held his breath, had he had any. "Look, Trynor! Look at their energy fields."*

"Yes! How wonderful! Let's help," Trynor and Jotin moved together and held the two humans' energies, encouraging the melding together that they had seen.

"Well done for noticing, Jo," said Trynor in awe, "We have something special here. It's really astonishing, when they aren't in the same soul group. That is a real shame, because one and one make more than two this time. They could work together at Home, not just in their lives. These cups will be more than beautiful. We must work together with them in as many future lives as we can manage: these two might create something astounding."

31

"Remember that couple who made the first wheel? Neither would have done it on their own, their guides said, but something extra happened when they got together. I wonder are Danthys and Alessia as significant as that?" Jotin passed his hands above the two heads that were bending together over the gold cup.

"I always put bulls, or flowers," said Alessia, "flowers mostly, they are easier. I put the new moon on the last jars I made."

"You mean on your pottery? Like the flower you wear?" Danthys indicated the pottery flower between Alessia's breasts. "Clever you, to draw attention so well to one, I mean two, of your most beautiful assets!" He dropped his head, to put a kiss just below the flower.

"I'm glad it had that effect," murmured Alessia, stroking his head, "even though I never intended it to."

"Haha. I'm sure! How can you not have noticed?"

"I'm behind it, looking out. I noticed you!"

"Yes, you did and everyone noticed you noticing me!"

"So?"

"So nothing! Let them! You're my woman now, aren't you?"

"Shouldn't we put away the cup before you do that again?"

Alessia took his hand from her bottom and held it towards the cup. Then, she found her hands tracing a shape, Danthys was tracing it with her, and she thought she could see the cup grow new handles, curled and beautiful. But she said nothing, as an idea came into her mind that she thought she would keep for Rasifi. She reached for the cloth and started to roll the cup into it. Danthys grabbed her hands and brought one to his lips, looking down at her with a smile in his eyes.

"You have just given me the most wonderful idea, Alessia! My father's cup will be spectacular."

"And you have given me one too. I hope Rasifi and Mikolos will like it."

"My woman could only have wonderful ideas. And so do I," he quickly put the cup away and turned again to Alessia, tracing his finger down over her skin to where the flower nestled. Alessia moved closer, her hands running down his back as she lifted her face to his. They moved together, barely able to keep still and their delighted laughter filled the dim room.

Chapter 5

Alessia looked up at the moon and tried to remember. Just how full had it been on the night of the grape harvest festival? She was almost sure she knew, but was confused because her body was not telling her. The days since had passed in a happy haze, seeing Danthys every day, sometimes taking their food out of the palace to eat together at midday. He had grown familiar to her, but not less exciting. In the evenings they met, often by the beach, to walk together in the moonlight. Several times they had found a sheltered place and had been able to lie down and enjoy each other all over again. The moon had shone down on them, but she had not noticed it properly. Just how full had it been? Was she right that it was the same now? For the first time in four years she had no certainty. Just a growing suspicion that the Mother had blessed her. She put a hand on her belly and asked it "is anyone there? I'll look after you, always!"

In the morning she was more certain of the blessing, when she found she could not eat. Rasifi looked at her and grinned. Nothing much got past Rasifi.

"You've been seeing a lot of Danthys these last weeks. Looks like you'll be seeing even more of him?"

Alessia looked up and blushed. "Yes, I think so. I will need his support when I can't work." A thought stopped her. "Will you allow me to keep working with the gold if I am with child?"

"Of course we will. Gold needs a female spirit to work it, to soften it. What is more female than a pregnant woman?"

"Will I be able to continue after the baby is born?"

Rasifi reached across the table and took Alessia's hand. "Not for a few months. You must rest and care for the baby. But when your strength is back, there's no reason why you can't start again."

"I must tell Danthys," said Alessia, "I hope he is as pleased as I am."

Rasifi stood up and started to clear the table. "He has to be. If the Mother blesses you and uses him, he is blessed too. He cannot reject a blessing, it would be bad luck. Not to say he won't be surprised. Amazing the number of young men who are surprised. You'd wonder what they thought they were doing when the night was warm and the woman was beautiful. The wine clouds their minds, I think." She bustled out, her hands full of dishes.

Alessia looked around the familiar room. She had been here only a few months now, but it seemed so comforting, so ordinary, so home. But now, with her baby on the way, could she call it home? Rasifi was kind and generous, but she might not want to support a woman who could not work, not to mention her child. What would happen if Danthys was not happy? She would have to go home and although she would be welcomed there, she would not be able to work with the gold anymore. Never to learn all the wonderful techniques that she had watched but not yet been allowed to try. A tear slid slowly down her face and she brushed it quickly away as Rasifi came back into the room.

"Why the tears?" Rasifi really did see everything. When Alessia explained Rasifi laughed.

"Even if you can't work the gold for a while, you can help us by being here and doing the gentle work around the place. You are going to be a great goldsmith. I won't let you give up so easily. But I don't think you'll be here, I think Danthys will want his woman by his side. So don't worry until you see how things turn out. Now come on, the others have gone ahead, they'll be wondering where we are."

"I don't think Kadmos will wonder for long. He's like you, Rasifi, he notices everything!"

At the midday break time it was still warm enough to take their food out into the yard outside the workshops. Danthys and his parents were there too. Danthys smiled broadly at Alessia and moved over to sit beside her. Everyone was used to this now and not even Kadmos made any comment. Alessia whispered to Danthys, "Can we go outside, down to the beach?" Danthys looked at her pretending to be shocked.

"You can't want to do that in broad daylight? I know they all know, but still..."

"I just want to talk to you without having everyone pretending not to listen and hearing everything. Just for a few minutes." Danthys agreed, so they quickly finished eating and went out past the guards and turned down the path towards the beach. There was a wind off the sea and the noise of the surf pounded in their ears. They walked along the sand, enjoying the feeling of it between their

34

toes. Alessia wondered how best to tell her news. She was so happy and excited, Danthys should be too. She looked up at him and took his hands.

"Something wonderful has happened. Something that makes us special to each other. We are truly blessed by the Mother!" and she stood, smiling up at him.

Danthys looked at her, puzzled. Certainly he felt blessed, to have found such a beautiful woman who seemed to love him as much as he loved her. Certainly, they were special to each other. He'd known that the first time they met outside the workshops and she had smiled back at him, such an open smile that the whole world had lit up. He put out his arms and drew her to him and kissed her, caressing her in the way that usually made her soften against him. But although she returned his kiss there was no softening and in a moment she pulled back from him and spoke.

"So you don't mind then? You're pleased?"

"Pleased about what? Certainly I'm pleased that I know you; that we have found each other. What could please me more?"

"Oh, for goodness sake, you dunderhead!" Jotin was standing beside Alessia in front of Danthys. "It is no wonder I can't get through to you when a solid flesh and blood girl standing here hinting her heart out means nothing to you." He started speaking slowly and clearly as though to the feebleminded. "Think, boy! Concentrate. And listen, to me too, but at least to Alessia." He sighed and stepped back.

"Our baby"

"Our.....so soon?" Danthys' hand shot up to his wide-open mouth. "The Mother blessed us, so soon? Oh, Alessia!" He was off, running, jumping, spinning on the spot and laughing. Alessia laughed too and joined him in his impromptu dance to the spirits: one that had never been choreographed but came straight from the soul and flew into the waiting arms, she hoped, of whatever spirits were looking out for her and her baby. After a while, they ran out of breath and slowed to a walk along the line where the sea met the land, so the waves washed over their feet. They walked for an hour, to and fro, talking of the future and their plans and hopes for their child: the 'greatest goldsmith in Crete'. The fishermen, pulling up their boats onto the sand and sorting their catches, watched in amusement and called out ribald suggestions for the cause of such happiness. When Alessia told them the real news they shouted blessings and grinned to each other. Eventually Alessia and Danthys realised that they had been out a long time, so they held hands and ran back to the workshops, where Danthys pulled Alessia into his parents' shop.

"Mother, Father! We have wonderful news! Alessia is to be a mother!"

"Oh yes," rumbled Bullneck, "and how does that concern us?" Alessia looked at him, startled and anxious, but was relieved to see he was beaming all over his broad face and immediately swept her into his arms in a huge embrace.

"Careful, Father, you might squash my daughter!" said Danthys as he hugged his mother. Bullneck bent down, searching in a cupboard in a corner of the shop. At last he came out slightly out of breath but triumphantly waving a wine jar.

"Kept to celebrate the choosing of our cup, but we can get another one for that. Go and fetch the others, we must drink to this."

So after pouring a small amount of the wine onto the feet of the statue of the Mother, to thank her for her blessing, the two families happily toasted the expected arrival.

Alessia moved to live with Danthys' family a few weeks later, because a pregnant woman should be with her man and her mother. Danthys' mother insisted that she was the nearest thing to a mother Alessia had in Malatos, although Alessia herself would have chosen Rasifi for the job. However, Danthys' house was not far and his parents were welcoming. Alessia still worked with Mikolos and Rasifi, so she felt included and happy. She and Danthys spent all their free time together, discussing the future and telling each other how special they were and how no-one had ever been so blessed, so beautiful, so special.

Hetrion, with whom she had travelled from her home in the west, passed the town with his troupe of bull dancers not long after Alessia realised she was pregnant and sent a messenger into the narrow streets to find her. She ran out to the road to see him and asked him to bring the good news to her family, along with a gift for her mother, a ring of gold wire that she had made herself. Alessia made sure Hetrion knew how hard it was to make the wire, so he could explain to her family. Just before the midwinter festival he returned, going east once again to dance for the festivities. This time he had gifts for Alessia, some pottery cups and plates for the baby and some baby clothes, one with slightly haphazard decoration on it that she guessed to have been made by her tiny sister. She pressed him for news, but the stories made her sad, as she knew that it would be even longer now until she saw her own family again. That evening she sat a long time holding her pottery picture, wondering how much everyone had changed. Danthys sat with her, his arm around her waist, letting her talk about them all. Then he told her stories of his mother's people, so far away in Egypt and he described a river so big it was as important as the sea. He promised to bring her and their child there some day, to take part in the dramatic ceremonies in the temple, as he had done.

Rasifi was beside herself with joy when her daughter Elena arrived with her family to visit for the Midwinter festival. It had been two years since Rasifi and Mikolos had seen their daughter and the grandchildren were grown 'beyond recognition, you're all such big little people'. Elena had married a farmer from the high plains, so they brought gifts of leather, wheat, apples and carrots. They had three children, one a girl just about the size that little Paslona had been when Alessia saw her last. Alessia loved the child immediately and played with her whenever she got the chance. One of Danthys' sisters also visited with her husband and toddler. Alessia revelled in all the female company and was fascinated by all their advice about pregnancy and childbirth. The women all agreed that the sanctuary cave on the high plain had powerful spirits, who looked after pregnant women and helped to guide babies into the world.

"Of course, it was easy for me" said Elena, "that's why I have three children so close in age. We live close to the caves, so I was able to visit often. The spirits of the cave are strong, you can see that in their pillars. It is too far to travel when you are pregnant, but I can bring an offering there for you."

So Alessia begged a piece of clay from a nearby potter and made a small baby out of it, to be left at the foot of one of the cave pillars. The potter agreed to fire it in his kiln; it would be ready for Elena to take with her after the festival. But five days before the midwinter festival they were all to be present at the palace with their cups. It was a strange morning for Alessia as she woke beside Danthys, both of them excited, but belonging to different teams. She decided to go and have her breakfast with Mikolos and Rasifi.

"But you should be with me, you are my woman. You live here," Danthys protested.

"No, Alessia is right," Bullneck rumbled, "she belongs to Mikolos this morning. She has helped with his cup. Off you go, Alessia, we'll see you at the palace."

At the palace, there was more ceremony than usual. The guards barred their way, crossing their crystal-pommelled swords until Rasifi declared her business within, whereupon the swords were removed and the guards bent one knee. Alessia found it amusing since they all greeted these guards every day, but she hid her smile as they passed. They gathered in the workroom, where Mikolos got out their cup and they all admired it again. Mikolos opened a jar of wine and poured a little into the cup and a little for luck onto the feet of the statue of Mother Diktynna, who stood at one side of the workshop. They handed the cup around, each taking a sip of the wine. Alessia marvelled again at the handles of the cup, that Rasifi had fashioned from Alessia's excited description. Three large flowers sat on the rim of the cup, some of their petals falling along its rim and one larger petal of each swooping up and out, then curving back in to meet the outside of the cup, forming three handles. At the base of each handle where the petal joined to the cup, Mikolos had placed a gold bee, the symbol of his family's workshop. It had taken hours of work and was truly beautiful, the flowers and the bees so real you could nearly believe you would be stung.

"Now the cup has been used it is launched on its journey," Mikolos intoned, "we ask the Mother to bless it and help the Queen look on it with favour." He dried the cup on a piece of rag and wrapped it again. At that moment there was a knock on the door and a palace page was outside, reciting in a reedy treble that they were commanded into the queen's presence. They left the workroom in line, with Rasifi at the front and in the courtyard found Danthys' family similarly lined up. They all grinned self-consciously at each other as they walked after the page towards the ceremonial arena. The sides of the arena were thronged with the

38

palace staff and other tradespeople. The priestesses were beside the queen at one end. The king stood behind his wife on a higher step, his advisors jostling on either side of him. The two goldsmiths were led forward to stand in front of the queen. Then the queen started on what turned out to be half an hour of incantations and prayers and Alessia found herself getting quite dizzy and weak. She was glad it was winter; that she was not standing in burning sun. Eventually the moment came: Rasifi and Bullneck were beckoned forward to unwrap their cups and put them on a small table which had been placed in front of the queen. Alessia's eyes were on Rasifi's hands, she was pleased to see the cup catch a beam of sun as Rasifi set it on the table, so it was not for a tiny moment that she heard the gasp that went round the audience.

"What is the meaning of this?" the queen demanded. Alessia looked at the table with more care and gasped herself, for there beside Rasifi's cup was its replica, with three curved handles in the shape of petals and the other petals lying smoothly along the rim. She felt herself sway and Danthys was there beside her, holding her. She leant against him, a tendril of anxiety curling up through her. Her vision clouded, the world looked grey, she felt herself falling. Then she saw Danthys' face above her and heard someone offering her water. She struggled upright, muttering apologies. The young page was beside her with a stool, explaining that she should have been sitting, if she was pregnant. "You should have told us," he hissed, "the queen does not ask pregnant women to stand for ceremonies."

Rasifi and Bullneck were explaining to the queen and her advisors that it was pure chance that they had chosen the same design; that they had not conferred. But in both their minds there was a doubt. Danthys and Alessia would have some explaining to do. The queen and the other priestesses conferred at length as the goldsmiths waited. At last the queen spoke.

"This is an omen. The Mother is telling us that we must celebrate doubly this year, that next year will be full of wonders,"

"Oh, really! She just knew she couldn't choose one of two almost identical cups," said Trynor.

"Yes. Wonderful to be in charge like that, making up the rules as you go along. Now she can blame everything that goes wrong on the cups, or take credit for the things that go right because she

39

ordered a double ceremony. Not that the cups are identical, ours has no bees."

"No, how could you? They are nothing to do with Danthys and Alessia's idea, they're just Mikolos' trademark added on. They look good though, don't they?" Trynor laughed, "But we shouldn't have let our pleasure, our confidence in Alessia and Danthys stop us discussing this, we should have shared the design!"

"I was enjoying the contest. I still have a strong human streak, don't you? Even if you were only a human once it must be in there."

"So there will be two ceremonies, one at dawn on midwinter's day as usual, and one at dusk. I will use one cup in the morning and the king will close the day with the other." The queen turned to Rasifi and Bullneck and her gaze swept over everyone in the two family groups, as she gave the tiniest of bows. "I thank you all for your participation. Your rewards will arrive tomorrow." She turned and swept out of the arena, followed by the king and both retinues.

Back in the courtyard, there was much laughter and teasing and excitement that both families would be paid for their work and neither cup would have to be melted down. They were all frustrated that they could not examine the two cups more clearly, to see how they had differed. Voices were raised as opinions were given.

"Alessia and Danthys know." No one was sure who had spoken, but all eyes turned to where Alessia and Danthys were sitting. Alessia blushed.

"Yes, you had better both explain," said Bullneck, "You suggested the idea to me, Danthys."

"And you to me, Alessia," said Rasifi, "Why?"

"Well, it just seemed that it would be pretty," Alessia said helplessly, "Danthys and I were talking about the cups and that idea just came into my mind."

"And into mine," said Danthys.

"But I did not tell Danthys my idea, only you."

"Is this true, son? Did you tell Alessia your idea?" Bullneck's eyes flashed. Eventually Alessia and Danthys managed to convince everyone that they were telling the truth and had not shared their ideas. As this realisation became clearer to the others, they fell silent one by one and looked at each other in amazement. It was Rasifi who broke the silence.

"We must give thanks to the Mother for guiding their minds, so that we would make two cups for the two ceremonies she needs."

"Oh, for goodness sake," muttered Trynor, "they are looking at a miracle of human and soul symbiosis and they ignore it entirely and give the credit to their god." He sighed and sat back in the wintery sunshine.

"Lighten up, Trynor, at least they have noticed and accepted, and are thankful."

"Yes, and we are going to have to sit through double ceremonies. We should have foreseen that."

"You are too anti-ceremony. They enjoy them and so do I, sometimes," Jotin was watching as Rasifi poured another libation onto the statue's feet. "Pity I can't drink that."

"I have reason to be anti-ceremony," Trynor shuddered, "it was my two year old blood my tribe were pouring on their statue's feet. It makes me nervous, I'm always afraid someone will revert to type and grab Alessia."

"I'm sorry, Trynor, I had forgotten. But this society almost never sacrifices their own people, I think you can relax."

The two goldsmithing families enjoyed Midwinter thoroughly. They were given front row seats at all the ceremonies and were excited by the rush of the bulls past their faces as the young athletes leaped over the animals' backs. Alessia was sorry that it was not Hetrion's bull dancing team, but she learnt some new and different steps for the earth walk by watching intently as the dancers moved through the arena. At the feasting after the ceremonies they were given seats at a long table near the king's and at last were able to study their cups again as they circulated, one filled with wine and the other with fruit flavoured water. They were not identical, but very nearly, and Alessia and Danthys marvelled together, that they had had such similar ideas without even discussing it. They went to bed happy and lay in the comforting darkness with their hands on each other's bellies, planning their baby's future.

When it was time for Elena and her family to return home, Alessia gave her the clay baby to remind the Mother that she hoped for a safe delivery and healthy baby. Elena pointed out that the priestess would ask for an offering of money also.

"Don't they always," sighed Trynor, "those priestesses are

always taking money, for nothing; we hear you perfectly well without caves or priestesses. But do it, if it makes you happy."

Chapter 6

Alessia was finding work very hot. Although the workshop was gloomy inside, the midsummer heat was beating through the flat roof and gathering in the room, unable to find a way out. They were all doing work that did not need the furnace, so it had been let go out. Alessia was making wire, pushing a thin cylinder of gold through a slightly smaller hole in a piece of wood, but it was difficult as her hands were constantly wet and the smooth metal slid through her fingers as though it was oiled. She wiped her hands on her skirt and tried again to get a grip on the slippery gold.

"I wish I had a piece a bit further advanced," she grumbled to Rasifi, who was beating a little sheet of gold with a tiny hammer. "It would be easier to get a grip if it was thin enough to bend." Rasifi grunted assent and wiped the sweat off her forehead.

"It's not really working weather at all, we never get much done in midsummer. But there's no point in wasting the time totally. Might as well do something."

This time it was Alessia who grunted, but it was with surprise. She put a hand to her apron, but could feel nothing out of the ordinary, apart from the huge bulge that sat on her lap like a soft boulder. She stroked it gently and as she did, she felt it change from a soft boulder to a hard one and she grunted again. Rasifi looked up.

"Is it starting?"

Alessia nodded, stunned into silence.

"We had better get you home, then. No baby wants to be born in a workshop. Come on, it is better to go while you can still walk." She explained to Mikolos and the boys what was happening, setting up a flurry of excitement, so they hovered about fussing while, Rasifi went to tell Danthys and his family. Although Alessia now lived with Danthys' parents, it had been decided that she would go to Rasifi's home for the birth of her baby. Rasifi had more experience of delivering babies than Danthys' mother, who had found her own experiences of delivery rather alarming and did not want to be too closely involved where, as she said herself, she was more likely to fret than be helpful. Rasifi on the other hand was a woman whose very presence was calming and other women of the town often called on her to help.

Danthys ran in from the shop next door, his young face pale. He grabbed Alessia's hand and stared into her face, his lips quivering.

"Oh, Alessia, my love, what have we done? I must be crazy to have put you in danger!"

"What danger, you ridiculous boy?" Rasifi bustled in behind him. "A baby is arriving, that's all. Danger indeed. If we do what we must and trust in the Mother, all will be well. Now instead of regretting what's past, which you don't regret anyway, you fraud, get your arm around your woman and help her back to the house."

They made slow progress back to the town, having to stop every now and then to allow Alessia to lean on Danthys and wait for the waves of pain to pass; and stopping more often to explain to passers-by what was afoot and to receive their good wishes for a safe and easy delivery, "and a healthy baby, if it is the Mother's wish." When they reached the house, Alessia refused to go inside, but sat outside in the shade where there was a small breeze making its way up the narrow street. There was still heat in the day and Alessia's face was red and damp. The three of them sat together in front of the house and in between Alessia's pains they talked of many things, including the little accidents of life that had brought them together at this time. *Trynor sat near Alessia, his hand out towards her, smoothing her energies, and not for the first time, wishing he could have a stronger effect on the breeze.*

"I should spend more time learning how to manipulate the physical world," he said to Jotin, who was sitting back observing, having made sure that none of his other charges had a greater need of him.

"It's hard. But you should work on wind. Occasionally I can get a gust to blow a bit harder, or in another direction. Not often helpful, but I did blow out a candle once. My person got away from an attacker as result. One of my high points."

"It looks so uncomfortable, being in pain, and hot as well."

"They are more used to it than you think. Lots of little pains all their lives, like a training, you could say. You really should take another body, then you wouldn't worry about a lot of it and pass less anxiety on to them."

"I'm not worried, really, Jo. I know it will all go fine, wasn't I with you at the meeting where it was arranged? Mohmi is waiting to join in. I just feel it would be nice to smooth it for my Alessia, make it easy."

44

"Not our job. We just guide them into it and through it. They have to work out how to make it easier, if they can; and they have. Rasifi has some herbs well stewed up that will ease the pain if it gets too much. The physical world provides a lot of the answers to its own problems."

"Quite the philosopher today, aren't you? Are you always this calm? Or is it just because it is Alessia going through it and not your Danthys?"

Jotin said nothing, as he let his memory go back over time, in Crete and before, and looked at his reactions to the troubles he and Danthys had gone through. At last he stretched slowly and said, "Yes, I think you're right. It is easy to be detached when it is someone else's pain. The same when I was a human, easier to bear another's misfortunes than your own."

Alessia groaned and clutched at Rasifi. Her eyes widened and she stared into the older woman's face, looking for reassurance.

"Come on, now. It's time to go indoors. It's cooler now and we can get you comfortable." She put her hand on Alessia's belly and stroked, waiting for the contraction to pass, before helping the frightened girl to her feet and into the house.

"I want my mother!" the helpless wail echoed in the narrow street. Danthys looked at Alessia and ran away, disappearing around the corner.

"Danthys, don't leave me, come back!" Alessia stared down the road.

"He'll be back soon, I'm sure; he's hardly running to Tylissos at this hour of the evening." Rasifi was business-like as she manoeuvred Alessia through the house and settled her on her sleeping mat, making her comfortable with cushions. In a few minutes Danthys panted back in.

"I didn't bring your mother, but I've brought your whole family!" He held out the clay picture Alessia's mother had made. Alessia smiled and ran her fingers gently over the faces, thinking she could feel her mother's spirit caught in the clay. She relaxed back on her pillows and allowed Rasifi to persuade her to take a sip of a herbal drink.

Hours passed and the room grew darker. There were sounds in the outer rooms as Mikolos and the boys returned from work and set about preparing food. They came in, one at a time, to see how things were going and to make cheering remarks. Alessia smiled to see them, but she was growing tired and she clutched her family picture to her and muttered to it occasionally.

"She is confusing her own mother with the Mother," said Rasifi to Danthys. "I think the herbs have befuddled her mind."

"No matter" said Trynor. "We're all listening to her intent, which is ours anyway. Why do you all think you have to pray for a safe delivery? We already know you want one. I suppose for the same reason that you tell your friends to take care on a journey, as though without your warning they would deliberately risk their lives. It's all an expression of caring, isn't it? And I care for you, I really do, my little one. Your baby is going to be just fine, as are you. Just keep going."

Alessia suddenly became agitated and tried to get up from the bed. When Danthys tried to stop her, she thumped feebly at his chest and raged at him that this was all his fault, that she had changed her mind about the baby and was going for a walk on the beach instead. Danthys stepped back astonished, but Rasifi laughed.

"It means the baby has decided to come. They are always like this when the baby joins them. The baby's energy and spirit has joined with Alessia's and shared with her the determination to get out. But the baby means out of Alessia, not out of the house. Go and fetch me a clean cloth and some warm water." With Danthys out of the way, she explained to Alessia what would happen next.

As Danthys came back into the room, the yellow light of the oil lamps was joined by a soft grey light, which fell across Rasifi from the small window. They all looked up, but Alessia could not see the moon from her place on the bed, so Danthys described it to her- nearly full, shining Mother Diktynna's good wishes down on them all. Alessia was cheered and calmed by the knowledge that the Mother was here and when the call came in her body to push her baby into the world, she obliged without any difficulty. The little girl rushed into the world on a stream of warm water and looked around quietly with big eyes. Rasifi lifted her up to the light from the window and as the moonlight fell across her face, she cried softly and waved her arms. Then she took another breath and roared. Danthys laughed, as Rasifi put his daughter on her mother's breast and he looked at his wife.

"She is shouting to the Mother! What is she saying, do you think? I hope it is polite."

"She is singing. Praises. So am I, inside." Alessia shut her eyes and stroked the baby's soft skin, unaware of Rasifi's activity as she cut the cord, delivered the afterbirth and then wrapped up the baby.

"Armishamai. Moonsong." Alessia opened her eyes and looked up at Danthys. "Would that be suitable?"

"It is a very pretty name. And she chose it herself." He put his hand out to touch the tiny form. "May the Mother always bless you, who sang to her in your first moment, my little Armishamai."

"A noble sentiment and a fine name. Now go away and let Alessia sleep. She has worked hard. Go and tell the good news." Rasifi shooed him out of the room and set about tidying up, not forgetting to whisper thanks in the direction of the moon.

"Thank you, too, for your help," said Mohmi, Armishamai's guide, who was sitting close to the baby, ready to soothe her if she woke and wondered what she was doing trapped in a body. The first few days were always the hardest, until they forgot and allowed themselves to become a baby.

Chapter 7

When Armishamai was a week old, Alessia started to discuss her naming ceremony and of course, the handfasting. Now that the baby was here, safe and well, it was appropriate to link her parents together formally, to work together to provide for her. Danthys suggested visiting Elena's sanctuary cave, but Alessia was firm. She wanted to go home to Tylissos and ask Planidi to perform the swearing ceremonies.

"After all, she's the reason I came here. If it had not been for Planidi, Armishamai might never have been born, we might never have met."

"We'd have got you here, don't you worry. We have Hetrion on our side, he hears his guide, so we only have to talk to her. Don't you worry, he'd have offered to bring you here anyway."

"I wonder if Hetrion is going that way soon, could we travel with him..." Alessia began to think about the phases of the moon, wondering if it might coincide with her needs and Danthys kissed her head and went back to the workshop. He knew that distracted look. There was no point in joining in the discussion, just wait and the ideas would brew. Then he could give his opinion.

As luck would have it -

"Luck!" says Trynor, "nobody ever realises how much we arrange..."

- Hetrion came past a week later and said he would be returning west in a month. He was delighted to take Alessia and the baby on one of the carts. Danthys could help with the bulls. So it was arranged and more than a year after she had travelled with him first, Alessia was again a temporary member of the bull dancing troupe. She sat up on one of the carts, holding Armishamai up to see her father walking in front.

"Look, little one! Dada is talking to the dancers." There was a burst of laughter from the group of young men and women walking with Danthys and a few of them glanced back at the cart.

"And I bet you he's telling them all about how we made you, my precious. Saying it was the dancing that did it." She watched with pleasure, but some envy, as Danthys started to dance with the troupe as they walked slowly along.

"Hey, I like that double dip, Danthys! Really feels like the earth moving." One of the bull dancers was copying Danthys, learning the Egyptian steps for the earth walk.

"Yes, it works, too," said Danthys, lowering his voice, pretending Alessia should not hear, "It was those steps that made her fall for me, the night of the grape festival. And maybe it was that night that the Mother sent us Armishamai!" Everyone laughed and two of the dancers started a very raunchy take on the earth walk, beckoning each other with sultry looks and tilting their pelvises on every dip.

"You'd better be careful, Danthys," giggled one of the younger women, "or you'll have dozens of babies," and she danced past him, trailing her fingers towards him as she did, "None of us would resist you!"

"Oh, Danthys will resist you fine, Dasi, look how beautiful Alessia is," said one of the men, before they started to teach Danthys the Cretan form of the dance.

The last part of the road to Tylissos was uphill, but Alessia got down from the cart and barely noticed the climb as her heart raced on ahead of her, anticipating their arrival. She scanned the hills for the first sign of the higher mountains that had watched over her childhood and when she saw them she turned to Danthys and put her arm through his with a contented sigh. Danthys was happy to be anywhere with Alessia, but he understood what she was feeling, as he had felt the same on his return to Crete from Egypt. He kissed the top of her head and whispered 'welcome home'.

As they came closer to Tylissos, Alessia saw a girl standing on the small promontory that overlooked the road. The sunlight was behind her, but she had a familiar outline and when she began waving and jumping it was clear. It was one of Alessia's sisters, who turned away now and with a flick of skirts, disappeared on the other side of the little hill.

"Gone to tell the others the news" said Trynor.

"I wonder will they like us," said Jotin, "I've been doing this for thousands of years, but I've never got over the nervousness of meeting new people. In one of my own lives it went very badly. I'm still waiting for people to reach for rocks again. It's hard not to let

50

my feelings leak through."

"They are going to love him. What is there to dislike? He's a nice, straightforward man, who loves their daughter. And they are straightforward people. Haven't been messed up by too many lives, like you! So stop worrying."

"Easy to say" fretted Jotin. "Worrying is something that sometimes creeps up on you, even when you aren't expecting it. You really should stop pussyfooting and take another life yourself. Then you might understand." He stopped, looked at Trynor and laughed. "But you don't, because you are worried. You are worried that you would make a mess of it, or feel the pain too much, or something of the sort. So you stay an observer. I tell you, young friend, it will get us into trouble sometime."

Trynor smiled. "Is that a prophecy?" He laughed. "Or just a threat?"

"Neither. Just a bad feeling for a moment."

"Well, stop it at once. Look at Danthys." Trynor pointed and Jotin turned to look. Danthys was walking slower than the others, falling behind. His expression was anxious and his smooth forehead was furrowed, maybe for the first time. Jotin moved quickly over to him and put his energy around the worried boy.

"Alessia, look!" said Trynor and Alessia turned to see Danthys' face. She waited for him to take the few steps to catch up with her, then put out her hand to him.

"That was my sister. She has gone to tell the others we are coming. Oh, Danthys, it is going to be so wonderful to see them again and to introduce them to Arma, and to you, of course. They will love both of you." She reached up and kissed him, and Danthys put his arm around her waist and drew her to him.

"I don't know why I got worried. Why should they not like me?" he said, in a puzzled tone. "But I just found myself wondering for a moment, how they would feel and whether I would be a threat to them."

"How could you be a threat?"

"I have no idea. It just came into my mind. Ridiculous really."

"You see the damage you caused, Jotin? And you were trying to blame me for causing problems."

"It seems this one is over," said Jotin, indicating the road ahead. There on the road was a group of people pointing and talking. A little girl was jumping up and down, and as the bull-dancing troupe drew closer she broke away from the others and ran towards them, her black curls bobbing. Alessia handed Armishamai to Danthys and knelt down, her arms out. Little Paslona, with squeals of "Alessia, Alessia!" threw herself onto Alessia's lap and buried her face in her older sister's shoulder. Muffled squeaks could be heard, as she recounted how she had missed her sister, and what skills she had acquired since Alessia went away. Alessia lifted her up and, carrying her as she had since Paslona was a newborn, she was gathered back into her family.

"So is this your daughter, Alessia?" asked her father after the first excitement had died down. "Isn't she a little beauty? And this fine man must be her father? You are very welcome. It is wonderful to welcome our daughter back as a full woman, blessed by the Mother and with her man beside her. Come , we must drink to this day. And you too, Hetrion, you must help us to celebrate, for you played a big part in this story."

The party lasted into the dark, as stories were exchanged. Alessia told of the earth walk, her new knowledge of gold, her love for Malatos and her adopted family there; and her family told of all the goings on in the town since she had left, the new births and the deaths, the celebrations and festivals. They included Danthys easily into the circle, sometimes remembering to explain to him who they were speaking about. As the time wore on, they explained less and less, as it seemed that he had been a part of their family always, and Danthys relaxed and told his stories too, of Egypt and the wonders there.

The two guides kept only a cursory eye on the proceedings, as they could see that all was well. They looked in occasionally, just to be sure, but as the evening wore on they could see their help was superfluous. Jotin was glad, as his attention was called for in no uncertain terms by one of his other charges. She had just noticed that what she had mistaken for a log in a river was actually a crocodile. So Jotin transferred his energy to the southern continent, to alert the girl's family.

Trynor's other people were all sleeping, as night had fallen on their parts of the world, so after a while he went back to his own home, to refresh his energies and talk to those who guided him.

The family, unaware of the wider world and secure in their own happiness, sang and laughed, the adults cradling the already sleeping children, as the moon set. It was only as the first tendrils of sunlight began to creep across the sky that they grew quiet, began to yawn and at last moved inside to settle for what was left of the night.

Chapter 8

Many days were spent in planning the naming ceremony. Alessia wanted all her old friends to attend, so she visited each one, to make sure they had no other plans for the day of the full moon. These visits took a long time, as Armishamai was admired wherever she was brought. Niklon's mother was fulsome in her praise and, because she had never known of Niklon's hopes, insisted that her son should admire the baby and congratulate Alessia. He did this with an empty expression, barely muttering 'yes, lovely' and not bringing himself to look Danthys in the eye. Everyone else was captivated by the baby's smile and the dimple it produced in her fat cheek. Danthys was equally admired, only a little less openly. His brown hair and his paler skin were remarked on and there was much discussion about Armishamai's colouring. It was wonderful to be back with friends and with so much to talk about. There were cousins and their families to see too as well as a feast to plan. Everyone offered to bring something, so there would not be too much extra work for Alessia's family, who still had to keep working in the pottery.

"So, did you ask everyone what they planned to bring?" asked Alessia's mother Tikda, as Alessia and Danthys came into the house one evening, laughing and chatting about who they had seen that day.

"No, but they all said they would bring something. There will be plenty. Oh, it will be the most wonderful feast!" Alessia, her eyes shining, danced around her mother. Tikda stood back and put out a hand to slow Alessia down.

"Hold on, hold on. Less excitement and more thought for just a minute. Do you not remember Tanthos and Falida's feast? I thought no one would ever forget!"

"Oh, yes!" and Alessia began to laugh. "I suppose we had better go back and ask!" She turned to Danthys and when she could catch her breath, she explained:

"They got offers of food, just like we did, but almost everyone brought olives! There were about seventy people there, with one loaf of bread, one dish of lamb and about fifteen big bowls of olives!! It's amazing we weren't all sick. It was so funny, we laughed all night!"

"I don't think Falida thought it was funny," said Tikda, "It nearly spoiled her day."

"It was her own fault," said Alessia without thinking, then she heard what she had just said and laughed again, "just like it would be mine. That's tomorrow sorted out, Danthys, we have to go and see everyone again."

"Except Falida" warned Tikda, "don't remind her."

"I imagine Falida will check around herself, after what happened to her," suggested Danthys, who had been falling more in love with Alessia as he watched her reaction to the old story. She was so straightforward, so quick to acknowledge her mistakes, so simply happy. He threw his arms around her and kissed her, then turned to Tikda, and kissed her too. Armishamai, caught in the crush of bodies, laughed and squealed and struggled. As Alessia turned to free the baby, she noticed a small dish on the table beside her. She picked it up and held it out to the others.

"Would you like an olive?" she asked, as a new wave of giggles bubbled out of her.

On the day of the naming ceremony, they were all up early, even though the guests would not gather till dusk. There were tables to be fetched from neighbours and set up on the flat ground beside the house. There were cups and plates to be counted and wine to be carried up from the shop in the town. There were dresses to be got ready, hair to be dressed and make-up to be applied. There were oil-lamps to be filled and wicks to be trimmed. They were all very busy, so in the middle of the afternoon when Tikda decreed that they should all go inside and lie down for an hour, there were cries of protest, particularly from Alessia's sisters, who wanted to continue making themselves beautiful. But their mother prevailed, telling them that an hour's sleep would add more to their beauty than any amount of kohl; so for a short while peace fell over the household.

At dusk, they gathered outside the house and their friends and relations brought their dishes and arranged the food on the tables for later. Two old women, who did not want to climb the hill to the sanctuary, because of bad legs in one case and shortness of breath in the other, were given seats near the tables and instructed to guard the food from marauding creatures, "with four legs or two!" They were given some wine to help them with their duties, and with much laughter about the value of two sleepy old ladies as guards, the rest of the group set off towards the sanctuary hill.

They were met on the way to the hill by Planidi, who called those people who could play an instrument to the front of the crowd and had a brief discussion with them. Then she turned and led the party up the hill, followed by the musicians. She sang an ancient chant to The Mother and the musicians accompanied her. The older people, who had heard this chant more often, were able to join in, so some of the group reached the top of the hill quite out of breath.

"Isn't it beautiful?" Alessia whispered to Danthys. "This is where I got the message that I was to go to Mikolos. It has to be a special place."

"It will be special for you, Alessia, because you make it special for yourself. It is beautiful. Always be aware of beauty, and teach Armishamai to see it too."

Alessia lifted Armishamai up to look around her, whispering in her baby ear. Planidi was drawing a circle in the dust inside the sanctuary stones. She called Alessia and Danthys forward to stand with her inside the circle and everyone else jostled around, to get the best view. Planidi held up her double-sided axe to the moon, now rising above them.

"Hail, Mother, guardian of us all, and especially this day of this baby, named in your honour." She went on with the prayer, mentioning all the spirits who would have a part to play in the lives of the little family beside her. Eventually she came to the actual naming.

"And she came into this world in your light, the light of the moon, and is to be named Armishamai which means Moonsong, so that she may sing your praise and walk in your light always." Planidi turned to Alessia, "hold her up to the moon, so that she is in front of it. That's right, up high." And when Alessia had stretched her arms up to the moon, holding her daughter, Planidi touched the end of the double axe to Armishamai's forehead and started some ancient incantations. The baby put out her fat little hands and gripped the blades of the axe, causing a ragged cheer from the watchers. Niklon, standing at the back of the crowd, smiled silently to himself.

"Stop reading bad futures into everything. It is not good for you

to be wishing bad for others," Roki was standing in front of Niklon, staring into the smug face. "Come on now, be happy for them and for this baby. Let go of wanting Alessia. She is not yours. Not this time."

"Why is it good if she grabs the axe?" whispered Danthys to Alessia, who although she was not entirely sure herself, whispered back that it was probably because Armishamai would be more connected with The Mother as she had grabbed her symbol herself.

"Now, the vows" said Planidi.

"Be careful, now. Don't vow anything you aren't sure you can fulfil." Jotin looked around at Trynor, who nodded. "Yes," he agreed. "we have to be careful here". They listened as Planidi asked Alessia and Danthys if they would vow to stay together, to look after Armishamai.

"That could be all right. Depends on the wording."

"So, now that you have named your baby in the light of the moon, you must vow to stay together and care for her until she comes safely to adulthood."

"NO!" said Trynor and Jotin together. "You can't vow that. Too much can go wrong. The world is too risky a place. Too many babies and children die. Just say you'll do your best. No Vow. NO!"

Alessia shuddered, as a sudden cool gust blew across her. Danthys reached out and took her hand. He smiled gently down at her.

"Of course we vow that, don't we? I want to stay with you for always."

"And I with you." Alessia looked at her feet for a moment, then up at him. "I love you more than anything."

"So do you vow to stay together?" Planidi raised her arms again to the moon.

"That is safe enough, just for this life," said Trynor.

"Yes, we vow to stay together," said Danthys and Alessia.

"And do you vow to care for this child?" Planidi took Armishamai from Alessia, and raised her again to the light of the moon.

"Of course you do."

"Yes, we vow."

"And do you vow to see her safely to adulthood?"

"NO, NO!" Trynor and Jotin shouted in unison. But Alessia and

Danthys saw only the moonlight, their precious baby, and their love for each other. And despite the feeling of cold that ran across them both, they joined hands and raised them to the moon and said

"We vow."

"Oh no, Trynor, what will we do now? They've vowed it, without any escape clauses. No 'with the Mother's help' or 'as long as we have the health' or anything!" Jotin's solid energy deserted him, so he sank down until he was sitting on one of the sanctuary rocks.

Danthys staggered slightly and put his hand to his head. He felt a little dizzy for a moment. Must be hunger, he thought, I forgot to eat at midday, with all the rushing around.

"It's not hunger, you silly boy," said Jotin crossly. You've just knocked all the stuffing out of me. The work you two are making for me and my friend here if anything happens to Armishamai, you have no idea."

"Come on, Jotin, pull yourself together." Trynor was fluttering around, his optimistic outlook to the fore. "We can help them fulfil that vow. It's only fifteen years, after all. There's a very good chance nothing will go wrong. And if you stay positive, Danthys will too and things will go better. They are both healthy, we don't expect any problems in the near future, do we?"

"No, I think they will both stay in good health, won't they? Barring accidents, of course. We'll have to keep a special watch to prevent those. No trip to Egypt, now. Too risky, pirates and storms."

"But if Armishamai is with them, what's the problem, if they all die together?"

"You must all be witness to the solemn vow taken here tonight!" Planidi's strong voice reverberated round the sanctuary, "The Mother will help those who try faithfully to keep their word, but terrible are the consequences for failure!" *Trynor paled a little as he listened to the woman pile on more awful warnings. He whispered to Jotin. "Do you think that priestess is going to insist the vow lasts forever? Would she have that power?" His slim energies stilled and he lowered himself to sit on the ground beside Jotin.*

Alessia looked around for a seat. She felt she could not hold the baby for another moment. She really was heavy for three months old. There was nothing near and Alessia's legs, feeling as useful as soup, bent and she sagged onto the ground. Danthys reached down to her and she heard a murmur of concern swell through the group of her friends and family, as several people came forward to help. There was a chatter of sound around her and she could pick out some phrases: 'too much excitement', 'overcome with the emotion of the day', needs some food inside her', but also 'not a good omen' and quickly, 'shh'. Alessia made an effort to clear her head. She did not want any rumours of bad omens to hang round her precious child. She looked up at her brother, who was reaching down to her and handed him the baby.

"Take Arma for me, will you? She just got heavy for a moment there. Must be having a name that did it!" She struggled to her feet despite the dizzy feeling that clung round her head. She took Danthys' hand and turned to Planidi, waiting for the next part of the ceremony.

"Look, Jotin, my little Alessia has more courage than us! She's up already."

"She doesn't know what has just been done to them," grumbled Jotin as he raised his energies to an upright position and started running his hands around Danthys, smoothing his energy and enlivening him. "It will be all fine in the end, so let's not get thrown by what might never happen." Trynor was on his feet now, also. Alessia and Danthys were standing happily in the sanctuary, listening to Planidi's closing incantations and waiting for the best moment of the ceremony, when she and Danthys would be ceremonially joined, hand to hand and would be truly a family.

Everyone joined hands around the new little family and danced. The circular dance around them sealed their energy in and surrounded them with love and support. These people would always help them in times of need and their other friends in Malatos would dance around them later, when they returned home. Alessia's eyes shone as she and Danthys danced in the sanctuary, in the circle of her family. She felt safe and happy, and truly blessed.

"We must be loved by all the gods, Danthys," she whispered so that only he could hear, "to be so blessed, and so happy."

Danthys swung her around, so that she squealed with delight and gathered her into his arms, crushing a happy breath out of her.

"I certainly am. To be loved by you and to have our little

Armishamai, our personal prayer to the Moon. I feel I will always be special." He closed his eyes and swayed in time to the makeshift orchestra's happy sounds.

Chapter 9

Alessia was busy in the gold workshop, with Armishamai sleeping in her basket in the dim corner. There was not much light left in the short day and Alessia wanted to finish the ornament she was making to protect Arma. It was quiet in the room, with just a sputtering of oil in the lamp that Alessia had lit to help her get the work done today. Everyone else was at home, starting the preparations for tomorrow's feast. A whole year gone, she thought, since we sent an offering up to the sanctuary on the high plain. It was a good idea, everything has gone well since. The Mother is watching us. She hammered the little piece of metal again, until it was as thin as possible. She had cut the other side of the double axe earlier and when this one was done she could put it on Arma and go home. The baby had been protected until last week by the pottery axe her grandfather had given her at her naming, but now she was beginning to crawl and it had cracked when Armishamai tumbled against a box in their sleeping room. So it was urgent to make her a new amulet. Alessia concentrated hard as she cut the half-moon axe shape and grunted with satisfaction as the tiny double headed axe appeared in her hands. I am only beginning, she thought, it will be many years before I have enough skill to show to the public, but I think the Mother will find this acceptable for a baby. She laughed as she thought ahead down the years to come and saw a line of amulets, each more skilfully made than the last, protecting her daughter.

A little wail came from the corner and a tiny fist appeared over the edge of the basket and grabbed the side. Armishamai was trying to pull herself up to look over the edge. Alessia bent down and lifted her to a sitting position in the basket.

"There now. You wait there for Mama for a minute. Good girl. Mama has to put a cord on your necklace. Then you'll be even prettier, won't you, my precious?" she babbled on in this way and Armishamai's round dark eyes followed her as she cut a thin strip of leather, and looped it through the little hole at the top of the tiny double headed axe. Then Alessia crouched down beside the basket and tied the ornament around the baby's neck, whispering a prayer to The Mother as she did so. She sat back on her heels and admired her daughter, now decorated with and protected by gold, instead of pottery.

"Now you are a beautiful girl, aren't you?" Alessia lifted the baby out of the basket onto her hip and, wrapping a large shawl around them both against the chill of the winter evening, went out of the shop, sealing the door behind her. She exchanged some pleasantries with the scribe, whose nose was down on her clay tablets as she wrote, then with the guards on the palace gate and hurried towards the town and home.

The midwinter festival was the next day and today's meal was taking second place to the preparations. The house was full of wonderful smells, as Danthys' mother and sister prepared the dishes they would contribute. Alessia sat in the midst of the activity and nursed Armishamai. Then, giving her a hard crust to chew on, she joined in with the work. Danthys and Bullneck were down in the square, helping to set up tables and raising screens across some of the streets to give protection from the winter winds. The festival meal would take place at midday, when the square might catch some sun and be warm.

Danthys and Alessia chatted as they lay in bed together later. Danthys had admired Armishamai's amulet and had praised Alessia for her skill after such a short time learning. They were looking forward to the festival meal tomorrow and hoping that Elena and her family might still arrive. As they talked, they felt a shake in the bed.

"Stop that, Danthys!" protested Alessia, prodding him in the side.

"I did nothing, love. I think it is the earth god, turning over again. She has been very restless these last ten days, had you noticed? Maybe she is looking forward to the festival, too. Let's go to sleep, it will come quicker."

But Alessia could not sleep without first getting out of bed and doing a few steps of the earth walk, "to let her know we heard". Then she got back into bed and fell asleep.

They woke again, when it was still dark, as another tremor shook them. This one was bigger and they could hear cups rattling in the other room. They laughed, a bit nervously and agreed that the earth spirits were really excited. Then another jolt in the earth shook their bed and as it settled, they heard a soft crack, as something fell off the shelf and landed on the floor beside them. Alessia put out her hand and felt around on the floor. A sharp point scratched her finger and she felt more carefully, her hands outlining two pieces of flat pottery, each with little lumps jutting out. Alessia gasped as she realised what it was and she traced her fingers around the outline, trying to assess the damage.

"It is the picture my mother made for me, when I left to come here. It is broken at the corner, I think my face has broken off."

"We'll look when it is light, maybe it can be mended. If the others are still recognisable that's all that matters.

"Let's get up, and go down to the sea," said Alessia, "And watch the sun rise." So they did, creeping out carefully so they would not wake the others and carrying Armishamai's basket between them, one handle each. The baby slept on, soothed by the rocking movement of her little bed. They walked through the sleeping town and down to the beach, walking carefully on the soft sand. The first blush of the dawn was beginning to light up the sky to the south-east and they could see each other's faces. There was a gentle wind, but chilly.

"It's a good thing we put up those screens in the town, the party will be warmer. It's cool here. Do you want to go further?"

"Let's go down to the wet sand and greet the god of the sea," said Alessia. "He has nothing to do with the midwinter festival, maybe he will appreciate a surprise visit!"

As they walked down the beach towards the boundary to the sea god's territory, the earth spirit shook again, fiercely. Alessia staggered, losing her grip on the handle of the baby's basket. The basket lurched and the baby let out a thin cry. Alessia laughed as no-one had been hurt and indicated to Danthys to put the basket down so that she could lift the baby out. As he did, the beach shuddered under them and their ears were assaulted by the loudest noise they had ever heard. It came from everywhere and nowhere, from outside them and from inside their heads. Alessia and Danthys clutched each other in fright, as they looked around to find the source of that huge noise. Armishamai started to wail. Danthys squinted up towards the hills, as he had heard stories that the earth spirit can sometimes try to escape through the top of a mountain, but there was nothing to see, except some people, running out of the town, also looking up towards the hills and gesticulating to each other.

"The Earth Spirits are angry," said Alessia. "I wish Hetrion was here, he could do a better dance. Come on, it's maybe up to us." She began the gentle swirling movements of the earth walk. Danthys joined in, to show support and because he could not think of anything else appropriate to do. Armishamai found the movements of the dance soothing and settled down in her mother's arms. After a few minutes a straggling group of people from the town came to watch and Alessia explained what she was doing.

"Maybe if you copy us, it will make the dance stronger and soothe the spirit of the earth as it has soothed my baby," she suggested. One of the women offered to hold Armishamai so that Alessia's arms could be free to honour the spirits more effectively. The dance circled on and after a few more grumbles the earth spirit seemed to settle down. Alessia led the group down to the water's edge, where it would be easier to dance on the solid sand, and as she moved along one of the other dancers suddenly stopped and pointed out to sea.

"Look, a light to the North! The sun has moved round!"

"No it hasn't, "said Danthys, "His light is still behind the mountains, look."

"Then what light is that?" They gathered to look out over the sea.

"Oh look," said Alessia, "our dance has worked. The Earth spirit is getting stronger. The sea is moving back to give her more space." They looked down and indeed there was now in front of them a wide expanse of wet, packed sand. It was the fisherman in the group who shouted first.

"Look, the god of the sea is giving us a contribution to the feast! Fish for the taking! Come on, everyone, help me!" He dashed forward to pick up flapping fish from the sand, laughing with the huge joy and the joke of it. Alessia and Danthys darted forward too, all other thoughts wiped out by the fun of picking up food from the bottom of the sea. They dashed to and fro, gathering the fish into Alessia's apron.

"We should get Arma's basket. That should hold more," said Danthys. Alessia looked at Danthys.

"Where is the woman with Arma?" she asked and stood up to

scan the group. She thought she saw her, over towards the rocks at the east end of the beach, but the shadows made it hard to tell. She looked out to sea, to look again at the light from the north, but she could not see it. The sea was black, not as it should be with the dawn light on it and the horizon was too high.

"Danthys, look, what is that?" but she did not need to ask more, as the horizon rose further and Alessia realised she was looking up at a mountain of water. Her hands went limp and she did not feel her apron-full of fish drop onto her feet, nor was she really aware of the warm flood that gushed down her legs onto the flapping fish. She vaguely heard screams and a cry beside her, "Alessia!" and barely felt Danthys' hand grab out for her arm, as the centre of desperation itself broke out from within her.

"Armishamaiiiiii!" Alessia lunged towards where she thought her baby might be, but the wall of water hit her and in the fraction of a moment before it knocked all the air from her body she barely had time for regret.

Chapter 10
Meeting Number Four

Jotin, Trynor and Mohmi, who had watched the baby Armishamai for her short life, sat in an area that seemed grassy, with a view of distant purplish hills. But they paid no attention to their surroundings. They looked at each other a little blankly at first. This was so unexpected it had knocked the stuffing out of them in the same way that the real breath had been squeezed from their people. Those people were in Healing at the moment, resting after their shock and being soothed by spirits with special skills. Soon they would be well again and able to join the group.

"Why were we not watching? We could have warned them," said Jotin.

"It was the night, or nearly," said Mohmi. "I'm off duty at night usually. My girl was asleep, I didn't hear her call until she had arrived home. That was too late. But it doesn't matter, does it? They are all fine, the lives were good, they can have another chance."

Trynor and Jotin sighed. "Yes, of course, that is true to some extent," said Trynor, "we know they are never dead. But you maybe weren't there at the naming ceremony. You didn't hear Alessia and Danthys vow to bring Armishamai to adulthood."

"Oh dear."

There was a long silence, as each guide thought through all the meanings and possible outcomes of this. At last Mohmi spoke.

"But it was not their fault. It was an earthquake, seventy miles away. How can that be held over them?"

"It won't be held over them by anyone other than themselves," said Jotin, "but humans are terrible taskmasters. They get notions and make up strange rules for themselves all the time. Look at some of those religious rituals. Some of them even sacrifice their children to appease their gods." He lapsed again into gloom.

"We should have been looking. We should have warned them." Trynor was shaking his head in disbelief that they could have made such an error. Slowly, a gentle light filled the grassy area

where they were sitting and each of the three guides heard an inner voice, reassuring and soothing.

"There were thousands brought back here by that wave and by the earthquake. None of us knew it was coming, not even at the highest level. No watching could have helped. But you know no harm is done, we are all still here and the human souls are unharmed. You know this. There is all of time to grow and learn. This is a brief sorrow and a misplaced one. They have a new chance now, to try something different, to learn more skills. You know all this. Why must I remind you?" With a gentle chuckle the voice faded away. The three guides were silent, feeling a little shamefaced after the gentle reproof. When their energies brightened they started to discuss what would be best to do next. Each one outlined to the others the special needs of their own human and they talked about ways in which they could help each other; in what ways it would be better if they worked apart or with other souls. As they chatted, they flitted in and out, going to discuss with other guides and friends, until at last it felt right to invite their charges to join them.

Armishamai arrived first and ran to Mohmi, throwing her arms around her guide. Mohmi wrapped her energies around Armishamai, who in moments was laughing, her white aura sparking with the joy of being alive.

"It's hard being in a body, Mohmi," she said, twirling around and allowing ribbons of her energy to wave around her, "particularly a baby one. You can't do anything, and you don't understand anything. I felt hungry most of the time I wasn't asleep." Her light dimmed for a moment as she remembered the water and how she had been ripped from the arms of the woman who was holding her. She had cried out in unformed baby fear for her mother, but in a moment the water had surrounded her and instead of her mother she had seen her true friend Mohmi, who she knew was with her always. Armishamai laughed now, as she remembered the other lives she had lived with Mohmi's guidance, and the memory of the dark water receded. Her white light shone again, young and simple, and she moved around the waiting guides like a puppy wagging its whole body.

"Danthys!" Armishamai saw him first and ran to embrace him. Danthys allowed her to throw her arms around him, but patted

her rather awkwardly, unable to meet her eyes. His light, pale cream, was less sparkling than Armishamai's and he held himself rather stiffly.

"What's the matter, Danthys?"

"That's the matter. You are calling me Danthys. You never called me Father. I let you down."

"Well, I couldn't call you anything. I was only six months old. But in my mind I was calling you father, even though I couldn't make the words. But it doesn't matter, we know we're friends, don't we? It wasn't your fault I died. You aren't so powerful you can affect the sea, are you? It was just a rough day, that's all."

"No, it was more than that. They have told me an island exploded. Maybe the people who lived there didn't know the earth walk and the earth spirit was angry."

"No, Danthys." Jotin was beside Danthys, reaching out to calm him. "The earth walk would not have helped. It is a physical thing, the way the earth is made. None of us can control it; certainly nothing you could have done would have made any difference. The earth walk is a lovely way to calm the souls of humans and make them aware of the world. But it doesn't affect the world, you know."

"Yes, I do know, don't I? Now. But I can't help feeling it is my fault. We promised to protect our child and now look. No, not promised, vowed. Much more important."

"Only in your mind, Danthys. No one here expects you to keep every promise you make. How could you, when the earth blew up? There have been floods all around the inland sea and dark clouds over the lands. There will be stories told that will last for thousands of years, long after everyone has forgotten what really happened. You are released from your vow, your teachers will tell you so; they have already told us."

Danthys sat and thought about this. He remembered those last few terrifying moments, his knowledge that he would lose Alessia, that all was for nothing. He put his head in his hands and his energies shrank a bit. Jotin sat beside him, touching, ready to help when Danthys was able to hear.

A pale yellow light appeared in the space and Armishamai danced towards it, singing, 'Alessia, Alessia!' Alessia reached out to Armishamai and drew her close, burying her face in her

71

daughter's hair.

"Oh, my baby, didn't you grow up to be beautiful! You were a beautiful baby, of course. Let me look at you." She held Armishamai away from her, drinking in the sight of her daughter, gone from her only a little time, now back after the separation of the grave. She smiled, hugged Armishamai and began to lead her in the steps of the earth walk, which had been so familiar and comforting to her.

"How lovely that you can do this with me, Arma," she murmured as they circled. If Trynor and Mohmi had been able to cry, they might have shed a tear as they watched the gentle reunion of the two friends. Jotin leant towards Danthys and whispered to him. After a while Danthys looked up, his face showing that he did not expect much. But he saw Alessia and jumped to his feet, ran over to her and lifted her high in his arms, spinning around with her as they had done on earth. The three guides looked at each other, smiled and let Danthys and Alessia have time together.

After a while, all was calm. Alessia sat between Danthys and Armishamai. When the guides approached, they could hear the human souls talking, quietly but intensely. The guides stood back and listened.

"I know, Arma, that it doesn't matter that we broke our vow-"

Suddenly there was a darkening over the group and a ringing voice spoke from the side.

"But you must! It is imperative! It was a VOW!" A faintly lemon light showed and they recognised it as Planidi. Alessia looked at her in astonishment. Planidi's colour showed that she was no older a soul than Alessia was herself, maybe even a bit younger.

"But you were a priest!" she gasped out, "How were you so much better than me and you have only my experience?"

"I can hear the guides when I have a body. They tell me I am better at it than nearly everyone else. So it is what I do. Listen for other people, while they are learning. But you must pay me, by doing what you have promised." The lemony light elongated, as Planidi drew herself up to her full height. The blue light of a much older spirit stood beside her and leant forward to talk to her privately. Planidi tossed her head and pouted. Then the blue guide spoke to Trynor, before encouraging Planidi away. Trynor watched them go, his edges softening as they went.

"Her guide says we must pay no attention. This happens sometimes, when a soul realises it has skills. He will bring her to teachers, she will learn. As you all will."

"You have a lot to learn yet," said Jotin, "You are doing well, all of you, but I don't think you are ready to be together again just yet. Even if Arma here wants you as her parents."

"Of course I do!" said Armishamai. "Though it means being a baby again. Your energies are special when you are together. It was lovely being protected by both of you at once. I felt invincible."

"Really?" asked Alessia. "You want to be our baby again? To set us free of the vow and of Planidi?"

"Of course I do, but not for the vow," Armishamai's tone was solemn, "for me. In fact, I insist on it. And as the baby, I might cry if I can't!"

"You'll just have to cry, then," said Mohmi, "I think you have other places to go and things to do that are more urgent. We will talk with your teachers and get their advice. When the time is right, you can all be together again. And maybe you can all use the experience to learn something, not just sort out a silly promise you made on a balmy hillside in a fit of romantic fervour. Right, Trynor, Jotin?"

The two guides nodded, smiling. "Yes," they said. "We'll let you know when it's a good time. In the meanwhile, go back to your groups, get on with other tasks. We'll let you know when you're ready."

Danthys looked at Alessia and reached a tendril of energy towards her.

"I wish we were in the same group," he whispered, "or even at the same level. Then we could see each other all the time and not have to wait to be given lives."

Alessia nodded and turned to Trynor.

"Can we not be put into the same group, Trynor? Soul mates ought to be together, surely?"

"When you have learnt more, maybe you will be put into a skill group together. But for now, you are more advanced than Danthys. He would hold you back."

"No!" Alessia was indignant. "Our energies match, you saw them, we would help each other. Please!"

"Not yet, my love. We will arrange another life together for you as soon as we can. And you can meet here sometimes, between classes. Be patient. Say goodbye, now."

Chapter 11
Dublin May 1972

David could hear the sounds of happy singing coming from the kitchenette of their little flat, along with the crashing and banging that indicated that a meal was being prepared. It was just over a week since they had arrived home from their honeymoon in Spain, a lovely sunny warm fortnight, when Kathleen had seemed to love him more than ever, had invited him back to bed at every opportunity and had encouraged him to love her in the most physical ways. Quite a change from the one hurried New Year's Eve fumbling before the marriage, which had resulted in the pregnancy. Maybe being married is the key, thought David, wincing at yet another crash in the kitchen. She just wasn't relaxed before. Pity we got pregnant so quickly though. Not enough time to think things through, to finish my course, to get those qualifications. Now I might have to do it as a night course. His mind wandered down the trail labelled 'night' and he felt a familiar frisson as he remembered Spain. Isn't quite so good the last few days, she's more inclined to huddle under the covers. Probably the weather, it's cool here and we were spoiled by that sunshine.

Kathleen came in, carrying two plates. "Ta Da!"

"I take it my beautiful wife has produced a masterpiece?"

"Don't I always?" Kathleen was flirtatious.

"Oh, absolutely. Puree of spaghetti, singe of chops, risotto a la carbon. Delicious."

"You ate them."

"Of course. Why wouldn't I? Didn't you make them? What is it tonight?"

"Ham salad."

"Great. Explains all the crashing. Lots of cooking to do. Oh Kath, I love you!" David reached out for Kathleen, who sidestepped him and put the plates on the table. Her hair swung forward and he put out his hand to stroke it. She flicked it back over her shoulder and smiled at him.

"Sit," she said as she took her own place, humming her happy little tune.

"Is your morning sickness still all right, love? It seemed OK in Spain. Mum told me it only usually lasts about three months."

"I'm not four months pregnant." Kathleen fixed her eyes on him and a chill ran down David's back. He looked at her, not having taken in what she was saying. "I'm just five weeks. Dr Holden told me today."

"What? How can you be only five weeks pregnant? It's May. Ages since New Year."

"I wasn't pregnant then. But I am now, isn't it great? Five weeks, counting from two weeks before we got married."

"You told me you were pregnant. So we had to get married. What happened?"

"I wasn't pregnant. But you were dithering and not getting on with proposing. I couldn't propose to you, I'm the girl."

"You could have asked me. It's 1972, not the Middle Ages."

"But what if you'd said no?"

"I would have said no. I didn't want to get married, to anyone."

"That's a horrible thing to say!" Kathleen put her head into her hands and stared at the table, "To say to your wife that you didn't want to get married!" She kicked the table leg.

"Well, I didn't. But I thought we had to," David stopped and looked at Kathleen, as realisation shot into his mind. His eyes widened and he continued "You fucking bitch, you tricked me. Seduced me into having sex with you -"

"I didn't."

"You did seduce me. You were all over me, your tongue was —"

"No, I didn't have sex with you. Not properly. You were totally pissed and you seemed to think we had, so...." Kathleen was smiling. No, thought David as his mind whirled and he tried to make sense of what had happened, she's smirking.

"You bitch! You trapped me into marrying you with a big fat lie!"

"Like I said," Kathleen said, her voice soft and silky, "you weren't getting on with it. You needed a push."

"I wasn't getting on with it, as you say, because I wasn't thinking of getting married. For God's sake, Kathleen, we're only twenty-two. I haven't finished college. And we certainly didn't need a baby."

"I want a baby," said Kathleen sullenly.

"So that's why all the lovey dovey in Spain? Because you want a baby. Not happy to trap yourself a husband, you then engineer a pregnancy too. Why didn't you take the Pill and put it off until I'd qualified?"

"I couldn't take the Pill. I was pregnant already, supposedly. What would you have thought if you'd seen me taking the Pill?"

"Who cares? What do you think I'm thinking now? That you are a scheming little slut who comes out of this squeaky clean, with a baby the regulation nine months after the wedding; unless I tell everyone what you've done."

"Please, David, don't do that. It won't change anything. I'm having a baby now. It's due at the end of January."

David stood up and reached for his jacket. "I'm going out."

"Where?"

"I'm going to see James. Tell him what an idiot I am. Get him to laugh at me, maybe it'll cheer me up. I can't stay here looking at you."

"That's horrible. When'll you be back? You haven't eaten your dinner."

"It won't go cold. It was never bloody hot. I don't know. Maybe I won't be back. Maybe I'll stay with James. He might not have rented out my room yet."

"You can't do that. You can't leave me!" Kathleen's voice was shaky. "I'm pregnant!"

"That's your fault. You should have thought it through. I'm going to. With a friend."

"But I'm your wife!"

"Unfortunately. But you're not my friend, are you? Seeya. Maybe."

David let himself out of the flat and walked quickly down the stairs. He felt as though he had just come through a wrestling match, he was winded and aching. His mind was whirring, but empty, except for two words, the bitch, the bitch, the bitch. He walked down Ranelagh and turned towards Rathmines, those two words rolling over and over, every step he took banging back up at him, the bitch the bitch, as he looked down a tunnel into his future, a tunnel that suddenly looked very narrow and dark.

"It's not as bad as you think, David. Just keep going, she'll die as arranged and you'll be fine with the baby. Your Mum will help. Don't give up." Jotin was plodding alongside, remembering all the

times he himself had been betrayed, all the different ways that humans managed to find to torment each other. "I haven't met this one before, David, it seems pretty vicious, but it'll all pan out in the end. Actually, I hadn't met Kathleen before either, so I couldn't predict this. But her guide tells me she needed a baby to fulfil her life plan. And look at it sensibly: you did need some distraction to keep you busy till Lucy grows up. Pity you couldn't have just had the sex without the getting married stuff. Lot of nonsense. Following silly rules. Daft. Specially now that they have invented such good ways to avoid pregnancy."

"She should have gone on the Pill," David muttered to himself as he climbed the front steps to what had been his home three short weeks ago. He rang the doorbell and after a minute an upstairs window opened and James stuck his head out.

"What are you doing here? Hang on." A moment later a key skittered across the pavement and fell into the gutter. David rescued it, let himself in and went up the stairs.

"Whoa, look who it is! The married man is slumming. You gone mad?" James was grinning.

"Yea, no girls here," added Paddy, "And if there were, they're ours. You've got one."

"All to yourself, lucky bastard," said Ken. The boys laughed and one of them made kissing noises. David sat down, suddenly feeling very old.

"Yea," he said, "Right."

"Of course," said James, "you're nearly a dad. Proves you've had fun. When is it, Halloween? 'Just six more months, that's all the time you've got,'" he sang.

"I'm being a Daddy in the morning!" sang Ken.

"Waa Waa the baby's going to cry!" added Paddy, as they got to their feet and started to march around the little room.

"Not till the end of January. I've been fool and she's a gold star bitch," said David. James stopped singing and sat down suddenly beside David.

"How come?" So David explained, leaving nothing out except the fact that he had apparently not actually even had proper sex with Kathleen on New Year's Eve. Ken and Paddy fell silent and listened. David was barely aware of their mutterings of "Jasus!" and "the hooer!"

"I feel such an idiot."

"Well, there's a reason for that," James said, punching his shoulder playfully. "You are. I told you not to have anything to do with her. She's not your type. I told you not to bring her to that party."

"It was only a party. I had nothing else planned."

"Rubbish. Everyone always has plans. You just succeeded with them. Lucky bastard."

"No, it was her idea, really."

"Well, don't tell too many people that part. Getting off with her is the only bit of this story that makes you look good. D'you want a beer?"

"Thanks."

The next morning was Saturday, so David stayed in his old bed and got re-acquainted with the furry mouth and drumming head that seemed to live in it. His head, the bits of it that were still functioning, was full of conflicting ideas, plans and thoughts about the future. Mostly he felt ashamed. Ashamed that he had let himself get drunk enough and into a position (literally, ha!) where he could be duped into thinking he had fathered a child. I'm an idiot, total. I wonder do I qualify for an annulment? Or would those bishops just say 'you had your willie where it shouldn't, tough luck." A long sentence for one small mistake. Eejit. Eejit. It wasn't even that much fun. Spain now, that was good. But that was only because she wanted to get pregnant. Oh fuck. David ran his hands through his hair and pressed his head, to distract himself from the pounding. He drifted off, into a dream where Kathleen was holding him at knifepoint and saying 'but you asked for kebabs!' and he was backing away, away, until he lost his footing and fell, the world whirling around him and he woke just in time to hold his head over the edge of the bed as the rush of vomit arrived.

Eventually he dragged himself out of bed and made feeble efforts to clean up after himself. He slouched blearily into the livingroom, accepted a mug of instant coffee from James, and sat on the sagging couch, holding the coffee, looking at it and every now and then steeling himself to take a sip. The steam was comforting, as was the warmth between his hands, but his stomach felt no better and his heart felt worse. There was a buzz at the door. James heaved himself out of his chair and looked out the window.

"Yes, Mrs Hyland, he's here. Come on up." He threw down the key.

"Oh, Jesus, not my mother. How does she know I'm here?" David looked wildly around for an escape route.

"We'll leave you to it. Come on lads." The three boys sniggered their way into the kitchen, where they turned on the radio, very loud.

"Hello, Mum." David closed the door behind her and sagged back to his place on the couch.

"So, tell me why you're here? What's your version of this nonsense?"

"What did Kathleen tell you? I presume she must have phoned you?"

"Yes. She was very upset, the poor lamb. After you telling her you didn't like her cooking and refusing to eat a perfectly good salad."

"Is that why she says I left?"

"Yes. Seems ridiculous, the poor girl is only learning to cook. And you're not that good yourself, that you can criticise. And it looks to me like you've been filling yourself with beer again with those pals of yours. That's what got you into trouble, my boy, drinking too much and losing the run of yourself."

"No, Mum, it was Kathleen that got me into trouble. Good and proper." David had decided he had been in such trouble already there was no point in trying to limit the damage. So he explained, as tidily as he could, what had happened. His mother sat quiet for once and her eyes widened.

"So she wasn't pregnant? Why did she want to say she was? All that fuss, getting a wedding organised in a mad hurry, for nothing? I wonder what her mother will make of it, when she hears. She had to make all those dresses in record time, three full sized and two flower girls, not to mention the veil. It would have been so much easier on all of us if we had had time to plan properly. I could have got a much better outfit."

"You might not have needed an outfit at all, Mum." His mother looked at him, her eyebrows questioning. "No," David continued, "I wouldn't have got married. I wasn't thinking of it at all."

"But you were in love with Kathleen!"

"No. I don't know. I didn't get time to think about it. I don't love

80

her today, that's for sure. How could I love such a cheat?"

"You are married to her. You will have to learn to love her. You should not have got yourself into a position where you could have got her pregnant. That is bad enough, you can't be all holy about it now. You did wrong."

"So did Kathleen. She..." David's eyes were beginning to prickle at the injustice of it. It was Kathleen who had unzipped his trousers, put her hand...He broke off the train of thought as his balls tingled and the blood that wasn't already on its way to his cock flooded his face.

"Well, there's two of you in it so. And a baby coming, who has done no wrong and needs his parents to mind him. So come on, Kathleen is in the car,"

"Mum!"

"and you're both coming back to Howth with me now for lunch and a good walk."

David sighed. He knew his mother's good walks. They would be out for hours and eat like monsters when they got back and everything would seem that bit simpler.

"Is Kay able for it? She might have morning sickness, she's only five weeks." He picked up his jacket from the floor and shook it out, before following his mother down to the car.

Chapter 12

It was a sultry afternoon in August and David was walking between his two jobs, trying to enjoy a few minutes of sunshine in the street before plunging into the gloom of the pub for the evening shift. By working every possible shift he could get both in the shop and the pub, he hoped he would be able to continue in College for his final year. The baby was due at the end of January, so there would be two terms to do after it arrived and it might be really tough to concentrate, but David reckoned it was worth it to try. 'Nothing ventured, nothing gained' his Dad had said and he would surely get a better job if he had a degree. And I'll need the money, he thought sadly, for baby stuff, instead of that camping trip the lads are going on. Eejit, Dave, you are one great eejit. Of course, Kathleen's life was changed too, but she was happy about it, she'd dropped out of her General Studies course without any regrets.

"There's graffiti over the loo paper in the College 'Ladies'. It says 'General Studies degrees, help yourself'," she had said, "so why bother? What would I do next anyway?"

He stopped on the bridge over the canal and looked down at the murky water, for once reflecting blue sky and one fluffy little cloud. The blue sky is Kath and the murky water is me, he thought sourly. She's all fluffy clouds and giggles now, now that her tummy is swelling and her baby is on its way. "What I've always wanted" she says, "my own baby - imagine!" Her own baby. Not ours. Hers. No interest in her husband since she got the positive test. Twice. Only twice in three months. The lads teasing me all the time about the sex life I'm having and does she have a sister. When I even get to see the lads. Oh, heck, it's five to. Better get inside. He lifted his face to the sun and walked over to the pub.

David was polishing glasses and hanging them up, when he heard his name called, jauntily, from the door. He looked across and there was Kathleen, her beautiful curtain of hair shining in the sunlight. She let the door close behind her and came over to the bar. David leant over and kissed her.

"What brings you here?

"Great news!" Kathleen was grinning.

"We won the Sweep? Did we have a ticket?"

"Twins!"

"Where?" David was puzzled. Kathleen pointed at her stomach.

"Here! Isn't it great? Two babies!" Kathleen leaned over the counter again, expecting another kiss. Davis felt weak. He looked across at this grinning girl and wondered what she had to do with him. Why he was married to her. Why he had even taken her out the second time. Lack of imagination I suppose, he thought. Or too busy studying for the honours degree to look for girls. Found one, or rather one found me and it was easier to keep her than think about it too much. A total eejit. He realised Kathleen was talking and tried to listen.

"Well? Aren't you going to say anything? Aren't you pleased?"

"Why would I be pleased?"

"Babies are lovely and now we'll have two instead of one. Doubley lovely. A whole family. And they might be born a bit sooner, the doctor says." She smiled at him again, her eyes crinkling. "Go on, say it!"

"Say what? That I'm happy to have been trapped and extra happy that I'm going to have double the expenses? How do I even know you're not lying again?"

"You're meant to say 'congratulations!' and give me a kiss," said Kathleen and her lower lip trembled. "You're spoiling it."

"Well, you're the expert at spoiling things, you should know. Now, you'd better go and let me get on. I need to keep this job."

"You're no fun. I'm going to go and phone Sandra and see if she's happier for me."

Of course she'll be happy for you, David mused as he cleaned out the coffee percolator. Sandra doesn't have to pay for the babies. Or look after them. Oh God, what am I going to do?

The advice from here is to hang on in. It's only for a few months. And you will love the babies – sorry about it being twins, not something we can always control, but you'll love them both. Like I said, your Mum will help. Once you're on your own, you can concentrate better on your studying and things should go fine. So, like you said, just get on with the job. One day at a time. Try to love Kathleen for the time you have her, it will be easier on you afterwards if you have been friends. She has beautiful hair.

I wonder if the babies will get Kay's lovely hair, or will they get mine? Nothing wrong with mine of course, but hers has a real gloss, just like a fresh conker. David's thoughts went blank for a moment and then he smiled to himself as he realised he had thought of the babies, not just as trouble, but as two people.

"Well, just about. They will be. The souls for them are chosen, I think you'll like them. You've worked with both of them before. Well done, keep concentrating on the positives. And on your job, looks like you have a customer."

David let himself into the flat as quietly as he could and hung up his jacket. He sat down by the window and looked out at the dark sky. Two babies, he thought. My sons, or daughters, or one of each maybe. Mine. Maybe they'll play football with me. Or tennis. They might like camping and when we have some money, maybe we can buy a dinghy and I'll teach them to sail. If I haven't forgotten how by then. No, Dave, no negatives. Try to think positively, like that mad drunk said this evening. Funny how someone half jarred can seem to make sense.

"Good, that, wasn't it? Though I say so myself. He was drunk enough to have let down some defences and his guide and I managed to get through to him. He told you what I wanted you to hear. Drunks will say anything, if we're lucky. Often they garble the whole thing, but he was a good one. You owe him a pint." Jotin laughed.

"'Just love her today' he said, 'and tomorrow love her tomorrow and if you don't feel like it, pretend and maybe you'll convince yourself'. So maybe I'll try it. How did he know it would make sense to me?" David was muttering under his breath, but even so, Kathleen must have heard him, as she stuck her head out of the little bedroom.

"Sandra says you're a callous bastard," Kathleen said, "and don't deserve a wife."

"Probably," David said and then bit his tongue to stop anything else coming out.

"And you stink of smoke. I can smell you from here."

"Your sense of smell has improved then?" David got up and went over to her. He held her face gently between his hands and tried to remember why he had fallen for her. He kissed her on the nose and she smiled. She was pretty when she smiled. He hadn't noticed earlier.

"She was smirking earlier. Not the same thing. Sorry, out of order. Carry on, bring her to bed and make love to her. I'm off."

"You're lovely. You smell good, unlike me and your hair is magnificent and you're sexy and cute and your breasts have grown..."

"And they're sore. You're not touching them," Kathleen paused. Her guide Haliken whispered to her. "But I do have other places that aren't. Come on to bed. I suppose you're sexy too."

Chapter 13
January 1973

Kathleen reluctantly turned away from the soft light.

"Why?" she said, to the listener. "Why must I go back? I'm meant to die from this infection, you told me I could try a sudden death. The babies are expecting me to go, aren't they? Please let me stay with you, please!"

Haliken shook his head. "I can't. We will have to wait."

"Why can't you? You have power, don't you? You can change things?"

"I don't have much power, almost none really. I didn't arrange this illness, so I can't make it worse. I'm only a guide, not an angel. But even angels couldn't fix this one. It can't be changed because time and science have moved on. Because very few can come Home now for such a reason. The humans have been too clever for us, they can cure this illness now. When I saw your life plan I thought it would be fatal. I was wrong. I'm sorry."

"Sorry?" said Kathleen. "What good is sorry? You tell me I have to go back, you don't tell me what I'll have to do when I get there, you put me in a situation where I'm not meant to be, without obvious help and you say 'sorry'."

"The help might not be obvious, but it will always be there. Just keep your senses open. I'll try to find a way out, or a purpose, so you'll get some value out of this life. You go on back now and I'll start working on it."

Kathleen opened her eyes. David was looking down at her, concern on his face.

"Kathleen, how are you feeling? Are you okay? I've been so worried."

"I feel lonely," said Kathleen.

"I'm here. You're not alone. And the twins are fine, the nurses have looked after them just as well as they looked after you," said David, as he stroked Kathleen's hand.

"I still feel lonely. I don't know why. It's like a dream that's just gone. I want to go back. Oh God, I don't remember!" Kathleen burst into tears. David stood up and leant over to kiss her head, but Kathleen turned her face away and the tears rolled silently down her face.

"I'll go and look at the babies," said David. "I'll bring one of them back to say hello, if it's allowed."

"Don't bother," said Kathleen, "just leave me alone. You got me into this. Just go away."

"What d'you mean, I got you into it? You pretended to be pregnant so I'd marry you, and then never said in time that you weren't, so we really got pregnant. We should have taken precautions. But no, you wanted a baby. You were thrilled when you got your test. 'My baby' you said and sent away for the Mothercare brochure."

"Baby" said Kathleen, "I only wanted a baby. And super-stud gives me two. Two the same, too. I'd have to go through all that again to get a boy."

"You were thrilled it was twins. And it's not my fault. Twins aren't in my family. But they're beautiful and healthy. We don't need a boy. You don't have to have another if you don't want. And this infection, it wouldn't happen again, Dr. Dempster says it's very rare these days to get one this bad."

"Dead right it won't happen again. Because I'm not doing this again. You can tie a knot in it." Kathleen turned on her side, away from David and pulled the sheet up over her head.

David walked down the corridor towards the baby unit. He watched another young father walk with his wife towards the lifts. She was carrying their baby in a bundle of soft yellow wool and her face glowed as she looked down at it and then up at her husband. They smiled at each other, that private, excluding the world smile that lovers share. 'Oh shit,' thought David, 'and Kathleen said she felt lonely.' He went into the baby unit and over to the corner where his new family was.

"Oh, hello, Mr. Hyland. I heard the good news about Mrs. Hyland. That's great. Not that there was any real danger, once they got the right antibiotic. How is she?" The nurse fussed round the babies.

"She's fine, I think, thank you. But down in herself. She doesn't want to see the babies. I'd thought I might bring one up to her to cheer her up. But she has her head under the sheet."

"Sure that's only a phase," the nurse was professionally cheerful. "Most mothers get a bit down on the third or fourth day; it's called 'baby blues'. Bound to be a bit worse when you've been ill. She'll be grand in a day or two. Won't she, my little darling? Won't Mammy be all better soon?" She handed one of his daughters to David.

David brought the tiny face close to his own. I'm not so sure, my little girl, that your mum is going to be all that much better in a hurry. She nearly died. But we'll manage, you and me and your sister. Somehow, we'll manage. He breathed in and the soft, powdery smell relaxed him. He looked quickly round for a chair.

"Whoa there!" the nurse was beside him, taking his daughter out of his arms. "You're done in, will you go on home now and go to bed early. We'll mind these lassies for you till their mam is on her feet. Have you work tomorrow?"

"What day is it?"

"Friday" said the nurse, as she tucked the baby back into the little plastic crib.

"Already? Oh dear. Or rather, oh good, I'm only going in in the afternoon. But I have to ring everyone with the news about Kathleen. Her Mum's on her way."

"Off with you then. See you tomorrow."

David joined the New Year Sales crowds, queuing for the buses. There was a comfortable anonymity in a city bus queue, no need to keep up a pretence, or smile. His thoughts freewheeled back over the past year. Less than a year since we decided to get married. What a lot has happened. Kathleen so driven to have a baby. I wonder why.

"Because she knew deep down that it was her ticket Home," said Jotin. *"Haliken told me that she wasn't meant to survive this infection. That's why I let you marry her. He was sure that this was so bad it would take her Home. He didn't do his research properly, he's about thirty years too late for a bacterium to be guaranteed to kill her. He should have given her a clot on the lung. Or found a viral illness, they still haven't a cure for those. So you and I are stuck with her for a while longer. Sorry."*

At least she's okay after that infection. I was really scared there, imagine having to bring up those babies on my own. It's hard enough making ends meet now and Dad is stretched helping us. I wonder how I would have coped.

"Your mother would have looked after the babies and then when they got into secondary school, you would have found a really helpful student called Lucy to fetch them from school and mind them for you. She was meant to be their mother, after all, even though neither of them is your Moonsong. Just as well we didn't go ahead and let Moonsong have one of those bodies. I don't know exactly what stopped us, at the last minute. We're not always wrong, you see. I'm so sorry this isn't working out. Though it's not actually my fault, blame Trynor and Haliken when you see them next. But we all get a learning experience now, not just those of you in bodies. We're going to be doing overtime, once Lucy gets old enough. You can just have a nice family time now, once Kathleen gets over the shock of being here, instead of planning her next life."

A nice family time, thought David. I'm a family man now. Oh, God, what a ridiculous thing to be, at my age. Dad was thirty four when I was born, I'm only two thirds that. And Mum was a nurse and knew how to look after babies. Kathleen doesn't know much that'll be useful. Maybe it's all instinctive, and she'll just know? He looked out of the bus windows, at the crowds going home, and realised all their mothers weren't nurses, and they all seemed to be upright and walking despite that severe handicap. Even Kathleen herself: her mother was the doziest woman he'd ever met, but so kind and so good for Kathleen.

"I'd like to call one of the babies Clare," David was sitting beside Kathleen's bed, eating her grapes. Kathleen was lying half propped up, staring out the window. She turned listless eyes towards him.

"Why?"

"I don't know. I just seem to want a daughter named Clare."

"Again? But this isn't her, neither of them are Moonsong, you can call her whatever you like. Be brave, live a little. Not that it matters."

"Clare's okay. Which one is she?" Kathleen swivelled her eyes to the two little cots by her bed. David got up and went around to look at the babies. They looked much the same, even though he had been

90

told they were not identical. He pointed at the nearer baby.

"This one?"

"Okay," Kathleen looked out the window again. "And what are you calling the other one?"

"You choose. Didn't you have a long list of names ticked in that book?"

"None of them seem right anymore. None of this does. I shouldn't be here, I shouldn't have babies, shouldn't be trying to work out what to call them, shouldn't have got sick, it's just not fair!" Kathleen started to wail. David sat on the bed and stroked her arm and shrugged apologetically at the woman in the next bed, who had turned curious eyes his way. Kathleen shut her eyes and slid further down in the bed. David fiddled with the controls of the little radio he had brought in for Kathleen, hoping she would be soothed by listening to music. It sprang into life with an Irish jig. Kathleen mumbled. David leant forward to hear her.

"Turn that rubbish off. Is there nothing decent on the radio these days? I wish they hadn't stopped Radio Caroline. Fascists." She fell silent.

"Yea, I liked Caroline too. Pity about it. Though there's a rumour it might get going again, off Holland."

"Caroline."

"Mmm."

"There. I made up my mind about something. I thought I never would again. Good for me." Kathleen shut her eyes again and gave a great sigh.

"What did you decide, Kay?"

"The baby's name. Caroline. Clare and Caroline. Now go away, I'm exhausted."

David stood up and leaned down over the babies. "Bye-bye Clare, Bye-bye Caroline. I love you. Love you too, Kay." He kissed her.

"Maybe."

Chapter 14

"Oh heck," said Kathleen, as she leant her arms on the bedroom windowsill and gazed out into the grey light of the February morning. "Would you look at that. Another dreary day to get through. It'll rain again. It always does. It's horrible here. What am I going to do with those babies?" A tear formed slowly in one eye and threatened to spill over.

"OK. I'm off. Mind yourselves, girls," said David, shrugging into his coat. He had his head into the bedroom and was grinning at the babies. They were head to toe in the cot, but both looking up at the mobile twisting above them in the draught, their newborn eyes still slightly crossed. "You too, Kay. Be good."

"What else can I do, stuck here with two squalling brats? It's fine for you, you get out of this tiny dump and see people and things. I just go on and on. I want to get away. Somewhere bright. Anywhere. Just away."

"It's February. Nowhere would be bright, it's the winter."

"I know it's the bloody winter. That's the problem." Kathleen sat on the bed and sighed, long and loud. "Just get me out of here before I go mad." She took a deep breath and let it out in a wail, as she ran her fingers through her hair, again and again.

"OK. Just leave your hair alone," said David. "I'll see what I can do."

"It's your fault I feel like this and it's my hair. I'll do what I want."

"No, it is not my fault. You wanted a baby. Your wretched sister had one, so you had to have one too. Amazing her name isn't Jones."

"I didn't ask for twins," Kathleen wailed again and threw herself backwards onto the bed, drumming her heels against it.

David watched her and wondered what he could do to help. Was she right to be angry, was it really his fault? Probably Kathleen was right and a week in the sun would help. He sat down beside her and reached out to stroke her hair, such beautiful hair when it wasn't sticking out like this.

"Leave me alone, you bastard." Kathleen sat up with a jerk and glared at David. "That's how you got me into this situation!"

David said nothing. Kathleen was too fond of the 'all men are raving sex-maniacs' argument, they had been down that road many times. But when she wanted a baby there were plenty of bedroom eyes and hands, he thought ruefully. And now the twins have spoiled my chances for a second go of being wanted in bed. Two babies for the fun of one. Great bargain.

He stood up and looked down at Kathleen. She had her eyes closed and her head turned away. She fidgeted.

"See you later, then. Bye." David went out to the front door. He could hear Kathleen, sighing and moaning softly in the bedroom. He went back, and hesitated in the doorway, looking down at her, wondering what he could say that would help.

"Nothing. She's not listening, not even to Haliken. Out, go on, leave. Or you'll be late for your lecture."

David looked at his watch and ran from the room. Kathleen followed him out into the sitting room and stood watching their front door as it closed behind him. Her hands twisted together, then ran through her hair, twisting and pulling.

"Get him to fix up a break, Jotin," said Haliken. "She's not meant to be here. Maybe if she got away for a couple of days she might remember that there is more to it than just this. I'll try and work on her patience."

"Good luck! Doesn't look like great material to work with."

"No, she hasn't signed up for patience training yet. She's not really ready. But we can always have a go."

"Haliken!" Clare's guide was in the doorway, "my little one is crying. Give her Mum a nudge, would you? Oh, hi, Jo. You not off to College yet?"

"I think he can manage the bus without his hand held." Jotin paused for a moment. "I hope." And he was gone.

Haliken turned and put his arms around Kathleen. "Come on, Kathleen. Listen. Little Clare is crying. Go to her. Go on, before she gets more upset. Come on, my love, you have to do this now. Come on, all will be well. All will be well."

Oh bloody hell, thought Kathleen. She could hear the wail from the bedroom. She stood still for a moment. The wail was joined by another more tentative cry, which grew as she listened, becoming

94

demanding. Bloody, bloody hell. She turned reluctantly away from the door, that elusive symbol of freedom, to go and investigate.

David's mind whirled as he stood at the bus stop. He did not notice the grey weather, the heavy mist obscuring the approaching bus, or the grumbling people jostling to be first in the queue. All he heard was the voice in his head saying 'There must be something I can do. She's so unhappy since the girls were born, I suppose it is sort of my fault. Our fault, anyway and Kathleen isn't in any fit state to sort herself out. But where can I get the money from for a break in the sun? Where could we go? London would be just as cold.' He didn't hear the voice outside his head saying

"It's going to be really bright and sunny in Wexford next weekend. Get the train. Book a bed and breakfast for two nights. That'll cheer her up. Wexford... Wexford... Wexford... Won't be too dear. The landladies in those B&Bs aren't too busy this time of year, they'll mind Kathleen for you. It could be just what you need, a home from home."

"Rome!" David looked round, not realising it was he who had spoken. The bus squealed to a stop beside him and he shuffled forward with the crowd. As he got on the bus and settled uncomfortably on the back seat between two large ladies armed with shopping bags made entirely of corners, he thought again: 'Rome?' Maybe Rome would be nice. It certainly ought to be warmer than here. How much would it cost to fly to Rome? It would show Kathleen I'm trying, he thought. She can't hold this all against me forever.

"Yes she can. Sometimes they do. Don't spend all the money you haven't got on a trip like that. It's over too soon and she'll want another. Come on David, just go to somewhere in Ireland. You can afford it, if you're careful. Then you can go again when she has another fuss."

"She does fuss so well. I'll go and ask about flights. Then she can decide, that should make her feel better"

"Bad move David, bad move."

But David had settled in his mind and now he settled back on the seat, as best he could without being injured, and allowed his mind to wander back to his little nursery. He smiled.

David straightened up from peering under the grill at the sausages and turned the heat down under the potatoes. He put his head out of the little kitchen.

"Do you want anything else done, or is it just sausage and mash?" he said.

"That's all there is," said Kathleen. She was feeding Caroline, whose little fists moved in the air and then stilled as she gave her attention to the serious business of sucking. Clare was lying in the pram, full of milk but not ready yet to sleep. "I've been so busy feeding these two and cleaning them, to think of anything else. You're lucky to get anything, stop complaining."

"I wasn't complaining, Kay. I was just asking was that it?"

"There you go again, criticising me when I've been slaving all day. I'm fed up of it."

"Kay, love, I know you've been busy. I know you're in bad form these days. I don't mean to criticise and I love sausage and mash. You're doing fine, look how well the girls are doing. And I've something interesting to show you, make you feel better."

"Please David, don't show her the Rome brochure. Please don't. Tell her you're enquiring about Wexford. Rome is too expensive. No, David, no no no."

David hesitated, but went over to the door to where he had dropped his briefcase when he had come in and smelt burning. He took out the brochure he had got earlier from the travel agent about short breaks on the continent. He looked at it and thought maybe this is overkill, maybe we can get through this some other way. This is silly. Then he heard Kathleen behind him as she laid Caroline down in the pram, saying now go to sleep the pair of you and leave me alone, and he clicked his case shut decisively and turned around with the brochure.

"I went into a travel agent today and got this. We could stretch to three days in Rome, I could miss a Friday maybe, if you think it would help? It should be warmer than here, anyway."

"Oh, David, what a great idea! Show me." Kathleen snatched the brochure out of David's hand and sat back down at the table. "Oh, this looks lovely. Look, Dave, a buffet breakfast with everything on it!"

David looked over her shoulder.

96

"That's a four star hotel. We can't afford that. I was looking at one on the next page," he turned the page over, "look, bed and breakfast, convenient to the station. Looks nice."

"Looks ordinary," said Kathleen, turning the page back and studying the photos of the big hotels. She started to daydream, room service, huge fluffy towels, endless hot water, wonderful meals, deferential waiters, sunshine, the Colosseum, the Vatican ....

"Meet him half way," said Haliken "any trip to Rome is more than you should afford just now. Don't push it for luxury too. Bed and breakfast is good, you're not tied to one hotel for dinner, you can shop around."

....shopping, drinks at pavement cafés, walks under the stars...

"this isn't a fortnight on the Riviera. This is three days in March, in a city. Come on Kath, I know you're not meant to be here and I'm sorry, but don't make it harder on yourself. Do something realistic. The Sunny South East would be better."

Kathleen turned the page and looked at the entry about the small hotel near the station.

"At least this would be better than this ghastly Irish weather. I can't stay here."

"We do have to come back, you know," said David.

"But not for a while. It'll keep me sane, looking forward to it, so I'll get weeks of value. Well, not too many weeks, I hope, I want to go quite soon. How soon can we go?"

"I have to let the pub know in enough time to find someone to fill in for me. And I can't go for long, or they'll find out they can manage without me and then I'm finished. We have to go at a weekend, because of college, but that's when it's most awkward for the job."

"You should be thinking of me, not of them. They're just a pub. There's loads of pubs. I need to get out of this place."

"I'm working on it. But if I don't have a job to come back to, I can't afford to stay in college."

"You can't afford to go to Rome. I told you. Wexford would be better."

"So how long will we be away?"

"The basic package is three nights, so out Thursday, home Sunday"

"That's only two days away! It's hardly worth going." Kathleen pushed away from the table and went into the kitchenette, switching off everything and snatching the potato pan up. She drained the potatoes and started mashing them with short hard strokes, throwing in a piece of butter which she cut off the block with the edge of the masher. She served out on two plates, banging the masher against them to dislodge the potato, and then put one plate approximately in front of David and sat back on her own chair with a grunt. Kathleen sat staring at her plate, saying nothing. David got up and fetched cutlery from the drawer.

"We could make it three, if we go on a Wednesday. But I lose more money by not working and miss more at College and have to copy someone's notes. So the longer I'm away the dearer it is. The flight out is early, so we'd have most of the day there and the flight back is late. So from Thursday it'd be nearly four days. More than half a week."

They ate in silence. David was aware only of the crashing of Kathleen's cutlery and the sharp clack of the salt cellar as she put it back down. Kathleen was aware only of her own over-riding misery.

Chapter 15

David gave a small tip to the taxi driver, picked up the bags and struggled up the path to the house, veering awkwardly into the flowerbed as Kathleen's overstuffed bag won the battle for his balance. The front door was shut. David let the bags drop and stood silently for a moment, wondering. It's not significant, he thought, read nothing into it. We're tired after the flight. He rang the bell. After a few minutes when nothing had happened, he rang again, longer. Eventually, the door opened an inch and as he pushed it further he could see Kathleen going back up the stairs. David heaved the bags into the hall, shut the door and hauled himself and the luggage up the stairs to the flat.

"I'll put on the kettle, shall I?" David asked as he pushed in through the half open door, "then we have to go round to your mum for the girls." There was an inaudible mutter from the living room.

"What, love?" said David, as he went into the room.

"I said do what you like and go if you want." Kathleen was lying on the couch with her eyes closed and her coat spread over her legs.

"Why don't you go in to bed if you're so tired. I'll bring you in a cup of something and then you can get some rest before the babies get here. I'll go for them, if it helps."

"I suppose." Kathleen put an arm over her eyes and stayed where she was. David went through into the kitchenette and put some water into the kettle. It's still cold here, he thought. Maybe a hot water bottle's a good idea. He set off in search.

After a minute or two more on the couch, Kathleen noticed David making noise in the bedroom. She sat up slowly, and swung her feet down. She sat for a moment, curled forward, trying to dispel the despondency that threatened to overtake her. Rome was all right, she thought. But it's over now. It feels like it's all over, all over again. She stood up quickly and swayed as the blood drained from her face. She sat down again and put her head between her knees. David came in.

"Kathleen! What's the matter?" he knelt beside her.

"I don't know, I feel faint all of a sudden. Maybe I caught a chill."

"Maybe you did, lying still in this cold room. Come on. We'll get you into bed. I'm organising a hot water bottle." David put his arm round Kathleen and gradually she allowed herself to be led into the bedroom.

David let himself out of the house and set off to walk the mile to his mother-in-law's house. As he walked he found his mood lightening as he anticipated seeing the girls again. He'd missed the softness of them, the beginnings of smiles, their happiness to connect with people without asking anything of them. So much easier than Kay. He pushed the disloyal thought down. Poor Kay, she can't help it, it's been tough on her, being ill and all.

"She could help it if she tried," said Jotin. "Haliken is working on her, trying to get through. It'll help if you don't fuss over her too much. Don't encourage her. Make her care for the twins when you get home. And tell your mum about what happened in Rome, how she behaved. Don't carry this all alone."

I'll talk to Mum, thought David. Get her advice, she's had babies too, she might understand. She had to look after us alone, too, with Dad being away so much. He had a frisson of guilt as he remembered; I still have to confess to Kathleen that I've applied to go on that field trip to Oxford. For two weeks. And I really would like to go and it really would help me, would look good on my C.V., never mind just impressing the Prof. And it will be interesting, seeing the labs there, how they do things. David rang the doorbell and waited, watching his breath make clouds, filling the porch momentarily with his own microclimate.

"You're back! Come in quick, before that damp gets in too. The girls are just back, they've been visiting,"

"Yes, and you didn't get him here fast enough, now he's missed her again."

"Who, Trynor?" asked Jotin.

"They were taken round the block to meet Mary and Peter, you know, half their garden backs onto ours. Their nieces were visiting, such nice little girls, Lucy and Alison. They came and wheeled the twins round. Much more fun than dolls."

"How are they? Did they miss me and their mum?" David went through to the back room, which was always kept snug. The babies would be there.

100

"Did you organise that, you chump?" Jotin looked at Trynor and tried to put on a stern expression. "Didn't I tell you, the age gap is too big now. And what if Lucy had met Kathleen?"

"What if she had?" said Trynor.

"She could have ended up as Kathleen's pal, as a useful babysitter in a few years, far sooner than she will be able to meet David on equal terms. That could ruin everything. Keep her away from those babies."

"But she was meant to be their stepmother and bring them up," Trynor protested. "How can she do that if she never meets them? As their babysitter at least she'd have some input."

"Yes, she was, before you fluffed by forgetting to get her born in time. She can't bring up these babies. And it's far more important that she gets together with David eventually. If we don't mess things up again. Now, go and stop her getting run over, or something."

"Nag nag nag. I'm gone."

Jotin followed David through into the back room.

David was holding Clare in the crook of one arm and was stroking Caroline with the other hand. A cup of tea stood cooling on the low table beside him.

"Why didn't Kath come with you?" Mrs Kearney was fussing around, offering cake and tucking in the babies.

"She's not very well. Nothing in particular, just low."

"After the travel, I suppose. You should have let us give you the money to stay longer, get more rest."

"Well, it's a nice idea, Mrs K, but I don't think it would have been better. Kay really enjoyed the first day, she came right out of herself, back to how she used to be. The second day she was okay, but by the third day she said Rome was horrible and she couldn't wait to leave. It was lovely to see her so well on Friday," he ended lamely. It had been. They had done almost no sight-seeing that day, had stayed in bed all morning, finding out again what the original attraction between them had been. He had had to get up eventually, to go out in search of more condoms. Easier to get in Italy than at home. He had bought a huge supply, but by the next day Kathleen had lost interest again and they were stuffed into his luggage, while he hoped the Customs would not search him and ask embarrassing questions about how many could be for 'personal use'. They had run the gauntlet safely, he had ignored Kathleen's suggestion to 'throw them away, we won't be needing them'; and they were now waiting to be unpacked into a safe place in the bedroom, tucked away with his hopes. He noticed his father-in-law was speaking.

"Is she depressed? I hear it can happen after a baby."

"I don't know. I'll get her to go to the doctor and see. But she seemed all right on the Friday. No problems at all."

"She's not really depressed, David. Nothing that medicines will fix. It's soul deep. But you work on it from your end, and Haliken will do what he can. He needs to find something to fill the void for her. Don't you start trying. Your responsibility is to the babies. And eventually to the baby you and Lucy will have, whenever we can get this mess sorted out."

"It's a mess," David said without thinking.

"What do you mean?" asked Mrs Kearney sharply.

"Uh, Kay being unwell and me with exams coming up."

"But surely you can do the exams again? The babies will only be babies for the one year. They should come first."

"Oh, they do. But I can't afford to repeat a year. I'd have to pay for it and a repeat looks bad on your C.V. I have to finish this time."

"Lot of nonsense, all this book learning," Kathleen's father leant back comfortably in his chair and lit his pipe. "I never went to any college, particularly not that Trinity and I got on well. Paid for all this," he waved the stem of his pipe at the ceiling.

"Yes." David stood up. "I'd better get going, see how she is. Come on girls!" He turned the pram around and headed out into the dank evening. Kathleen's mother came running out of the kitchen with a little parcel in tinfoil which she tucked into the pram.

"Cake, for Kath. Cheer her up. Bye now. Bye little darlings, be good girls." She kissed the babies and went back in to the warmth.

Chapter 16
Dublin 1976

David brought his coffee out to the back step and sat down carefully, lifting his face to the low rays of the dying sun. He rested his head back against the wall and allowed the warm light to wash over him, as he took a huge breath and let it out in a rush. He imagined all the bad stale thoughts he'd been having all day rushing out and smiled slightly as he thought of the effect on his struggling garden. Maybe he would wilt the purple sprouting broccoli. A little hand stroked his face.

"Why you sad, Daddy? Why you smile and being sad?" Clare was trying now to climb onto his lap.

"Because life is very confusing, poppet." David put his mug down and lifted her up, so that her dark curls were just under his chin and he could see grubby hands playing with his collar. Clare grinned up at him.

"Am I 'fusing too, Daddy?"

"No, you are probably the only thing that is straightforward. You and Caroline. You keep me balanced." It's true, he thought, if it wasn't for the girls I'd be totally at sea. Though Kath would be happier. He stopped, his mind freezing over under the onslaught of the idea that had just surfaced. No, that can't be true. How could she, she wanted a baby so much. She would miss them, she'd have to be mad not to. But in behind all these thoughts that he was desperately reciting like a mantra, was a bigger thought that might never go away, now that he had allowed it in. Kathleen would be happier without the girls. Oh no, he thought, oh no. Are they in danger? Surely not. Surely Kath wouldn't do anything to harm them?

"Daddy, you're squishing me!" Clare was pushing at his arms with her pudgy fists, her little face getting flushed. David opened his arms and kissed the top of her head.

"I'm sorry, Clare. I didn't mean to squish you. I just had a confusing thought again." Clare nodded solemnly.

"You forgot me. Mummy forgets too. Is Mummy 'fused?"

"Yes, I think sometimes Mummy is very confused. I think maybe all the grown ups are. I don't know what to do about it."

"Listen."

David waited, expecting a bird to sing, or Caroline to come singing through the house, but there was nothing.

"Listen to what, love?"

Clare was climbing down. "Listen" she said again and ran inside. David sat on, on the step that had been in the sun, wondering what he was meant to hear. There was traffic in the distance and a group of children were shouting and laughing in a nearby garden. A plane crossed the sky almost overhead, but he could barely hear it. Inside, he could hear Clare explaining something intently to Caroline, who as usual ignored her and carried on humming. It was all very normal and peaceful in its way, but nothing that was going to solve his confusion.

"Oh, God, what'll I do?"

"Clare's right, just listen," said Jotin. "You're still hopeless at hearing, I do wonder if we're ever going to be able to get through to you all. I'm not God, as you could see if you knew how to look, but I'm in charge of answering you. But you really must start listening. I'm run off my feet here trying to get your attention, sometimes."

"All I can think of, is carry on. The girls need me. They need a proper mother too, one who would put them first. But how can I arrange that?"

"Carry on is good. Lucy's still too young. The girls do need you. And listen to me carefully for a minute – Kathleen will not harm them. You can forget that. She may not be terribly good for them, but she won't harm them. And listen to me in future. Actually...... listen to Clare, too! I'll have a word with the guide who looks after her. She can filter some messages through. LISTEN TO CLARE."

David smiled. He could still hear Clare trying to boss her sister. David always thought that Clare was the younger twin, but Kathleen said that as she always took on the lead role that she must be the older. Such a pity they weren't sure, so silly. Clare could probably settle that argument, he thought, she seems to have an answer for everything she doesn't have a question for. 'Listen' indeed! Little Miss Smarty Pants, people would call her, or 'precocious' if they were feeling polite. That's all it is. High I.Q. probably. Hope it is, would be great if she does well in school. In the distance he could hear the front door opening and then a crash as it was slammed. David tensed and froze and heard, as he expected, two little voices shouting 'Mummy, Mummy,' as the twins launched themselves at Kathleen; and heard, also as expected, though he could not stop hoping it would be different, her tired voice saying 'not now, girls, Mummy needs to relax.' Then there were footsteps on the stairs, as Kathleen went up to the bedroom. And another door slammed.

"Mummy's tired, Daddy," said Clare. "Maybe she needs a cuddle."

David smiled and pulled Clare onto his knee again.

"Give me a cuddle first, lovekin. Then my cuddle meter will be full and there'll be some over for Mummy." Clare planted a wet kiss on his ear.

"Do you want Caro cuddle too? Caro! Caro!" Caroline ran in from the other room and seeing Clare on David's lap, started to climb up too. David scooped her up and hugged the two girls fiercely, his face between their heads, feeling curls on one side and silky smoothness on the other.

"Hello, love, how was your day? Did you get what you wanted?" David sat down on the side of the bed, where Kathleen was lying with a damp cloth across her eyes.

"Of course not," her voice was just above a whisper. "When do I ever? You'd think it was difficult. This lousy city has nothing." David picked up her hand and squeezed it gently.

"What were you looking for?"

"A last-minute holiday. Nothing. All sold out, not just the cheap ones. I went to every agent. You'd think they'd have something left for September. Not a fecking thing. I can't bear it."

"But we already had our holiday, Kathleen. You know that. We agreed before we went that that was it for this year. We're spent up, if you want the kids to go to the Montessori this term."

"You agreed. I never agreed. You just said it and I was supposed to go along with you. You know I can't survive without getting out of this place every now and then. And foreign travel is good for children. Broadens the mind."

"Maybe. Routine is good for them too. And you have 'got out'– we're only back four weeks. It was a good holiday, wasn't it?"

"It was OK. But it's over now, nearly a month and this place is killing me. And those girls are just whine whine all the time, I can't hear myself think." Kathleen turned over with her back to David. "They don't think of me at all, just themselves."

"Kath, that's not fair, they're only three. And actually it's not true either. I came up because Clare noticed you were tired and told me you needed a cuddle!"

"Well, she's wrong. I don't want you pawing me. Particularly if you didn't even think of it for yourself. Go away." Kathleen flung back the duvet, got in under it and pulled it over her head. "Go and cuddle Clare if she thinks it's so great."

"Don't be put off by Kathleen, David. Clare was right. A good cuddle would have helped. I'll have to try to get through to Haliken, to tell Kathleen to listen to you! Oh dear, oh dear. It really is difficult this time round. What is it about the world now that none of you hear us? Arranging chicken entrails was messy, but at least you paid some attention to them. Much easier way back then. This scientific mindset is really hard to get through to. Listen to Clare, David. Listen to Clare."

"Mummy better now, Daddy? Not tired?"

"No love, Mummy is tired. We are going to make the dinner now."

"I help. Caro too," Clare went to the drawers and began taking out forks.

"Good girl. You lay the table, that's right." David started preparing food, listening to his daughter working her way around the table counting carefully as she laid out four forks, four knives – 'careful, sharp!', four spoons. Her high voice was strangely soothing, with its repetitions and gentle confidence. As David chopped vegetables and peeled potatoes he thought back to the holiday. The girls had loved the beach, and despite his distaste for sand he had enjoyed their pleasure. They had built sandcastles with moats and he had even allowed them to bury him up to the neck, very inefficiently. Kathleen had laughed at his screwed up face and expressed pleasure that for once he had not been 'disgustingly happy' as she put it. She had been happy the first day in Spain. She was always happy on the first day of a holiday, amazingly so, as though a switch was thrown. One of the reasons I keep agreeing to

106

go on trips, he thought, is that I get to have a proper wife for just one day. He smiled. I should go on loads of trips, short ones, two days each. Twice a week, then I could say I had a sex life. Maybe I should apply for a travelling job, then she might be happy.

"Yes, probably. But I don't know of any jobs where you can bring your whole family. Maybe the circus! And of course you have to come back here to meet Lucy."

She was happy the first day we moved in here, too. Our own house and it was like being on holiday for a day. But now it's just boring her. She does nothing with it, doesn't want to help with decoration, or new furniture. Not that we can afford much. Particularly with all the trips we have to pay for. Just as well I stuck it out at College and got the good degree and a decent job. Maybe when the girls go to Montessori Kath will relax a bit.

The doorbell rang. David wiped his hands and went to answer it. Caroline was dancing up and down beside it, shouting 'who's it? who's it?' David opened the door.

"James! Come in. Look, Caro, Uncle James!" Caroline held up her arms for a hug and Clare ran out to join them. There was a squealing bundle in the hall as Kathleen came down the stairs.

"Hello, James," she said, "would you like to borrow them?"

"Hi, Kathleen. You look brown. Holiday not worn off yet?" David flashed him a warning look. Don't mention holidays, he begged silently. Kathleen just smiled distantly and went into the kitchen.

"I brown too! And Caro!" Clare took James' hand, to pull him into the garden, explaining earnestly about the new ball game they had acquired in Spain.

James stayed for dinner, causing great excitement for the twins, who pushed and shoved each other to be first at the cutlery drawer to get him a knife and fork, so that Kathleen screeched at them and had to go into the garden to get away. She came back after a few minutes and was tolerably polite to James, who she had never really spoken to since the night David had run away to him when she broke the news of her pregnancy.

"Do you mind putting the girls to bed?" David asked after dinner, "James and I would like to go round for a pint."

"Oh, all right. Out you go. I can't stop you, anyway. Come on girls. Bed."

"Night-night Daddy. Have nice pint." Clare kissed David.

"Night-night, big ears!"

"I haven't!"

"Not really, it's a joke. Night-night Caro."

"OK, so what's new? Or did you just come round for a feed?"

"Met a girl," James' face was beaming. "Last week. Gone out with her three times."

"Whoa there! Careful. You know what happened to me. Go on, tell all."

"She's gorgeous. Blonde, slim in the right places," James' hands moved down through the air in a familiar gesture, "and clever too. And when she smiles, the world stops." There was a long silence. David watched James staring into another place, where there was only himself and his girl. He thought back to when he had met Kathleen, years ago. Had she smiled at him then?

"What are you shaking your head for?" James asked.

"Just thinking. How quickly it can all go wrong."

"Nothing's going to go wrong. Julie is great."

"Not with you. With me."

"What's wrong?"

David looked up, straight at James. James was looking puzzled and he blinked at David.

"Your girls are gorgeous. You're so lucky."

"Hmmm. Kathleen's a handful, though."

"Well, I know she's not fond of me. But she's pretty."

"Pretty is skin deep," David paused, wondering if he should say more, what to say.

"Go on. Nothing to lose. Maybe James can help."

"Oh, Jim, I don't know what to say. It's too late for me, I'm stuck. Just don't make the same mistake I made. Make sure Julie loves you, not your wallet, or your sperm-bank." And David explained how difficult he found Kathleen, how lonely he was. "If it wasn't for the girls, I'd have given up long ago. They keep me hopeful. But it's still lonely, with no adult to share with."

"Oh." There was a long silence. "Can I get you another?" James turned towards the bar.

"Seems he can't help you at the moment, Davy. His guide tells me he's too excited by his Julie, who is right for him, that he just

108

can't imagine anyone being unhappy. Talk about something else."
Jotin sat close to David and stroked him gently. When James came back with the drinks, they discussed football, what news they had of Paddy and Ken and the benefits of camping holidays. Apparently Julie was happy with the idea of living under canvas and David damped down his regrets and tried to let James' happiness rub off on him.

Chapter 17
May 1979

"Mr Hyland. Yes. Dr McCarthy will see you shortly. There's a bit of an epidemic, he's a little delayed."

"No problem." David went into the waiting room and sat down. His last week in this job and he was moving on. Out of drugs sales into medical equipment, a different firm. Into management. A miracle really, a much more interesting job. Not that he minded visiting all the doctors. They were tolerant, for the most part and didn't rag him too much about the quality of the free pens he had to give out. But it would be nice to be in something more productive. He closed his eyes and rested his head back. More money, too. When he'd told Kathleen, on their wedding anniversary, she had been delighted.

"Can we go somewhere, to celebrate?" He had thought she meant out to dinner, but when he had said of course, let's arrange a babysitter, she had snorted and pointed out she meant away, for another week off. He had sighed. If only, even just once, she would want something else, something solid, that would last. A piano. A good sofa. Or even new clothes.

"Must we? I am tired, with all these trips."

"I hope it's not the seven year itch."

David wondered. Can you have a seven year itch for seven years? Just as well we had the girls, he thought, smiling. He had left them to school this morning and loved seeing them run in with their friends, so carefree, so cute in their little uniforms. I love them so much, he thought, so much. Caro, singing all the time, copying any new tune she hears and dancing as though there are springs in her shoes. And Clare, so different. So serious and wise. She's said funny things more than once, that seemed to make sense. Odd coincidences.

"Coincidences, huh! Will they ever cop on?" Trynor was in the waiting room, his energies sparkling. *"Get him to open his eyes, she's coming!"*

"Lucy? You have her coming here, now?" Jotin was puzzled.

"Yes. She's seventeen, I reckon that's old enough to be interesting? Her little sister is certainly interested in boys and she's only fourteen."

"Isn't Lucy busy with exams?"

"Oh yes, that's how I got her here. She's not very sick, but her nose is running, so she wants it fixed before the Leaving starts. I hope it isn't too red to be attractive."

"I don't think David will notice anyway, but we can try. His wife is being a bit less ghastly at the moment."

"Jotin – you mean he's still entangled with her? You haven't found a way out yet? If I wasn't mad at you I'd be sort of pleased. Proves it's not only me that gets things wrong." Trynor shimmered with amusement.

"I haven't exactly got anything wrong. I just haven't done anything. After all, none of us were meant to be in this predicament, it was Haliken who made the big error. Those girls were expecting to be left motherless at three days old."

"Tragic."

"Yes, so the humans would have said," Jotin and Trynor nodded wryly.

"Actually," said Jotin, "it's more tragic this way. She isn't meant to be their mother at all. And it shows. She's miserable about it, but of course she doesn't know why. David has to stand up for them all the time."

"Can you not get Haliken to arrange another infection for her? One that works?"

"Difficult. They're so good at curing them now. Killing off a healthy young woman isn't as easy as it used to be. Time was, we could arrange nice short sharp lives for people, one lesson per life. They've messed it up. Pity, they're all so determined to stay alive forever. They're not at all convinced there is anything after. We'd have to arrange a much more complicated disease now. I died three times of things that are really easy to fix now. And anyway, the girls' guides won't let us kill her, we did discuss it. We thought of a car crash, nice and quick. But the girls aren't meant to have a grief like that in their lives. It would have been all right at three days, or even three months. But they're too old now, six is much too vulnerable." Jotin looked over at David. "Looks peaceful and happy, doesn't he? We'll change all that if this works." He went

112

over and pinched David on the cheek.

David opened his eyes and looked around, rubbing his cheek. He couldn't see any insects, but something had bitten him. At that moment, the receptionist put her head round the door and said, "Lucy? The doctor will see you now." David looked across and saw the back of a girl in a school uniform follow the receptionist out. He closed his eyes again.

"Drat! Why didn't we rope in that woman's guide? She came in at just the wrong moment." Trynor was agitated.

"Does Lucy have any flowers? I didn't see them." Jotin was sitting beside David, wondering whether to pinch him again, or to wait until Lucy came out of the surgery.

"No," said Trynor, "how could she? She has to wear that uniform."

"Well, let's try to get them together in the hall when she comes out. But without flowers will it work?"

Lucy was talking on the phone to her friend. She had a plate of crackers, cheese and paté beside her on the floor and was showering crumbs around as she chewed slowly, her eyes closed, the better to enjoy the flavours, as she nodded and exclaimed at Sally's news.

"Did he? Wow! And what did you say? Yea, yea,.. really?" This went on for some time. She licked her fingers carefully. "No, nothing much. Well I went to the doctor today. No, not too bad. Just my nose, runs like a tap. Distracting. So who could I meet at the doctor's, he's about a hundred. Well, there was quite a dishy guy waiting to see him, but he was ancient too. And sick, probably."

"Not ancient, not sick." Trynor was sitting on the floor, playing cat's cradle with a thin looped strand of his own energies, twisting the coloured thread over and under itself in intricate patterns in the way he had watched Lucy play with wool in many lives.

"Well, let me see. Quite tall, I passed him in the hall on the way out. No, he didn't see me. What guy would ever notice us in this lousy uniform? Totally de-sexing. He had nice hair, really thick. Hm?. Oh, brown. And a nice nose and his mouth was nice too. What else can I say except nice? He was just sitting there with his eyes closed. ...Yes, that's how I got to look at him. Otherwise I'm too embarrassed... No, the hall was too dark, I couldn't see what colour they were. He didn't look at me. ... So what? Like I said, he was antique. ... Oh, twenty seven at least... "

"Just twenty-nine. Not antique. About the same as you, if you count the centuries."

".. no, nothing serious. Bit of hayfever, he said. Gave me an antihistamine, but I've to try it out, it might send me to sleep. Listen, have you tried that Question three on the biology sample paper? Yes.. No, that's what I thought..." *Trynor wandered away. He didn't have to mind Lucy too much when she started talking schoolwork. It was stuff from other lives she needed help with. She used to be terrified of beaches, but that had almost worn off. It was more recent things that were problematic now. Fear of loneliness. Walking in the dark. Knives. Railway stations, she got very wobbly in those. But talking to friends on the phone, not too much problem there.*

Alison ran down the stairs, stopped and pouted at Lucy.

"I need the phone. Hurry up."

"Go away. I'm discussing important study with Sal."

"Well, I have to find out what the homework is. From Deirdre. So hurry up, or I'll tell Mum you're eating all that expensive Magill's paté."

"It's me that asked her to buy it. So I don't think she'll mind if I eat it."

"Doesn't seem to matter how often they've worked together, sisters still fight. They were the same as Eloise and Pascale. Until Eloise married, then she had the power."

"Yes" agreed Alison's guide. "And I think Alison remembers being Pascale and feeling grateful and is trying to get over it by being pushy. Maybe she should be the older one next time."

"Probably. Make a note. Not that any of this is important really." The two guides stood together and watched with amusement as the two girls began to shout at each other, and as Alison cut her off with a quick finger on the button and then pulled the phone out of Lucy's hands, Lucy picked up her plate and stomped off into the kitchen in search of more paté.

"She really learnt to love food in France, didn't she?" mused Trynor, "nothing like being hungry first to give you an appreciation."

Chapter 18
North Médoc, France 1789

"Sainte Vierge, aidez-moi!" The scream echoed through the room and the midwife gripped the struggling woman's hand.

"Calm, now, calm, all is going well." The nurse reached for the sponge, dipped it in warm water and gently wiped the sweating face that was tossing to and fro on the pillow.

"How can it be all right, when it hurts so much?" Eloise cried, fastening anxious eyes on the older woman. "How can you just sit there, saying all is well?"

"Because I know it is. Nothing is out of the ordinary. You are just like your mother, she bore you with no trouble at all."

"Where is Mother? She said she would be here! Oh, no, it's coming again! Help! Help!" Eloise tossed and writhed and repeated her prayers to the Blessed Virgin, who knew what this felt like.

"We're all here for you, little Eloise," said Trynor, "and Mohmi is here with the baby's spirit, waiting to see her come back into the world. So all will be well. Calm, now. Calm." He passed his hands over Eloise, stroking just above her body and she relaxed a little, just before the contraction faded.

"That's better, you're doing well. Our Lady heard your prayer."

"I do not want to do this," Eloise whined and she began to raise herself up. "I'm going to go downstairs and talk to Daniel and tell him that he can do it, if he wants a son so much."

The midwife gently pushed her back and began to adjust the covers. She had seen this before and knew that the baby was nearly on its way.

"You tell him that later, dear. I'm sure he'll be interested in your suggestions."

On the dark landing, Jotin stood with Daniel who was trembling with fear. He was not downstairs relaxing as his wife imagined. He was more afraid than he could ever remember being. Why, oh why did I do it, he thought, forgetting in his panic that Eloise had loved him as much as he loved and wanted her. Wanted her, he thought, yes, I wanted her, ever since I saw her breasts heaving with the exertion of dancing at the village festival last year. Couldn't take your eyes off her, could you. Behaved shamefully, too, plucking a flower from one of the stalls and placing it between her breasts. His face coloured again at the memory of his rashness. Imagine what could have happened. She should have slapped my face, even though she was only a peasant. But I thank God she did not, he thought, as he began to smile at the memory of how she had looked up at him and laughed, their eyes connecting in a wave of amusement, that brought their hands together and swept them off into the next dance, while he watched her hair swirl around her as they turned to the music. She was made for me, he thought and now I'm going to lose her. Oh, God, protect her.

"But of course. And us. It's all right, tout va bien. Your Eloise will live to be a good mother to your child, you know that, inside. Stop trembling now. Go in to her, go on," Jotin spoke soothingly and moved the air currents on the landing, so that the light from the guttering flame of Daniel's candle flared for a moment and lit up the handle of the door.

Daniel put out his hand and turned the handle; quietly the door opened a little. He could see Eloise, lying on the rumpled bed, which had seemed so full of magic when he brought her there as his new wife. So full of magic until yesterday, when they could lie, their limbs entwined, talking about their baby and the wonderful future he would have. It seemed so special, this baby, so important. And now Eloise was struggling alone. He watched, standing in the open door, holding his light out of sight of the midwife, hoping to escape discovery, to be able to pray with Eloise, to help in some way, to promise God money for the church if Eloise was spared. To watch. To be where he should be, with Eloise.

"In the name of the saints and all that is holy, oh, forgive me, Mon Seigneur, but what do you think you are doing?" The voice cut harshly across his thoughts, as his mother-in-law bustled up the stairs. "Please come out of there and shut the door. That is no place for a man." She reached past Daniel, pulled the door shut and turned towards him, shooing him towards the top of the stairs, her lowly position forgotten in her anxiety for her child. "Go down and get them to boil some water. We will tell you when you are needed.

Go on, down you go." She curtseyed perfunctorily and opened the door again, only to shut it in his face as she went into the bedroom. Daniel could hear Eloise, with a different tone in her voice, as she wailed - "Maman, oh, Maman, where were you? I've been so frightened."

"Come on, Daniel, even I have no power against the taboos of women. On we go downstairs and do what you are told. All will be well. Viens, ne t'inquiete pas." Daniel stood, unmoving, straining to hear through the door, to guess what was happening inside. *Jotin blew and* suddenly Daniel's candle went out, leaving him in the dark. He sighed and began to go down the stairs, to wake the servants. The house was quiet, creaking ominously as it settled into the night and a chill crept in from the darkness outside. Daniel decided he would boil the water himself, to show his mother-in-law that he was not entirely useless. She certainly thought so and his own mother's behaviour tonight would not have impressed the busy peasant women now upstairs delivering the new landowner. I wonder why the peasants help us, he mused, as he started to rake up the ashes of the fire and set about boiling some water. It is nothing to most of them what happens in the château. My own mother and sisters just went off to bed and left Eloise alone. Didn't even tell me, or send one of the servants to the village for Eloise's mother. Why didn't Maman tell me, when it is her grandson who is coming? He shook his head and began to search for the kettle.

Daniel woke up suddenly, with the room full of steam and an ominous hissing coming from the kettle. As he feared, it was boiling dry, the last bubbles chasing themselves around and a white film forming in their place. He felt guilty, partly because there was now no hot water, although he did wonder what it was needed for, as no-one had come to fetch it; but mostly simply because he had slept while Eloise was suffering. He listened to the mumble of voices above and then he heard her, her voice barely audible. It sounded like she was pleading with someone. He pulled the kettle from the heat, left it on the tiles by the fire and dashed up the stairs, not waiting to light a candle.

"I'm hot," whimpered Eloise, "I need air. Open the shutters, Maman, please."

Her mother looked at the midwife. "Is it safe to let in the night air? My Tante Louise says that night air is dangerous for babies."

"Never mind the air. All sorts of things could fly in and bite the baby. Leave it closed."

"It's for me, Maman, not the baby. I'm hot. There's no baby. I'm hot!" Eloise's voice was rising to a shriek. Her mother wrung a cloth out again in cool water and was laying it across Eloise's forehead, murmuring soothing words that had been familiar to her children when they were tiny. Eloise began to relax, until the next spasm hit her and she cried out again. There was a crash, as the door was flung open. Daniel strode across the room and fumbled with the shutters.

"I do not care if you say this is a women's place only. Madame de Vrac needs help and you are standing discussing it. Do something."

The shutters creaked open, several large flakes of paint falling from them as they moved and fluttering down into the courtyard. A cold breeze came into the room, accompanied by a lone and probably confused moth. Daniel went to the bed and knelt beside Eloise, bringing her hand to his lips. He stroked her face and looked into her eyes.

"I'm here, my precious. I'm not leaving, no matter what they tell me." Eloise tried to smile, but another wave of pain and a huge shuddering urge broke over her body. She cried out and as her body heaved it was as though her movement created a break in the clouds that allowed a stripe of silvery grey to fall across the bed. There was a slither and a tiny body emerged into the moonlight. The little face crumpled and let out a wail. The two older women sighed with relief and grinned at each other.

"A perfect little girl." The midwife lifted the baby, wrapped her in a cotton cloth and laid her on Eloise's breast.

Eloise leant back on the pillow and closed her eyes. Her body sagged and her whole face softened as she whispered "it's over, it's over. The saints and Our Lady be praised, it's over."

"No, my darling. It is just beginning." Daniel's face was shining and the corners of his eyes glittered, where the tears were gathering. He had put his finger in the baby's hand and she was gripping him tightly. "She is beautiful, is she not? Just like her mother!"

"You flatter me, Monsieur. Maybe she's beautiful like you. Look at her hair. So soft and dark. I'm sorry, I did not give you your son.

118

Are you angry with me?"

"No, she's too lovely to want anything else. We can have the son next time."

His mother-in-law grunted. "Hm. They always say that, men. As soon as you're through one danger they want to put you in a new one. Now come on, Monsieur, out! You're in the way, this little lady has to learn how to feed."

"What will we call her, Monsieur?" Eloise looked past him out of the window and up to the crescent of the moon, shining sedately down on her and her daughter. "The moonlight helped. As soon as you opened the shutters, and it shone in, she was born. It is so pretty, look!"

"Au clair de la lune," sang Daniel, "she was born by the light of the moon. Claire is a pretty name."

"Lot of nonsense," said the midwife, as she bundled used sheets into a sack. "It was the Blessed Virgin who helped. Did you not hear Madame cry out to Our Lady for help? And it was given. Perfect baby, healthy mother, or she will be if you go away now and let me get on."

"Marie-Claire" said Eloise, "my little Marie-Claire," and she looked up at Daniel for his opinion. He nodded and beamed down at her. One of the tears broke free from its mooring and dropped onto the baby's face as he kissed his little family and was then shooed from the room.

Chapter 19

The sun was settling onto the treetops as Daniel came out onto the terrace of the little château of Merillac. The long shadows crept across the grass towards the house and birds were beginning to congregate on the ridges of the barns, chirping and cawing and nudging each other. As the air cooled, the cicadas set up their strumming in the trees, seeming to call that work was not over while nature was still busy. The leaves of the trees barely moved in the heavy air and Daniel could see a shifting patch of greyness in the air a few feet away, rising and falling a little as the tiny insects that it was went about their miniscule business. Between the trees he could see the neat green lines indicating the gentle undulations of his vineyards, and two fields full of golden wheat. Further off, he could see the last of the sun reflecting off the shallow water covering the salt marshes and imagined that he could see as far as the estuary beyond, where ships sailed with precious cargoes of wine. He stood, his hands on the smooth wood of the balustrade and looked out over his land, his mind running idly over the tasks achieved today on the farm. The wood was warm under his fingers and he stroked it, pleased by the silky texture and momentarily aware of the three generations of related hands that had done the same thing on hundreds of other satisfactory evenings. He turned towards Eloise's favourite chair and only then became aware of her, curled up tight, her eyes closed. The baby was quiet, dozing in her crib at Eloise's feet.

"What is it, Eloise? Are you ill?" he crossed over to her and touched her back, alarmed at how stiff it was. Eloise stiffened more at his touch and mumbled something. He had to bend close to hear.

"No, Sir. The baby is beautiful and healthy. And I am well and healthy and blessed to be safely delivered. They tell me often how lucky I am and how happy I must be." Eloise tucked her head further down into her chest and sighed.

"But I am not happy to see you like this, ma chérie. Where is your smile and the flashing eyes I love? Stolen away by this beautiful evening?" He was stroking her back as he talked and gradually she began to uncurl and smiled wanly at him.

"The baby is beautiful, they are all correct. And I love her. But I am not me anymore, not Eloise. I am just Madame."

"You are always Eloise to me, always. Even if we have a dozen children, you will always be the reason for me."

"The reason, Sir? I do not understand." Eloise was pulling herself up more now.

"My reason for bothering, for running the farm, for caring about the crops. Because I know my Eloise is here, looking beautiful and ready to smile at me."

"I will try, to please you, but it is difficult to smile, I am so tired." Eloise sagged back in her chair and looked out past Daniel, towards the sunlight, setting amongst the branches of the trees. The rosy light seemed to warm her and she smiled down at little Marie-Claire, whose little mouth was working as she dreamt of feeding.

"She'll cry soon, again, look. She is always hungry. I will have to go in."

"She is making you tired, my love. Why do you not let me find her a wet nurse from the village? Then you could rest more."

"I am from the village. I will feed my own child. I have seen what can happen to a child when its mother must give her milk away to another. I will not cause a child to starve." Her eyes flashed defiance and Daniel looked at her with surprise, mixed with delight that his wife seemed to be recovering her energy. He decided to fight back.

"But a woman can feed two babies. Why else would God give her two breasts?" He leant back and grinned, his argument complete.

"If both of the children are with her, yes. But if a woman goes to the big house to feed the little Duc, do you think her own baby may go too? No, her own child must stay in the village, fed on whatever can be found. Such children do not thrive. My cousin's baby died of a fever, which he could not fight because he was so weak, after she went as wet nurse to the château. She needed the money for her other children. It was a big price to pay, I will not ask it of anyone. I am sorry to speak thus to you."

"I did not know." Daniel was silent now, his eyes troubled. He knew he had been fed by a nurse, in fact he remembered her with affection, as she had also fed his younger sisters. Now he wondered how her own babies had fared.

As the last rays of sun slid away from the house there was a little wail from the crib and Eloise struggled to her feet. She lifted the baby and carried her indoors, to feed and clean her. Daniel called one of the servants and asked for a glass of wine. When it came, he sipped it slowly, wondering what he could do for Eloise to lift her spirits. Half way down the glass he had an idea. As his mind worked on it he began to sing softly under his breath. By the time dinner was announced the plan was formed and he explained it with great excitement.

"A picnic!" exclaimed his mother, looking for a moment just like a little girl. "Where to?"

"The beach at Soulac. It is very lovely." He smiled at Eloise and she smiled back. It was very lovely to the two of them, as it was where Daniel had taken her, very daringly, on horseback to ask her to become his wife and where, an hour later, she had agreed. It had taken an hour for her to recover from the surprise of being asked to marry into the château, even a château as small as Merillac.

"I would like to see the beach," said Catherine, Daniel's youngest sister. "The sea must be bigger than the Garonne, is it?"

"Of course it is, silly. You have been to the beach, we all have," Charlotte said, as she helped herself to more bread and began pulling it into tiny pieces, "you just do not remember as you are far too young. Maybe your brain is not fully grown yet."

Catherine stuck out her tongue at her sister. "I'm ten, not a baby. Stop pretending I'm a baby."

"You were a baby when you were born. I remember it very well."

"And I remember you as a baby very well too, Charlotte," Daniel said, "It is a condition most of us recover from. Stop teasing Catherine and tell her what you remember about the beach."

"The beach is very inconvenient," Madame deVrac was grumbling again. "All that sand. And it can be windy."

"I agree," said Jotin. "Think of somewhere other than the beach. I do not think you will like it as much as you think, now that the baby is with you."

"The beach is special to us, Mother. I think we will like the beach. And on the way we can stop at the Church of Notre-Dame. They say that this year a priest has set up a shrine beside it and is saying Mass for the pilgrims who pass. Like in the old days, before the sand swallowed the church."

"Like I said, too much sand. My mother always talked of the

people who came looking for work when their town was overcome by the sand. I was only a child at the time, but I well remember the stories. The houses filled with it." Madame deVrac shuddered, but then brightened. "But a priest, you say? Saying pilgrim Masses? That would be something to see. Are there many pilgrims still?"

"I am not sure, Madame. There should be, it is still on the route to Compostela. We will have to go and see. We will bring two carts, and rugs and musicians. Then we can dance!"

Eloise's eyes shone. A dance on the beach. She loved to dance and with Daniel it was so special, they had first noticed each other at the dance in the village. Of course, they should have paid no attention to each other, she should have looked at the ordinary boys, not at a landowner; she took big risk, smiling at Mon Seigneur. Many aristocrats would have used her and cast her aside. But she had taken the risk and he had offered her marriage. She grinned at Daniel and he was happy, her spirits seemed to be lifted.

The picnic was arranged for three days later. The cook had worked hard, producing baskets full of terrines and patés, cold meats and ripe cheeses, their aromas escaping out of their straw wrappings and making everyone's mouths water. There was bread, soft and crusty, and pastries and bottles of fruit juices, and of course, wine. Two carriages rattled up the drive shortly after breakfast and their neighbours from the next châteaux jumped down, full of excitement at being invited to join in. Madame deVrac rushed to greet them and there was a wonderful chaos as everyone milled around, getting in the way of the three musicians who had been hired from the village and who were packing their instruments onto one of the carts. Daniel put his own violin in too, though as he said to Eloise, if he wanted to dance he could not play – 'or at least not very well!' Eloise was installed on the other cart, on cushions, with the baby on her lap. Her spirits were still a bit low, but she expected they would improve soon. Rosemarie the midwife had visited and told her that many new mothers felt as she did, that it was maybe God's way of making them rest instead of trying to work too hard, 'and have no time to make milk for the baby'. So she was content to be tucked up in a rug on the cart and to watch idly as the countryside passed by. As they passed through the village she called out to many old friends, who ran over to kiss her and congratulate her on the arrival of 'la petite'. Etienne the blacksmith came across and clasped her hand in his huge fist.

"I am so glad to see you well, ma petite," he rumbled. "I was worried for you when Rosemarie was up at the château and so glad when she got home soon with the good news. Not a boy this time, he'll have to try again for an heir, this one's another little dancer for me to teach, do you think?"

Eloise laughed with him and settled back again, remembering the times when Etienne had allowed her to hold the horses while he shod them, trusting her to manage their huge power; and afterwards how he had taken out his fiddle and played and had showed her the steps to old dances, laughing that if she could dance well her feet would always avoid the hooves. But it was not necessary to avoid hooves with Etienne, he had such a way with animals. He was the doctor to all the local animals, just as his wife looked after most human maladies. Lost in a happy memory, Eloise began to relax and Daniel, watching from horseback, was pleased to see that his plan seemed to be working.

None of the party noticed the figure in a doorway at the far end of the street, hanging back, but unable to tear himself away from the sight of the woman he had hoped to win laughing so easily with another man. And such a man, thought Nicholas. Why did she have to get mixed up with the aristos? Bastards, every one of them. Look at them, three families, doing no work, able to take time to go on picnics, for God's sake and still able to eat well! They will ruin her, my Eloise, he thought, turning away at last. She will turn into one of them, mother to another landowner in time. He shuddered, thinking of what would have to happen before Eloise could become mother to a boy and muttering set out back to his work.

The countryside became sandier and a salty tang drifted on the air. Daniel allowed his horse to walk beside the cart in which Eloise and Marie-Claire were riding. He could see Eloise's face, she was looking into the middle distance, seeing nothing, but with a small smile on her lips. Daniel reached out with his riding crop and gently lifted a lock of her hair away from her face. Her smile broadened and slowly her eyes turned to his. They just looked at each other for a moment, but that was enough.

"Monsieur," said Eloise, "is that the chapel up ahead? The one we went into after our Walk on the Beach?" Her voice put an importance into that event that they both understood. Daniel nodded.

"May we stop and go in? To give thanks again?"

"Good idea" said Daniel.

"Good idea" said Trynor and Jotin together. "But not for the reasons you think," continued Trynor.

The carts were pulled up to the door of the chapel and Eloise was helped down. Her mother in law in an uncharacteristic burst of generosity offered to hold the baby, but Eloise insisted on bringing her into the chapel, so the little family went in together. Daniel's mother stayed beside the cart, giving orders and fussing about the picnic baskets, hoping for compliments on her lunch arrangements from the ladies in the carriages. The other young people got down and walked about and sized each other up. No one seemed to feel the need of prayer.

It was cool inside the little chapel and the sun slanted in from one of the side windows, lighting up the flagged floor and the few simple seats. Someone had left a jug on the altar, with some wild flowers in it and they were drooping a little. Eloise went over to the side of the little church and sat facing a statue of Mary, who looked down on her with stony peacefulness.

"Our Father, which art in heaven..." she began, her eyes shut and her lips barely moving as the familiar words soothed her. Daniel knelt beside her and joined in. Marie-Claire lay on her mother's lap, her eyes open wide, as she listened to a voice only she could hear.

"Marie-Claire" said Mohmi, hovering beside the baby's head, "you do not need to be in a church to hear me now and I want you to remember, when you get bigger, that I will talk to you always, not just in churches. Your parents have forgotten, like the others. Maybe you will be one of the few who will always hear us?" The baby waved her arms and gurgled.

Eloise looked down as she continued to pray, and hugged her baby.

"...the fruit of thy womb, Jesus. Look, Daniel, Marie-Claire is joining in! She wants to thank God too. Holy Mary, Mother of God...."

"No, Eloise, she is talking to her guide. So could you. Better still,

126

you could listen. I'll wait till you finish your prayer. Just keep quiet after it, would you, and not start gabbling again?" Trynor waited, leaning up against the statue, smiling down at Eloise. Jotin was prowling the chapel, waiting for the prayer to stop.

"Amen" said Daniel and Eloise, and they sat for a moment in silence.

"Eloise, do not go to the beach," said Trynor, "you would be happier in the meadow behind this chapel. You could dance there without a shadow of memory."

Eloise shifted in her seat. A picture had come into her mind of the dance in the village square and she felt a frisson of happiness.

"Why are you wasting good chances worrying about the beach?" Jotin was frowning at Trynor. "They will not like it and they will go somewhere else. It does not matter, really." He turned towards Daniel. "Listen Daniel," he said urgently, putting out a hand towards Daniel's back and stroking him gently, "I want you to listen to the farm workers when they come to talk to you about their wages. Be fair to them. Discuss with Eloise how to treat them, she will understand. I'll remind you, I'll be there. When I stroke you, you will remember, please?"

"He might," said Trynor. "Then again, he might not. It's too vague. Much easier to concentrate on immediate things. Like the picnic. Talk to him about the workers when they are with him."

"Oh, I will. But he just doesn't listen when he is not in a church, haven't you noticed? Not since he was a baby. We have to use our opportunities."

"Yes, I suppose so. At least they do listen a bit when they are in here. Once they stop talking."

"Isn't that the truth? They are so uncomfortable with silence, always having to fill it with something. Quick, they're leaving!" Trynor and Jotin rushed over to Eloise and Daniel and started to talk, rapidly adding suggestions, one after another.

"They won't hear anything, if you say so much," said Mohmi. "Isn't that right, my precious?" She smiled down at the baby, who cooed back up at her again.

"You are a precious thing, my little treasure," Eloise snuggled her face down into the shawls and breathed in Marie-Claire's baby smell, sweet and soft. "Look, Monsieur, she is smiling!"

"Of course she is not smiling, she is too young, she is hungry.

What could she have to smile about, at her age?"

"*The joy of being alive*" *said Mohmi, as they all moved out of the chapel into the sunshine.*

Chapter 20

As she handed her daughter back up into the cart, Eloise turned to Daniel.

"Would you mind if we do not go to the beach? We could have a good picnic in the meadow." She indicated the area behind the chapel with her other hand.

"Why?" Daniel was perplexed. Eloise had been so enthusiastic when he suggested the outing. In fact, it had brought some life back into her. "I thought we were going to walk at the edge of the water?"

"Yes, we were. I do not know. I just had a feeling that The Blessed Virgin does not want us to go to the sea."

"Why would she object? Her Son's friends were fishermen. You are having fancies. Come on, we will breathe good salty air and dance on the sand. Anyway, we have to go on, to see this pilgrim shrine." He swung himself back up onto his horse and, standing up in the stirrups, pointed forward dramatically with his crop.

"Onward! We will vanquish all foes and take the sea before the day is out!"

Eloise giggled and settled down again in the cart, as it started to lurch back toward the road towards old Soulac.

The sand became more plentiful, drifting between the tufts of rough grass and moving a little in the breeze. They crossed the brow of the hill and thought they could see a distant horizon, but there on their right they could just make out the ruins of the old church of Notre Dame, which had been engulfed by sand more than sixty years before. There was no roof, but they could see walls here and there, poking out of the sand. There was a small tent at one side, made of rough canvas and a table outside it, with a candlestick on it. A man with wild hair and a beard was sitting in the shade of the tent, but he stood up to greet the party. He was tall and gangly, but imposing, and wore a monk's habit, with a large crucifix at his belt. He approached, his arms open.

"Welcome, pilgrims! You make the long journey to God's house in Spain! He will reward you well for your determination. Come, I will say prayers for you and you will make an offering to the Glory of God. Or I can say a Mass?" His hand pushed forwards in the age old gesture of the beggar. Daniel stepped forward.

"No, we are not pilgrims, we live to the south of here. We are here to see the sea and have a good day on the beach. But some prayers would be welcome, thank you." He put his hand in his pocket to find some coins. His mother started to rummage in one of the baskets and at last pulled out a purse.

"No," she said with dignity and for the benefit of her audience in the carriages, "we will have a mass. For the health of my daughter-in-law and grand-daughter and that the crops this year will be successful. This should ensure both, I think?" She pressed a gold piece into the priest's grimy hand. The priest bobbed his thanks and the coin disappeared inside his robes. He bustled away into the tent and came out with a book and a small flask, which he laid on the table with exaggerated reverence. He indicated for them all to stand in front of his makeshift altar.

"No, Father," said Daniel, "we will allow you to say the mass after we leave. We have come out to give my wife a good day at the sea, to bring some colour back to her cheeks. We will not spend it in church," He lifted Eloise up onto the cart and told its driver to move on. Madame deVrac's eyes flashed.

"How dare you speak to a man of God like that! And in front of our neighbours too," she hissed. "It is my cheeks that will have colour, I'm so embarrassed. To walk away like that is shameful. You should be more mindful and remember we have a position to keep up, it is too easy to lose it. You read too many books and are getting heretical notions." She paused, till a new thought struck her, "also, we need to check that he says the mass."

"He will say it. What else has he to do? No crowd of pilgrims here today. I suppose it depends on the weather, whether they can get a boat across the estuary. Maybe no one was coming this way today." Daniel swung himself up onto his saddle.

"Come on Madame, back up into your place."

They continued on down the slight hill and made their way across the rough tussocky ground towards the low dunes that blocked their first view of the sea. The air was fresh here, blowing in from the ocean and the cries of gulls filled their ears. Eloise got down from the cart, which could not go further and followed the track where some of the servants had gone ahead with the rugs and the children had run, keen to reach the freedom of the beach. The coarse grasses tugged at her skirts and sand poured into her shoes. She bent down and emptied them out, causing a scandalised rush of opinions from her mother-in-law, who was following behind, grumbling. Daniel finished tethering his horse to the cart and ran forward to walk with Eloise as they returned for the first time since their marriage to the place where they had truly fallen in love. He took the baby from her, so that she could manoeuvre her long skirts more easily through the long reeds. Marie-Claire was quiet and still, her eyes wide open, her little nose twitching, smelling the sea. Mohmi, beside her, was saying "you do not need to worry, nothing will happen to you this time. You are safe." The baby closed her eyes and yawned.

Eloise was ahead of Daniel as they went over the last dune and onto the beach. She looked at the sea, rolling and grey, and held her breath.

"It is so big," she said and stopped walking.

"Go on," said Daniel, pushing her a little, "let us all see." Then he too came past the dune and stopped. He clutched the baby tightly as he looked down the beach towards the waves. His mother was coming just behind him and reached forward.

"Give me that child," she said, "before you squeeze her to death."

Daniel looked at his mother, without seeing her. He looked down at the baby, now sleeping quietly.

"No!" he said and pushed the baby into Eloise's arms. "She should be with her mother here. Then she will be safe." Eloise took the baby and hugged her tight. She walked a few more steps onto the beach and turned, tears beginning to form as her heart started to pound.

"I cannot bring the baby onto the beach. It is not safe. The sea...." She looked at Daniel, whose face was white and sweating. "I'm afraid, Monsieur. I do not know why. Can we leave, please?"

"If you like, my love. You do not have to stay anywhere that does not please you."

"Cheat!" said Jotin, as he stroked Daniel's energies to calm him. "Go on, admit you are afraid too."

"He won't" said Trynor, "He thinks he has to stay strong, or he is not a man. Come on, let's get them out of here. If you had joined with me in warning them, they could be dancing by now."

Daniel and Eloise were walking quickly back to the carts, leaving one of the musicians to go onto the beach to explain to the servants that the rugs had to be folded up again and the children rounded up. Daniel's mother grumbled even louder to his sisters when they reappeared, about people who could not make up their minds, caused disruption, and wasted time before lunch; and that it would be their fault if the food was spoiled. She apologised fulsomely to their friends, putting the blame on Eloise and forgetting the need for discretion − 'not used to the beach, you know, she's from the village. I warned Daniel, I begged and I threatened, but he would not listen. Insisted on ruining himself, bringing shame on the family. After his grandfather and father were so careful...' She broke off in confusion before she let out any more about the family's humble origins, now thankfully almost a hundred years and more than fifty miles away.

They got back up onto the carts and into the carriages and made slow progress up the hill towards the church. The little shrine seemed deserted, but from his better vantage point on horseback Daniel could see the priest, stretched out on the ground in the shade beside his tent, his head on the book and the flagon lying on its side on the sand. He sighed. It had been a short mass. He hoped that it would work and that his mother would get her value and also that she would not notice the sleeping priest. He spurred his horse on, back the way they had come.

The party stopped again at the little chapel and walked around the side of it, to a large open meadow, down the edge of which there was a row of shady trees. The rugs were laid under the largest tree, the table was set up and at last the food could be unpacked. Eloise chose a place on the rugs and listened to the wind in the leaves above her.

"The wind is making a lovely sound, Monsieur, listen. Gentle. I did not like the sound of the sea, it was too big. I do not want to see it again."

"No, we will stay away from it in future. But we should never forget that it brought us together, never forget its power. Its power..." Daniel fell silent as he felt the hairs on his spine rise in a ripple that ran up to the back of his neck. He looked at Eloise in sudden concern and knelt beside her, raising her hand to his lips.

Her hazel eyes looked into his, puzzled, then she smiled and squeezed his fingers a little as he let go.

"Oh Sir, you should not blame the sea. It was you and your flower that really had the power over me. I would not have been there at the sea with you if it had not been for that flower and the dancing!" Their hands had just met again when Madame deVrac's voice broke through their self absorption with enquiries about their preferences for duck breast or leg and a complaint about the cheese having been stored on its side.

"I do not know, really, what these servants are thinking of sometimes. That lovely cheese has leaked all over the fruit. Such a waste."

"Just as well really," whispered Daniel to Eloise, "if it had not, she would have been berating us for unseemly behaviour in front of the servants!" He squeezed her hand and got up to help with the food and mollify his mother.

Eloise, alone for a moment, picked up Marie-Claire and spoke softly to her.

"My precious little one, I will protect you always, for ever. You do not need to fear that big rough sea, you are never going near it again. I am going to keep you safe." Marie-Claire slept on, comfortable in the warm shade.

Eloise sat in the shade, nibbling at the pastries spread out on the table and sipping a glass of rich red wine. Her fingers were still greasy from the confit and cheese and she rubbed them with the stiff linen napkin. Her eyes closed, and she could hear more clearly the musicians clattering about as they got out their instruments, the ladies and gentlemen chatting, laughing, and in one case snoring, and the servants gossiping as they packed away the leftovers. She could distinguish very little, but because they were village people and spoke in her dialect, the odd word came through with startling clarity. As she drifted on the edge of sleep she heard 'Nicholas ....anger...Nantes ....Paris ....cousin ...trouble ....good man' and her mind drifted back to her childhood, when her brother's friend Nicholas had teased her, catching her hands and swinging her round, telling her it was only a matter of time and she would dance with him, to his tune. I wonder why Luc liked him, why he never asked him to stop? It seemed he had assumed that if he liked

Nicholas, I must too. Of course, if Nicholas had behaved like all the other boys in the village, I would have liked him better, maybe even enough to dance with him, or more. But that air of ownership he put on, that was unattractive. As though I had no mind of my own. Well, I showed him I have a mind, when I danced with Daniel. Though I didn't dance with Daniel to show Nicholas anything, I wasn't thinking of him at all. So why am I thinking of him now? He does not matter to me.

"Not directly, you're right. But get Daniel to listen when he comes to talk to him. Everyone will be happier if they hear each other, including Luc and your father."

Eloise opened her eyes and looked around, puzzled. Then she saw Daniel holding out his hand to her and heard the music starting up. She jumped to her feet and under the shade of the big trees the dancing started. Eloise found her feet moving with the music and she threw herself into the dance, enjoying the turning and circling of it, catching the hands that were held out to her, letting go, weaving the pattern to and fro. She began to smile and then to grin and by the time the circle had moved her round to Daniel again, she was laughing aloud. Daniel matched his steps to hers and moved her out of the group into the sunshine. They danced circles around each other, slow and stately, in rhythm to the music. They locked eyes and laughed again, not knowing why they were suddenly so happy, but not caring.

They were brought back to the present by Madame, calling them back into the shade, back to the proper behaviour of the gentry.

At the salt marshes, Nicholas was scraping the thin layer of salt to the side of the section and his cousin Jean-Marc was lifting the little pile into a small sack. They were sweating in the afternoon heat.

"This is slow work," Jean-Marc said, as he wiped his streaming face again, "it would be quicker just to sweat into the bag and squeeze it out. And it would be pure white salt off us, not this cowardly stuff. What makes it that colour anyway? Who ever heard of yellow salt!"

"It is the way it is here. I suppose it must be because the silt underneath it is yellow." Nicholas stretched across to gather the last thin scraping of crystals, being careful not to gather the mud underneath. "We get less for it than if it was white, of course. The cheese makers over in Cantal like it, their cheese is yellow anyway. But it is hard to sell privately, you know what I mean?" Nicholas winked at his cousin, "though I do keep a bit the nuns never know about."

"The nuns sell to the cheesemakers for you, then?"

"Yes, and take half of the money. And the taxes are terrible. That is why I keep some back."

"It is the only way the common man can survive. It is the same in Nantes. Maybe when the summer is over and things calm down, I can find you a market there. Can you get the colour out of the salt?"

"I don't know. I never thought of it."

"That is why we are poor. We just accept. We must stop behaving like sheep, we must take control like the Parisians. We must insist on better conditions."

"They tried that in Bordeaux once, I heard. There were riots about the price of bread, but nothing changed. Look at the price now."

"But if you never complain, nothing will change, that is for sure. The rich are not going to wake up one morning and decide to give away their money, are they? So go and ask your landlord – I challenge you! Don't be lily-livered like your salt."

Nicholas looked out towards the estuary, hidden from them by the dykes and saw the thin stream of water beginning to make its way towards them.

"Quick, get that salt off the ground, they have opened the sluices." The two men worked quickly to save the last of the salt and pulled the bags up onto the higher ground between the salt pans just as the first of the high tide snaked over the low barrier and covered the silt again. Nicholas ran around to close the little gate that would hold today's sea water on his patch of marsh.

"It is so hot, we might be able to be back here in two days for the next lot. The summer is good, more chance to salt away a little of our own, huh?"

Jean-Marc laughed. "Not a good reason not to put in for a share of the seigneur's. Get him when he is feeling richer, too!" He flung an arm round Nicholas and patted his shoulder boisterously.

Chapter 21

It was a bright evening a week later and Eloise was sitting at her dressing table, getting ready for dinner. Marie-Claire was fed and sleeping under the watchful eye of Eloise's youngest sister, recently hired as a maid to help her with the baby. So Eloise was free to sit and think, and she was enjoying letting her mind roam, still very aware of her good fortune at having married into a wealthy family.

The best bit, she thought, of having money, was not having to work. She thought of the village and of what she might be doing now if she had not married Daniel. Helping her mother to make food for all seven of them. Having to stoke the fire, then struggling with that big pot over it. Brushing the hair away from her sweaty forehead with the back of her hand, trying not to let her greasy fingers touch it. Instead, here she was, with clean hands, dabbling them in her jewellery box. The late sunshine was coming in the window and lighting up a corner of her dressing table. Eloise plunged her hands into the box, scooped out her necklaces, bracelets and rings, and spread them in the triangle of sunlight. The little pile gleamed. Eloise gazed and touched. There was the string of pearls, glowing softly in the reddish light, which had been her betrothal gift, reluctantly passed on by her mother-in-law, who had told Daniel privately that Eloise's coarse peasant skin would ruin them. Daniel, in the first flush of excited love and made bolder by his surprising choice of bride, had passed this opinion on to Eloise, along with the assurance that her skin was as smooth as mother-of-pearl. He told her that the pearls had been bought by his great-grandfather, a year after he had won the land around Merillac and with it the chance of respectability. Eloise had been pleased to receive them and often wished she could have met him, a stevedore who was lucky enough to be challenged by a passing Duke.

"I'll bet you my land in the Médoc against your sweaty shirt that you cannot get my luggage aboard before the noon bells ring," had been the wager, and great-grandfather, who liked to test his strength, had bent to the loads and done the job in the four minutes remaining, to the chagrin and amusement of the Duke, who had reached into his pocket and thrust some papers towards the bewildered but triumphant man. "I have not seen it," the Duke had said, "it is new land, not good for much. A tiny island until recently, when the Dutch engineers drained the marshes. But if you can work as hard as you have shown me today, you will get more good of it than I would." And he had walked aboard the ship bound for the Indies, leaving great-grandfather a small landowner.

"But do not tell Madame deVrac you know this. She is embarrassed to think she married into such a family," Daniel had warned her.

"I am proud to be part of such a family. He must have been a remarkable man, to build this château and become so rich."

"Not rich enough for Maman. And no title. It is a great grief to her to be plain Madame, a new name too, there were no deVracs before great-grandpapa made it up. To keep us humble, he said."

A remarkable man indeed, thought Eloise, not one to be ashamed of. I wish my brother Luc could win such a wager and buy his wife pearls. And his grand-daughter could have diamonds like these. She picked up her diamond bracelet, which was glittering and seemed to be shouting out you have real money now, you lucky woman. And there were rings, with different stones, all beautiful. But best of all, there was her gold filigree necklace. She picked it up, feeling a reverence towards the man who had made it. She had often watched Etienne as he worked the iron for horseshoes and knew the skill needed. Had she been a boy, she would have asked him to take her on as an apprentice. It was so satisfying, watching the raw lump of metal turn into something with a planned shape and a real use. But this necklace was on a different level. The man who had worked this metal had used fine skills and delicate care, to create these tiny flowers and birds, interlocking and held by the finest wires. Eloise looked at the beautiful piece lying there in the sun, glowing with a rich colour and felt a happiness fill her as she traced her finger around the gold.

"I watched him make one like it," Daniel had come into the room behind her. "I wondered why you did not hear me knock, but when I saw what you were looking at, I understood. When I watched him work, time stood still. I could have stayed all day, but I was in his way, just a gentleman whose place was to pay, not watch. So I paid and never regretted. I knew I would have a beautiful wife to wear it one day. Will I help you to put it on?" He picked up the necklace, carefully straightening it out so that it would lie flat. Eloise watched his fingers handling the gold wire and flowers so delicately and felt a huge surge of love for him. Then she blushed. Daniel stepped back from her and laughed.

"What wonderful thoughts are going through that pretty head?" he mused. I think I would like to know, maybe they could be to my advantage!"

Eloise shook her head. She looked away from him, confused and wondering what to say. She was sure she loved Daniel just for himself, but here she was admiring him with the gold. To love gold was unworthy, unless it was to give to the poor in the village. She was not sure what she felt, except hugely lucky. Daniel's hand crept round her neck, fastening the necklace in place and then his fingers moved downwards across her chest. He left one finger between her breasts and pointed to her reflection in the mirror.

"The only thing wrong with this necklace is that it is too short. There should be a flower just here. And here, and here." Eloise turned towards him and raised her face. She would say nothing, he would never understand how she could be ashamed to be rich, even just for a moment. He had been rich all his life, nearly thirty years. He did not know what it was to be hungry, or exhausted by work. And now she could share in his good fortune and employ Pascale. Things were better all round; and he had such soft hands. She shuddered as she returned his kiss, feeling it getting more insistent and his hands moving downwards towards her hips. Suddenly he slid one arm under her and lifted her up, burying his face between her breasts as he carried her towards the bed.

Eloise sat up and straightened out her skirt. The sunlight had gone from the room and the little pile of jewellery no longer gleamed. Daniel lay beside her, breathing gently, a slight sweat on his face just visible in the dying light. As she stood up, he opened his eyes.

"Where are you going?" He sounded puzzled.

"You have kept us late for dinner, I'm sure. What will your mother think?"

"She will think the truth. That I have a very beautiful wife, who makes eyes at me instead of changing for dinner."

"I am changed for dinner. It is you who must rush into your

clothes so as not to be embarrassed any more than absolutely necessary. Come on, get up, hurry!" She pulled his sleeve and sidestepped him, giggling, as he rolled towards her and off the bed, putting his feet deftly under him as he landed. He stood up and looked down at her, lifted her face with one finger and kissed her nose before sauntering towards his dressing room, smiling back at her with mischief in his eyes.

Chapter 22

Nicholas had taken care of his appearance this morning, he had washed his hands and face and shaved as best he could. He was going to talk to the Patron and get him to see sense. He set his cap firmly on his head, covering his unruly hair, and set off for the château, early enough that the talk would be over before work and the foreman could not complain. He would get his piece in first. He would tell them about the news from Paris; that would frighten them all right. Make them realise it could not be all their way for ever. It was a while since his cousin had ridden from Nantes to bring the news and to get out of the way, of course – Jean-Marc had always got into trouble, he was the most tactless man in France. The only safe place for him was somewhere the trouble was not and with his advancing years he had at last realised it.

"But Nicholas, you have not. Not yet. You are too like him, be careful. Do not say too much. Remember Eloise never gave you any reason to hope. You were just her brother's friend." Roki followed along beside Nicholas, talking to him, trying to slow him down, but Nicholas broke into a run as he got near the gates of the estate.

"I'll tell you. You will have to listen to me."

Daniel was in the room called the *chai* looking over the fermenting vessels when Nicholas appeared, breathing heavily. He looked over to the door, puzzled to see one of the men here without the foreman. He was even more puzzled when the man walked towards him.

"Yes?"

"Mon Seigneur, I am Nicholas Martin. I speak for all of us." Nicholas took off his cap and twisted it in his hands. He looked at Daniel's feet.

"Yes?"

Nicholas was suddenly silent. He had no practice at talking to the gentry. He had expected Daniel to be angry and then he could have been defiant. That was how he had practised this conversation. He had talked to Daniel several times now, in his head and it had always gone well: Daniel had always apologised for stealing his woman. But that was not the point of coming here. He could not have Eloise now. But there were other things he could have.

"Mon Seigneur, we need money." There, it was said. The sentence hung in the air between them.

"You do the work, you get your piquette." Daniel was still puzzled.

"Piquette is a tasty drink, but it is only the rinsings of the vats, not wine. We must pay high rent for our little pieces of land and everything we earn is taxed. We cannot live like this, seigneur."

"But you do. Here you are, alive. What do you mean?"

"We can save nothing. If a man is ill for one day, his family starves. When he is too old to work, he dies."

"He is right, Daniel. Listen to him, he is telling the truth. You could afford to charge lower rents without suffering." Jotin held his energies around Daniel, trying to help him to hear this strange new thinking. "Remember those books your mother disapproves of? 'Voltaire' I think wrote some of them. Those ideas aren't just for fiction, they could be true. Come on, don't just annoy Madame with your new liberal opinions, develop some that can benefit people."

"But all the landowners charge the same," said Daniel, thinking fast. "If I reduced my rents, I could not compete. My products would be the dearest."

"Your wine is the best, Seigneur" said Nicholas with what he thought was a flash of genius. Daniel smiled.

"Well said, Monsieur, but unfortunately not true. Our wine is average. It would be difficult."

"It is difficult now, Seigneur, for us. We only ask that you pay us some wages for our work."

"Money? Not goods? Can you not sell what I give you?"

"No, Seigneur. No-one will buy piquette, it is.."

"That is enough, Nicholas. Stop now. He called you Monsieur, he is hearing you." Roki's hand was on Nicholas' arm.

"All right. I will think about what you have said. I will talk to my wife, she knows the village."

"Your wife?" Nicholas' voice was rising. "This is men's business, what does 'your wife' know?"

"STOP! Stop now!"

"She knows nothing about the happenings in Paris, about the new way of things!"

"Nicholas, enough! He was listening. Say no more." Roki's hand was now at Nicholas' mouth, stroking.

"What about Paris?" Daniel was puzzled again.

"My cousin has come from Nantes with news from Paris. The Bastille has fallen, the people are in charge. The days of the rich are over."

Daniel put out a hand to steady himself. "When did this happen?"

"Last month, he said. He came ten days ago. Who knows what happened since. But the rich will be finished. You might as well pay us. Only Christian, after stealing my woman and setting her up in your little palace. Tempting her with gold."

"Your woman? Are you talking about my wife?" Daniel was back to being puzzled.

"Do not say any more, Nicholas, or you will lose what you have gained. Apologise and leave. Come on."

"She was going to be mine. She was my best friend's sister. We were going to be brothers."

"Did Madame deVrac know this? Or was it just a plan between the boys?"

"Madame deVrac indeed! She was Eloise Seurin to me and it was good enough for her! Now, are you going to be a Christian and pay us in money?"

Roki moved over to Nicholas and tried to urge him away, muttering at him softly.

"I am a Christian, as you say, but I seem to remember a piece where Our Lord states that the owner of the vineyard may choose the wages and the workers have no right to complain. Now get out and say no more, before you find yourself without any job at all."

"Oh, Daniel, shame on you, using that story. These men have not enough, he is right, even though he is a fool. And new times are coming, I have had a look at Paris. It is not a pretty sight. Talk to Eloise anyway. Give them some money, enough to save a bit for the lean times." Jotin drew Daniel's attention back to the vats, to allow him time to mull over what had been said while engaged in repetitively calming work.

Daniel sat on the terrace, deep in thought. He did not notice the evening light, or the familiar noises that usually soothed him at the end of the day, because his mind was in Paris, remembering a visit there years ago and trying to picture it now. He would have to get more information about what was happening there. How could 'the people' suddenly be in charge? Did he mean the Third Estate, the ordinary people? How could that be, what about the nobles? What about the King? Surely he would always be in control, he was the King, after all, appointed by God to rule France. It was not his fault he was King, it happened if your father was king. No escape. Just like me, Daniel thought ruefully, I only own this estate because Papa died. No-one asked me if I wanted to be born here and produce wheat and wine.

"Well, not strictly true, but you don't remember us asking. At the time you were quite keen on living in a château near the village where Alessia was likely to choose to be born as Eloise. It is so funny that you don't remember discussing it with her. But it has to be that way, or you would not be able to choose now. Make a good choice now. Let go of your irritation with Roki's boy and give them all a bit of money. Might be best for you, too."

Nicholas is an idiot, thought Daniel. Jealous of me! Eloise has not once mentioned Nicholas to me. His thoughts stopped, as a new one arrived – maybe she had never mentioned Nicholas because there was something to hide? I'll ask her sometime. His eyes followed the flight of a swallow, swooping over the barns in search of dinner, its forked tail flicking this way and that as it steered past the best morsels. The trees were loud with the song of the cicadas. The sun was setting and the countryside was settling down under the soupy air, with only a small movement in it to carry away the perspiration that was prickling out on Daniel's face.

Eloise came out onto the terrace, fanning herself. There were damp circles under her arms and tendrils of hair stuck to her forehead.

"Bonsoir Monsieur. Pascale is bringing some white wine. It is too hot for the red." She plopped down onto the rocking chair and pushed it a little with her foot, trying to make some more movement of the air. "I left Marie-Claire inside, it is a tiny bit cooler there. She does not like feeding in this heat, we get so sweaty where we touch."

Daniel felt himself perking up a little as this image went through his mind, rather quickly, before it flowed downwards, causing a slight frisson as it went. He grinned at his wife, forgetting momentarily the worries of the morning, which had been followed by grovelling apologies from the foreman and mutterings through the workforce.

"I suppose we could try producing some sweat ourselves...." He broke off as Pascale came out onto the terrace with a tray. She had brought the wine and glasses and also a plate of slices of saucisson and pickles. She put these onto the table and with an exaggerated curtsey to Daniel and a mischievous grin at Eloise, fled back inside. Daniel raised his eyebrows in a question at Eloise.

"Did she hear me? I mean, did she understand?"

"Yes, and probably yes," said Eloise, smiling at his obvious discomfiture, "she's a peasant, remember? Not a protected flower from the aristocracy. She knows what goes on, how could she not, there are only two rooms in the cottage. Not a lot of privacy, you hear most things. And smell them. We know what our parents and our brothers were doing." She blushed, thinking she had gone too far, been indelicate. After all, Daniel was of the gentry himself. She tried to rescue the situation.

"But she will say nothing. We have that training too. Never say what you think, you have no right to opinions," she broke off, aghast, her hand flying to her mouth as though to prevent the escape of any more dangerous words. Daniel was silent, looking past Eloise out across the garden, his eyes on the barns, but his mind on the morning. Several long minutes passed, and Daniel remained still. Then his eyes slowly turned and fixed on Eloise, their unusual light brown glowing in the evening light.

"Is that how it is?" he asked, his voice low. Eloise said nothing, she was afraid she had already said more than was wise. Daniel stayed quiet too, her silence answering his question very fully. Then he seemed to shake himself, as he brought out his real worry.

"Nicholas came to see me this morning."

"Nicholas?" Eloise was puzzled.

"Yes, 'your' Nicholas," he said, a bit put out at her lack of reaction, "at least that's what he said he was. Or rather that you were his. I was alarmed to hear it."

"Oh, Mon Dieu!" said Eloise, taking a gulp of wine and then leaning her head back against the chair, "is he still at that? I thought that marrying you would get him off my back. He is such a fool." She shut her eyes, remembering many occasions in the past when

145

Nicholas had tried to force his unwelcome attentions on her. Her brother had tried to persuade her that Nicholas was the one for her, just because the two boys were friends. But she had never been interested in Nicholas, he seemed more like another brother really. And she did not like how he smelled.

"Madame, do you promise me it was all in his mind? That you were never his woman?"

"Daniel, I was never anyone's woman, until you. You know that. I hope."

"Yes, I do. I am sorry. It is just that when he accused me of stealing his woman, I ...."

"He what? How dare he say that of me!" Eloise stopped and in an awestruck tone she added "and how did he dare to say that to you? When you have such power over him? Has he gone mad?"

Daniel took her hands and began to stroke them as he told Eloise about Nicholas' visit, leaving nothing out, including his own mystification at the idea that the king might fall. Eloise, knowing nothing of kings, heard only the part about his request for money. She had never handled money herself, but knew it was there and the power it had over people, particularly when there was not enough of it. And there never had been enough of it, which meant that everyone she knew was almost always hungry. Only those who could afford to rent a patch of ground, or who could use the narrow strip of land around the salt marshes to grow food, as well as the money they earned from the gathering of salt were comfortable; and sometimes Etienne, when he got a big job to do. Three years ago there had been an accident between two carriages not far from the village, and he had been busy for weeks, mending the axles and other metalwork. He cared for the horses too, it had been wonderful to watch how he soothed them and got them out of their harnesses and back on their feet. Even the one with the broken leg had been calmed by him, as he talked gently all the time he was strapping on a splint and extricating the frightened horse from the mess of splintered wood. The horse had not survived, of course, but only because it was a horse, whose function was walking. If it had been a cow, it could still have given milk, even with the limp. Eloise smiled as she remembered the disdainful gentleman telling Etienne he would not pay for the care of 'a useless beast' and offering to shoot the horse then and there. Etienne had refused, saying that if the

146

horse was not wanted, he would give it a home. The gentry had laughed at the ridiculous sentimentality of the peasants, but they would have laughed on the other side of their faces if they had been present at the feast that was held a month later, when the whole village joined in to roast the horse steaks and joints. Etienne had waited until the horse was rested and healing, "so that the taste of fear is not in the meat". Yes, Etienne understood animals alright and Eloise's mouth watered at the memory of the happy result. There had been no feasting since, times were harder and no village could survive on accidents. Nicholas is right, she thought, they do need more money.

"It is hard, Sir, as a peasant," she said carefully. "Even when you can grow some food, you owe most of it in taxes. I do not know the details, it is men who have what money there is. But you have a lot, I think," she looked at Daniel, trying to gauge the effect her words was having on him. "I love my jewellery, but I think its price could keep my family for many years." She stopped, hoping she had not said too much.

"You must never think of selling your jewellery. If you need I will give you its value for your family. You would not get a fair price for such workmanship, people around here would pay you only for the gold." Daniel stopped and smiled at Eloise,

"This is a very solemn conversation for such a pretty woman. Come, smile again and let me see again why I buy you such beautiful things. That is better. I will talk to the foreman and some of the workers and see what I can do. Do not think about it again, no one will starve on my property. Maman will see to that - even if the villagers have to survive on her hard jam!" He laughed and Eloise joined in, as they thought of the unspreadable concoction the senior Madame deVrac had once amused herself by making.

Chapter 23

The days were getting shorter but the weather stayed sultry. The sun shone hot through a pale grey sky, the air was still and tempers became short. Waiting for the time of the grape harvest, Daniel shut himself away in his office with his ledgers and did calculations. This year would be a good one, God willing, as there had been rain in the spring and there was good sunshine now, so the vintage should be high quality and command a good price. Maybe he could afford to pay the workforce a little. But what if he did this year and then next year it snowed? Or if there was a storm between now and the harvest? It might be dangerous to commit himself. He wiped the sweat away from his forehead and neck and looked at his figures again. Abruptly, he stood up and strode to the door, calling out for a servant to send for the foreman.

Eloise was sitting in a rocking chair under the cherry tree opposite the house. Marie-Claire was on her knee, waving her pudgy fists and smiling at her mother, who was singing her a simple nursery song. The baby's tiny dark curls were plastered to her scalp with sweat. Eloise had taken off Marie-Claire's little bonnet, but there was no breeze to cool her head. Eloise had no energy: in this heat it was hard to gather any enthusiasm for anything. She sat and sang gently, smiling at her daughter, and wondered how she had managed in the old days eighteen months ago when she had been a peasant and been obliged to work. She could barely recall, it seemed another world. Eloise rocked her chair harder and managed to create an illusion of a breeze, which lifted one of the baby's curls. Marie-Claire gurgled.

Another voice called to Eloise and for a moment she thought it was the baby, and started. Then she realised it was coming from behind her, behind the hedge. It came again –

"Eloise!" it was a throaty whisper. "I need to talk with you. Come here."

"Who is it? Come round to me, it is shady here." Eloise was looking round, trying to see through the hedge.

"No, I do not want your husband to see me." Eloise recognised the voice now, it was Nicholas. She thought for a moment.

"And I do not want my husband to see me creeping away to talk to you. Not after the nonsense you told him about us. Such fibs!" She straightened back in her chair and closed her eyes.

"Not fibs at all. The truth as it would have been if you had not caught the rich man's eye, you lucky hussy."

"You might think so, I do not. Do you not remember I kicked your shins for trying to kiss me, years ago? I never wanted you, you were just my brother's friend. Now, go away."

There was a rustling of branches behind Eloise and suddenly Nicholas was beside her, his rough hand on her wrist. She pulled back, but he held tight and spoke in an urgent undertone.

"I always loved you, Eloise. The most beautiful woman in the village. I love you still. I would do anything for you, remember that. Times are coming when you may be glad I am your friend, glad you can still claim to be a peasant. But now, you can help me. Not just me, all of us, we are all in the same need. Luc would tell you so too, if you asked him."

"My brother has the sense to leave me out of men's affairs. He is glad for my good fortune and knows I will help everyone if I can. I asked my husband to give our sister work, so now that she is fed here, there is more to go around at home."

"But you must tell your husband that we need more. You must." Nicholas's grip was getting harder on her wrist. Eloise reached across and slapped his hand. He let go and sat back on his hunkers, looking at her with a strange expression in his green eyes. Then Eloise explained, as patiently as she could, that she had already talked with Daniel about the wages and that he was working out what he could do about it.

"So, you see, there is no more I can do. No more I *will* do. Now go away." Eloise fastened the baby's bonnet onto her head, its curls a little drier now and stood up, holding Marie-Claire against her chest. She set off towards the house, with the determined firm walk of the working woman she had once been. Nicholas sat in the shade watching her go. Frustration and longing welled up in him and he thumped his fist into the ground.

"I will have you, I will. Sooner or later. You'll need me sometime, then you'll see."

150

"Come on, Nicholas, leave her. She is not yours to have this time. I wish you would remember that," Roki added ruefully, as he passed his energies around Nicholas, to smooth down some of the spikes that were sparking and shooting in Nicholas's energy field. *"Tell you what, there is no work to do now and Luc and the others have gone to the river to swim. Come on."*

Nicholas picked up his hat, squeezed his way back through the hedge and set off at a brisk walk towards the river. He hoped he would find some of the others there.

The foreman perched uncomfortably on the edge of a chair in Daniel's office. He was not at all sure that it would hold his weight, with thin little gold legs like that and he was poised to stand if he heard a crack. He was finding it difficult to concentrate on what Daniel was saying. He understood vines all right and could take a good guess at foretelling the weather, he knew what the wine would fetch, but he left the detailed calculations to others. But he would not mind a bit of a raise in his wages, either. Those children were getting bigger all the time and so were their appetites, particularly the boys'. Only yesterday his wife had told him she thought there was another on the way. That would be seven, when would it end? His oldest was only twelve years old. I sometimes thank God for calling two of them home to Him, he thought, so why does He keep sending these expensive blessings? That rabble-rouser Nicholas has nothing to complain of and yet it is him who is stirring up this trouble; hope it doesn't backfire on all of us.

"So do you think that would be acceptable?" Daniel's voice broke through the foreman's reverie. He had no idea what Daniel had just suggested, but reckoned that with all those big ledgers open on the desk, Daniel must have done some good work.

"Oh, I think so, Mon Seigneur. Very good."

"Excellent. I will tell them at the harvest festival dinner. Thank you so much for your opinion." Daniel stood up and indicated the door. The foreman leapt up with relief off the delicate chair and scuttled out. Daniel sank back into his own chair and sighed with relief.

"Not so soon. I do not think it will work as well as you do. And that man heard nothing, he agreed to nothing. And you are so used to being deferred to, you did not notice. You must realise not

everyone is hanging on your every word. You are not all that special in the world, you know. Special to me and to Eloise, but not to that foreman. You are simply his means to an end, his children must eat and you have the money. Simple. But you must share it more fairly."

"So this will be fairer. I think they will be pleased." Daniel leant over and shut the ledgers. *Jotin sighed.*

"He did not hear you. You did not hear me. I wish you would listen more."

Daniel went to the door. It was very hot, nearly midday. Just time for a cooling drink before lunch.

Chapter 24

September stayed hot and heavy. There were morning mists now, rolling in from the estuary and bringing the salty tang of the marshes. Daniel watched the grapes anxiously, for signs of the mould that would spoil his wine, but the days were dry and the grapes ripened well. It was a quiet time on the estate as they waited, hoping the grapes would mature enough before the inevitable storm that would end the sunshine. On the marshes the collection of salt continued, the evaporation a little slower now because of the shorter days and morning mists. But not many workers were needed for the vines during this waiting time, and now that Daniel had been alerted to their dissatisfaction, he imagined he could hear the grumbles of those he had not hired. Not all of them had concessions on the salt-marshes, and for the first time he found himself wondering how they fed themselves during these slack times.

"They often do not," said Eloise when he asked her.

"What do you mean?"

Eloise looked at him, and shook her head. "Just that. If you have no food and no money, you do not eat. The neighbours help if they can. But they do not often have much to spare."

"Did you have enough to eat?" Daniel looked at his attractive curvy wife and found it impossible to imagine her starving. Though come to think of it, she had not been so plump when they met.

"I always had something. But mostly not enough, never enough. Well, enough to stop you dying, but not enough to fill your belly. I do not think anyone in the village knows what it is to eat enough. You always want more. We were luckier than most. My father collects salt and has some small crops from the edges of the marsh; and my mother has a goat so we often had a little milk, and now and then the kid, of course. But we had to share that with the man who owns a billy, because he made the next kid." She fell silent, remembering the time she had gone with her older brother to bring the goat to visit the billygoat. A long walk to the village of Jau, but a good day.

"Same as us. We have to pay for the bull." Daniel was thoughtful. "But of course, a calf can grow bigger, so there is more meat; and we

153

are a smaller family, so we can sell some."

"In the village, there is never anything to spare. Only the men get money - from what they can sell, like the salt. But the nuns take half as rent and the taxman takes most of the rest. If there are surplus crops they can be sold, but that is rare. Nobody can sell the piquette: who would buy it? After all, that is why you give it away, it has no value. You would pour it away after rinsing the vats, except that it has a little flavour."

"They like it, otherwise why would they do the work? It tastes good, I drink it too sometimes. Anyway, I think we will invite the wives and families to the harvest supper this year. I think we will have a little good news for them, so it would be good to give them a pleasant evening too."

"That would be kind, Monsieur. I hope we do have good news. I do not like this weather, it is too warm, maybe it is too good to last."

Luckily Eloise was wrong. The weather lasted through the harvest, which was one of the best Daniel could remember. The crushing of grapes started at once and spirits were high. On the day of the fête Eloise helped in the kitchen whenever Marie-Claire would stay quiet, despite the older Madame deVrac's extreme disapproval. She enjoyed it too much to stay away pretending to be a real lady, even though that would have been 'more suitable'. Several women came up from the village to help, so there was great merriment in the kitchen and despite the heat tempers stayed cool. The prospect of a large and delicious meal had everyone in good form. There were joints of beef to roast and a large pot was simmering, full of pieces of beef and onions, garlic, beans, herbs and wine. The aroma was heavenly and the temptation to dip a spoon was not being resisted. The hunters had been out, so there were several rabbits and a few hares to make another rich stew. The baker had been working overtime and had delivered several sacks full of large loaves as well as some tempting cakes. The cook was making several dishes of terrine from her own recipe and Pascale was grating stale bread in huge quantities to mix with flour and eggs to make big dumplings to cook in the stews. Several large cheeses had been ordered from the town and delivered last week, they were maturing nicely in the pantry. Everywhere you looked there was food, but you did not even have to look as the smell was everywhere, a new delicious odour came to Eloise's attention every time she stopped noticing the last one. She stopped for a moment and leant against the door jamb as she came in with more ingredients from the vegetable garden, to feast her eyes on the busy room. I am so lucky, she thought, to be at home here where there is so much, such plenty. I am blessed. What did I do to deserve such wealth?

"Nothing in particular, this time. You are able to share, to help Daniel see that things can change a bit, that it should be fairer. And because your energies work so well together you are succeeding, he is hearing you and maybe this small corner of the world will become more equitable. I just wish you could share some of it with me. Judging by all your behaviours, that food is a real pleasure to the senses." Trynor was thoughtful for a moment. "I should take another body sometime, to get a taste of that food."

"You are all very welcome to this wonderful meal, in celebration of a spectacular harvest. Later I will talk more about how you have all played your roles in this year's bounty, but for the moment, let's not waste time with these wonderful smells in our noses – Bon Appétit!" Daniel raised his glass towards his employees and their wives and sat down, to applause. The food was handed around and wine was poured. Bread was broken and dipped in the aromatic sauces, and the gathering became noisy with laughter and joking between the cries of 'pass me that' and 'more wine anyone?'

Eloise sat happily at the top of the long trestle table to Daniel's right and revelled in the feeling of belonging, to her husband on one side, and her parents and brothers and Pascale and many other old friends from the village, sitting all along the table. If only it could be this friendly all the time, she thought, as she looked up at the starry sky so calm and unhurried above her. And if only it could be a good harvest every year, then even the poor might get a chance. She looked along the table, noticing who was not there, who would never be there again. The last two lean years had stolen so many friends, particularly the old, who could not manage in hard times. Of course, it would still be hard for them, even if Daniel gave wages in money to his workers. The old could not work as fast and could never hope to earn enough. I hope everyone old has a young person belonging to them, to earn for them. Please, God, she thought earnestly.

"You are thinking well, Eloise, not just of yourself. That is good. Well done." Trynor turned to Jotin and smiled, a bit smugly. "My girl is progressing well, isn't she? How do you feel about Daniel? Is the energy-meld working for him?"

"It is a bit harder for him, nothing in his daily life supports what he has read. Also the class system in this country nearly overpowers the equality he feels with Eloise." Jotin was thoughtful. "He took on a hard task. Learning to think of others when you have not suffered yourself is much more difficult. I think he is doing all right, he is beginning to hear Eloise and Nicholas when they point out the sufferings of the poor. But he is not doing enough about it to save himself problems in the future. Oh dear, here we go!" Daniel was getting to his feet and calling for silence. The hush that fell over the table came so suddenly that Eloise could hear her own heart beating. She clutched her napkin and found she was twisting it through her fingers, round and round. She looked up at Daniel, standing so confidently beside her, and then down the table. Her mother in law was nibbling a pastry, breaking off tiny pieces to bring to her mouth on a tiny spoon, apparently entirely absorbed in this activity. Charlotte and Catherine were ignoring each other even more carefully than they were ignoring the momentous event that was about to occur. The villagers were staring at Daniel as though at a priest on the altar, as though he could offer them salvation; only the foreman looked a little unsure. Nicholas looked smug. Then her eyes came round to Pascale and she relaxed. Pascale was smiling her big open smile as usual. Eloise found that she could smile back and her hands stilled. She only slowly became aware that Daniel had finished speaking and that changes were happening around the table. The village women were clapping, a little uncertainly, but the men were getting to their feet, their fists clenching, their mouths working. Nicholas was shouting.

"How dare you insult us! After all I said, I thought you understood. You understand nothing, you, you ..." Luc was beside Nicholas and pulled him into his seat before he could find an insult to throw at Daniel. Eloise pulled at Daniel's sleeve and he sank down into his chair.

"Why are they angry, Monsieur? What did you say to them?"

"I told them that as this year has been a good harvest after two bad ones, I am going to pay them a bonus and give them two pints of wine each as well as the piquette. I think it is a good offer." Daniel was quiet, watching the arguments that had broken out around the table with an air of puzzlement.

"How big a bonus? And what about next year? Will you pay the bonus all now, do we have that much money? And when will they get the wine?" Eloise was full of questions. Daniel looked at her and smiled ruefully.

"My little village wife. That is what they are all asking, all those questions. Except the size of the bonus, they know that." He told Eloise what he had offered.

"Well, that will be helpful, but it will not keep anyone from starvation if anything else goes wrong for them. It is less than a loaf a week. And did you not tell me that tax must be paid? Oh, Daniel, I do not know what to suggest now."

The foreman came over and touched his cap. "Mon Seigneur, I am sorry. I did not understand what you planned. I would have advised otherwise. Good night and thank you for a lovely meal." His wife, standing just behind him, curtseyed and added her thanks, "and for the bonus, Seigneur."

The other villagers left quickly once the foreman had gone. The women mostly expressed thanks with a little curtsey, but the men were less respectful and confined their thanks to 'for a pleasant evening'. Eloise's brothers were more fulsome, but Nicholas did not say goodnight at all.

Madame deVrac finished her pastry and dabbed her lips with her napkin. She took a delicate sip of wine and looked around, her eyebrows rising.

"They have all gone? Just like that? Dreadfully rude, but then, they have no breeding." She looked pointedly at Eloise.

"Yes, Maman. They have gone. My speech was not the success I thought it would be."

"So there!" said Charlotte, "you're not so clever after all."

"Will they be friendly again?" Catherine asked, her eyes round. "They were all very cross. And it was such a good dinner. It should have put them in good spirits. I am."

"You only think of your stomach, that's why." Charlotte got up. "I am going to bed. So should you, Cathy. Come, Maman, the party is over."

"Yes, the party is over. I have been talking with Roki and the others in the village. They will be angry now. We must be careful." Jotin was beside Daniel and looked at Trynor solemnly. "We had better suggest moving out of the area for a while, until tempers cool. I had a quick look round the rest of the country.

It has been a dangerous summer for the landowners." Daniel shuddered, then took a deep breath and stood up, helping Eloise to her feet.

"Come indoors, Madame. I cannot think any more tonight. It will be better in the morning, I can talk to the men when they are sober again and we can be reasonable."

"Of course!" Eloise was relieved. "It was because they had wine. They are not used to it. Piquette is so weak no-one ever gets drunk on it. Even I feel a bit light headed and I am used to wine now. I will go and look at the baby, then go to bed. Good idea."

Chapter 25

"Go, now! Run, behind the barns, make your way to the village, to your mother's. You can hide safely there, they will not harm a village girl. No-one will see you, they will not know you have left. I must fetch some papers, some other things. When it is safe I will catch you up." Daniel pushed Eloise and Pascale out of the back door into the dark evening, kissed Eloise quickly on the cheek and ran back inside, waving his hand towards the barns, saying "I love you, go quickly now," before closing the door. After a few moments Eloise heard the bolts shoot across behind her and was appalled. He had locked them out. But she could hear the mob shouting at the front of the house and knew that Daniel had gone to meet them, to talk some sense into them. There was no help she could give, nothing she could do anymore. She was a village girl who had become a lady, she belonged nowhere in these confusing times. Eloise stood uncertain, in the shadow of the house, sure no one would see her here. Marie-Claire, in her arms, stirred and whimpered. Pascale put her arm through Eloise's and they stood, shuddering.

"I think Daniel thought we had already run away," Pascale said, squeezing her sister's arm. "I do not think he intended us to hear the bolts, he does not mean to shut us out, just those noisy ones." The noise from the front of the house was growing louder, a thumping started. Eloise thought she could hear Daniel's voice, remonstrating. The baby wailed and as she did, a dark shape moved around the house. They pressed themselves harder into the shadow of the porch.

"Come on," a raucous voice cried, too close. "We can get in the back here." Feet pounded and Eloise heard laughter. She broke away from the house and ran towards the barns, not looking back, trusting Pascale to follow, hoping the moon's light would not betray them. The noise of the crowd grew louder behind them, laughter and angry shouts in equal measure.

In the shadow of the barn, she stopped, leant against the wall and tried to catch her breath. She rocked Marie-Claire, hoping she would not cry, would not hear the mob and be alarmed. But you should be alarmed, my little one. Your Papa is in there on his own, trying to protect the house, to keep it for us, to look after us. She put her hand to her neck and fingered the gold flowers that hung there.

"He looked after me, until now, when he locked us out. Why did he not run with us?" Eloise asked.

"I do not know, he must have some good reason, he is a man," Pascale muttered, her bravery deserting her as she cowered beside Eloise.

"Because he knows they do not want to hurt you, you are not in danger, so long as you keep out of sight. It is the master of the house who is at risk. He is going to get out another way and draw them away from you." Trynor hovered, looking back towards the house. "Jotin is encouraging him to leave, now, out of the far windows. He will be safe in the marshes. The crowd will find the wine and get drunk and do no more harm. Come on, away we go, into the wood." Trynor pushed Eloise, hoping she would feel him and Eloise turned away from the house and walked around the back of the barn. From there it was not far to the little wood. She gathered up her skirts in her free hand and ran the short distance. Once they were between the trees they had to move more slowly as the undergrowth tore at their hems and branches flicked into their faces.

Eloise stopped as a branch caught her hat and nearly pulled it off. She grabbed at it and her hold on the baby loosened. Marie-Claire began to slide towards the ground. Eloise stooped quickly to save the baby and sat down with a bump at the foot of one of the trees. She gathered her cloak around her, settling the baby on her lap. The air was cold, a white cloud billowed from her mouth and nose, and she could see Pascale because of the sharp puffs of vapour she was producing. Later in the night it might freeze in the air. She shuddered and tucked the baby close against her, to share her warmth with the tiny body. Pascale sat down beside her and they huddled together, tucking their feet up under their cloaks. Eloise put her arm around her sister, throwing her cloak around Pascale, so that they were sharing their heat.

"I am too upset to go further now," Eloise said, tucking the cloaks together. "Tomorrow we will go to the village. We will be safe there with mother. Surely they will remember that I am one of them, when they are calm in the daylight." The baby sighed and mumbled in her sleep. Eloise closed her eyes and let her head nod forward.

Daniel waited inside the door for a moment before he shot the bolts, picturing his beautiful wife running away to safety. He muttered a little prayer for her safety.

"Trynor is with her, and Pascale with her own guide. They will do their best. They are not in real danger, anyway. Go on, do what you have to do quickly," said Jotin.

Daniel hurried through the house to the study and set his oil lamp down on the desk while he opened the drawers and took out the important papers. He stuffed them into his pockets and turned to the safe, putting the money into a leather purse. There was not much, he had sent most of it away yesterday with his mother and sisters, but it would maybe be enough to buy off the crowd and allow his safe passage. I wonder did Eloise take all her jewellery with her, he thought, or was she too hurried?

"Do not waste time on jewellery" Jotin was shimmering on the spot, trying to encourage Daniel to leave now. "They will prefer money. You can buy more pretty things later. Goodness, you could even make them, if you could only remember. You'd think you had handled enough gold back in Crete to last you several lifetimes. Listen, they are getting excited. Come ON!"

Daniel stopped and listened. The crowd were singing now, he could not make out the words but it sounded aggressive. He turned and ran for the stairs, Jotin at his heels shouting 'No! No!' taking them two at a time. He dashed into the main bedroom and stuffed the contents of Eloise's jewel case into his pockets. Then he went to the window and opened it, leaning out to pull the shutters closed. The crowd roared and someone threw something, which hit the outside of the shutter with a dull thunk. Daniel rushed from room to room, closing the shutters. Under one window was a group of men he recognised from the farm.

"What are you doing here?"

"Come to tell you we need more pay, Seigneur!" The man swept off his cap and made an exaggerated bow.

"But I know that already, I am making changes, you have been told. The money must come from somewhere." Daniel reached for one of the shutters.

"Out of your pockets then!" a shout came from behind the men he knew. "Down with the aristos!"

"Explain to your friends that I am not an aristo, would you?" Daniel sighed. "I just work the farm, organise things. I do not organise how society is run."

"Death to the rich!"

"And I am not rich, either. Each year pays for itself." Daniel pulled the second shutter in and fastened the two together. The jeering and catcalling outside continued.

"Quickly, now you are here, shut all the shutters. They are getting dangerous. Come on, the baby's room . . ."

The baby, thought Daniel, smiling. He set the oil lamp down on a table. She is such a pretty little thing. Safe in her mother's arms, being carried swiftly to the sanctuary of the village. I'm glad I sent them away, but a pity they did not go yesterday with Maman.

"No, you idiot, do not think about the baby – go to her room!"

Daniel ran back down the stairs, wondering why there was a sensation of cold on his face. *Jotin ran backwards in front of Daniel, trying to stop him and blow him back up the stairs to the baby's room.*

"A window must be open," Daniel muttered.

"Yes! Upstairs! You missed one! One over the terrace, they can climb onto that. Go back up!"

"And if there is a window open, I can climb out. It must be the pantry, if the people outside have not noticed it." Daniel ran towards the kitchen. As he opened the door to the pantry, he heard cheering, and overhead, the sound of running footsteps. He froze, listening.

"Oh, God, help me. They are in the house."

"I tried to help. You did not listen. Now, quick, out!"

Daniel felt for the pantry window and was confused when he found it shut and barred. Oh well, he thought, there is a dark corner outside, so it is a good choice. He opened the window and was reaching for the bar holding the shutters when he heard screaming overhead. The voice sounded young. Then there were screams outside and cries of 'Fire!' Daniel ran in the dark for the stairs, but found he could see his way up them easily. Light flickered in one of the bedrooms and the screams were coming from there. Daniel moved quickly but carefully into the room. Outlined in the window was a young boy, his jacket on fire. Daniel pulled a blanket off the bed and threw it over the boy, hugging it to his writhing body. The carpet was smouldering and there were flames on the other bed where the oil lamp had been overturned. He pulled the boy from the room and unwrapped the blanket. The boy was not moving, but he was still breathing.

"What have you done to my son?" said an angry voice at Daniel's shoulder.

"If this is your son, I have put him out and pulled him away from the fire. What is he doing in my house? And how did he, and you, get in?"

"From the terrace roof. Give him here, before you kill him," The man lifted the unconscious boy and strode towards the baby's bedroom, where he shouted down to friends below and lifted his son out onto the roof of the terrace. Daniel went back to the room on fire. The heat was now too great, he could not go in. Smoke billowed out into the corridor and made his eyes sting. He ran to the next room and grabbed the ewer from the table, making his way back now into the smoke and also into the crowd of men who were streaming into the house through Marie-Claire's room.

"Help me put out this fire," Daniel shouted at the men, who pushed roughly past. One of them aimed a blow in his direction, but the flailing fist caught one of the other men on the side of the head, knocking him into the wall. Within moments a fight had broken out and the staircase was full of kicking boots and grunting men. The ewer went flying out of Daniel's grasp, its contents sloshing uselessly over the melee. The smoke was beginning to creep downwards now and the men began to cough.

"Come on, help me get water," Daniel said, desperation taking the usual authority out of his voice. Several of the men laughed.

"Why should we? What have you ever done for us?"

"Nothing, of course, as I do not know you. But I have done plenty to help people like you."

"No one ever helped me when I needed it. You are not my boss. Get lost, with your big house and your airs and graces." The man pushed past him and went into the dining room. Daniel went down the stairs and along the hall. On his way past the dining room he could see the man helping himself to the brandy on the sideboard and threatening another of the raiders with a silver candlestick.

Daniel ran to the back door. Maybe I can organise a chain, he thought and we can pass water from the pump.

"No." *Jotin was ahead of Daniel. "No, just run. Your life is important, Eloise and the baby are waiting in the wood for you. She was too upset to go to safety, she wants to stay near. You can be with her."* Jotin stopped and watched Daniel. *"Oh no, I am babbling. He isn't hearing me. Try again, clearer. . .Daniel! Go to Eloise!"*

"Eloise!" Daniel stopped and thought. He looked back at the house. The upstairs windows were glowing now and men and women were running in and out carrying his possessions away. I cannot save the house, he thought, it is too far gone. But I could loot it too and save some of the things for Eloise.

"No, you do not need things. She just wants you. No more pretty things."

"Pretty things," Daniel ran towards the house, *Jotin in his wake, shouting "He is hearing me at last, but only in part. Help, please help!"* A deep purple glow appeared in front of Jotin.

"You need help?" Jotin could hear the question deep within him.

"Yes. Daniel is hearing me, but only some words, not my meaning. And he is running back into a burning building. Not to save a person, just for things."

"Stay beside him. That is all you can do. They are given free choice, sometimes they choose wrongly. You are doing well, I have been watching. It will all be well, you know that." The soft voice soothed Jotin, even though it did not supply a human scale solution.

"Yes, I know. But I grieve too. We are trying so hard to help them."

"You are all learning. Go now and be with Daniel. He will soon need you."

Daniel ran into the living room, covering his face with his handkerchief to keep the worst of the smoke from his nose and mouth. He opened the cupboard, trying to decide what to rescue. Then he saw the painting above the fireplace and remembered Eloise on a winter's evening telling him how she felt safe, that summer would always come again so long as she could see that picture. He reached up to lift it down and other hands reached out to help him. It was heavy, they could not get it off its hook. He pulled a chair over to the fireplace and climbed up. His throat stung and his eyes watered as he wrestled with the heavy frame. Eventually he worked the wire up off the hook and the picture's weight fell into the arms of his assistants. Daniel climbed down and turned to thank them, but there was nobody there, nor was his picture.

"You thieves! You have taken everything," he searched around for something else to take, but could see nothing, the smoke was choking now. He turned to the door and could see a couple of people outlined by the flickering orange, with more of his things under their arms as they ran along the hall. He ran towards them and saw that one had a small picture in his arms. He looked towards the stairs and could see legs coming down and then stopping, turning towards the wall, and he remembered the row of smaller pictures hanging up the stairs. Daniel turned and lunged for the stairs, his hand up feeling along the wall, as he closed his eyes and held his breath against the pungent smoke. An empty nail caught his hand and tore it and he swore under his breath, but continued to feel, climbing the stairs as he passed two more nails, their contents already stolen. Then he felt a picture. He went up two more steps, to be high enough to lift the little picture off its nail and felt the skin on the side of his face begin to blister.

"Leave it. The paint is blistered too, it is not worth saving. Run DOWN."

Daniel lifted the picture, held it against his chest and turned to go down the stairs. As he did, there was a crack and a whooshing noise and a huge weight fell on him, engulfing him in flames, which rolled on into the hall, setting light to several people who were running for the door.

Daniel got up and looked around. He could see very little, just a mass of burning timbers and scattered tiles. He climbed over the flames, marvelling at the fact that he was feeling no pain and still clutching the painting to his chest. The paint on it bubbled and steamed, but then he realised it was no longer in his arms. The house was quiet, most of the raiders seemed to have left. No, there was one of them, but he was just standing, watching Daniel. Strange, he was standing on top of the burning roof, which was now lying on the floor of the hall, setting fire to it and the

165

downstairs rooms.

"So why have you no loot? I thought that was all you people wanted, to take my things and destroy my house. You've had a success there- look at it!"

"Look at it closely yourself and see what is wrong," Jotin came closer to Daniel.

"It is burnt down, that is what is wrong! What a stupid question."

"And are you burning? Do you feel pain?"

"No." Daniel stood and thought for a moment, then looked down at himself and at his hands, which were smooth and clean. He looked up at Jotin. "And I can see myself," he said, "when there is no light. And I think I know you," he peered at Jotin, squeezing up his face in the effort to remember. "I do know you." There was a long pause.

"Oh, Jotin, I'm sorry. I was meant to survive, wasn't I? And I got tempted by temporary things and now I'm dead. And Eloise will be on her own, with no house, no money," his voice began to rise to a panicky shriek and Jotin stepped forward to put his arms around Daniel.

"Come, we will go and see Eloise, watch how she is getting on. Last I heard, she had reached the marsh."

Eloise was woken suddenly, by a hand pulling at her arm.

"Quickly, get up, come with me," Nicholas pulled her again, "come, ask no questions, just come. We must be quick, they are coming this way."

Eloise and Pascale got to their feet and Eloise allowed herself to be guided through the trees, away from the house, away from the barns, the heat.

"The heat? What is it?" Eloise turned to Nicholas, her eyes wide.

"Fire. Come." They stumbled on, through the dark wood, with occasional bursts of orange light helping their progress. Then they were out of the wood and into the vineyard. Nicholas guided Eloise ahead of him between the vines and she allowed herself to stumble on, with the hand in her back pushing her forward. At the end of the row she stopped and turned to face Nicholas. As she did, she looked past him, back to the barns, to the château, and her eyes widened with horror.

166

"Look!" Eloise said, all other comment dying in her throat. "The house. Look!"

"I know," Nicholas said, putting an arm around her shoulders and holding her tight to him. "The house is gone. The barns too. It is a shame, there was wine in those barns."

"Daniel? Where is Daniel?" Eloise's voice was becoming shrill. "Let me go and see!" she began to pull him back towards the house.

"No, Eloise. It is better if you stay with me. Daniel...."

"NO NO !" Roki said, as loudly as he could. "Do not tell her. She will save herself if she does not know."

"..is saving the horses. He will ride them away. Tomorrow he will come back for you. Come, we must hurry." Nicholas pulled Eloise around so that she could no longer see the burning house and they ran and stumbled on through two more fields of hibernating vines, then across a field which was waiting for the spring ploughing. The slight dip in the land hid the house from them and the triumphant cries of the crowd were less insistent. They slowed to a walk, moving more carefully now in the total darkness. Thick clouds were covering the sky and there was no more moonlight. Nicholas kept his arm around her shoulders, Eloise barely noticed it, accepting it as a guide. She was comforted by Pascale's hand holding her skirt, the slight pulling reminding Eloise of when they had been children and she was given the care of her little sister.

Water filled Eloise's shoe and her foot squelched on the bottom of the salt marsh. She recoiled, but her shoe stayed behind in the silt, and her skirt, its sodden hem clinging now round her legs, prevented her from feeling for it with her toes. She stood again on the grass, her foot chilled.

"We will fall in, Nicholas. My shoe is gone, my skirt is soaked. We should wait here for the dawn."

"That will be hours yet. We should get to safety, into the warm. Hold my left arm and I will put my right foot in the water. So long as you are on the dry and my foot is wet, we will know we are following the edge of the marsh and will come to the village. Pascale, you hold Eloise on the other side." They walked like that for several minutes, silent except for the rhythmic splashing of Nicholas's foot. They did not speak, Eloise thinking of Daniel and the horses; Nicholas looking forward to the day when he could at last marry Eloise, now that she was a widow. Pascale was thinking

167

of getting back to her mother.

A light showed ahead.

"Look, Nicholas. Is it the village?"

"I do not think so. It is moving. Stop," he held still and the comforting splashes stopped. "Listen," he whispered and she heard singing. The light bobbed as it approached and Eloise could see that it was three torches, carried high.

"Close your eyes. Get down." Nicholas pushed Eloise to the ground and crouched beside her.

"Our Father, who art . . ."

"Shut up, you idiot," Nicholas hissed. "The devils will hear you faster than God." Eloise swallowed her prayer and continued it in her mind.

"I hear you," Trynor said. "I'll pass it on. Keep still now."

The singing got louder and was interspersed with jokes and banter. Whoever they were, they were going to the château to 'see the fun'. The voices were strange, the accents unfamiliar.

"Who have we here?" A foot pushed at Eloise. "Someone who should not be here. Someone who is trying to hide. Up to no good, I'll bet. On your feet till we look at you!"

Nicholas got up first and helped Eloise to her feet. She held tight to Marie-Claire under her cloak and looked at the strangers. There were five men, bedraggled and unkempt, but looking strong and healthy. They gathered round and examined Nicholas and the sisters, as though they were cattle at a market.

"A lady, what d'you reckon, Henri? Not a useful person to know, no good these days, ladies and gentlemen. A waste of space." He drew his grimy finger across his throat as he grinned, drawing a ragged snigger from his mates. *Roki and Trynor were in anxious discussion with the group of guides who had arrived with the strangers and there was much gesticulating.*

"What do we suggest? We suggest you calm your people down and get them away from here," Roki said, waving his arms about.

"It is not easy," said one of the guides. "We stay with them all the time, but they do not hear us and do not listen. They are very young souls, they think everything is simple, do you remember?"

"Oh yes," Roki said. "Not that long ago either. But it is not an excuse, you still need to get through to them. You lot do not belong here, where we are busy trying to rescue our people. Just as things

are going well for my man, you turn up with a bunch of vagabonds and threaten to spoil everything. Go away, go on. You agree?" he turned to Trynor.

"Yes I agree they should go, not get mixed up with our plans. Our plans which are already in tatters, but which can be saved, so Eloise can still be with Marie-Claire. But I do not agree that things are going well for Nicholas. In what way?"

"He can marry Eloise, as he has always wanted."

"But there is no plan for that. They are friends only."

"Fuss, fuss. What harm if he does? It would free him of wanting it, then they could be friends next time."

"The harm is that it would be wrong for Eloise. Oh, why are we discussing this when so much is happening? Look!"

The gang was circling the shivering fugitives, feeling their clothes, staring into their faces. One put his arm round Pascale's waist and tried to kiss her. She pulled away, trying to laugh it off. Nicholas raised a fist, but his arm was pulled roughly down by the biggest of the gang, a burly man with a manic glint in his eye. Nicholas stood as quietly as he could, hearing his heart thumping and feeling sure it could be heard all the way across the marsh. The big man stopped in front of Eloise and ran his eyes over her. She shuddered. The man grabbed a long stick from one of his companions and used it to lift the hem of Eloise's skirt. He pointed to her bare and muddy foot.

"The lady lost her pretty slipper, then? That will be a new idea for you, to go without, hein?"

"We are from the village," Eloise said, in her strongest local accent. "I am not a lady."

"Then why the servant girl, and what is this?" The man lifted her filigree necklace away from her neck on the point of his dagger and beckoned for one of the torches to be brought closer. "Gold, I think. How do you explain that?"

"Whore!" The man with the torch spat at Eloise's feet.

"No!"

"She is not a whore," Nicholas said, putting his arm around Eloise again. "She is a decent woman; from the village, as I am. Just as she says."

The bandit looked at them again, still holding the necklace on his dagger, teasing it back and forth. Eloise tried not to move, aware of the blade so close, the man's thick breath in her face. He snorted. "Maybe you are telling the truth. But then, maybe you stole this gold and you have no right to it, eh, my pretty one? And if you have no right to it, then you could give it to us and we could let you go, even with this evidence of crime hanging around your pretty neck. Too pretty for Monsieur Guillotine, I think, not that he is fussy."

"I did not steal it, it was bought for me by my husband." Eloise stared into the man's face, suddenly made brave by the memory of the first time Daniel had shown her the necklace and how he had put it on for her.

"And where is this rich husband now?" the man pulled himself up to his full height and tossed his head back. "Keeping his appointment with the executioner?"

"Of course not," Nicholas said. "The girl is her sister and I am her husband."

"No!" Eloise turned her head to look at Nicholas and as she did, the point of the bandit's dagger ran into the side of her throat. The man pulled it back roughly, twisting the point up to sever the delicate links of gold. He grabbed for the necklace and stuffed it in his pocket as he backed away. "Sorry, didn't mean to hurt her, just a bit of fun," he mumbled, as the group turned and ran into the darkness.

Nicholas put his hand up to Eloise's neck and felt the slippery stickiness. Eloise leant heavily against him.

"Does it hurt?" Pascale asked, standing on tiptoe, trying to see the wound, straining her eyes against the night.

"No, it is not bad," Eloise's voice was soft. "But hold Marie-Claire for me."

Pascale reached out, took the baby and tucked her into the crook of her arm. The clouds parted and a bit of light shone through. Nicholas peered round to see the wound and turned Eloise's chin towards him. The wound gaped, but there was very little bleeding.

"Lie down for a moment, and rest." Nicholas supported her weight and lowered Eloise to the ground.

"Daniel?"

Nicholas and Pascale looked around, but there was nobody there. Nicholas looked back at Eloise, who was very still. Her eyes were wide and there was a little smile on her face. He picked up her hand and it was limp.

170

"Eloise! Oh no, my Eloise!" Nicholas laid his head on her silent chest and wept. Pascale's eyes were wide with horror, as she jiggled the new little orphan, who had begun to cry.

"Daniel? Oh, my love, you have caught up with us! But where are the horses? And who is this?" Eloise got easily to her feet and turned to look at Jotin, her brow furrowing. "I know you, I think? We have met before."

"Yes, Eloise, you have met before," Trynor said, stepping forward to stand beside her.

"Oh, hello Trynor," said Eloise, as she leant over to kiss him on the cheek. "Nice to see you again." Eloise stopped and grew very still. Then she moved over to the little group huddled on the ground and looked down at them. She turned to Trynor.

"But how did I die? It was not a bad cut?"

"Not deep, but it opened the vein in your neck. Air got in and stopped your heart."

"And Daniel? What happened to you? And what will happen to Marie-Claire? Oh, my poor baby, poor Pascale." Eloise went to Pascale and hugged her.

Pascale looked around, her wet eyes bright. *Eloise kissed her on both cheeks.* Pascale smiled and wiped her hand across her face. *Eloise leant over the baby and pulled a face at her and* Marie-Claire stopped crying, smiled and gave a little gurgle. Pascale got to her feet, lifting the baby and holding her close. She spoke to Nicholas, although she was not sure if he heard her.

"I am bringing the baby to Mother. Then I will send the men out to bring Eloise home. You guard her till they arrive." She set off into the murky night.

Chapter 26
Meeting Number Sixty-four

Eloise looked at Daniel. He was watching Pascale as she walked away. His shoulders shook and he put his face into his hands, shaking his head gently from side to side. Eloise moved over to him and put her arm around his shoulders.

"Our baby, gone." His tone was bleak. Eloise squeezed him to her.

"Yes. But Pascale is a good girl. She will make her a good mother."

"Not as good as you. She needs her own mother. And her father, such as he was. A useless idiot who got bamboozled by wealth and lost everything as result." Daniel turned to Jotin. "What will we do, Jotin? What can we do now?"

"We can leave here and go Home. Time passes differently there, everything will seem easier. Come." Jotin and Trynor wrapped themselves around Eloise and Daniel and lifted them off the ground. There was a sensation of pulling, then of floating, the light grew brighter though still soft, then they landed without a bump on a beautiful lawn. The sky was like an upturned bowl, stretching pale above them. Eloise lay down on the grass on her stomach and watched the daisies that were blooming just in front of her. They were beautiful, perfect. She looked at Daniel. He too was beautiful, without any trace of the fire that had taken his life. The two guides were sitting nearby, watching. Time passed. Eloise did not know how long, but she did not care, it was enough simply to be here in this lovely space. Time enough later to explore, or meet old friends. She turned over onto her back and watched the sky. Small clouds drifted across it and like on earth they resembled animals. There was a rabbit, yes, its ears were growing, and there it had a tail, and look, its nose is twitching! Eloise laughed and sat up.

"Trynor, am I making the cloud into a rabbit?"

"Yes, of course. It can be whatever you like. It is for you to play with."

Eloise lay back and made a cloud horse in the sky. Another one appeared beside it and she and Daniel raced their horses around and around as they shouted with laughter and happiness. They sat up and hugged.

"We made another mess of it, didn't we?" Daniel's tone was calmer this time. "Earth is a hard place, no matter how much practice you get."

"What happened to Marie-Claire?" Eloise asked Trynor, "Did she grow up happily?"

"She was happy for as long as she lived. She can tell you herself now, look!"

Marie-Claire walked across the lawn. She glowed a soft yellow and had taken the shape of a young woman. Eloise ran to meet her.

"Oh, my child, you grew up to be so lovely."

"No, Maman. I am this size now because it is awkward to be small. I lived to be just three."

"Oh, Marie-Claire! I am so sorry. I should have protected you better. What happened?"

"I should have protected both of you," said Daniel, as he joined them.

"Pascale was my Maman after you left. She was a good mother, milked the goat for me, mashed up her food for me, played with me. Loved me. Even after her own baby was born."

"Little Pascale had a baby? Tell!"

"She married Nicholas. He said your sister would have to do, that he would take second best."

"Poor Pascale! She married him, when he said that?"

"Yes, and it is working well. He has fallen in love with her. Actually, I think it will be better for them both now that I am not there. No reminders of you, or, worse in his eyes, of the wicked landowner who stole his girl. Their son is just a year old now, a sturdy little fellow. He did not get sick."

"But you did? What was it?"

"Mohmi tells me it is called diphtheria. All I know is that I could not get my breath. It was terrifying. Such a relief when I came out of my body and didn't need to breathe any more. But I watched Pascale cry and that hurt. She feels you are truly dead, now."

Eloise sighed. She remembered the horror of losing her little brother, the fear, no, the knowledge that she would never see him

174

again, then the awful length of the time without him and his funny ways. She remembered, from other lives, having to live a long life without someone she had loved. She shuddered. Even if she had remembered that she would always eventually come back here, it would have been tough, putting in the time. She hugged Marie-Claire again.

"Well, we don't seem to be much good at raising you. Maybe it will be third time lucky. Do you want us to try again?"

"Of course," said Marie-Claire, "as often as you are willing to have me. It's not as though I'm going anywhere!" They laughed and the guides joined in. There was a voice from the shadows-

"I'm glad to hear it. You still have to keep that vow. Only one stopping my figures being one hundred per cent." It was Planidi, a very slightly darker shade of yellow now, suggesting she had made a little progress, but not much.

"We are going to have Moonsong again, Planidi, but not because of the vow. Because she wants us to and because it feels good when we work together," Eloise stopped and looked at Planidi, realisation spreading over her.

"You were Madame Plantier? The market woman who encouraged me to dance with Daniel?"

"Yes."

"Well, I suppose I should thank you. Even if you were only doing it to make your own records look tidier. It was going quite well until the revolution."

"I'll be there next time, too." A dark bluish purple light formed beside her and they were aware there was something being said.

"Ah, I'm sorry, but I am being told to say that I do not need to watch over you," Planidi grimaced, "It's hard to let go of wanting perfection. I have to do more work on it. Let me know when the vow is fulfilled," there was a pause, "No, sorry, I am going to erase my records. Carry on." Planidi walked away in a rather meandering path. Jotin laughed.

"Well, you just saw someone being given a very strong lesson. I hope she is able to do it."

"Will her guide not erase the records for her?" asked Daniel.

"No," Trynor sounded shocked, "It must always be voluntary. Everything is your choice."

"Even being my parents again," smiled Marie-Claire, "Though

175

why not find a simpler situation?"

"Maybe we should be poorer next time," suggested Daniel, "so that we concentrate on the important things. I am so ashamed of myself, dying for a silly painting."

"Don't be too hard on yourself," Jotin was by his side. "You really were thinking of bringing something for Eloise. It wasn't the monetary value. The other looters were just thinking of money. Didn't do many of them much good, they couldn't find buyers for a lot of the things. It's their descendants who will benefit. We'll look round for a life for you that isn't too poor, you don't want to be distracted by poverty either."

"It was lovely, having that good food," Eloise was reminiscing, her eyes closed. "I enjoyed that, after being poor as a child, though it was still hard, knowing others had so little. And I learnt to cook some of the things. The cook was kind, she let me and some of the village women help her and showed us what to do. I would not enjoy being hungry again, but I'll do it, if it helps."

"I would like to do something creative. I watched that jeweller with a great sense of frustration. I must have known I could do it myself! Was it easier for you, Eloise? You could do embroidery."

The discussion of what they would like and what they would need, carried on a long time. It was companionable, sitting there on the grass with old friends, chatting, joking, and later, playing music together as they allowed the sky to dim and points of light to shine out. Eloise put her head back and looked up at their night sky. She focussed her attention, gathered three small clouds together into a circle and shone a gentle light on it.

"Look, Marie-Claire," she breathed, "The moon!"

Chapter 27
Dublin, autumn 1979

"What's wrong with Kathleen now? Oh dear, I'll run so," Jotin reassured Haliken, then blinked into David's office and set about making a nuisance of himself, trying to attract David's attention.

David was sipping coffee out of a paper cup while running his finger down a list of specifications, trying to guess if his firm could easily meet them and if it was worth tendering.

"Come on, Davey, ring home," Jotin concentrated hard and the phone on David's desk rang once and stopped. David reached out and picked up the receiver. The dialling tone puzzled him, but he listened for a moment then put it down, trying to look at his watch at the same time. His sleeve caught the paper cup and tipped it over.

"Yes!" shouted Jotin, "and I didn't even have to help."

"Fuck," said David, snatching the paperwork out of the way, not noticing the splash of coffee on his trousers.

"Go on home David. It's a lovely stain, couldn't have done better if I'd planned it. But you need those trousers for tomorrow's meeting, so go home and change. NOW!"

David sat down, wiped his desk with a tissue and threw it and the cup into the bin.

"You wretched human," Jotin cried, "How am I ever going to get through to you? The girls need you, now!"

David looked up at the photo of his twins and smiled. Just as well the coffee hadn't splashed that way, he thought.

Now there's an idea, thought Jotin. I certainly need one. Quickly.

Kathleen sighed and put her feet up on the coffee table. Just enough time to read another chapter before the walk up to the school, she thought. Maybe it would cheer her up. Those tablets are awfully slow to work. They never seem to do more than take the edges off the dull ache. "Why do I always feel like this?" she said to the walls. "What did I do to deserve feeling this bad all the time?"

"Nothing more than I did for letting you get yourself in this

mess," said Haliken. "I didn't notice they had invented a cure for that infection. You were meant to be out of there pretty quickly, remember? You might have even been in a new life by now, learning something else. We'll just have to make the best of it, Kathleen, my own. We're here for the duration. No short cuts. Now, go on up to the school. Being normal and looking out for the girls should dull the pain."

"I need to dull the pain. It is pain. If you felt this bad in your body, they'd give you morphine." Kathleen pulled herself to her feet and shuffled over to the sideboard. The first mouthful of whiskey shocked her, the effect rushing up her nose and hot-wiring her brain. But then she sat down and picked up her book, in a big effort to be calm and not go along with the rather giddy feeling that was overcoming her. She sighed, put her head back and gradually the alcohol pulled the book from her hand and dropped it on the floor.

The telephone shrilled, jolting Kathleen awake. She stared at it, wondering where she was. It rang again, insistent. Kathleen at last reached over and took the receiver off the cradle and laid it down on the table. She could just hear a tinny voice rattling in its depths. Her glass was still on the table, with a tiny brown stain at the bottom. She picked up the glass and held it upside down, watching intently as the drop rolled towards the rim, then put out her tongue and caught it. The voice in the phone stopped and was replaced by a buzzing. She put the receiver back on the cradle for a moment and then laid it down on the table. A different buzz continued.

"There. Now you have to leave me alone. I know you weren't Sandra, she'll be at work now. Only ever rings in the evening. When I'm busy. Never when I need her." She got up and went back to the bottle on the sideboard. Half a glass, she thought, that will get me back to sleep and out of here. She lay back on the sofa glass in hand, and watched the rain pour down the window. Ghastly climate. Indoors, only place to be in this weather. She sipped, and once more sleep took over.

David let himself into the house and ushered the two children in ahead of him.

"Go upstairs quickly, take off all your clothes and put on your pyjamas and dressing gowns." he said.

"Why?" the girls looked up at him. "It's not bedtime yet?"

"No, it's not bedtime, but your clothes are sodden and I don't want you catching cold. Now on you go. I'm going to put on the kettle for hot drinks." He hung up his coat and watched the girls as they chased each other up the stairs. They recover so quickly. They'll be loud and exhausting again in no time. Wish I could be the same. He went into the kitchen and shivered as he put on the light and threw the switch for the heating. So dark already and only just after Halloween. He put on the kettle and started getting out mugs and drinking chocolate.

"Who's that?" Kathleen's voice from the front room startled him and he dropped the sugar bowl, watching helplessly as sugar spiralled onto the floor as the bowl revolved.

"Why are you here?" David went into the room where Kathleen was lying on the sofa in the dark.

"I live here," Kathleen said. "Why shouldn't I be here?"

"Why didn't you fetch the girls from school? They were standing out in the rain by the railings for ages. The caretaker saw them as he left and phoned me at the office. He said there was no reply at home. I thought you were stuck in town."

"I took the phone off. Every time I try to relax the bloody thing shrieks at me." Kathleen shut her eyes. "Switch off the light."

"Did you hear what I said about the girls? Why didn't you go for them? They were on their own in the rain. Anything could have happened to them."

"Oh, fuss fuss fuss. Nothing happened. They're here now aren't they?" Kathleen pushed herself up on one elbow and pulled a glossy brochure towards her. "Look at this one, this looks really special. Three Greek islands in one fortnight. Transfers included, one child free if you take half-board." She lay back again and started to hum 'Never on Sunday'.

"Kathleen, we can't go on another holiday, you just have to stop daydreaming like this. Please. We haven't paid off the last one yet." The kettle began to sing in the kitchen. "Do you want a hot drink? The girls are soaked, I'm making them one."

"Why?"

"Why what?"

"Why are the girls soaked?"

David stared at Kathleen, and past her at the rain streaming down the window. It was dripping heavily onto the windowsill.

Must get a ladder and get up there and look, he thought. Maybe there are leaves in the gutter.

"Go on then, ignore me," said Kathleen, "alone all day in the house and now no-one is paying me attention even when they are here. Is it any wonder I have to keep myself going with plans to get out of this dump?" She sighed loudly and threw an arm across her eyes.

"I'm not ignoring you. I'm just amazed that you need to ask why the girls are soaked. It's lashing, didn't you notice? And two six year olds were abandoned at the school gate because their mother couldn't bother to remember to go and fetch them."

Pounding could be heard on the stairs as the girls fought to be the first down. Clare got to the living room door first and rushed in. She ran up to Kathleen and jumped up on her.

"Why did you forget us? Why? We were in the rain, all alone!" A thought struck her and her eyes shone with the drama of it, "we were like Babes in the Wood! The birds would have to put leaves on us!"

"Wouldn't need to," said Caroline, who was sitting by her mother's feet. "We could just have scrunched down. There were loads of leaves off the trees. Too soggy though, not a nice blanket. I'm glad Daddy came."

"There, you see, it was all fine. Daddy came for you and you got to practise being babes in the wood. What fun!" Kathleen hugged Clare, who broke away and threw herself in under the hearthrug, shouting "I'm dead in the wood, look!"

"I hope it's not really a practice, Mummy," said Caroline, "I don't want to do it again. Daddy mightn't remember either next time."

"One of us will remember, love," said David. "We just have to arrange better whose turn it is to remember." He glared at Kathleen and went into the kitchen.

The next evening when David got home from work the house was quiet. He sat at the kitchen table wondering where everyone was, anxious in case his daughters were on their own again. There was a Greek phrase book on the table. He looked at it dully, realising what this meant. The campaign was on for a holiday in Greece. She has such restless feet, he thought, only really happy when we're planning to go somewhere, or going somewhere. Even

180

when we're there she's not that content, as though it wasn't quite right. Maybe I should be firmer, because we really can't afford it, and I don't enjoy it that much when I'm thinking all the time about the bills when we get home. If it worked and made her happy, it might be a good idea. Maybe if she could remember the holidays for longer, look back on them more. I wonder would a better camera help? If she had a really nice album?

"No point. She's searching for somewhere forgotten. We'd bring her back Home to us if we could. If she killed herself no-one here would be cross with her, she wouldn't be cutting her life short. She's had six more years than planned already. But I hope she doesn't, for the girls' sakes. Too messy, too unfinished. We don't want them to lose a mother who they remember, even by accident. You need to be firm. Just say 'no'. I'll hang round and remind you, again. But you have to listen."

The front door opened and the twins, coming in in front of their mother, saw the light and came into the kitchen.

"Mummy came today," Clare was bouncy, "and then we went to the shops and got ice-creams. Mine was a Brunch, I like the pink bits. But Mummy says it's not as nice as Greek ice-cream. Greek ice-cream is like Italian. Yummy. When are we going?"

"We aren't going to Greece, Clare," David sat down and leant his arms on the table, "We'll all just have to prefer Brunches."

"I like choc-ices better," said Caroline, as she climbed up onto David's lap, "I like it when they go all slidy."

"They have no flavour. Nothing here has any flavour." Kathleen was leaning in the doorway.

"Well, come on, Kathleen, let's find something better for you. A life with flavour. Will excitement do? You could do something really different, train in mountain rescue maybe," Haliken ran out of ideas.

"Someone has to rescue me from this. I have to get out. I've said."

"So go. Come on."

"So I'm going into the travel agent in the morning. It's the only thing that makes it bearable. Often I think I'll leave it and be strong and stay here. But I can't. I can't."

Haliken sagged. Kathleen slumped onto a chair. Then slowly she reached for the brochure.

"Put the kettle on and I'll show you which holiday I have in mind," she said, her eyes beginning to shine.

Chapter 28
Spring 1983, Dublin

Lucy stuck her head round the door of Alison's room. Alison was on top of the chest of drawers, holding a poster of David Bowie against the wall and trying to push a drawing pin into one corner of it. She had another pin between her lips.

"I'm just going to borrow your eyeliner, okay?" Lucy came into the room, heading towards the little dressing table.

"Hep me wiv vis!" Alison's words were garbled around the pin. Lucy pulled a chair over, got up on it and helped to hold the poster up. Alison fixed in the second pin and turned to Lucy.

"If you're using my make-up, you can bring me home another fellow. The last one was no use."

"Cheek of you! Pinch every guy who ever looks at me and then chuck them away; or they get sense when they realise you're only a kid. But they don't come back my way. You're in debt to me, I reckon you owe me a whole set of makeup, the work I've done trying to get a boyfriend."

"You're better off without them, those creeps."

"Don't steal them if you think they're creeps! Go and find your own."

"I will, as soon as Mum lets me go anywhere interesting. I'm nearly eighteen now, surely that has to help."

"Just means you're more dangerous. If I was Mum I wouldn't let you anywhere."

"She can't stop me when I get into college."

"You mightn't, if you spend all your time mooning around after pop stars and not studying."

"You're not studying and you have Finals."

"Yes, and I have a study plan which I stick to and it includes seeing the girls one evening a week." Lucy found the eyeliner and went back to her room.

"OK now," Trynor said to Kumbal, Alison's guide, as they moved through the corridor between the two girls' rooms, "Lucy's going out again. Your job is as usual."

"Not hard. The little minx loves making eyes at Lucy's boyfriends. And with her being prettier, it's easy to let her do enough to unsettle the boys. Of course, now that Alison is old enough, we can let her actually go out with the next one, without her parents having a fit."

"Yes," said Trynor, watching Lucy's careful attention to her eye make-up, "we have to be careful and remember what the current society's rules are. It was so much easier back when women had more freedom. After all, when she was Alessia, my Lucy was a mother well before she was Alison's age and everyone rejoiced."

"Mmm," Kumbal agreed, "it did seem simple back then. The lives were shorter, too. How old was Alessia when the Wave came?"

"Seventeen. We were caught out that time." Trynor stretched out on Lucy's bed. "I hope nothing ghastly happens this time round. We have great plans, everything arranged for the best, but we never foresee the unforeseeable. That's why we're here now, Haliken's mistake about Kathleen's infection."

"No, we're here because of your mistake, don't try to wriggle out of that one! We were all meant to get going ten years sooner. They'd have met and married, and had Moonsong again by now. Providing of course, you had put her into the same denomination as David. Ten years ago that would have been an even bigger problem."

"Yes, it's easy to forget how important it is to humans. Silly now, not to have remembered when I actually got killed only thirty-eight earth years ago for being the wrong religion. Of course at the time I didn't realise that was why, I was only a child. And now, with the rush getting her to earth when I realised I was late, I've put Lucy into a different group. It was such a good family for her and for Alison. I really don't know why it should be so difficult for her to meet David, why they all make such a fuss about it. We don't care what religion they have. Except for the ones with child sacrifice. I really object to child sacrifice."

"I know you do. We understand." Kumbal sat on the bed and let some of her energy flow over Trynor, quietening his indignation. "But I don't think there are any of those left, are there?"

"Not officially." Trynor was subdued. Kumbal brightened deliberately and put on her most cheerful voice, the one that

184

human listeners might have recognised as an exasperated nursery teacher.

"Well, anyway, the religion thing will probably cause fewer problems the older she gets. It's never impossible, there are always ways to get them to meet, don't we all make sure of that, when it's necessary? That's why the humans get so fussed about their taboos, they know they can't trust themselves not to fall in love with the wrong people!"

"But they fall in love with the wrong people all the time. Look at David wasting his time with Kathleen. And she with him."

"Ah, but the humans think it is a wonderful match."

"Shows how much they know." Trynor sat up. "Looks like we're ready. So I'll go and see if I can keep her out of trouble and you watch over my back-up plan!"

Lucy looked at herself in the mirror once more and pulled a face at her reflection. She had done her best and she thought that with such indifferent materials to start with she didn't look too bad. *"You look lovely, Lucy. You are perfectly nice looking, with some very good points. Now stop worrying, far too many young men find you attractive for my peace of mind as it is."* She put her new bag over her shoulder and admired the effect. That would do. It was only a drink with a friend in the Pavilion in Trinity after all. Nothing special.

"That's good. The special nights are an even worse strain, worrying that you'll set your eye on someone new. And then trying to convince you to bring whoever it is home. Just talk to the girls, Lucy. Okay, I'm coming. Bye, Kumbal."

Two hours later Trynor was backing away in front of Lucy, trying to block her view of a group from the rugby club. They were pushing and jostling to get to the bar and Lucy had just stood up to make her own way there to get more drinks for herself and her friends. *Trynor was in as much of a panic as he could ever remember being, in spirit. Being locked into the gas chamber was worse, he thought, but not more significant. Not for me, anyway. I wish I could turn opaque, so they couldn't see through me.*

"Hello Trynor!"

Oh shit, thought Trynor, maybe I should be even more transparent and then he wouldn't have seen me,

185

"Hello Roki."

"Fancy meeting you here!"

"Fancy."

" Is it Eloise you're with?"

"Yes. She's Lucy this time."

"Great! A woman again. It was crap when she was a guy. As Lewis she was almost no fun at all." Roki was looking round and caught sight of Lucy, where she was at the bar, trying to attract the barman's attention. "That her? I'd have known her anywhere!"

Trynor sighed. "Of course you would, her energy pattern hasn't changed. Now please leave her alone. We are working a plan and it's hard enough without you two mucking it up."

"What's the plan?"

"Get her together with David-Daniel-Dorothy and let them have the baby again. The 'baby' insists, says they have great energy when they're together."

"Still at that?" Roki looked around. Lucy was still waving at the barman, with gradually decreasing enthusiasm as he ignored her once again.

"Hey, Martin! Look who I've found!" Roki was gesticulating at one of the rugby group, a tall well built young man, who was reaching in to the bar over the other customers and lifting the full pints out, distributing them to his friends. He kept the last pint and lifted it towards his group.

"Cheers, lads!"

The other boys echoed him and they all drank.

"That's enough, Roki, don't try again, please!" Trynor was dancing on the spot, trying to attract attention from the barman's guide, who was sitting on the back counter, between the spirits bottles, watching the melee in front of him. "Get your man to serve my girl, please!" Trynor shouted, through the hubbub. The guide, a very old calm soul, apparently had a hands off approach. He smiled. Trynor was not sure whether it was in response, or in general pleasure at the world around him.

"Martin, look! There she is!" Roki was nudging Martin. Martin looked round. "He heard me, look, at last he heard me!" Roki was jubilant.

"Sod's law. He hears you just when it isn't right. Come on Lucy, you don't want another drink. Go on to McDonald's instead."

"Tut tut. Promoting junk food. Shame on you." Roki grinned as Martin leant forward a little to the barman and spoke in a firm voice.

"There's a lady here trying to get served, I think." He smiled at Lucy. "What were you trying to get?"

"Two glasses of Guinness and a vodka and orange. Thank you."

Martin repeated the order to the barman and looked down at Lucy. He saw a medium height, medium pretty girl.

"Must be tough, trying to get attention, when you're small."

"I'm not small! I'm average for a woman."

"Oh, I'd say you're more than an average woman," Martin grinned and his eyes crinkled. "Martin Fitzgerald." He put out his hand.

"Lucy Browne." Lucy shook the proffered hand and then found she couldn't take her hand back. Martin was holding it. He lifted it to his lips and made an exaggerated gesture of kissing the back of it. Lucy was still, looking with amazement at the top of the head bent over her hand.

"Cheap move, Roki. And untrue. He never kissed her hand like that in France. It was Daniel who made the gallant gestures."

"So? My man has become more gallant, now he's not trapped by class distinctions. Look, she recognises him."

"Unfortunately. Lucy, put him down!"

Lucy watched as Martin straightened up. She found herself tongue-tied as she looked at him. The barman put her drinks on the counter and announced the price. She fumbled for her purse, but a large firm hand came out and held hers.

"Put your money away. I'm getting these." Martin paid and then looked round for his friends. "Where are your friends sitting? The lads were looking for some beautiful ladies." In a daze Lucy led the way back to her table and introduced Martin to Sarah and Jen. His four friends jostled over, gave their names and made attempts to shake hands without spilling drinks. They pulled stools over from other tables and soon they were all a noisy group together. Jen leant over to Lucy.

"Nice find! How did you do that? Men to choose from," she whispered under cover of a gust of laughter from the boys.

"Tell you later. Hands off Martin, he's mine."

"Fine. Four others."

The girls had a wonderful evening, as three girls will in the company of five boys all vying for their attention. At closing time, phone numbers were exchanged and they all spilled out onto the street and separated towards their bus stops. Martin took Lucy's elbow.

"I'll walk you to your stop."

"Thank you. Bye Sarah, bye Jen." She grinned broadly at them and they smiled back. Jen gave a surreptitious thumbs-up and Lucy laughed, feeling very happy.

The bus came into view almost as soon as they reached her stop, rattling round the corner and up Nassau Street at a great rate. Martin only had time to take Lucy's hand and again kiss the back of it. Her heart sang and she promised him she would be at home tomorrow if he phoned.

At home, the house was quiet. Lucy tiptoed to her room, wishing she could sing and dance her way there and express some of the excitement that was fizzing out of her. 'I could have danced all night!' she hummed softly to herself as she let herself into her room and closed the door. It immediately opened and Alison looked round it.

"Well, how'd it go? D'ya find me one?"

"I found five. You can have four of them. One of them's mine." Lucy sat down on the bed and patted the place beside her.

"Yes, tell her all. Then Kumbal can get working."

"You know, I can't explain it, but I feel as though I've known him for years."

"You have. It doesn't mean he's good for you. Cut loose now, before it's too late."

"He's lovely. Kissed my hand. Made me feel really special."

"He sounds a real creep. Kissing hands. Yuck!" Alison made vomiting sounds as she poked her finger into her open mouth. "Did he kiss you properly?"

"No, of course not. He's a gentleman."

"Oh my god, you've gone mad. Since when did you want a 'gentleman'?" Alison made it sound as though a gentleman was the next thing to a rapist. *Kumbal nodded her approval of this approach.*

"And he's phoning me tomorrow. So get out and let me get ready for bed. He might ask me out."

"Ask him round. Let me check him out for you, you're not in a fit mental state to make judgements."

"Yes, Lucy, she's right. Ask him round. Go out for a walk or something, so your head isn't turned by a romantic date." Trynor was walking to and fro, twisting his hands together. *"Kumbal, what am I to do? This is the worst thing that could have happened and she's gone all gooey on me. Jotin will kill me!"* The idiocy of this comment made them both laugh, so they missed what Lucy said next.

"A romantic date. Yes, I think he'll do romantic really well. I'm not showing him to you, you ruin everything."

Several times over the next months, particularly once her finals were over, Lucy sat with Martin and listened spellbound to his stories about himself and his family. She was mesmerised by all they had in common and told Alison about it when she got home. Alison was unimpressed.

"So what if he's interested in rugby? You aren't. You like badminton."

"It's sports, isn't it? Healthy. Gets you moving, stretching," Lucy paused and then continued in a dreamy voice. "Actually, rugby's probably better, gets you out in the open air too. Maybe I should take it up. Martin's been explaining it to me."

"Girls don't play rugby. It's rough, Dad thinks. He stopped; it was dangerous, he said."

"He goes to the Internationals."

"So? Lucy, don't be an idiot. You're good at badminton. Look at your cups," she waved a hand towards the shelf of awards. "All you'd get from rugby is bruises. Or a broken neck. You should know. You're the physio."

"He loves dogs. I'd love a dog."

"Me too. Most people like dogs. What does that prove?"

"And he has a younger sister. So he understands what I have to put up with. Now get out!"

"OK, I'm going. Bring him home, so I can see him."

Lucy was reluctant to bring Martin home. She wasn't sure of him yet. She wanted to be sure. She had met his parents and his siblings, and their dog. She preferred the dog.

"Of course you do, Lucy, the dog is the most sympathetic soul.

189

None of them are meant to be in your life, but it doesn't matter for dogs. They can love anyone."

"So when am I to meet your family and get to know the people who are important to my girl?"

"Not yet Martin my pal. Steer clear of them if you want this girl, her sister will recognise you and give you your marching orders. She had enough of you, being your wife in the Médoc." Roki was watching, amused.

"Roki, why do you persist in trying to ruin everything? This is not the right woman for Martin and certainly not the right man for my Lucy. Now, work with us on this. Stop him taking advantage again."

"Surely she should learn from this, how not to be taken advantage of?" Roki grinned. "Excuse my grammar."

"Hump your grammar." Trynor was getting angry. "And I don't excuse the content of what you're saying. This is not a learning opportunity for Lucy. But it could be for Martin, to learn to stop taking advantage of her. Have you forgotten what he did in Scotland? That was bad."

"She got her own back. Wouldn't give us a job when she could have. He had a bad time after that. Had to 'go on the parish'. Lost all his self-respect. Can you blame Martin for trying to get it back? I'm not going to stop him. Why's it so important they get together? They've done it already, starting thousands of their years ago."

"She and David have excellent energies when they can be together. And their baby has asked us to let her grow up with them. She felt it was helping her to develop something special, but never got past a few months. She's had lives with each of them separately, but the energies just weren't the same, she says. She wants to be a child with the two of them."

"Do you think you want to have children, Martin?" Lucy asked, very quietly.

"Oh no, she always hears me when it isn't appropriate!"

"I suppose. Haven't thought about it." Martin stood up. "Will you have another?"

"Good man, Martin," Trynor was relieved, "avoid that question." Trynor and Roki continued to argue, as they watched Lucy and Martin talk. Lucy's eyes were shining and she looked quite beautiful. She listened to Martin as though he was the only

thing in her world, and Martin believed he was.

Chapter 29
Dundee, Scotland, 28th December 1879

Lewis glanced at the clock for the hundredth time. The hands had barely moved, maybe less than a minute since the last time he looked. He sighed, turned his body on the chair so that the clock would be behind him and picked up the piece of wood and his knife. He was making another figure for Dawn, this one would be a cow. By her first birthday, next June, he planned to have a whole Noah's Ark finished. He whittled carefully for a few minutes, tiny curls of wood coming off under his fingers and falling to his lap. The light was dim in the small room and the wind howling outside crept in occasionally round the edges of the window, making the candles gutter. He could just see the tiny horned head beginning to stick out of the little block of wood.

The clock whirred, then struck the quarter. Just another fifteen minutes and it would be time to set off for the station to meet them. He hoped Dr Ross had been able to help the wee one. Dorothy had such faith in the old doctor back in Cupar and had insisted on bringing Dawn to see him. It seemed as though they had been gone for weeks, but it was only two days. Not long now and they would be home, and with Hogmanay coming soon, maybe he and Dorothy would dance again. His hands fell still as his memory took over.

Lewis was in the forge, the sweat pouring down his body as he manoeuvred the hot metal in the flames. It was an unusually still day and though the doors were propped open no air moved, except for the tiny gusts from the bellows, when young Robert remembered to pump. Robert was the new apprentice, taken on a few months ago, so that he would be of some use to the master when Lewis got his papers next year, and moved on.

"Come on, lad, a bit harder!" Edward McIntyre came back in from the office and immediately noticed the slacker. He was a tough master, thought Lewis, but that suited me and I have learnt a lot

193

from him. Maybe I can run my own forge one day. He gave the horseshoe another tap and held it back into the heat, wiping the sweat out of his eyes with the back of his wrist. Mr McIntyre was watching him, so he worked carefully, wanting to demonstrate his skill. He wondered later how long the girl had been watching from the doorway, and blushed often when he thought of how she had seen him stripped to the waist.

When the shoe was finished and given its last dowsing in water, steam billowed in front of Lewis, adding to the wet on his face and chest. He took a handful of hay out of the bale they kept by the door for the occasional bribery of their reluctant equine customers and rubbed it over his face and chest. It was not very absorbent, but he enjoyed its fresh smell. He became aware of a tiny gasp from the doorway and looked up. There was a young woman looking at him. At least he assumed she was, but as the light was behind her all he could see was a slim curvy outline, the shape of a hat, and a glow of gold under it where the sun was shining through her hair. He whirled around, reaching for his shirt.

"Ach, no, do not bother. I...." She broke off in confusion. Lewis shrugged into his shirt, pulling it closed across his chest and moving into the doorway so that he could see her better. Her face was pink, but her eyes still strayed to Lewis' chest, where he could see bits of hay were sticking to him. He picked off some of the bigger pieces and dropped them on the ground. The young woman watched them fall, and it seemed for a moment that she would pluck them out of the air, but then she was reaching into her bag and pulling out a buckle, which she held towards him with a trembling hand.

"Can you mend this? The tongue has broken."

Lewis took the buckle and turned it over in his hands. It was big and heavy.

"This is not yours, I think? It is too big for a pretty girl." He stopped, astonished at himself for being so forward and very slowly raised his eyes to look at her. Then his world stopped and his heart flipped over, settling down eventually to beat forever in a totally different way, even in a different place. Unable to think clearly about anything, he stared at her smile. It seemed to light up the forge, light up the street, light up the...

"Yes, yes," said Trynor, "the smile always gets you, doesn't it? Just as you get the result by having flowers on your chest. Not

194

quite flowers this time, but grass seems to have done the trick. Too good a signal to drop. We'll use it again, I suspect."

"Take the young lady into the office, Lewis; and take her order properly," said the master smith, "while I try to get it through this thick young skull here how to keep a fire hot."

Lewis did up his shirt buttons with shaking hands and led the young woman through into the little room so grandly called the office. He offered her a seat, then took her details into the big leather bound ledger. Aware of her eyes on him, he tried not to let his tongue creep out from between his teeth as he concentrated on making the pen do his bidding. He formed the letters as well as he could, to suit the importance of the occasion. He had noticed her before, in the town, but did not know her name.

"Dorothy Milne? Then are you maybe related to my cousin, Neil Martin?"

"Yes, he is my cousin, too!" They laughed and fell into a discussion about their families, how they shared a cousin and yet were not related. And eventually they found themselves agreeing to go to the Martin family's harvest ceilidh the next week.

And we did, thought Lewis, as he glanced again at the clock, and we danced as though no one else mattered and were noticed by everyone, including the minister, sour old killjoy that he is. Neil and the others had good fun laughing at my expense over that. And I got teased unmercifully when I got back into the forge that first day with the buckle in my sweaty hands. Lewis grinned as he remembered how easy it had been, getting to know Dorothy, and how he had been able to say pretty things to her that would have tied his tongue with any other woman. None of their teasing matters now, he thought, because she is my own sweet Dorothy, we have our little Dawn, I am saving a bit from my work in the foundry and I will have my own smithy one day, maybe over in Dairsie, to be nearer the family, so Dawn can play with her cousins. Of course, he thought with a happy sigh, she will have brothers and sisters of her own to play with. It was not too bad for Dorothy, giving birth to Dawn, so maybe we can have many more. We will have to give the next one an ordinary name, or they will all think we are mad. But she was a beautiful new baby, who cried to greet the dawn. So what else could we call her?

"What indeed? Why break a habit of millennia? Even though it was actually the moon the baby was looking at, not the dawn," said Trynor, smiling indulgently at his old friend.

There was a crash in the street and Lewis went to the window and looked down. It was too dark to see, but he could hear the wind howling. The clock chimed seven, so he began to put on his coat. It could take longer in this wind to get down the hill to the station. He banked down the fire, to hold its heat for their return. Bitterly cold draughts sneaked in around the window frame and under the door from the stairwell, defying even Dorothy's rag snake, which was pushed against the bottom of it. It would have been cold on the train too. Maybe the tearoom at the station would be open and they could warm themselves before setting off on the walk back home. Lewis went quickly over to the shelves and took a few coins out of the jar behind the saucepan, locked the door of their room and clattered down the stairs to the front door. As he opened it, it flew inwards with the force of the wind and he saw a large hoarding bowling along the street. He dragged the door shut, gathered his coat tightly around him and strode as fast as he could towards the station. It was a wild night and chimney pots flew through the air, one crashing at his feet. Lewis turned up his collar and broke into a trot. He always felt uneasy walking through the dark and this was particularly unpleasant, with a disembodied enemy throwing missiles.

At last he reached the station and ran down the steps. It was a little less windy on the platform, as it was below the level of the street, but the crashing noises had not stopped. As he watched, a tile fell from the roof onto the platform.

"All into the waiting rooms, please!" The stationmaster was raising his voice to be heard over the wind. "It is dangerous to stay on the platform. Thank you, ladies and gentlemen." Lewis did as he was told and joined a large crowd who were waiting for friends and relatives. There were no seats left, but he squeezed into a corner and leant against the wall, closing his eyes and allowing himself to daydream again.

It had been a Saturday night, so they were going to the music hall down near Greenmarket, hoping for a good show, with some of the new songs the lads at the foundry had been whistling. It was a mild night and Dorothy suggested they set out early, to have time to walk down to the harbour and look at the boats.

"I thought you did not like to see the sea?" said Lewis, as he put on his jacket.

"I do not like the real sea, it is too big. But the harbours do not worry me, when there is a wall around the water. It makes it look safer. But it is thrilling to look at those boats and think of how far they have been, how brave they are to go. All the way to the South Pole!" Dorothy's eyes glowed.

"I do not think you can get to the South Pole in a boat. I agree, though, they are brave to go so far. I am uneasy on the ferry. It is good there is the bridge now, it does not wobble like that little boat." Lewis stopped and looked at Dorothy in alarm. "But do not say so to Neil, or I will never hear the last of it. He is a terrible tease."

"I will say nothing. My sister always grumbles about how she had to do all my share of the work looking after the fire when we were young, even though I did all the washing. I could never manage the ironing; the irons get so hot in the fire and you have to get so close and spit on them to test them. It's worse now, that we do not have a range like mother's. Heating the irons against an open fire is even more nerve wracking. You see the result." Dorothy smoothed her wrinkled dress and smiled up at Lewis. He leant forward and kissed her quickly, appreciating the relative anonymity of Dundee compared to their home town and silently promising to buy Dorothy a range as soon as he could.

"I do not know how you can work with those hot fires in the foundry, it makes me feel weak even thinking of them." Dorothy grinned at him again, her blue eyes flashing mischievously. "It is a small miracle that we met. If I had had to come any closer to that furnace you would have had to pick me up off the floor in a dead faint!"

"Well, that would have been even better. I could have held you straight away, instead of having to wait for the ceilidh." Lewis took Dorothy's hand in his and they walked comfortably together down the gentle hill towards the riverfront.

They spent a while looking at the ships in the dock and, in plenty of time for the show, walked back across to the music hall and bought tickets for the cheapest seats. There was a gentle breeze

197

blowing and on it came a most tantalising smell, unusual, but definitely delicious, as Lewis found his mouth filling with water.

"Can you smell that? What do you think it is?"

"Let's go and see," Dorothy was already moving in the direction of Greenmarket. "We have time before the show, I think?"

They soon joined a crowd outside a small tent, from where the hot sharp smell was emanating. They could not see its source, but there was a crudely lettered sign outside the tent: 'chip potatoes, 1/2d'.

"Stop pushing at the back!" A voice roared from inside. "Plenty for everyone, wait your turns please!"

"Well love," Lewis turned to his wife with the air of a grandee inviting a lady to a banquet, "Will we try these potatoes? I have a penny to spare."

"Oh, yes please, Lewis. The smell is so good."

And at last they had been at the front of the queue and had bought two portions of the fried potatoes, had sat on the simple boxes and enjoyed this new delicacy as though it had indeed come from the grandee's kitchen. They had eaten with such slow appreciation, that they had missed the first half of the show in the music hall entirely, yet neither of them had resented the waste of money at all. One penny for chips and on later visits, extra for two portions of peas as well, was so enjoyable, better value than the theatre. Salt and vinegar are a fancy enough sauce, thought Lewis, when you are with someone you love. And now that little Dawn can join in and have a bit of mashed peas, well, we are as lucky as kings.

"Ladies and gentlemen!" The stationmaster's voice cut into Lewis's musings and he tore himself away from the delicious thoughts, back to the noisy cold station.

"Ladies and gentlemen, you are all advised to go back to your homes. The train will not be crossing the bridge tonight." There was a bit of grumbling, but people could see that there was no help for it, they would have to return in the morning. The station emptied quickly and Lewis tucked his head down against the gale as he trudged his way back home. He hoped that Dorothy had heard that the train would not run to Dundee and was now sitting in her mother's cosy house, not stuck in a draughty waiting room on the other side of the Firth.

Chapter 30
Earlier that evening

The little station at Cupar was packed with people, some waiting to buy tickets and many here to see off their friends. Many were with fractious children, jiggling after their long exciting day. Dorothy followed in her mother's wake, as the older woman pushed a way through to the ticket office. Rose Milne was a solid woman with a gentle manner. She had brought most of the population of Cupar into the world and many women had reason to be grateful to her. Her neat deft hands had lifted numerous reluctant babies out of their desperate mothers. She was recognised and greeted and space was made for her in front of others, but she did not like to take advantage of what she considered God-given talents, so they joined the end of the queue.

"I should have bought a return ticket, I do not know what I was thinking on Friday," said Dorothy, as the baby in her arms began to fret.

"What difference?" said her mother. "The train will go when it goes, whether you are sitting on it for one second or two minutes."

The queue shuffled forward. At last it was her turn and Dorothy laid her money on the counter.

"One to Dundee, please"

"Now you yell," said Mohmi, *"you have to keep her off that train."*

Dawn screeched. She screeched as she had never screeched before, as though the worst pain in the world had just been visited upon her. Dorothy nearly dropped the baby onto the counter.

"Here, give me the baby," said Rose, "while you get the ticket. There there, my precious, did the pain come back, then? A naughty pain, when Dr Ross says there is nothing wrong. We do not need to worry, just a bit of colic." She shifted Dawn up to her shoulder and patted her back with a practised hand.

"I had reason to be worried, mother. She pulled up her little legs with the pain."

"Every baby has colic. You would think there had never been another baby in the world, the way you and Lewis fuss over this one. No good doctors in Dundee! What nonsense."

"I trust Dr Ross," said Dorothy, as she took her ticket. "Now he says there is nothing wrong, I can relax."

"Hmm. Until the next time. Are you going to come running home every time she has a fever?"

"I might. Will you not welcome me?" Dorothy patted the baby's back, making no difference to the grizzly wail that Dawn was making.

"Of course, hen. This is your home. We never wanted you to go to Dundee. And I do not think this little lady wants to go to Dundee either."

"You are right, Rose" said Mohmi, "at least, not on this train. Go on, Dawn, shout. You must not get on the train." Dawn wailed, louder. Two other babies were crying, one very loudly.

"Maybe we should bring her back to Dr Ross," said Rose. "He could see her tomorrow and there would still be time for you to get back to your husband before Hogmanay. I'm sure your ticket will do for another train."

"Yes, maybe that would be better." Dorothy took the baby back and kissed her. Dawn stopped crying and smiled at her mother.

"Come on." Dorothy turned and made for the station entrance. A porter pushed across her path with a heap of luggage and she stopped. She turned to face her mother.

"But what will Lewis think? He will go to the station to meet us and we will not be there. He will go mad with worry." She turned back.

"Worry does not hurt, in the long run, Dorothy, if there is no reason for it," said Jotin. "Go home with your mother now and get the ferry tomorrow. Then you will know why I stopped you buying a return ticket yesterday."

Dorothy hesitated. Then she started moving back towards the platform. Dawn began to grizzle again and her mother stopped and looked down into the little face.

"So, what do you think, hen? Will we go back to the nice doctor? Or home to Daddy?"

"Ask one thing at a time, you silly girl. How can she answer that?" asked Jotin.

"She does not expect an answer," said Mohmi. *"It is so frustrating. They are so deaf this time. Getting deafer all the time. Learning as souls, progressing in other ways, but getting more and more difficult to guide. Come on, Dawn, yell again, it is the only way they will hear us."*

Dawn yelled again.

"Oh the poor mite," said Rose, "she is frightened. Maybe of the doctor."

"No, No, No," shouted Jotin, Mohmi, and Rose's guide together. *"Of the train!"*

Rose shuddered and pulled her shawl tighter around her.

"Someone's walking over my grave," she said.

"You go on home, mother and get warm. No point in us all shivering. Dawn and I will be all right, the train will be here soon. I hope I can get a seat away from a window, so I do not see the sea."

"You and not looking at the sea! You will not see it anyway now, it is pitch black out there."

"Another good reason for going now and not waiting for tomorrow."

"Well, goodbye, my love. Write to me tomorrow." Rose kissed her daughter and bent forward to kiss Dawn, whose tear-stained face looked back up at her with an unfathomable expression.

"TaTa little one. Be a good bairn for mummy. Wouldn't you love to know what she is thinking? Such a face, wee Dawn." She kissed the baby and turned away.

"Wouldn't you just? It would be so much easier for all of us, if the people who could hear us could talk. Little Dawn will stop understanding us soon," said Jotin, *waving ruefully at Rose's guide as she and* Rose walked away.

Dawn wailed and howled all the way through the queue, past the ticket inspector and onto the train. Dorothy took a seat and tried to nurse Dawn under her shawl, but Dawn just cried. Another young mother got on and sat opposite Dorothy. They smiled at each other as the two babies protested.

At last the train doors slammed shut, whistles were blown and the train began to move. Dorothy stood up and went to the door, her hand going impulsively to the handle.

"Yes, yes ! Pull it, quickly. Or better, pull the cord!" Jotin's voice was full of energy. Dorothy looked up at the emergency cord and

at the warning sign beside it about improper use. Her hand fell to her side and she turned and sat down, smiling a little shamefacedly at the woman in the seat opposite, who looked at her with raised eyebrows.

"I do not know what came over me," Dorothy said, surprising herself utterly, "I just suddenly wanted to get off. Whatever would they have thought of me if I had jumped out when we were moving! Or worse, if I had pulled the cord, for no good reason."

"That's what you think. You should stop letting your fear of people's opinions cloud your judgements. You wouldn't have burnt to death in France if you hadn't been so keen on making the peasants like you and had just run away like I told you. Oh, no, here I am babbling again. It gets so frustrating, when you do not even hear my clear instructions." Jotin slumped down onto the seat and leant his head against the window. The train gathered speed and swayed a little as it rattled through the night.

"I don't think there is any more we can do," said Mohmi, her *voice and her energies wilting, "except get ready to speak to them face to face again. I do not think she will get out at a strange station, no matter how hard Dawn cries. Especially not at night. You can stop crying, Dawn."*

"We can put them to sleep, so they do not know. One less fear to carry forward, maybe," said Jotin, as he hovered beside Dorothy, *trying to soothe her energies with his, and directing her attention to her ticket.*

Dorothy took her ticket out of her pocket and laid it on the seat beside her. She looked at it, wondered why she had done that and was about to put it away again, when Dawn cried. She lifted the weary baby to her face and kissed her.

"Well done, Dawn. You can go to sleep now. Night night, Dawn, I'll see you soon. I have the easier job, look. Crying babies are always tired," said Mohmi.

"I will give Dorothy a dream. She can remember when the baby was born and the moon was setting in the summer sky, and sunlight was just beginning to tinge the horizon. And her Moonsong arrived once more into the world and cried with happiness to see the moon again, and once more was named for it. As near as her parents could manage, in this culture with meaningless names. And how the baby smiled, only a few minutes

after her birth, to be welcomed so. There, she is asleep, and remembering." Dorothy's eyes were closed and her breathing was steady, blowing a tendril of golden hair with each breath. *"I will just go and warn Trynor, to be ready. Poor Lewis." Jotin was back in a moment, his face grim. He and Mohmi sat,* as the train rumbled north, through the night, juddering in the wind. It stopped at several stations, there was a noise of slamming doors and whistles, but Dorothy and Dawn slept on. At St. Fort station the train stopped again and in a moment the door was pulled open, allowing a gust of smoky air into the compartment. The ticket inspector stuck his head in.

"Anyone getting off in Dundee? Tickets please."

"The other lady put hers on the seat," said the young woman as she handed over her ticket. "She must be exhausted, she has slept the whole way."

The inspector picked up Dorothy's ticket, nodded to the young woman and slammed the door. A whistle blew and the train shuddered forwards. In a few minutes, the noise of the wheels changed as the train rattled out onto the bridge over the River Tay. Dorothy and Dawn still slept. As the storm winds hit and the bridge suddenly gave way, the night filled with screams and the noise of grinding metal as the train fell. Dorothy heard nothing as she and Dawn shot out of their seats, hitting their heads on the roof of the carriage as it came down to meet them. They were both unconscious as the train plunged down into the dark water and silence closed over it.

Mohmi and Jotin were waiting to gather them in.

Chapter 31

Lewis woke early and lay listening to the quietness in the street. The wind had dropped and the sun was trying to break through. He stoked up the fire so that it would be bright and cheery when he got home with Dorothy. It would save her having to think about the fire, which always seemed to bother her. Strange, when she had never been burned. "Far too careful," Dorothy's mother had said, when he asked her once, trying to find a reason for such a strong fear. "No, she never went near the fire, even when she first crawled. I never needed to watch her, not like the others, who all seemed bent on getting themselves burnt: many's a time I had to butter sore little fingers."

Lewis put the guard in front of the fire, bundled himself up in his warm coat and set off again for the station. It was a pleasant walk, with a watery sun warming him. He hurried as he got closer to the station, anxious to hear when the train was scheduled to arrive, hoping Dorothy had not had to wait for him. He began to notice groups of people, standing around the entrance to the station, and an unnatural stillness, punctuated by crying. He stopped at the top of the stairs, suddenly frightened. He looked at two young women who were coming up, tears streaming down their faces.

"What is it?" Lewis's voice was barely a whisper "What has happened?"

"Gone" The young woman's voice rang out, startling the stillness.

"Gone? What is gone?"

"Our brother. On the train." She started to cry again.

"The bridge." The other woman put her arm around her sister and led her away.

Lewis put a hand to the rail and gripped it. His heart fluttered weakly, his bowels seemed turned to water and his legs sagged.

"When?" he whispered, but no one replied. He forced himself upright and walked down the steps to the stationmaster's office. There was a crowd around the door, shouting and weeping, demanding explanations. Lewis listened. It seemed the train had crossed the bridge last night and had fallen into the Tay before they had all been told to go home.

"You lied to us!" a voice in the crowd shouted.

"There was nothing any of us could do on such a night, Madam. I thought it better to let you have your rest." The stationmaster was dignified and sombre. Lewis turned away. He slowly pushed his way back up the stairs, heard himself saying "gone" to the new arrivals who were asking for news. He walked across to the edge of the river and looked upstream to the bridge. The central section was not there, the ends of the rails stuck out, twisted. He walked towards it automatically, not thinking at all, his mind crying out 'Dorothy! Dorothy!' *Trynor walked beside him, holding his energies around Lewis, as though to protect him from the wind. He talked, but knew that he would not be heard. Eventually he called out,*

"Roki!"

"Yes?" Roki was there, dancing around mischievously as usual.

"We need your help. He needs a friend who is in a body. He is too shocked to hear me, and later he will be too sunk in grief. Get Neil, will you?"

"Down to the river? He is on his way to work. He knows nothing of this. What has happened, anyway?"

Trynor explained. Roki mocked- "and they let them get on, when it was not in the plan? Rather a habit of messing up, haven't you? Well, let me see what I can do..."

"If you get Neil to come to the flat at the dinner hour, I'll try to get Lewis back there. Please, he needs someone to talk to."

Lewis reached the end of the bridge, where the tracks turned to run along the shore and found he was joining a small crowd of people jostling for news, information, answers. He stood with them and listened, but his mind shut away the dread and he said to himself 'no, they were not on the train. It was not crossing the bridge, so they went home. They are still at home with Mrs Milne. They will come across later on the ferry. I will have to go and meet it. I had better buy some food to have for their dinner.' He straightened up and strode back to the town, full of resolve and plans for a hot meal. Dorothy so loved hot food, despite being so cautious about making it herself. It was always the way to give her a treat and himself too, to have something interesting to eat. He remembered when they had no money at all, before he got the job, Dorothy had experimented with different quantities of salt in the porridge, to 'ring the changes' as she said, to make their food more varied. So I will buy something special, to welcome her home after giving me such a fright.

"What kept you from work? The foreman is not pleased with you!" Neil was in the doorway, stamping his feet and rubbing his hands together. . "Are you coming for the afternoon shift?"

"No."

"Just 'no'? Are you sick? Or rich all of a sudden?"

"Did you not hear? Are they not all talking?"

"Hear what? I have no time to listen to gossip and tittle-tattle."

"It is not gossip. For some people it is the end of the world." Lewis let his head fall forward again, and his hands twisted together.

"The end of the world? I did not hear the last trump, did you? Come on man, what can be that bad?"

"The rail bridge collapsed. The train fell into the firth."

"Oh, that! Amazing that a great bridge like that could just collapse. I wonder why?"

"How do I know? It makes no difference how. I only know the train is at the bottom of the Firth, but I must go and meet Dorothy off the ferry. She was staying with her mother."

"You never said Dorothy was away. Why are you bothered about the bridge if they went by ferry? What time are they due back?"

"They went on the train." Lewis began to tremble. "But they must be coming back on a ferry. They cannot be at the bottom of the sea. They cannot."

"Did Dorothy have a return ticket?" Neil's face was pale and his eyes were round.

"No!" Lewis jumped up, smiling and rushed to the window to look out. "No, for some reason she only bought a single. Waste of money, I thought, but she had some reason. So it is all right. Come on, come with me down to the ferry."

"If they are safe you have no excuse to miss work and nor have I. I will walk part of the way with you, but it is in the wrong direction. You will have me late."

"You can explain, you have a way with words."

Lewis waited at the ferry's landing place for most of the day, but no one he knew got off the ferries, until just as the short day was drawing to a close, the very last boat of the day pulled in to the shore and Lewis, sitting despondently on a bollard, saw at last the comfortable figure of his mother-in-law. She was first onto land and walked slowly towards him, her stout figure looking too heavy for her. She had never looked heavy before.

"Lewis, pet!" She put her arms around him. As he returned her embrace he could just see, in the dim light, the tracks of tears on her face. He took a deep breath.

"Were they on the train?"

"Yes," her voice was gentle and sad. Lewis slumped down onto the bollard again. "I went up onto the bridge to watch the train leave and she was on it in Cupar, so unless she got out somewhere, she was on that train. I'm sorry to have to tell you so."

"Oh, Mrs Milne! My Dorothy, my Dawn!"

"Yes. Our beautiful girls." She lifted Lewis's arm. "Come, on, let's go home. We can talk as we go." But they walked in silence for most of the way, as the tears spilled out of Lewis's eyes and poured unchecked onto his collar. They got into the little room and Rose stirred the fire into life and put on a kettle to boil. They sat and looked at each other.

"How were they, when you saw them last? What did the doctor say?" For several minutes Lewis listened intently as Rose described their visit and all the now irrelevant, but so interesting details of the doctor's opinion.

"So there was nothing wrong. They need not have gone. And they would be here now."

"No.... They could have stayed longer with me. They nearly did, you know." Rose explained how Dawn had cried and they had considered taking her home.

"So Dawn knew."

"*Yes!!*"

"No. How could she? She was just upset by the noise."

"Poor little mite. She did not want to be there, one way or other."

Footsteps thudded up the stairs, the door burst open and Neil came in, his cheeks red and his eyes shining from the cold and exertion. He looked quickly around the room, leaning over to see into the tiny bedroom beyond and then his eyes settled on Rose and the stuffing went out of him.

208

"Mrs. Milne? What..." He broke off.

"They were on the train, Neil. Mrs Milne saw them leave, saw the train leave with my girls in it."

"Oh." Neil was silent and stood turning his cap through his hands.

"Go on, say something sympathetic. 'Oh' is a bit feeble."

"I ah, uh, I, I mean, oh dear." Neil's cap was now a small twist of cloth in his white knuckled hands.

"Brilliant! What happened your 'way with words'? Easy to see you were never an orator," Roki was grinning.

"Come in properly, Neil, stay awhile," Rose was indicating the stool under the table. Neil pulled it over to the fire and sat down. His eyes flitted uneasily between Lewis and Mrs Milne.

"Keep quiet. Listen. Maybe you will be useful just by being here."

They sat in silence for a long while, watching the fire, the slow steady burn of the coal and the spit and hiss of the wood Lewis had thrown on. Lewis looked up at the noise and gazed sadly at the half finished carving on the table.

"She will never play with it. It was for her birthday. She will not have a birthday, not even one. The best Noah's Ark in Dundee, it was going to be. Wasted."

"It will not be wasted, Lewis. You can keep going and in time you will meet another woman and have another daughter. I will like to meet them," Rose's voice began to shake, "to fill the gap." She fell silent, her hands busily dealing with her nose and eyes.

"No. That was my family. My only family. Gone. How could I replace them?" There was a long pause.

"They must have been so frightened, to be suddenly falling into the sea. And the sea so cold, and dark. Trapped in the carriage, maybe, struggling to escape. The water rising." His voice rose to a tremulous shriek and he started to shiver violently. Neil put out a doubtful hand and patted Lewis's shoulder. *Trynor and Roki were talking together, discussing the best way to handle this unexpected disaster.*

"I'm worried, Roki. He might get through this, but he has to get through his life now. We have no plan for it. What will I do?"

"What can you do? Just stay with him. I'll encourage Neil to be his friend, if I can. Pity Neil's not a woman this time, it could have

been their chance to marry."

"Just as well he's not. That would have been an extra complication. A friend will be enough, but can you stop him trying to be funny? That is too exhausting."

"I can try. But that is his nature. Listen!"

"Come on, Lewis. You will feel better soon. After all, did I not hear you complain that the baby cried all night and you wished she would stop? You can sleep well now!"

"I will never sleep again."

"No, you will. Once the funeral is over, you will feel better."

"There can be no funeral. There is no body."

"Oh."

"We have to wait until they are found. Oh, I hope they will be found."

They sat in silence until the clock whirred again. Neil jumped to his feet.

"Oh my goodness, I will have to run, I said I would meet someone." He was gone, banging the door behind him with his usual exuberance. Lewis and Rose could hear his feet running away and the endless ticking of the clock.

Chapter 32
Meeting number 70

Dorothy found herself on a hillside, looking down over a beautiful valley. It looked like home, but when she looked again, she realised it was not quite the same. There were houses, but they were bigger and in the wrong places. She felt confused and shook her head, trying to remember.

"It was dark, it was late. We were on the train. Why am I here?" her voice rose. "Where is Dawn?"

"She will be here in a moment. I wanted to talk to you first."

"Jotin!" said Dorothy straight away, then stopped; a puzzled look came over her face. "Why do I know your name? Who are you?"

"You know me. You have forgotten for a moment, because you have come home so suddenly. But I am always with you, always have been with you."

"Are you God?"

"No."

"Are you Jesus? You do not look like Him."

"No, I am not Jesus, though we are often mistaken for him."

"Who is 'we'?" Dorothy looked around at the empty landscape.

"Me and the other guides. You humans have one each. Come, you need to rest and learn to remember." He led her to a waterfall and handed her over to a woman with a soft face, who encouraged Dorothy to sit under the gentle water and sang softly to her.

Mohmi arrived with Dawn, who was dancing around her guide and laughing.

"I did what you said, didn't I, Mohmi? I yelled. It was hard work, all that yelling. But I heard you, even in that little body and I yelled as hard as I could."

"Yes, you did. Every time I hope you will always hear me, but when you grow up you always go deaf. It is fun for the first months, but so difficult when you cannot talk their language."

211

"Why?"

"Because if you could you would not be back here so soon. You would be in Dundee getting ready for your first Hogmanay."

"Would I have liked that better than being here?" Dawn danced around Mohmi, waving her arms.

"Maybe not, but you would not have to go back again, like you must now."

Dawn stopped dancing and sat down at Mohmi's feet. Her energies stilled and she grew pensive. After a long time, she spoke.

"I remember now. I was the baby again. What went wrong?"

"The train you and your mother were on fell into the sea."

"Where is my mother?"

"Coming now, see?" Dorothy was walking towards them and the cleansing waterfall was fading into the surrounding scenery now that it was no longer needed. As Dorothy approached she saw Dawn and broke into a run.

"Oh, Dawn, how wonderful that you are here, safe. Haven't you turned into a beautiful woman! But I failed, again. I didn't bring you up." She paused. "It was interesting, being your mother for a change. How did it seem to you? Where is your father?" she looked around in increasing panic.

"He is not here, Dorothy," said Jotin. "This time he did not die. He is in Dundee, grieving for you. We tried to stop you, Dawn cried, but you did not listen."

"I must go to him, see if I can help him. Can I?"

"Yes, of course. Come."

Dawn and Mohmi sat together and discussed the events and what could be done next, until Dorothy got back.

"Did you get through to him?" Dawn asked.

"Not really. When we have bodies we are all so sure there are no spirits or ghosts. So he cannot hear me, because to him, I am gone. Rose felt me a little and is encouraging him to finish the Noah's Ark. That is a good idea, it will keep his hands busy. Maybe for a moment or two he will think we are still alive."

"Maybe if I go?" suggested Dawn, "when he has finished the ark. I will go and admire it and be happy, then maybe he will feel me."

"A good idea," said Mohmi, "but now, come, we have to decide what to do next. So do you, Jotin."

Chapter 33

"Mrs Milne, wake up, they have found someone off the train!" Lewis was flushed and excited, barely able to stay still enough to hear Rose's voice on the other side of the thin door. "Will you be ready to come with me?"

Rose opened the door and looked out, holding a wrap around her. "Yes, I will come, but I think we should be careful not to upset ourselves by hoping. Is it a live person they have found?"

"It is a woman. It might be Dorothy."

"It might." Rose closed the door gently and Lewis sat down to wait. He had not slept much, on the rug in front of the fire, and when he had his sleep had been filled with scraps of dreams, of trains, wind and crying. He put his head in his hands and wondered how long he could bear to feel like this, so at sea, so alone.

You are not alone. I wish I could make you hear me. You have time to pass now without Dorothy, but you will see her again. Keep making the Ark, keep your hands busy and your skills sharp. Trynor *moved over to the table and blew on the half-made carving.* Some sawdust rose into the air. Lewis looked up and stretched out his hand to the little figure. It will need a bull, he thought, I cannot leave the cow half made and alone. And then maybe there will be a calf. How long was the ark at sea? Was there time on it to grow a calf? I must read more carefully and find out. Lewis smiled at his idea and was still smiling when Rose came out of the inner room, where she had spent the night in the bed.

"It is nice to see a smile, Lewis. I must confess I do not feel much like it myself. Is there a happy thought you can share?" Lewis explained about the calf and Rose did smile a little, remarking that it was wonderful how the mind went on thinking of little things even when it seemed that the big worry was so huge there would never be space for anything else.

Down at the shore they joined hundreds of people jostling and calling out. Eventually news filtered back to them. The woman found was not alive and was older, definitely not Dorothy. A search operation was being got under way, divers were coming to help.

"I must get home, Lewis," said Rose, turning towards the dock, "send a letter if they find her and I will come to help. I pray that they are found."

After seeing Rose onto a ferry, Lewis walked slowly back up the gentle hill towards his home. Pray, he thought, that is a good idea. I should pray that she swam ashore and was able to keep hold of the baby. Or that their bodies will be found. Or that I will die soon and not have to put up with this any longer. I will go to the kirk and say a prayer. St Mary's church was just in front of him and he went to the door, but it was shut. He turned away and tried St Paul's further along, but it also was closed. He felt desperate, that God was turning him away, after stealing his wife. Then he saw St. Andrew's Cathedral and took a breath. I must say a prayer, he said, under his breath, as he watched himself walk up the steps.

"You did what?" asked Neil later, when Lewis was confessing his strange compulsion, "You went into the Roman Church? Why?"

"I do not know." Lewis shook his head slowly.

"In his confusion he thought he needed to be in a church to say a prayer, some of his other lives' beliefs got through. He forgot the religion here teaches that God can hear you anywhere. But any of us might think we needed a church, if we got that distressed," Trynor was sitting on the table in Lewis's room, swinging his legs. He addressed Lewis: *"Look, we're here, all ears, ready to pass any messages you have. And we can sometimes fix the small things ourselves. Actually, we fix a good deal you don't even ask about."*

"What was it like?" Neil was captivated.

"Like a theatre. Very decorated, fancy, with gold, you know. And the seats sloped a bit, so if you are at the back, you can still see. Lots to look at, pictures, statues."

"Statues? Idols?" Neil wanted to know more.

"Oh, I do not know, Neil. Go and look. I was so surprised I forgot to say any prayers."

"Just as well, you do not want idols to be hearing you."

"Pity. If you had sat down and been quiet for a moment you might have felt me there." Trynor was quiet. *"What do you suggest, Roki? How do you get through to Neil?"*

"Once he heard me, when he was fishing. Of course he does not know it was me, but that is not important. He acted on my advice. And very good advice it was, too."

"Only once? Never in the kirk?"

"No. They talk too much in there."

214

"Isn't that true?" Trynor laughed. "But once or twice I have worked with the guides of priests and they have encouraged the priests to say things that were useful to my people. Hard work though," he sighed. "Maybe I will bring him on a quiet walk."

"Get him back to work," said Roki.

"Are you coming back to work?" asked Neil, "I'm keeping your place open for you."

"What do you mean?" asked Lewis listlessly, his mind beginning to dwell on the possible chances of finding Dorothy by walking the shores of the Firth.

"What I said. I'm doing your work, one of the lads is doing mine. Anyone can be a stoker. Takes brains to be a smith." Neil smirked, hitting his fists together, "tap, tap!"

"But you are not a smith. You are a farm worker turned stoker. You have no papers."

"The foreman did not seem to mind. I said I could do it and so I can. I have been watching you for more than a year."

"I watched my master for seven years and he watched me. It takes care and practice to be a smith. I will come back tomorrow, before you hurt yourself. I will have to trust that someone else will find my Dorothy."

"I will tell them to expect you. Tap tap!" Neil was gone, leaping down the stairs, singing in his off-key voice.

It was a week before another body was found, but then over the next few days, many, mostly men, were brought ashore and funeral services were held in the waiting rooms at the station where they should have arrived tired and happy after their journeys. Lewis went down to the shore every time he could and the cold seeped deeper into him each time as he began to realise that his wife would probably never be found. He went once to eat the fried potatoes they had enjoyed together, but they were ashes in his mouth and no amount of vinegar could help. It was a waste of a halfpenny, he thought, that I cannot afford now that I am only being paid as a stoker.

"You must fight that, Lewis. You are a skilled man. You wanted to be a smith back in the Médoc and couldn't because you were a woman, but you are a man now. Don't let being a smith go to waste. At least you can enjoy your skills." Trynor had been

involved in this one-sided argument ever since Lewis had gone back to the foundry and discovered that the foreman had given his job to Neil. Lewis had just said 'oh' and looked around him with dead eyes. *"You have to care about yourself, Lewis. That Neil has been making lives difficult for you for a long time. It is time to fight back."*

"I wonder..." Lewis stopped, hoping the people sitting around him on the benches, enjoying their chips, had not heard him talking to himself. I wonder, he thought quietly, why Neil did it. He said it was to keep my job open and it did, for him. How can the foreman have been taken in by him, pretending to be a smith. 'But Mr Martin, why did you not bring your papers with you?', 'Oh, I am sorry Sir, but I left them safe at home in Fife. You know how it is in a rented room, nothing is secure. Will I send for them?' The cheek of him, thought Lewis, taking a risk like that. The foreman had not demanded to see the papers and Neil was settled into Lewis's place. 'You can have another position when one comes available, Mr Lindsay,' the foreman had said to Lewis on his first day back after the accident, 'you have not been reliable this last week. I think it would be easier for you as a stoker for the time being.' Lewis said nothing, but wondered how reliable all the other people whose relatives had drowned had been this week and how it was that anyone in this town had been so untouched by the tragedy as the foreman seemed to be.

"Why have you stolen my job?" Lewis asked Neil, as they left the foundry that evening.

"I have not. I have made a job for myself. I need the money more. You have only yourself to keep, but I have my eye on a bonny lassie who works in the grocer's in the street behind. I will need to buy pretty things for her. You will be fine as a stoker for the next little while and then he will give you another job."

"But you are not a smith, you are not qualified. You will make a mistake."

"No, I will not. You will stop me." Neil was jaunty, his eyes were flashing with mischief.

"And why should I do that?" Lewis was having difficulty keeping his concentration on Neil. He was bewildered. He would have to ask Dorothy how to handle this situation. His eyes overflowed and his attempts to hide his tears were in vain. Neil chuckled.

"Because if you do not, I will tell the boss that you are trying to put out the fire by snivelling onto it!" Neil turned in at the door of a public house. "Come on, I will buy you a drink!"

"No, thank you, Neil. I just want to go home." Lewis trudged the rest of the way to his quiet room with a heavy heart and picked up his knife and the little cow. As he carved, he relaxed and thought of his baby and her gurgly smile. She will love this ark, he thought, as he carefully trimmed the feet of the cow so that it stood sturdily.

Mohmi sat quietly as Dawn paced to and fro, thinking out what to do; remembering when her mother Eloise had died in France; and when they were both killed by the tsunami in Crete. Mohmi glowed with a soft blue light, which she occasionally stretched out to Dawn to soothe or direct her.

"It is so hard, Mohmi. The other times I did not have to wait and watch like this. And Lewis is so sad. He does not know I am safe and that we will be together in an instant."

"It does not feel like an instant when you are in a body. Even those people who are sure they will see each other again feel the pain of a long separation. But most of them are not at all sure. Such a pity they do not remember."

"Have you been a human, Mohmi?"

"Yes, many times. It is hard, when you feel you are on your own in a hard world. But it is hard to be here watching too. Trying to get through to the deaf! It was a bit easier in times gone by, you all heard us a little. But now, they are all so sure they understand the world, they hear nothing."

"Would Lewis hear me, if I went to him?"

"He might. Why don't you try?"

Dawn came into the little room on a June morning. The sun was glinting between the curtains and slanting across the floor and up onto the bed. *She sat on the end of the bed and watched as* Lewis began to wake. *Mohmi was with her, standing in the shadows, waiting.* Lewis stretched and opened his eyes. He looked at the sunlight and reached over to the window, to chuck open the curtain, allowing the warm light to flood into the room.

"Happy birthday, little Dawn," he whispered and shut his eyes.

"He sees me!" said Dawn to Mohmi.

"No, I don't think so. He just remembers. Talk to him."

"Hello Lewis. No. Hello Daddy! I came to help you remember my birthday, but you don't need me for that. But do you remember me? My smile?" She smiled broadly. "Does that look like my baby smile, Mohmi?"

"Not much."

"Oh well. Remember how I used to cry when I woke up first and you could not calm me?"

Lewis stirred. "You were such a quiet baby in the mornings. Smile smile. Like the sunshine in the room."

"Oh dear. Was I wrong?" Dawn looked at Mohmi.

"Yes. It was as Marie-Claire you were bad-tempered first thing. As Dawn you were much better. But it doesn't matter. Stop talking so much and try to touch him with your energies."

Dawn moved closer to Lewis and stroked his forehead. She concentrated hard and tried to get inside his mind, to plant a happy memory there. Lewis got out of bed and went to into the other room to rake up the fire and heat water. Dawn followed and went to the table where the ark was set out.

"Oh, Mohmi, look! How beautiful! All the animals are perfect, so real. Nearly a whole farm. Look at the dogs, I can almost see their tails wagging. And the pigs look muddy. He is skilled, my father."

"Yes, and you are appreciating the gift more than if you had been alive. You would have just chewed them to pieces and been forgiven because you were teething."

"Oh, Lewis, thank you!" Dawn sat down and looked with pleasure at her birthday present, the joy of seeing such skills lighting up her being. Lewis came to the table and looked at the ark with dull eyes.

"I wish you could see your ark, little Dawn. It has kept my hands busy and my mind quiet for half a year. But who is it for? No-one will play with it, now."

"I can't play with it, but I can look at it. I love it. I love it better than the gold amulet in Crete, or the crochet bonnet in France, because you made it for me even though I was not there. But I am here, Daddy. I am here now!"

"I will build a shelf for it. Then I can see it. Maybe I will add more animals. I need to do something interesting."

"Why does he say that, Trynor?" Mohmi asked and Trynor

218

arrived.

"Because no smith's job has come available. I keep telling him to move to another place, but he is stuck. The only thing he seems to have energy to do is carve these animals and go to eat fried potatoes. When I see the way those simple chips are keeping Lewis alive and connected, I really think I must experience food again."

"Again? I thought you said you had not had a body?"

"No, I did, once. A long time ago. They sacrificed me to their god before I was three years old. The world seems a bit kinder now. At least child sacrifice is no longer sanctioned, so maybe I will risk it. I will ask for somewhere with really interesting food, so I do not have to go back again! I am not brave."

"Do you remember food?" Dawn was intrigued.

"I think I remember honey. It used to be put on our bread, or porridge." Trynor stopped and indicated Lewis with his head, "Look- he is hearing me a little!" Lewis reached a jar of honey down from the shelf and trickled some over a slice of bread. "But he hears unimportant things like why not have honey, but not the tough stuff like why not get another job. It is such hard work, trying to get through."

"I think he hears you, Trynor," Dawn was kneeling with her eyes at the level of the table, admiring her wooden animals. "I just think he ignores you when it is difficult to do what you say. It is easy to decide to have honey. Getting a new job is hard."

"Yes," said Mohmi, "and it works the other way too. We provide the easy stuff much quicker, don't we? After all, 'Please let there not be a queue ahead of me at the post office' is so much easier to manage than 'Please let the man who is making my life a misery drop dead of something painful!'

Chapter 34
January 1884

Lewis was sitting by the fire, holding a small lump of wood, turning it this way and that, feeling for knots, wondering about the grain. He had finished the second badger just before Christmas and had carved nothing for over a week now. It was bad planning, he thought, to have had empty hands over the New Year. I thought more of them as result. But it was good to have the badgers ready for Christmas. I wonder what this wood will make, it is a good solid piece. It needs a big animal.

He heard familiar boots clumping up the stairs and moments later Neil's cheerful face poked round the door, followed by a smaller replica. Little William ran across the room and held up his arms.

"Hup knee, Unc Lewis?"

"Of course. Hup you come." Lewis breathed in the sweet smell of the child's hair and hugged him close. "And how is your little sister?"

"Sleep." William was unimpressed by babies. "More animal?"

"Yes, another animal. What would you like?"

"We came to tell you," Neil cut in, "They have found the Tay whale, floating north of here. They could not catch it, but they injured it enough to kill it, it seems. It is being towed ashore."

Lewis fingered his lump of wood again and felt a shiver of excitement. "Will we go to see it? If it is ashore. I am not going out to sea."

"Big wale," William held his hands apart as far as he could, "big fish. Make wale, Unc Lewis!"

"Two whales, for a Noah's Ark," said Neil, looking proudly at his son

"No, I do not need to make two, Noah did not have to save the swimming things. But we could have one whale, swimming beside the ark. I will make a whale for Dawn's fifth birthday."

"Oh, Lewis. Can you not let it go? Dawn does not have a birthday. Go and find a woman and have another Dawn. Or make toys for William. He loves you."

"And I love him. How could I not? Of course I will make him something, when he is older. I must keep my hands busy."

"Well, will we go and see this whale?"

So on the next Sunday, Lewis joined Neil with his wife Margaret, baby Isabelle and a very excited William, to make the short train journey to where the whale was on show. It was sixpence each to see it and Lewis hesitated.

"Come on, man, not to worry. I will pay for us all. I can afford it, after being promoted!" Neil was expansive, enjoying the moment. He flung an arm around Margaret and kissed her.

"Neil! Not here!" Margaret was embarrassed. Neil fished a florin out of his pocket and handed it to the ticket seller with a flourish.

"Three, please. I am treating my wife and my staff!" It was Lewis's turn to be embarrassed and he turned away, to hide his expression from the others. 'His staff!' How dare he, Lewis thought, as they shuffled forwards towards the whale enclosure.

"Yes," said Trynor, "he is rather overstating his case. But he is the foreman now, you cannot deny it. You will be working for him. You should leave and get another job. Show your papers to a new boss, one who has not seen Neil's forgery and believed he was your friend. Come to think of it, you should get a new friend."

Of course, thought Lewis, he is my friend. He did not have to pay for me; it could have cost me twelve portions of chips just to see this lump of rotting whale. He is a good man.

"No, he is not."

He persuaded the boss to keep me on after Dorothy died. I could have lost my job.

"He took your job. You only got his."

A job is a job. I only need something to get up for. To take my mind off my girls.

"It has been three years, now. You could do more. What about your skills? Don't waste them just making these animals."

Making the animals has been good. I wonder how this whale will turn out?

"Lewis, you just aren't listening! And when you do hear me, you get it all wrong. How can I help you if you don't listen?"

"Listen!" Lewis held up his finger, and cocked his head to the side.

"Shhh!" said William, holding his pudgy finger in front of his mouth.

"Listen to what, Lewis? I can only hear the crowd talking," Margaret was looking up at Lewis, a puzzled look on her usually smooth face. Lewis stopped and smiled down at her.

"I do not know, Margaret. I thought for a moment I heard something important. Just my mind playing tricks again," Lewis pulled his scarf higher and lowered his face, partly hiding himself from the others' curious looks.

"Oh Lewis," Trynor's voice was soft but full of frustration.

"Never listens, does he?" Roki was laughing. "They don't, mostly. Makes the job easier, in a way."

"How?"

"Well, if you know they won't listen, you don't have to bother exhausting yourself trying. They misunderstand, so say nothing. Just watch. My Neil is doing all right without my opinion."

"And is it your opinion that it is right to lie and steal Lewis's job by fraud?"

"No, of course not. But he will learn that in time."

"At the moment he is learning that dishonesty pays. Lewis is too sad to fight back."

"When I see him face to face, I will tell him. As will his teachers. He will know, anyway. He will just need to be reminded."

"Would it not be better to learn now? What if the manager finds out what he has done?"

"He might. We will see."

"Really hands-off, aren't you? Just allow anything to happen and watch. Call yourself a guide?" Trynor turned away. Roki walked on with the little family, pulling faces at William and pretending to wrestle with William's guide. William laughed.

"What is funny, pet?" Margaret asked.

"Oki fighting! Oki bad!"

"Who?" Margaret was interested, but the baby gave a little wail and the business of tucking the shawls tighter and settling her daughter more firmly in the crook of her arm distracted her, so the moment passed.

The whale was satisfactorily huge, its teeth could be seen and wondered at and children could stand in its mouth. Lewis took out his notebook and made sketches, holding his pencil out and

223

squinting at it as he recorded the proportions of the whale. He studied the tail and climbed up to see the blowhole. He felt the skin and looked closely at the teeth and eyes.

"This is so much better than working from a picture. The books in the library are good, but from now on I must try to see the animals I carve. It was easier with the first ones, the cows and horses, I was so used to them. The badgers were hard, I only once caught a glimpse of a badger."

"Yes," Neil said, "Your cows are very good. And the dogs and cats. Just like real. Be careful you do not carve a dead whale by copying too faithfully."

"You are right. I must see the animals alive." Lewis was thoughtful for a moment. "I know, I'll save up and one day I will go to the zoological garden in London."

"Why not just go to the circus, when it comes to Dundee?" sneered Neil.

Chapter 35
Cupar, Fifeshire, Scotland 1909

"Mohmi?" called Dawn, *"Can you come and help me again, please? I am going to see Lewis. It is that time of year, he is sad again."*

"Certainly. Let's see what we can do this time. You are learning a bit, maybe one day you will reach him." They flew in an instant to Lewis's little house, on the outskirts of Cupar. It was June, a bright evening, with the sun glancing in through the windows and lighting up the table. There was a large wooden Noah's Ark on the table and Lewis was setting out animals in pairs, in a long line snaking to and fro, queuing them up to gain entrance to the ark. A large wooden whale, worn smooth by years of handling, swam at the bow of the ark as though guiding it. Lewis handled the little animals delicately, looking with love at each one as he unwrapped it from its tissue paper and set it up in the line. He hummed to himself as he arranged his handiwork and occasionally spoke to the empty room.

"I will have to stop this soon, Dawn. I am running out of animals. Look, the newest ones have a branch to hang from. They live in South America and they move slowly. Like me these days." He hung two wooden sloths on the branch of a carved wooden tree and placed it at the end of the queue. He sat back beside the table and sighed.

"Happy Birthday, Dawn. Wherever you are."

"I'm here, Daddy. Thank you. The sloths are beautiful. I can see them moving slowly." Dawn put out her hand to the sloths and then towards Lewis. She sent her love as best she could from her hand to Lewis's cheek. Lewis put his hand to his cheek and his eyes widened.

"Dawn?" He looked around the room and straight into Dawn's face. "Dawn, are you here?"

"Yes, Daddy, I'm here. I have been here on all my birthdays and sometimes in between. You don't usually notice."

"Dawn. You came back. Oh Dawn..." Lewis's voice choked and he fell silent. *Dawn wrapped her energy around him and sent a calming wave into his mind. Mohmi stood by and helped, reminding Dawn of the best ways to do this.* Lewis relaxed and looked again at his life's work, his nearly two hundred tiny statues, and smiled.

"I did them for you, Dawn. To keep you with me. But you were not here. Are you really here now?" He looked around the room again. The sunlight slanted in, lighting the animals and showing up dust in the air, which moved occasionally as the summer breeze wafted through the room.

"Which is your favourite animal, Dawn?" Lewis stared at the table.

"Oh, Mohmi, Trynor, help!" Dawn was agitated. "I have to show him, to help him believe. How will I show him I always loved the whale?"

"You can't," Mohmi was brusque. "We cannot move the whale, or get the light onto it. You will have to fib. Come on, if we join forces, we can use the wind and blow something over." They stood together and when the next soft gust came in through the open door, they pushed with all their combined skill and one of the two little giraffes toppled and fell. Lewis gasped and picked it up. He looked around, but saw nothing. He stood it on the table and looked at it. I wonder, he thought, was it just the wind that did that? Lewis blew at the giraffe *and on the other side of the table three sets of energy blew back, as hard as they could.* The giraffe did not move.

"So this was your favourite then, Dawn? You were seven when I did this, copied it from a picture in the encyclopaedia. I'm not sure how good it is. When I get to London I will check. I have the money, but now when will I find the time? My elephants are accurate, I saw several at circuses. I'm glad you like the giraffe, I thought you would like the long neck. I suppose you did!"

"I do now, Daddy. I love it the most now, because it has helped me make you notice me. I hope you can live your life more peacefully, now that you know I am always here. And Dorothy is too."

There was a knock at the open door and the Reverend Reid stepped in.

"Evening, Mr Lindsay. My word, that is some Ark! Where did you get it?"

"I made it. For my daughter."

"I did not know you have a daughter. I thought you were a single man."

"I was married. My wife and child died. The Tay Bridge."

"I am sorry to hear it. How old was your daughter?"

"Six months. I have been making it ever since. It is her thirtieth birthday today."

"You have spent thirty years making a toy? For a dead child?" The minister was politely puzzled.

"It kept her alive for me. It helped me go on, when I had lost everything."

"You did not remarry?"

"No. I never noticed another woman, after Dorothy."

"Where are you from originally, Mr Lindsay?"

"From here, Minister. From Cupar. I lived in Dundee a long time. I was apprentice to old Mr McIntyre before I left. He taught me to shoe a horse, to work metal, everything I know. He left me his business. Had I known that, I would have come back and learnt the new ways with him. He used to keep hay for the horses, now I keep petrol for their replacements. These motor cars are a big change; I am having to learn a great deal."

"Where are your wife and daughter buried?"

"They were never found. They have no memorial, except this ark. There was a fund set up to help the dependants of the victims; I went to a concert in aid of it. It was lovely music, for me it was my Dorothy's funeral, she had no other. I always wished they would put up a memorial, but they never did." Lewis wiped a quiet tear from the corner of his eye, hoping the minister would not see. *The minister's guide, who had been standing quietly, watched Lewis and leant over to whisper in Reverend Reid's ear..* The minister straightened up and cleared his throat.

"Why not come on Sunday, and show the Sunday School children your Ark, and tell them about the little girl it was made for?" He broke off abruptly and coughed, looking around as though wondering what he had just said.

"Oh, what a lovely idea!" Dawn thanked the minister's guide. "I think he will like that and it will help. I would like to be there."

"Thank you. I would like to do that. And I think my daughter will come with me."

"What nonsense. You have just told me she is dead."

"Yes, she is, but she is here. Or at least, she was a little while ago." Lewis explained about his musings and the fall of the giraffe. "So it was her favourite. I will tell the children."

"You will do no such thing. I will not have their heads filled with fanciful nonsense!"

"Unless you tell it to them yourself," said Trynor; the minister's guide nodded in agreement.

"Well, I could tell them the story, say I imagine she was here and that it is comforting."

"She is with God. That is what you will say." The minister was stern.

"All right." Lewis wilted a little and looked at the minister. "Why did you call, Mr Reid? Can I help you in some other way?"

"A long story about a hinge to his gate. Concentrate, Lewis, it is good business. Then listen to us again." Trynor stood back and waited.

"I'm sorry I couldn't manage better," the minister's guide was contrite, "but he only occasionally hears me at all. It was really only because I mentioned Sunday school that he switched on. He is full of firm ideas that are very hard to shift."

"It is all right. Lewis will enjoy meeting the children and seeing them play with the ark. It is a long time since children saw it, since he stood up to Neil. Neil was so annoyed, he stopped bringing William and Isabelle to visit. Isabelle loved the ark, particularly the elephants."

"I watched them, once, playing with my ark," Dawn chipped in, "it was fun to lend it to them. They were lovely natural children. And for years William saw the guides. His mother thought he had imaginary friends and indulged him. It was amusing. I wonder where they are now. They grew up, I suppose."

"It is common, I believe," Mohmi was grinning at Dawn.

"Ha Ha Ha. You wouldn't guess it from watching me when this set of parents try to rear me." Dawn was smiling, too. "Mind you, I have been adult many times with other parents and that isn't easy either. Dying at six months old is a doddle in comparison to some lessons I have had to slog through. Particularly the death in the train, when I was out cold and felt nothing. Well organised."

"Thanks. We aim to please." Mohmi was laughing now.

"Sh, listen." Trynor silenced them.

"So you will come on Sunday? And do come back with me for tea after showing the ark. My wife makes a good cake."

"Thank you, Mr Reid, I will enjoy that." Lewis showed the minister out and sat down to look again at his animals.

"Tempted by cake. Always the same, kept going by food. I wonder how you would react if you ever tasted a proper French paté! Would you guess that it was what you had been searching for?" Trynor turned to Mohmi, *"What do you think? What is this about food?"*

"I don't think it is any more special than anything else they carry forward from life to life, really. I mean, you told me he would not challenge Neil for years because he was afraid of being killed again, even though it was accidental. It is just that you notice his interest in food, because you don't remember much in the way of sensory pleasures."

"No. But you're right, I do remember being killed. I have no desire to do that again, but it's always a risk."

"So, Dawn, will I risk bringing the ark to the Sunday school? Will it survive all those children? What harm if it does not, I suppose. It should have been loved to sawdust by now."

Lewis was in the garage, as he was learning to call the forge, with the bonnet of the doctor's car up and his head under it, trying to see what the problem was with the engine, when a familiar voice called out from the doorway. He straightened up suddenly in surprise. He rubbed his head where it had hit hard metal and squinted towards the door, where a silhouette was outlined by the warm autumn sun.

"Neil?"

"Yes, of course, can you not tell?"

"I can tell your voice. Hold on a minute till I wipe my hands." Lewis found a piece of damp rag and wiped off most of the oil and grease. He held out a hand to Neil, who shook it firmly. "What brings you here?"

"I'll come straight to the point. The foundry closed." Neil shuffled his feet.

"A pity for you. You were well set up there. So where are you working now?"

"Nowhere. You see, I made a mistake and some girders we made were faulty, and..."

229

"Did anyone die?"

"Oh no, not as bad as that. It was discovered in time, but the customers lost confidence and orders were cancelled and, well: I was sacked before they closed. No one will hire me now, they have all heard."

"Apart from the fact that you had no proper papers, you mean?" Lewis was angry with Neil for working in a job he was unable for and angrier at himself for helping him to do it for so long. "I should never have let you away with that. I should never have given you advice all those times you called with questions to bail you out of a difficulty. I suppose you got into trouble because I had left Dundee?"

"Yes. If you could have put me right..."

"I put you right too often. And got nothing for it. You even stopped me seeing your children to punish me for moving to another factory. I should have given you the wrong advice the first time. I was a fool."

"You were grieving. You were a great help to me and to Margaret and the children of course. She sends her love and says she hopes to see you soon. Of course, when the children visit, you will see them and my grandchildren. They are lovely, but a bit of a crowd if they all come at once."

"I am sorry, but why will I see your children when they visit you? Not that I would not love to, of course."

"Well, we will be in Cupar again, or maybe out the road a bit. My cousin.."

"Why Cupar?"

"Well, I am hoping you can find space for me in your new repair shop. These motor cars are getting very popular, I hear."

Lewis went pale. He stood quite still and looked at Neil, whose cheerful ruddy face looked back at him, smiling. Lewis opened his mouth to answer, but nothing came out. He shut it again and stared. At last he found some of his voice.

"I am surprised, Neil."

"Surprised? You are shocked to your core. Tell him so." Trynor was shaking his head at Roki, who raised his hands out from his hips in a 'what can I do?' gesture and stayed silent.

"You stole my job when I was grieving. You came asking for my help every time it was too difficult for you, you practically forbade me to see your children once I stood up to you, when you knew seeing them was keeping me sane and now you have the gall to come and ask me to employ you, when you are known in Dundee as a fraud and dangerous?" Lewis broke off, winded.

"Think about it, Lewis. I will not ask you to make up your mind today. I will call again tomorrow." Neil turned on his heel and stalked out of the workshop. Lewis leant against the doctor's car, feeling as though he had just run a mile. He wondered what he could do. It is not fair of him to ask me such a thing, he thought. He would take over here as he took my place in Dundee. But I cannot let him starve. He must work.

"Not for you. He can go back to the farms. He has plenty of cousins and nephews with land to work."

And poor Margaret. She must be distraught. I cannot see her with nothing.

"Poor Margaret knew her husband was lying and using you. She could have stopped him. Do what is right for you, my Lewis, not what you imagine is right for the Martins."

It is wrong to be so weak and let Neil ride roughshod over me again. But it is unchristian to see him and his wife hungry.

"Come on, send his karma back to him now, or you'll have to do it again in the future, maybe in your next lives. Get it over with." Trynor was getting exasperated. Lewis stood up.

"I cannot decide. Maybe if I tidy the garage, things will come clear." He moved around for a while, picking up tools and returning them to their places on the wall. As he reached out to hang the heavy wrench on its peg, he felt a sudden pressure in his chest and his breath caught in his throat. He grabbed for the worktop, but missed and watched his hands blur as he fell to the floor.

"Well, that's one way of avoiding the decision, I suppose," said Trynor, as he went to warn the others that Lewis would be coming.

Chapter 36
Meeting number Seventy-one

Lewis lifted slowly away from his body, looking at it sprawled on the ground. He put a hand on his chest, relieved to find that there was no pain. His arms felt normal and when he looked at his hands, they were clean, not a trace of oil remained. His head felt clear. He looked around the workshop and felt a regret that he had not moved back here sooner. Only two years my own master, he thought. I should never have stayed in Dundee, even with the new factory. And now no one of my own to leave this to. That apprentice is a good lad, but too interested in motor cars. Not enough attention paid to the skilled work. I wonder where he is?

A boy of about eighteen ran into the workshop, calling out "Mr Lindsay? Did you call? I heard voices." He stopped short when he saw Lewis lying on the ground.

"Oh, my goodness, are you all right? Mr Lindsay?" He knelt beside Lewis and watched his chest intently.

"I am perfectly all right, silly boy. Just not breathing. Now, tidy me up and get on with that repair for Dr Stewart. He has to drive his motor to Glasgow tomorrow."

"Help, Help!" the boy was running to the door, "Something has happened to Mr Lindsay!"

"Oh, dear, do I have to sort this out as well?" Lewis stopped to think. "But I cannot, because I am lying there, yet I am here and can change nothing. I think I will leave him to it. He likes me well enough, but he does not love me, so he will be well able to manage."

"Of course he will, Daddy."

"Oh, hello Dawn, how did you know—" Lewis stopped short, "Dawn!! Oh, my Dawn, you beautiful girl, you came for me?"

"Yes. I came every year."

"I thought so, recently. Did you see your ark?"

"Yes. It is beautiful."

233

"Would you like to see it again? It is on a shelf, we will be able to see it easily. Am I allowed to do frivolous things when I have just died, or is St Peter waiting impatiently for me?" He winked at Dawn, who giggled.

"You believed that sort of thing, an hour ago," she said.

"Yes. It was easier, believing something. It stopped me worrying about the possibilities all the time. I was reasonably sure I qualified for Heaven. Some people really suffer imagining hellfire. Neil, maybe. Though I don't know if he really has much conscience this time."

"Oh, look, it really is beautiful. And my favourite whale out in front, showing the way." They had arrived at the house and were hovering at the level of the shelf.

"Your favourite whale? I thought your favourite was the giraffe?"

"No, it was just the one we could move. But it worked for you, didn't it?"

Lewis threw his arms round Dawn and hugged her tight. "Yes, it did, my pet. You did well. I am donating the Ark to the children's hospital, with a little plaque in your memory. It is there, behind the animals." Dawn moved over and read the brass plaque. Her eyes glistened.

"Oh, Lewis, I'm so sorry you had to go through all that all alone. I did try to stop Dorothy getting on the train, but she didn't understand me, even though I cried like anything. Next time, we must try to get it right."

"Do you want to try again? We haven't been particularly good parents so far."

"Of course. It hasn't been your fault and I'd love to see you both together for a full life. You deserve to have a long time together, after all that's happened. Come on now, the others are waiting."

"There's Trynor!" Lewis broke into a run and Trynor held out his arms.

Dorothy and Lewis were sitting on a marble bench in a sunny courtyard, vines and bougainvillea trailed over the walls above them, a hot sun beat down. They were talking intently, filling each other in on the thirty two years they had spent apart, catching up with news of those still on the earth and those in spirit. They sat close, occasionally stretching out their energies to interlink, or to remind each other of fun times they had had in their bodies.

"And what did you think of being a woman?" Lewis looked suggestively at Dorothy and she laughed.

"You forget, I have been a woman many times."

"All right then, what did you think of being my woman?"

"Actually, being your woman was fine. Being a woman in that society was not particularly easy. Everything had to be so polite, so well behaved. It was stultifying at times. And hard work."

"Yes, hard work – like being a peasant a hundred years earlier. I worked hard then and got no respect. Crete was easier, at least in the body." Lewis stopped, remembering Eloise and Alessia and how it had felt in those bodies. "Rasifi was just as skilled as when she was Rosemarie, but less relaxed about it. And as Rose she was comfortable- got you through Dawn's birth well, didn't she?"

"Yes. Lovely having her as my mother, you usually get that honour."

"No, never my mother. Just a mother figure."

"Pedant!" Dorothy found some of her Danthys energy and pulsed it out towards Lewis/Alessia, who responded with a coil of energy in return. The two strands of energy met, the colours scintillated and the two energy beings that were the souls of Dorothy and Lewis twined together, rising higher, moving in and out, twisting around, chasing each other to the ground, taking it in turns to surround and be surrounded. A musical note hummed from the centre of their mixed energies and harmonics joined it, so that the note became a perfect 'ohm' as they melded and parted and came together again, their energies vibrating faster and faster, the pitch of the note rising and expanding so that the music filled the courtyard and spilled over, rustling the plants that were hanging on the walls. Their colours shone brightly, pulsed in circles, squares and spirals, coming and going and changing and growing brighter, so that the whole courtyard glowed, as though with an inner sun. Then slowly the glow dimmed and the music faded and the two energies settled and parted, just enough that they could sit again side by side on the bench and laugh together.

"We could never do that in Scotland!" Lewis said with a mischievous grin at Dorothy.

"Nor in Crete, be fair."

"No, nowhere on the Earth. But the food tastes better there than the imitations we can make here."

"Yes, I suppose there must be some compensation for taking a life," Dorothy was wistful for a moment. "I watched you eating all those fried potatoes and envied you at times."

"They killed me in the end," Lewis paused and then said very firmly "so I love fried potatoes!" They laughed.

Trynor and Jotin were watching from the doorway.

"I thought we would find you two somewhere warm and sunny. Reliving some long ago lives, were you?"

"And connecting properly again. We have been apart a long time by earth standards. Harder for Lewis than for me."

"You were making beautiful music. We enjoyed the concert."

Lewis was beginning to look apprehensive. He clutched at Dorothy's hand and gripped it. When he spoke, it was very quietly.

"Have you come to tell us we have to leave again? So soon? I don't think I can face it just yet. It was so lonely there, all on my own. Of course, I had brothers and sisters and some friends, but no one who was special. None of my soul friends were there." He fell silent and looked at his feet.

"No," Trynor said, sitting down beside Lewis, lengthening the bench so that they would not feel crowded. "No, it will be a while before we are ready for you to go to Earth again. That is what I have come to tell you. I am going to take a body and it will need a lot of my energy, as it is only the second I have ever had." He sat back, looking a bit surprised at his own disclosure.

"Why do you need to do that? You are so wise already." Lewis looked at his guide with a worried face. "If you need a life, what hope is there for all of us? We'll be going back and back for eternity!"

"Well, I don't exactly 'need' to take a life, though I will build in some learning while I am there to justify my ticket, but I really want to taste all that food you have been waving under my nose for the past two hundred years. Those patés, the cheese, the wine,"

"Oh yes," said Lewis and Dorothy, their faces lighting up, "and the soft bread and the stews and the herbs..."

"And then the chips!" said Trynor, "You were very keen on the chips. Maybe I will take a life in Belgium, where that chip seller came from. Or maybe France. Somewhere with interesting food; I am doing research. And when I am finished, then you can have a life together again and raise Moonsong. Planidi is still grumbling about it. Her guide threatened to send her for partial remodelling if she didn't stop worrying about earthly things, so she does try. It seems difficult for her. You all need to make a bigger effort to get rid of your fears."

"And Dorothy, you need to learn not to let other people's disapproval sway you so much. You need to learn to follow your inner voice more."

"You mean you!" said Dorothy.

"Not always. You have good ideas of your own, too. Of course, when I hear you having one, I try to make it louder for you, but it doesn't always work. You can all be very cussed sometimes."

"So, can I hang out here with Dorothy and have some interesting classes, while we wait for you?" Lewis was holding Dorothy's hand tightly.

"Well, you can spend a little of the time together. But you do have individual stuff to work on, too. So you won't be in each other's arms the whole time. You can have as long as you want now and then Jotin will supervise while I'm away."

"Trynor, who is going to guide you while you have a body?" Lewis was curious. "Do you need a guide?"

"Yes, I'll have someone, don't worry."

"I hope you'll hear her," said Lewis.

Chapter 37
Dublin, summer 1983

"Should be easier," said Jotin to Trynor, "now that Lucy's working. All I have to do is get David to sprain something and Bob's your uncle!"

"Yes! Why hadn't I realised? Could have saved all that stress over the past few years. And wondering why she wanted to do physiotherapy. Maybe she knew more than we did."

"I doubt it. Didn't you say it was from when she hurt her ankle at that school Sports Day?"

"Yes, you're right. She enjoyed her visits for treatments then. Got better so soon she thought they were magic," Trynor smiled at the memory. "Good thing, it seems, in the end. So when are you going to push him over?"

"Haha. The tennis season is on, maybe something can be arranged. Leave it with me."

David ran to and fro across the court, fielding the ball as the two girls joined forces at the other side of the net. One and a halfles, they called it, when he played the two of them, and they loved it, declaring that as their ages added up to twenty and he was just thirty three he had an advantage and should be handicapped. This took a different form each time. Today he was playing left-handed. This was Clare's idea, as she was left-handed herself. She and Caroline could never decide whether it was better for her to play on the left, so they could catch the wide shots, or on the right so they had 'good coverage of the centre' as Caroline put it. Either way, they often beat David, who ended their matches out of breath but elated. On this early summer Saturday, the sun was trying to peep from behind some heavy clouds and Herbert Park was looking a little windblown. These winds would be good for sailing, should take it up again, he thought, as he lunged to reach another ball that had just made it over the net. He forgot he was holding the racquet in his left hand and reached out with his right, of course missing the ball entirely.

"Love forty," shouted Clare triumphantly.

"Is it? Are you counting properly?"

"Yes, Daddy, we're winning!"

"Again. I'm no good as a left hander."

"Not when you forget, silly!"

"I'll try harder."

"Or what's the prize? Two Cokes?"

David lobbed the ball over the net and Clare took a turn at serving. The ball came over the net at speed towards David's left and he did remember and put his racquet out, Jotin adjusted the angle of it slightly and the ball caught the frame, jolting the racquet in his hand and sending a sharp pain through his wrist.

"Ow!" David dropped the racquet and held his wrist, rubbing it. "I think I'm finished with being a lefty for today."

"I think we win," said Clare, "how about Cokes now?"

"Ducks first," said Caroline, as they put away their racquets into the bag and gathered up the balls. She was a champion of ducks' rights, declaring that the ducks could not be allowed to starve just because she had got 'too old to feed ducks' as her mother had said. So they crossed the road to the other part of the park and gave the ducks the bread that had been saved for them. David watched his girls, glad they were still able to behave like children, sorry that the baby years were gone and aware that all too soon the childhood years would be over too. He rubbed his wrist and wondered suddenly what it would be like at home when the girls had gone and he was alone with Kathleen. He felt a sudden chill and put it down to the wind that was still whipping across the grass. He called the girls, they waved goodbye to the ducks and ran in front of him towards the shops and the prospect of fizzy drinks.

Kathleen was lying on the couch when they got home, surrounded by travel brochures and a couple of guidebooks. David leant over and kissed her.

"Researching Portugal?" They had booked earlier in the year for a fortnight in the Algarve, a resort with good amusements for children.

"No, that's sorted. I'm looking for something for the autumn."

"What? We haven't even gone on our holiday yet and you're on to the next one? That's ridiculous, Kathleen. We can't afford to go away all the time. And you shouldn't live your life from one trip to the next. Just enjoy today." He sat down in the armchair opposite his wife, and looked at her. "Why not come and play tennis with us? We could play doubles instead of one and a halfles. It's fun with the kids."

"Yea," Kathleen continued flicking through her brochure. "There's a nice autumn break here, to the Italian lakes. We haven't seen those."

"We haven't seen the Great Wall of China, doesn't mean we have to go." David stopped. He knew there was no point, Kathleen was tenacious, would hang onto a holiday idea forever. "Why don't you ring Sandra and see if she'll go with you? She might like Italy."

Kathleen started to cry. "You're horrible. You never want to come with me. You're nasty when we're away and you're mean when we get back. And now you want me to go on my own." The sobs grew louder. *Haliken tried to soothe Kathleen, stroking her and singing gently. Then she turned to Jotin and shrugged. "I'm sorry. I don't seem to be getting anywhere with her. I'll try and work on the Sandra idea, talk to her guide. Then if Kathleen realised her disenchantment while on holidays wasn't because of David, maybe we could move on a bit. What d'you think?"*

"Sounds a good idea." Jotin turned to David. "Come on, out of here."

David pushed himself up out of the chair and gasped. His wrist was sore. He wriggled it experimentally, it hurt. Kathleen paid no attention, her hands were over her face as she cried. David went out to the kitchen to see what needed to be done for dinner.

An hour later, David went up to the girls' room and knocked. He stuck his head round the door and asked the girls to come down and help him with dinner preparations.

"My hand is still sore. I didn't know I needed my left hand so much. I can't hold anything properly. Come on." They followed him down and they did a strange five-handed act, with much laughter. Kathleen came in to see what was happening.

"We're doing one and a halfles dinner!" said Caroline, as she held the handle of the saucepan that David was stirring. "If I don't hold it, it goes round and the sauce will stick. It's called co-operation." She pronounced this very carefully. New words had to be minded and then stored away.

"Another game," said Kathleen, sitting down at the table and running her hand across her eyes, "to steal my children away from me."

"I'm not." David felt cold again. "I'm just making the dinner, but I need help. My hand is sore. You could have helped, but you wouldn't. I asked you."

"You also told me you didn't want to go on holidays with me."

"We're going on holidays, aren't we?" Clare was puzzled, "all of us? To Portugal?"

"Yes, we are. But Daddy doesn't like coming."

"Now, Kathleen, you know that's not true. I love our summer holiday," David was brisk. "Come on, girls. Let's dish up." He still had the spoon in his hand and with the other he picked up the pan from the stove. His wrist gave, hot sauce splashed onto his shoes and all over the floor. The pan rattled into the corner. Both girls giggled, but their mother got up muttering 'now look what you've done' and 'get this mess cleaned up', so they bent their heads and fetched cloths.

"I'm sorry Jotin, that she's being so awful. I'll try to calm her down." Haliken was beside Kathleen, talking gently to her.

"No, it's fine this time. We have a plan. He's going to show Lucy his sprained wrist, then we'll be on the home straight. Trynor is encouraging her to go shopping, to find something flowery she can wear."

"Doesn't she have a uniform?"

Jotin looked stricken. "Oh, yes. Oh well, we'll get them together anyway. It's still best that he sees Kathleen's worst side."

A week later, as Lucy was walking into work, a charity collector rattled his tin at her. *Trynor jumped with surprise and looked over. He nudged Lucy hard.* Lucy stopped and looked at the man. He was holding out a little bunch of flowers to her.

"We're asking for a pound for the flowers, or for less you just get the sticker! It's a good cause…"

"What is it?"

"Who cares what it is. Give him the pound." Trynor turned to the collector's guide. "What brought you here? It's not a good place for collecting, I wouldn't have thought."

"I'm a friend of Jotin's. He told me you need flowers. So I got my guy here. Not too difficult, he hears me sometimes."

242

"One of the few, then. Thanks a lot. We'll owe you one."

"No. I'm repaying Jo. He's helped me out often. You're welcome and the charity gets the money. No losers." He nodded towards the tin and they watched Lucy drop her pound into the slot. She took the flowers.

After changing into her white tunic in the hospital, Lucy pinned the flowers up near her shoulder, hoping they would be allowed. She went into the treatment office and looked at the appointments book. Mr O'Leary, Miss Hutchins, little Emily Nolan..

"A new one at eleven?" she remarked to the secretary, Fiona.

"Yes, his letter is here."

Lucy scanned the letter. Nothing much, a sprained wrist.

"Nothing too difficult, so. Mr O'L here yet?"

At five minutes to eleven, David came into the reception area and gave his name to the secretary.

"Yes, Mr Hyland, Miss Browne will be ready for you in a few minutes. Take a seat and fill out this form. Can you do it with the bad hand?"

David smiled at her. He was feeling inexplicably cheerful this morning. "No problem, it's the other hand."

"Oh, that was lucky!" Fiona started typing again.

"Cheerful, for a very good reason. Because I have been telling you all day, since you opened your eyes, that today is the day. That's why you have your best tie on, that brings out the blue in your eyes. And why you shined your shoes. You're looking good and we are going to win the girl today. And have the baby, well, not today, but we're on our way! There's a song for this," and Jotin began to sing, *"Oh what a beautiful morning!"*

"Oh, what a beautiful morning, oh what a beautiful day...." David sang gently, wondering why he should think that, as the weather was not particularly wonderful this dull day.

"Fiona, who's the gorgeous man in the waiting room?" Joanne, one of Lucy's more senior colleagues, was leaning over Fiona's desk.

"Lucy's eleven o'clock."

"I'll take him. I have a gap. I could do with a good view for a change." Joanne's last patient, the very old and wheezy Mrs Dunphy, was now waddling her way back to the main entrance.

"O.K. All the same to me."

"NO!" Jotin was out of his chair, running towards the desk.

"Tell your people no! This one is meant for Lucy, we've been arranging it for years."

"More my Joanne's age, don't you think?"

"Long story, don't argue. Tell you later. PLEASE!"

"Tell her Lucy was pleased to have a new client." Fiona's guide was leaning over the desk, pointing at the space in the appointment book. Fiona looked down.

"Though I don't know, Joanne. Lucy was pleased to see a new name."

"She won't mind. I'm doing her a favour, really."

"No, Joanne, apparently this one's not for you. There is one waiting, next year. Wait till then."

"It could be next year before I get another decent man. After that bastard Seán dumped me I deserve a break." She picked up the new chart that was waiting on the desk.

"Mr. Hyland? Come this way, please." Joanne led the way to one of the little treatment rooms. David followed, admiring the way her hair curled at the back of her neck and the shape of her bottom. When she smiled at him as they both got into the room, his heart skipped. For a moment he was glad he had hurt his wrist and had had to reschedule the whole day for this appointment.

"Trynor! The other physio has taken him in. We'll have to co-ordinate a meeting in the corridor after his treatment. Get those flowers more prominent, the time for subtlety is over."

Trynor talked rapidly to Lucy and then to the guide of Emily Nolan, whose stiff little legs Lucy was stretching, to prevent the muscles seizing up. Emily reached up and touched the flowers.

"Pretty flowers. Like mam's." Mrs Nolan was wearing a similar bunch, right on the front of her cardigan. "Put here!" Emily pointed imperiously at Lucy's bosom.

"I can't, Emily. I really shouldn't have them on at all. They're out of the way there."

"Pretty here!" She poked Lucy's tunic.

"OK, I'll move them. Just for you, sweetheart." Lucy moved the flowers to the front of her tunic, just beside the zip. "How's that?"

"Nice."

"Thanks. That should do it. Tell your Emily thanks. She's a good one."

"Isn't she? She has them all organised at home, even with her

rudimentary language. 'Our Special Boss' they call her. We have a lot of helping and persuading to do this time, me and Emily."

"What are we going to do?" Trynor wailed. "That was our best chance for ages and we fluffed it." He and Jotin were sitting together in a quiet spot at Home, allowing soft lights and gentle music soothe them after their frustrating day. "I can't even get her to stay in the office and do paperwork until David comes out of his session, no, she trots off and has a longer coffee break. And then you fail abysmally to get him to come for another appointment. It was just awful, watching him walking out of there two minutes before she came back from the canteen and knowing he wouldn't be back."

Jotin lay back on the soft surface under them and looked at the lights. He ran his mind back over the day.

"Yes, we failed badly. David had every right to feel down. That was one of the worst bits, him suddenly feeling so low after being so cheerful and not knowing why."

"Was that after he left?"

"No, it was when Joanne turned around, to start taking his history and he sort of knew it was the wrong woman. I could see his heart sink. He checked for the flowers, I'd told him to and she thought he was looking at her breasts. Would have been funny, if it hadn't been so sad. Joanne tried really hard to get him to notice her. Told him all about Seán and how he's gone. Only thing she didn't ask was if David was married. Didn't want to know."

"She saw his ring, I suppose."

"Hadn't you noticed? He stopped wearing that after Kath accused him of not wanting to go on holidays. He felt if she hadn't noticed that the start of a holiday was the one time they felt together, they didn't have much. I didn't try to discourage him."

"But he'd still have the mark on his finger, takes a while to wear off."

"Maybe. Wouldn't have bothered Lucy."

"No." They lay together, pondering. After a while that older wiser energy filled the space and spoke softly inside their heads.

"You are doing your best. That is all any of us can do. Yes, they are remarkable souls who should be together for a whole life. They are more than the sum of their parts and might even work

245

together in a future life, but if not it does not matter. If the Curies had not been there to work with radioactivity, someone else would have been found. Gilbert and Sullivan could have been replaced and the humans would have been no worse off. Watson and Crick would have discovered DNA alone, though maybe not as quickly. Lucy and David are a wonderful pairing such as these, but just think in terms of simply letting them enjoy that they are so well suited."

"I was hoping they might be able to do something to help the Earth," Jotin ventured.

"We have people and spirits working on that. The Earth is a magnificent creation and it would be a pity if it was lost. But remember, there are other worlds which we can use if we must." The light faded, leaving Trynor and Jotin feeling gently sad, but relieved.

"OK, then. I suppose we just watch and wait. We'll get another chance. Dublin isn't such a huge place."

Jotin chuckled. "Yes, the humans never tire of saying that. But they don't stop to realise how many old friends they never bump into. Always astonished when they meet someone, never astonished they don't. I mean, Ken is still in Dublin, but I don't think David has seen him since the twins arrived."

"No, and Lucy hasn't seen Sally. Though she's in London the last few months, I think. They were both in College at the same time, but no need for any contact, so we didn't arrange any. Imagine the exhaustion if we had to keep them in touch with everyone they had ever known." Trynor leant back again and stretched luxuriously. "I'm going to have a rest. I'm knackered, to borrow a phrase." He closed his eyes.

Chapter 38
March 1984

Lucy's mother Betty Browne put the last plate onto the table at her own place and sat down. She took a deep breath and let it out, looking at her family as they sat waiting for her to start.

"Sorry it's a quick one again," she said, picking up her fork, "I seem to be in a constant rush these days. Understaffed as usual and I have to make sure nothing goes wrong. So you're the ones who suffer."

"It doesn't feel like suffering to me," said her husband Robert. "It looks fine. But I ought to learn to cook, then we could all help out. Why didn't you do it tonight, girls?"

"No ingredients," said Alison, with her mouth full of fish finger. "I can't cook if there's nothing to cook."

"I'm sorry, Mum, I didn't even think of it. I was looking something up. I have an unusual patient." Lucy was miles away still.

"Thinking about Martin again. No time to notice anything else."

"Yes," said Mrs Browne thoughtfully, "Martin. When are we going to meet him? It seems a long time now since you met him."

"She's ashamed of him," crowed Alison, "Doesn't dare let us see him, he's so ugly."

"He isn't," Lucy said mildly. A year ago she would have kicked Alison under the table for teasing her like this. These days she was happy. She had managed to keep Alison away from her rather delectable boyfriend for nearly a year. She had received a huge card for Valentine's Day and was hoping Martin would bring her out for dinner for their anniversary in May. Her new job, though still exhausting, was going well, she had nothing worrying her.

"That's because you are DEAF. I have been at you and at you to give him up, or to bring him home. So I agree with your Mum. Bring him home."

"You can meet him if you want."

"Good. Invite him for dinner on Saturday. Does he eat everything?"

"I think so. He has a sweet tooth. His Mum always makes

desserts."

"Oh, I'll have to compete with that,"

"Please don't."

"Would he like pavlova, do you think?"

So the following Saturday there was a huge pavlova and Martin made many complimentary comments. Alison had admired him hugely when he arrived and sat beside him being winsome, asking him all about himself, so no one else had to say a thing. Martin answered at length, explained carefully how he thought his old College rugby team were doing and how the Irish team was likely to do next season. He told them all about his job, how he had dealt with one of the customers and made a big sale and how he hoped to be sales manager before too long. He told them all about his family and how his mother had been ill last year and his sister was in France for a year, studying; how their dog had recently had mites in its ears. By the time they all moved into the kitchen to have dinner around the big pine table, Alison had fallen silent. Martin was a perfect guest, polite and deferential. He held Lucy's chair out for her and she blushed and thanked him quietly. He passed the dishes to Betty Browne first, then to Lucy, then to Alison.

After he left, not too late, thanking them all again for a perfect evening, the four Brownes sat silent. Lucy watched them all, her heart bursting with pride that he had been so charming and with relief that Alison had not made a play for him. None of the others was looking at her. Her mother's eyes were closed, her father had picked up a paper and was looking at the sports results. Alison was looking at her hands.

"Well? Isn't he lovely?" Lucy was buoyant.

"Oh god Luce, he's so boring." Alison broke the silence.

"Sums it up." Robert turned the page of his paper.

"What?" Lucy was stunned.

"Well, dear," her mother started more gently, "he is very good looking. And very polite. And he's been to Trinity,"

"Yea," said Alison, interrupting, "and he lives on the southside."

"And you tell me he has a good job," Betty continued, ignoring the joke. This time it was Robert who interrupted.

"He told us himself about the good job. At length. I was a salesman once myself. I know how it is. He didn't need to explain it

248

all so carefully."

"So I don't think there's anything actually wrong with him, dear,"

"He's Catholic." Alison's voice broke across her mother's and caused a stillness in the room.

"Hallelujah! I hadn't paid attention to that. We're home clear. Thanks Kumbal, everybody, looks like we've found a get-out clause." Trynor smiled and the other three guides smiled back and relaxed, allowing their energies to flow, after keeping them tight all evening as they tried to control some of what their people were saying. Betty made an effort to relax and be reasonable. She smiled. "Well, I don't think we should hold that against a person, Alison."

"But you don't want us to marry Catholics, do you?" Alison wrinkled her nose at Lucy and stuck out her tongue.

"I would be sad to see my grandchildren grow up in a different culture to mine, that's what I said."

"You're making Martin sound like a Martian..." Lucy was indignant.

"Only takes an A!"

"....but he's not different from us really. And he almost never goes to church."

"Oh dear."

"Does his mother?"

"Yes, Mum, I think so."

"Oh good."

"It'll come out when the chips are down, then. He'll want his children Catholic."

Robert Browne folded his paper and put it down. He looked round at them all, sitting on the edges of their seats and settled himself more comfortably, as though to prove that he was in control.

"I think we should all stop worrying. There isn't going to be a problem, because Lucy isn't going to marry him, are you love? Not because he's Catholic, or a salesman, or a southsider, but because when the rose coloured glasses wear off, she's going to realise he's as boring as hell and her busy mind would freeze over in a nanosecond if she did. So I don't think we need to discuss it. He didn't ask you to marry him, did he, Lucy?"

"No. But Dad, he isn't boring, not to me. He's lovely. Funny, and witty, and charming."

"He flatters you, you mean," said Alison. "I'm awfully glad I learnt the knack of finding my own boyfriends and I'm not dependant on you anymore, if that's the new type you're going for. Philip was far nicer."

"Philip was lovely. But you stole him and now, just 'cos you don't want Martin, you don't want me to have him either. You're all just jealous!" Lucy burst into tears and ran from the room. Robert put out his arm, to stop Betty or Alison from following.

"Leave her alone. It'll blow over."

"He's probably right," said Diljas, Robert's guide, to Trynor, who was heading off after Lucy. "Let her stay with Martin a bit longer, till she gets used to her job and has the energy to look round again. Then you and Jotin can pull out all the stops. But you're acquainted with Roki, it should be easier to work with him on moving Martin on. Could be harder to get her away from a brand new boyfriend just as you're ready to roll. The humans have a saying, 'better the devil you know'."

"The devil you know certainly suits Roki when he's being difficult! I suppose you're probably right. We'll wait and watch. She is really busy studying up on her patients, worrying about them. I think she finds Martin soothing just now. It's good that she's learnt some science, but I'm still wondering why she decided to become a physiotherapist, when she has all that experience as a craftsman. Still work with her hands, but not creative. I didn't encourage it, I'm not sure it'll make her happy."

"She can do the creative stuff as a hobby. They have more leisure time nowadays, can try all sorts of things. Look at Robert, he'd have marquetry all over everything if he was let. But just paperwork at the office."

"I'll go up and get her to sleep. Thanks, Diljas."

Chapter 39

Kathleen flung a magazine onto the table in front of David.

"Explain this!"

A worn copy of Penthouse stared up at him, accusingly and apologetically.

"It's a copy of Penthouse."

"Yes, I know that, you bastard. What is it doing in your drawer? You filthy bastard, looking at all these, these, whores! And you a married man. Meant to be respectable. And I'm meant to be respectable too. How does this make me look? A wife with a husband who looks at filthy pictures. As though you didn't have a woman of your own.!"

"I don't." David's voice was almost inaudible.

"What?"

"I don't have a woman of my own. That's why I have that magazine."

"Fuck you! You have me."

"Do you know how often you let me come near you? Have you counted?"

"Don't be disgusting!"

"Well, I have. Twice, this year. And it's October. That's once every five months. Not enough."

"It is for me."

"Good for you. But not for me. Which is why I own a copy, one single copy, of Penthouse. To help me forget that I have some needs. To release some of the tension of being rejected all the time."

"You mean you're- ugh! I thought you were just looking at the pictures, but you say you're, oh god, I can't even say it, you're..."

"Wanking."

"What? Is that what you call it? That's revolting! How did you expect me to feel about it?"

"I didn't expect you to know about it. I didn't expect you to go delving into the bottom of my drawers and opening the bag I'd hidden there so it wouldn't upset you. I thought I could have some privacy."

"Secrecy, you mean. Married people aren't supposed to have

secrets."

"Who says? I don't remember promising to tell you absolutely everything I ever do or think."

"Well you should."

"I pooed twice yesterday. Used seventeen squares of paper altogether."

"What?" Kathleen stopped pacing up and down the side of the table.

"You suddenly seem to think I should tell you all my private business. So I thought I'd oblige."

"What you do in the bathroom is nothing to do with me."

"Precisely. So my masturbation habits don't concern you either."

"They do. It's sex. It's for me."

"Now you're deluded. How can what I do in private be for you? After you've rejected me yet again? I've counted the number of times I've tried to make love to you and you didn't allow me. I ran out of fingers a long time ago on that one."

Kathleen stopped pacing and looked at David.

"Do I?" she said.

"Of course you do. Is it such a habit you don't even notice? I want to have a normal marriage and you don't. I don't know what you want."

"We do have a marriage. We have two daughters to prove it. And I look after the house for you, and you give me housekeeping money and, and everything."

"Sounds like playing house." David looked up at his wife, wondering where everything had gone so wrong. "Sit down, maybe we can talk." Kathleen pulled out a chair and sat opposite David, picking at her nails and occasionally running her hands through her hair, as she always did when she was unhappy. She glared at David and began to sniff.

"Don't cry. Nothing has happened."

"Yes it has. I've discovered my husband is being unfaithful."

"I have not. I could have been, but I haven't."

"What do you mean, you could have been? Who is she?"

David ran his hand across his eyes and closed them. He let his mind go back to that young receptionist at work, who had flirted with him so delightfully, the time they had had that impromptu party in the office, after landing the big order. They had all been a

252

little giddy after working through most of the duty-free brought by the English supplier and she had begged him to accompany her to a party that weekend. He had wanted to go, oh how he had wanted to go - he had almost succumbed, particularly after she had cornered him in the kitchenette and kissed him, and he had held her bottom for thirty glorious seconds and felt it tighten as he gently squeezed. It had reminded him he was an attractive man, not just a nuisance, as Kathleen seemed to think.

"Oh yes, Davy, you're attractive. She was a nice girl, you should have gone to that party. It would have got you away from Kathleen in time. We could easily have got the girl to move on to someone else and got you to Lucy. But no, you had to refuse her and go and buy that magazine to help you over it. It's a bit ragged, why don't you get a new one?"

"The only thing I have been unfaithful with, Kay, is a copy of Penthouse. And only because you are frigid."

"I am NOT! How dare you?" Kathleen's eyes flashed.

"Well, you are doing a damn good imitation, then. I've tried everything I can to turn you on. But nothing works, unless we go on a holiday, then you're sexy for one day. Hence twice. Two trips this year."

"I might get pregnant."

"I use condoms, always. And so what if you did get pregnant? We can afford another baby."

"The girls are nine. What would people think?"

"I don't care what they think. They'd know we had had sex. That wouldn't be so bad, would it?"

"I can't get pregnant, I just can't." Kathleen started to cry in earnest. *Haliken leant over to Jotin:*

"She's right. She doesn't know why, but she really can't bring herself to have a baby. It wasn't in the original plan."

"You'd think all bets were off on that, we've made such a mess of it. But she doesn't have to get pregnant, does she? There's all sorts of things she could do."

"You'll have to tie a knot in it, if you want to come near me again."

"What?"

"What?"

"You can have a vasectomy."

"No! You have to have the chance..."

"But it's you who doesn't want another baby, not me. Why should I have the surgery?"

"Are you saying you'd have another baby if you could?"

"Well, if you died..."

"Yes! Go on, Haliken, can you work on her dying?" Jotin was getting agitated.

"I thought we went through that. Agreed it's too difficult. But I'm still trying to work on getting her away."

"Oh, if I died, you'd find some floozy the next day and fill her full of all the babies you haven't forced on me. Well, that tells me a lot. You're waiting for me to die. I wish I could, make it all simpler for everyone."

"How right you are." Jotin smiled. "Funny, they think they're being ridiculous, but they're on the button, sometimes."

"No-one wants you to die, don't be ridiculous. We all love you."

"Funny way of showing it," Kathleen flicked at the magazine. "Vasectomy, or forget it." She got up and ran out of the room. Sounds of sobbing could be heard going up the stairs. David sat at the table, his coffee cold beside him and the crumpled magazine looking cold to match. He stroked it, feeling the skin of an old friend. But no part of him responded with the buzz he usually felt when he got it out. She's spoiled it for me, he thought. Even that release is gone now. He sighed and the soft pages riffled. What'll I do? I don't want to prevent another baby, really. I'd like to have another. Why shouldn't we have another? We're only thirty-five, hardly geriatric.

"No, and Lucy's twenty-three. Don't do anything rash. Stall. Go on, put your magazine away safely, you'll be needing it."

There was a buzz in the energy of the room. The lights flickered and David looked up. *Trynor arrived, his energies in disarray, wild points of red and orange light jagging out of him. Jotin got up, startled. He moved over to Trynor and tried to soften the points of energy, to smooth his friend down to a state where it would be worth asking questions. Some of his own energies began to fizz in harmony with Trynor and he struggled to maintain his calm.* The lights went out. David sat for a moment and when nothing happened, got up and began to feel his way towards the cupboard where the candles were kept.

"Come on, friend, calmness now, calmness. Tell me what has you like this and I can help." Jotin continued to move his energies across Trynor's and gradually the colours muted and the jags of light softened. Trynor's mouth opened and shut several times and at last he croaked-

"He proposed. And the idiot girl said yes. Come and look." The two guides flicked out of the room. The lights came back on, just as David was lighting a candle and a voice from upstairs asked 'what have you done to the lights?'

"Nothing. They just went off. Seem okay now."

"Come up. I'm lonely."

I wonder does that mean anything, thought David. Maybe, if I'm positive about the vasectomy idea...He picked up the Penthouse off the table and went over to the bin, but as he was putting his foot on the pedal to open the lid, a thought struck him and he turned. He pulled over a stool, got up on it and slid the magazine onto the top of one of the high cupboards. I'll get it down when everyone's out, he thought and put it back upstairs. Just in case I need my Clothilde-on-page-seventeen again, who knows. This might be a flash in the pan. If anything even happens. He switched off the lights, blew out the candle and headed hopefully for the stairs.

"Look!" Trynor was still upset, but was trying to calm down. Lucy was in Martin's arms, her hands were at the back of his head and a diamond ring was on her finger. They were kissing deeply. Roki was sitting in the other armchair, sprawled out in it, relaxed and amused. Trynor rounded on him.

"How could you? How could you? You're wasting this life. We'll have to start again, yet again."

Jotin was calmer than Trynor. It was a bit easier for him, he thought, he had watched David make this mistake years ago and was more used to it.

"Yes, Roki," Jotin joined in, "They are meant to be together and with Moonsong. She's sitting there at Home waiting for Lucy and David to be ready for her. Just waiting, when she could be getting on with things. And if Lucy and David don't marry this time, she'll have to find something else to do, or another life to live. We could be centuries before we can get all three of them free at the same time."

255

"And this world might even be gone by then," Trynor added, "so we have to hurry."

"Chill, man," said Roki, "look at my guy. He's happy. So is your girl. Doesn't happiness count for anything?"

"It must be guides like you in charge of a lot of humans. Inexperienced souls, not interested in the big picture, with no foresight. Meanwhile the ozone layer thins, the glaciers melt and species become extinct."

"So what is Lucy going to do about that?" Roki's mouth lifted into a sneer.

"I didn't say she was going to do anything. I just want her to be with David and Moonsong."

Roki yawned and stretched. Martin moved suddenly and Lucy gave a little cry of protest as she began to slide off his knee. Martin pulled her back, ran his hand up under her jumper and began to unhook her bra. He fumbled with the catch and Lucy reached back and pushed his hands away as she undid the familiar hook and eye. As Martin's hands moved up under the edge of her bra and his fingers began to make circles over her nipples, she closed her eyes and allowed herself to concentrate on the delicious feelings that were beginning to flood her. Her head fell back a little and Martin leant forward and kissed her neck. She could smell his hair and she nuzzled her chin into it. Martin pulled her jumper up further and bent his head. As he did, Lucy began again to slip towards the floor, but this time she did not protest. *But Trynor did protest, his energies spiking orange and red* and Lucy shuddered with pleasure, as Martin slid off the chair also, his hands moving all over her.

"*Come on, Trynor, you aren't helping," Jotin was pulling his friend from the room. "Your anger is only making her excited. Maybe if we leave she'll come to her senses."*

"I doubt it," said Roki, "I'm staying. How about we make a baby for her now?"

Trynor raised his fists and moved towards Roki, who backed away, laughing.

"Only kidding. We'll leave that for later." Martin reached into his pocket and pulled out a little packet. *Jotin pulled Trynor away, trying to keep both their tempers.*

Chapter 40
1986

Lucy woke early on a bright May morning and stretched lazily. Strange but wonderful, she thought. Imagine, I'm getting married today! Not just any old wedding, but actually mine. Why do I want to get married? ...do I want to get married? Well, I don't particularly want to stay here putting up with Alison's Finals all next year and listening to her bitching about Martin. I can't help it, just 'cos she doesn't fancy him – I do and I'd like to do my fancying in peace and not have to listen to 'why are you still with that boring guy?' all the time. So, maybe he doesn't fascinate her. You don't have to be scintillating to be a good guy. He's decent. Why do I want to marry him- is that the best I can think of, decent? His indecent moments are the best! She flung herself out of bed and over to the mirror.

"OH MY GOD- you couldn't, that's just not fair! LOOK at the spot on my nose, I can't go out in public with that, I just can't!"

Alison came in. "What was the screech? Have you seen sense at last, or do I still have to make a show of myself in that stupid dress?"

"Not as much of a show as I'm going to be- look" wailed Lucy, as she contemplated her nose again, peering at the mirror for a closer look. "Have you any good concealer, or any better ideas, or are you just going to gloat?"

"Don't get her anything, please! It's hard to make a good spot that quickly. Don't spoil it!" Trynor sat fidgeting on Lucy's bed. "Alison, come on - you've heard me and Kumbal before, we've got to stop this. Time's running out."

"Hey. Lucy!! Hey Lucy!" Trynor got up and looked in the mirror over Lucy's shoulder. "You don't want to go out in public like that, do you? You don't want to stand beside that drop-dead gorgeous guy with a beacon on your nose. It's good, isn't it? Even though I say so myself, it's a pretty good bit of creation. I should feel proud of it- what d'you think?"

"I should feel proud to be standing next to Martin. I'm not going to let a silly spot stop me having My Day- he should love me even with a spot. Maybe a bath will relax me, I'm starting to feel jittery. Can I have some of your bubbles, Alison?"

"Yeah, I suppose. I don't think I can talk any sense into you anyway."

"Jittery is good. Proud is not good. That was for me, you silly chump. You really will have to tune in better. I'm trying my best here. Now listen to me- YOU DO NOT WANT TO MARRY MARTIN. There is a much better plan for you, just be patient. You'll attract another guy, you're pretty enough. In fact WE HAVE A REALLY NICE GUY FOR YOU-you just have to wait a bit. What's your rush?"

"Are we in a rush? Alison, what's the time? Oh, God, should I have set my alarm?" and Lucy fled into the bathroom, still calling out in a frenzy to the household.

Three hours later, Lucy came into the living-room. The spot on her nose was almost invisible, due to Alison's grudging ministrations with a makeup stick. Her hair was finally up, held with a veritable porcupine of pins, as it had inexplicably kept escaping, no matter what they did with it. Mum and Alison had stood by, with combs and mouths full of hairgrips. As Mum said, it really seemed as though her hair didn't want to stay up. But they had got the better of it and it looked OK. The dress looked all right, too, despite a bit of the satin shrivelling up under the iron. They had pulled it flat again almost immediately and there was only a tiny tear. If Lucy kept her hand by her side it would never be seen. The arrival of the bouquets an hour earlier had caused a wave of hysteria. "But I told them I wanted the greenery to trail, not stick out all round like a tacky Christmas decoration" Lucy sobbed. "Anyone would think I wasn't meant to get married, the way everything is going wrong."

"That's right- you're getting the point at last! You have me in a right tizz here, trying to think of what to do next. That's a problem of never having been a human adult, it's harder to think of good annoying ideas. I wish Jotin was free. But really, a famine is more important, he's looking after a few souls starving over in Africa who really need him. Come on, Lucy, call it a day and let me go and check on some of my others."

258

Robert kissed Lucy on the nose. 'Careful, Dad, you'll rub off the makeup and I'll look like Rudolph again.'

"I don't care, you're my pretty girl anyway and if that idiot Martin can't remember what you looked like yesterday without a spot, he deserves you even less than I think."

"Not you too, Dad! What is wrong with Martin?"

"Nothing, that's probably the problem. Do you not remember your mother listing out his good points when we met him first? Once he said he wasn't interested which church he got married in, we couldn't find a thing wrong with him. We could never stay awake long enough to notice anything."

"Oh, Dad. Do you still think he's dull? He has a good job and we talk about all sorts of things."

"Does he make you laugh?"

"Should he? Laughter isn't everything."

"It is, you know. We laugh nearly all the time here. So do you, when you're here. Laughter is the whole point, really. And I don't hear much when you're with Martin. Too many intense discussions about the future. This future you should not be sharing. Your future is waiting for you in a house in Donnybrook, trying to realise he has the wrong wife. Jotin is working on him, he's depending on me to work on you."

"I like to hear you laugh. You always did when you were little. You got a bit serious when you got to college."

"It was hard work. I had to concentrate. It would have been easier if I'd met Martin earlier, he could have been supportive."

"Would have been better if you'd met David. There's real support. Though the temptation to have the baby would have kicked in. At least this way you can earn your own money." Trynor was rambling, feeling desperate, wishing his friend Jotin was here to help share the agony. But he had refused to come and watch 'the last chapter of our disaster' as he had named Lucy's wedding day. He had gone off to Ethiopia and was doing his best there. Diljas, Robert's guide, was standing with Robert, but not sure what to do. At last he leant forward and talked softly to Robert.

"Come on, if we're going? The car has been waiting for ten minutes and the posse of girls has been gone for ages. They'll be shivering on the church steps by now." Robert stopped and looked at Lucy. Always in a rush, he thought, always wanting the loose ends

259

tied up. Is that why she's getting married? Just to have it behind her, one less uncertainty in the world. Oh, my poor little girl, he thought suddenly. Always afraid of the dark, of strangers, terrified of sharp knives. Cautious on beaches, not like Alison, who ran carefree. Did I not protect her enough, make her feel everything would be fine no matter what happened? Maybe I've really let her down, maybe school fees and nice clothes, a warm house and plenty of food isn't where it's at these days. Maybe I've missed something; is she scared of the whole world? Time to put it right.

"Lucy."

"What?"

"Lucy, if you don't want to go through with this, if you think it might be a mistake, or too soon, that's not a problem. You stay here and I'll go on down to the church and explain. Don't worry about the reception or anything, it doesn't matter, compared to making a huge mistake." *Diljas nodded his thanks to Robert.*

Lucy stared at her father. He was normally so jovial, so sure about things and here he was suggesting she might be making a mistake. Why, she wondered. He never made mistakes, why should she? *Trynor stilled his energies, pulled them into a concentrated ball and beamed his thoughts as hard as he could towards Lucy. 'Mistake, mistake, mistake' he thought, as hard as he could.* Lucy took a deep breath and looked firmly at her father.

"I think you're making the mistake, Dad," she said. "I know what I'm doing." She reached for her bouquet. "I'm ready to go." She walked firmly towards the door, *with Trynor running beside her, mumbling as he went,*

"You're making the mistake, Lucy, not your Dad and here I am not stopping you, they'll all say I'm a useless guide, I'll never be able to hold my head up again."

Lucy, preceding her father out of the house, straightened up, threw back her shoulders, took a deep breath of her wedding day air and forgot to duck her head to get into the limousine. Her headdress caught in the top of the door and fell backwards into the dirt. Lucy took a deep breath, picked it up and fixed it on as best she could. Alison could check it later. She sat back comfortably onto the leather seat and sighed with pleasure.

Trynor and Diljas got into the car too and took the jump seats.

"Much comfier than those ordinary cars they have nowadays,"

said Diljas. "You have to sit on top of people. Unless you can run along outside, but I find I gauge the speeds wrong and either get left behind, or get too far in front. This is nice. I remember a Bentley I had once, well I didn't have it exactly, but my human did and there was always plenty of space for me. The only thing I had personally, in the vehicle line, was a rather nice cart. Back in 1123. Dodgy axle though, in the end."

"Diljas, shut up a minute. We're not just here for the ride. My girl is about to make a terrible mistake and I can't get through to her. Can you get her father on our side again? It's for his good, too. He won't be happy if his girl is miserable."

"He knows, and I know. I've tried. You heard him, already. He thinks of these things himself most of the time, he's had a bit of practice. But she is the most stubborn human I've ever seen and I've worked with some beauties, I can tell you. Free choice was a crazy idea. They use it for all the wrong things. Well, here goes....Robert. ROBERT- tell Lucy again you'll get her out of this! Come on ROBERT, listen to me!" Diljas leant over and poked Robert in the chest. 'Come on Robert, you know she shouldn't do this. Tell her to stop NOW!!"

Robert rubbed his chest thoughtfully. I really must give up fried breakfast, he thought sadly. It seems to be giving me indigestion again. He cleared his throat. "Lucy, like I said, if you want to back out of this, I'll go in there and tell them you can't do it. You can go home and not have to face them."

Lucy looked at her father thoughtfully. Why is he going on like this, she wondered. Have I said anything to give him the idea I don't want to get married? I want to get married- I suppose. It's just nerves and a trail of mini disasters today. It'll be fine once the church bit is over. The church, where Martin's family might feel out of place and be upset for him, or blame him. He's doing a lot for me, being married in my church. "No thanks, Dad" she said quietly. "I'm getting married and I'm going to enjoy today. Please enjoy it with me."

"Flippering fruitcakes," said Trynor with such venom that it sounded obscene. "I'm going to have to do something drastic," and he shut his eyes, took a deep breath, and

"I think we have a puncture, Sir," said the chauffeur, as he pulled the big car to a halt at a bus stop, the only available piece of kerb.

He got out and walked around the car. Lucy was horribly conscious of the queue of curious faces, watching her. I have to stay dignified, she told herself resignedly. I mustn't go to pieces, I mustn't. What would Martin think - he's always so calm and in control. It won't do any good to cry and it would add to the red splodges on my face. Take another deep breath... *Lucy...Lucy...this car won't get you there-sit back and think of all the wonderful alternatives, no need to go at all, just sit back, sit back and think again...*

"DAD - does this bus route go past the church?" Lucy twisted around on the seat to look out the back window. "No bus just now, but maybe one's due soon?" Putting her bridal dignity aside, she wound down the window and asked a woman in the queue.

"Supposed to be,' the woman replied glumly, 'but you know the buses, nothing for hours then four in a row."

"Dad, have you any money? If we're getting a bus we'll need a fare.'"

"Just a twenty. No coins. I'll just get out and help with the wheel."

So, thought Lucy, in mounting frustration, which is more dignified on your wedding day, sitting in a jacked-up car at a bus stop, or getting on a bus in a wedding dress? At least the photographer isn't here, at least I can pretend I was just late. So I think I won't move, I'll just stay here and rest.

The chauffeur was avoiding Robert's eye.

"I'm afraid the spare is flat too, Sir. I don't know how that can have been allowed to happen. I'll radio in for another car."

"It's OK, if you can lend us some change. We'll get this bus now. It'll leave us at the side gate of the church, I think." Robert leant back into the car. "Are you still game to get the bus, or will we just go home?"

Lucy looked up: "Well, if that's my choice, I think the bus it is!"

"Why did you let a bus come? We could have delayed her for ages, maybe Martin would have got fed up and gone. Remember 'Far from the Madding Crowd'?"

"Firstly," said Diljas patiently, "I have no control over Dublin Bus. Does anybody? I can't even control my own man here. Secondly, that was only a film, a work of fiction. That young man didn't want to marry anyway. He set up the delay. What I've seen of Martin makes me think he'll hang on all day. He likes the idea of

marriage. Conventional thing to do. Come on, I want to get on this bus, not jog along beside." Diljas grasped the pole on the platform and with a flourish, swung around it into the interior.

Fifteen minutes later, Lucy and her father got off the bus and followed by shouts of 'Good Luck' and 'May all your troubles be little ones!' walked in through the side gate to the church grounds. The ground was muddy and Lucy's white satin shoes were soon the worse for it. *"Yes!" said Trynor.*

"Oh, please, Trynor, just stop," said Diljas "You're not going to stop her going in at this stage. Don't make it worse for her. Wait till she's inside. Maybe we can silence her."

The ushers quickly went inside to signal to the organist; the bridesmaids, whispering excited questions, gathered up behind and Lucy and Robert walked slowly into the church. Calm, thought Lucy, desperately, Calm. She held on tight to Robert's arm. Dad's solid, she thought. I'll never be alone with Dad around. She turned to him as they reached the top of the church and smiled. 'Thanks, Dad !' She turned towards Martin, who was grinning at her. She looked at him for a long moment and she was seeing a stranger. Nerves, she thought again, just nerves.

"No, Lucy, not nerves. Me, trying to TALK TO YOU." Trynor was beside Martin now, pushing his way in beside Roki, looking Lucy in the face. "Come on, girl, please, LISTEN TO ME. You aren't meant for this one. He'll be happy with someone else. You'll make each other miserable and I don't want that. Come on, kid, tell him you don't want to marry anyone today. Roki, help me on this one, please. You know my girl here's meant for someone else."

"Hey man, what's that to my guy? He wants to be married, she's nice. He's been wanting to marry her for hundreds of years. Come on, let's get this over with, I believe there's a party after these things?" Roki waggled his hips and clicked his fingers rhythmically. Trynor rubbed his eyes.

"Oh no, I forgot what you're like. If you'd paid attention before you'd be less interested in the party and more aware of the pain later. It'll hurt Martin too, you know."

The rector had started talking-"We are gathered together in the sight of God.."

"and some very pissed off angels!" said Trynor. "Would anyone just listen to me! 'or forever after hold his peace'- huh! That does

263

NOT apply to me, my good man. You'll all be hearing from me. Or would, if you'd only listen." He stopped for a moment, thinking, and then muttered *"and by the way, sorry for calling myself an angel back there, but that's what the humans understand."*

"Who gives this woman to be married to this man?"

Robert started. He had been dreaming, a thought was just there on the edge of his consciousness. Maybe he should say 'no-one'. She'd thank me later, he thought - if she ever spoke to me again. Betty poked him in the ribs and hissed 'Robert - your turn!' Robert smiled over at Lucy, who was looking at him like - like what, he wondered later. Was she waiting to be thrown a lifeline, or hoping he didn't embarrass her?

"I DO," he said firmly. *Diljas sat down heavily, narrowly missing Betty's handbag.*

"Oh, Robert," he mused sadly, *"All we can do now is watch and hope."*

Trynor grabbed Lucy's shoulder and shook her. Lucy shuddered, as though a tremor went through her. Alison caught Jen's eye and they smiled helplessly at each other.

"Come on Lucy, this time all you have to do is nothing. Just keep your mouth shut and say nothing. I'll sort out what comes next. Jotin says he'll get it sorted with David, pretty soon. Just say nothing. Just keep mum, that's my girl. You're good at silence, do it now!'

"I do," said Lucy in an almost inaudible voice.

"Well, folks, that's it," said Trynor, *"I've had enough. I obviously can't do this job and I can't stay and watch the partying,"* he turned to Roki. *"Over to you, you can keep an eye on them both for a while. I need some time out and maybe a spot of counselling."* *And he blinked out.*

Lucy felt lighter all of a sudden. Martin was putting the ring on her finger and it was the first part of the service she had really noticed. She smiled at him and his infectious grin shone back at her. Her voice gained strength as she went through her vows and the atmosphere in the little church lightened. Robert took Betty's hand and squeezed it. 'It worked out for us, why not for them?' he whispered.

Later on that evening, in their hotel room, Lucy recounted all of the day's disasters to Martin.

"But, you know," she said with a laugh, "I had been beginning to wonder if I was actually meant to get married at all, everything was going so wrong. But as soon as I said 'I do' I felt calmer, as though everything would be all right now!"

"Of course it'll be all right, you silly. Come here and let's start making it all right straight away."

Roki put his hands over his eyes. But he couldn't resist peeking.

Chapter 41
A month later

Lucy pulled open the curtains and looked out at their little garden, the early summer sun just creeping over one hedge to attack the dew on the grass under the other. There was nothing in the garden yet but grass, tussocky and full of clover. Maybe I'll make a flowerbed at the far end, she thought, in the sun. Pity we couldn't get a house on the other side of the road, where the sun would have come in the back windows, we could have built a little patio outside the kitchen.

"What are you looking at?" Martin had come back into the bedroom, wrapped in a towel and was now struggling to put socks onto feet still slightly damp from the shower.

"I was just musing about the garden. Maybe we could build a little sitting area down at the end, where it would be in the sun. But I don't want to cover too much grass, we'll need that if we have a baby, for kicking a ball on."

"Grass is easier. And like you say, we'd need a rugby pitch. When are we having this baby?"

"I'd like to try soon. I thought, it's June now, so if I stay on the pill another month? Then from July, I'd be due in..." she counted on her fingers, "April." She turned to Martin, a broad smile on her face, watching for his reaction.

"April? Is it not a bit soon? I mean, we won't have been married a year."

"It's more than nine months. Everyone will know it's legal." She sat down on the bed and watched as Martin buttoned his shirt. "I don't know why, but I really want a baby soon. Lots of babies."

"I'm quite happy to help you make lots of babies. But I'm quite happy to 'make babies' without the babies!" He pushed her backwards on the bed and, putting his knee beside her, looked down into her face.

"Now you see why I put on my socks and shirt first and leave pants till last. Just in case I get a good offer like this." He bent over to kiss her and his other knee slid between her legs.

267

Six minutes later, Martin was lacing up his runners. Lucy lay back on the bed and watched. The dampness between her legs was the beginning of her interest and the end of his.

"Are you going somewhere?" She tried to keep the irritation out of her voice.

"Training, I told you," Martin was rummaging in a drawer.

"Oh. I thought you said we were going into town. Window-shopping and a spot of lunch, you said."

"Yea. Sometime. Maybe next week."

"Why maybe? Can you not be sure?"

"No. Depends on the lads. When they're free."

"Well, you're part of 'the lads'. Tell them you're not free next Saturday morning."

"Can't do that."

"Why not?"

"I am free. Nothing's forcing me to go into town." He stuffed his shorts into his sports bag and straightened up. "Well, I'm off. Don't do anything I wouldn't do. At least, not if I'm not here." He bent over, kissed the tip of her nose and left the room. Lucy looked at the door and listened to his feet running down the stairs. She felt empty. The fortnight on Crete had been magical, they had spent every moment together and gone to see all the sights. The ruins at Knossos and Malia had been creepy but amazing. Her spine had prickled nearly all the time. Her Granny would have told her someone was walking over her grave. Martin had laughed at her, told her she was imagining things. He had loved the beach and wanted to spend all day there, but she had not liked it, preferring the pool at their apartment. They had gone out for dinner every night, the food was cheap and delicious and they had walked home tipsy under the stars. Lucy had felt at home, had known that marrying Martin was the right thing to do.

"No, my dear one, going to Crete was the right thing to do. Pity it wasn't with David, he would have remembered Malia too. But it would have been an unpleasant few minutes, with both of you shuddering on the 'Malatos' beach. Martin never moved far from Tylissos when he was Niklon, so you never visited anywhere where he felt at home. He was just pleased to have got you at last."

"Okay, Lucy, organise your day and do something useful with it," she said to herself as she showered. So she went to the supermarket and the butcher's and bought some steak for dinner. At four o'clock she had finished all the housework, not difficult in a house with as little furniture as they had and was sitting at the kitchen table with a mug of coffee, doing the Simplex crossword. The phone rang. It was Jen.

"You busy tonight?"

"I don't know, Martin's out at training. I don't know when he'll be back."

"Well, if you can, come round for dinner. Peter's coming over, and Sarah and Mark. It'll stretch, you don't have to let me know till later," Jen paused. "Luce, are you OK?"

"I'm fine," Lucy straightened up. "Just did all the housework. A bit tired, I suppose, wrenching people this way and that all week and then hoovering all day."

"I'm glad I'm not one of your patients," Jen laughed, "it sounds painful!"

"Figure of speech."

"Yes. OK, Hope we'll see you." Jen rang off.

"Put the steak in the freezer section. Now. And plan to go out to Jen's. Martin will go if you're decided. Go on." Lucy went to the fridge and took out the meat. She held it for a moment, then opened the little freezer section and rammed it in, on top of the bag of peas. She shut the fridge and looked at it, why did I do that, she wondered, after going out to get it?

"Because just occasionally you hear your old friend. About something trivial like going out to dinner, but it gives me hope. Now, go and have a long hot bath, and relax. You'll enjoy the evening."

At half past seven Lucy phoned Jen.

"I'm sorry, Jen, I don't think I can come. Martin isn't back."

"Come on your own?"

"How would I get there, I've no car."

"Maybe I can get Mark to swing by you. I'll give them a buzz, if they haven't left yet." Jen rang off. Lucy heard Martin's key in the door and ran into the hall.

"We're invited to Jen's for dinner!"

"Oh, God, Lucy, I'm knackered. I don't want to go anywhere. Been with the lads all afternoon. Had a few. Just want to sleep. After dinner." He pushed past her into the living room and spreadeagled himself on the couch. "What is for dinner?"

"Well, it was steak, but I put it into the freezer after Jen phoned. I think she's probably doing spag bol, she said it would stretch. Come on, I'll drive."

"No."

"No?"

"No. I'd prefer steak with my wife to spag bol with her friends and their dreary boyfriends."

"They aren't dreary and the steak is frozen now."

"Go out for fish and chips, so. Like I said, I'd prefer to be with my wife."

"He had that chance all day, Lucy. Go on, you're ready to go out and have a fun evening."

"I'd like a fun evening."

"Can't we have a fun evening together?" Martin reached out, grabbed Lucy's hand and pulled her towards the couch. "I know a great game for two people. Did I ever tell you about it?" His hand pushed up under her blouse. Lucy giggled.

"Oh dear. We're still at that stage. Go on, enjoy!" Trynor left.

Lucy was sewing a sheet together to make a ghost outfit. Big tacking stitches, just enough to last the night. And I'm not going to be naked underneath, not at his rugby club. So if it rips I'll be safe. I won't need make-up, if I'm as pale as I feel. At least it's not in the morning, I would be useless at a morning party. Martin came in, dressed entirely in black plastic, with red horns on his head and a long forked tail.

"How do I look?"

"Ravishing. But you'll melt in that. Bring some ordinary clothes in the car, to change into."

"I can't wear ordinary clothes to a Halloween party. Everyone will be dressed up. Is that all you're doing?"

"I've been at work all week. And you know I'm not feeling great. I'm looking forward to lying in in the morning. Dry toast and nothing to do."

"You wanted to be pregnant."

"Doesn't stop me feeling sick. You try it sometime."

"He did, more than once. And once he had appalling vomiting. Died of it. Roki was telling me. It shocked them both. You don't

270

look as pale as you think. You're nearly at twelve weeks, it will be better soon. Put some white stuff on your face, and enjoy the party. Roki loves parties even more than I do. It could be a good night."

Dawn was looking for Mohmi. It would have been enough just to call her, but Dawn was playing, trying to guess where Mohmi might be and going to each place in turn. There were some places she could not follow her, where Mohmi would be private; or she might be on earth looking after one of her other humans, so she had not found her yet. She had some wonderful news to share. Eventually her excitement got the better of her and she called, very gently.

"Mohmi?"

"Yes?" Mohmi was there beside her. "Have you a problem?"

"Well, I had a small one, I was trying to find you..."

"Hide and seek again? You would think you had never had an adult life, the way you love the childhood games." Mohmi wrapped some of her energy around Dawn and hugged. Dawn leant into the embrace.

"I met Trynor while I was looking for you. Then it got more important to find you. Did he tell you? Lucy is pregnant. So I need to know, can I have that body? Please?"

"We'll have to think about it, discuss it with Trynor and Jotin. And Roki. Come on."

The three guides were waiting. Mohmi greeted them, then asked them if it was suitable for Dawn to listen to the discussion. They agreed and showed her where to sit, a little separated from the four guides, but able to join in if invited. She listened avidly to the discussion about her next life.

"Well, really I don't see what it has to do with Jotin at all," said Roki, "David is married to someone else, with their own children. This baby is my Martin's."

"And Lucy's. And she's meant to be with Dawn. Has Martin any souls he has unfinished business with who are free at the moment?"

"Not now." Roki grinned. "Not now that he has got his girl."

"And do you think that will be the end of that? You're a bit naïve if you do." Jotin was puzzled. Roki was quiet for a moment, as he thought about it.

271

"No," he answered eventually. "It's complex, isn't it? Martin is completely happy right now, but it's not really right. I should have known. I get carried away, sometimes. I'm sorry."

"That's OK," said Trynor. "WE all know it can be put right. It's just that this time, Jo and I really want Lucy and David together, to raise Dawn. Then we can be relaxed about their next lives. See if they can produce anything more significant than beautiful vases together."

"Cold fusion?" Roki's tone was sarcastic.

"If we knew what, we could do it ourselves. Alexander Fleming's guide didn't know anything about penicillin. Found it quite mystifying actually, all her own lives had been in societies with witch doctors."

"So you don't know what you're doing at all, then?"

"Look, Roki," Jotin was firm, "it is perfectly simple. This life was arranged so that Lucy and David could get together and enjoy a whole life, instead of those three interrupted ones. Then you wrecked the plan, Lucy got confused and is having a baby with the wrong man."

"Plenty of people do the wrong things," grumbled Roki.

"Yes and plenty of guides work themselves to a frazzle trying to stop them," said Mohmi, "It's up to all of us to accentuate the positives. Actually, I think I remember a song the humans used to have about that." She began to hum.

"So, do we have any idea whether Dawn should take this one?" Trynor looked around the guides and then smiled at Dawn.

"I'd be a bit nervous of it, really," said Jotin, "We can't be sure of getting them together. If they don't, Dawn will only be with Lucy and she's done that before."

Trynor turned to Jotin. "Do you think we'll be able to get them away from Kathleen and Martin?"

"Hey, hold on a minute!" Roki was on his feet. "Are you trying to get her away from Martin now? While he's happy?"

Trynor sighed. "Oh, Roki, I thought you understood. It is a mistake. Just because Neil wants to get his own back on Lewis for getting his own back, he goes and marries Lucy this time. Neither of them should be together. You know that. We have been discussing it for four thousand years. You agree with me, mostly. Why not now?"

"Because I see him happy now. It's hard to resist. He makes such trouble for himself, he's not happy too often."

"Well, you should help him to work on that. Stop him depending on other people to make him happy."

"I'll try." Roki sat down and put his head in his hands. "Just don't take her from us just yet."

"I don't think I could," Trynor looked at Mohmi, "So what do you think, listening to us all bickering?"

"I think Dawn should wait. You might get them free. Let's give it a while. Have you any other souls in mind for this baby?"

"Yes," said Trynor, "Quite a few possibilities. We'll have a chat, see who would be most helpful to Lucy in this situation, or who could get most out of it. Sorry, Dawn. I hope it will work out, and we'll be working with you soon." Trynor went over to Dawn and wrapped her in energy. Jotin joined them and the two guides stood for a while with Dawn, exchanging love and good wishes. Then Dawn moved away, smiling at them all.

"It's a pity for me, but listening to you, I think you're right. Let me know when it's the right time. I'll be around." She flickered and her light went out.

"Probably gone to the library," said Mohmi, "she likes to review old lives, to do the next one better."

"She does them well as a result. Almost an expert. We chose well, by chance!" Trynor hugged the others. "I'd better get going. Have to hurry up on finding someone to take this new body."

273

Chapter 42

Lucy sat up a little gingerly in the high hospital bed, a bit tender after the baby's sudden arrival. Three days early and in a great rush to be here.

"I was only here an hour and there she was," she told Jen, who'd popped in on her lunch hour to view the new arrival, "and isn't she beautiful?"

"She is," said Jen, looking enviously at the pink face, its little mouth working, "and I think she thinks she's feeding. Look!"

"She's dreaming. Takes after her mother. I dreamt about her the night before she arrived. How she would look when she's older."

"What are you calling her?"

"Aisling. Because of the dreams."

Some of those dreams were of Dawn, how she would have looked, had she grown up. How you saw her in spirit." Trynor was *sitting close by, taking care of Lucy and standing in for Aisling's guide, who wasn't really needed much at this early stage, particularly when Aisling was asleep.*

"It's a pretty name."

"Yes."

"Yes, that's why I like it, apart from meaning 'dream'. Martin liked it too. We went through lots of names, he was really fussy."

"Who was fussy?" Martin was standing in the doorway.

"You, I was just telling Jen about the struggle to find a name."

"God yes." Martin sat down heavily on the end of the bed. Lucy moved her feet out from under him.

"Some of your ideas were really crap," she said.

"And I didn't like yours, so it was even."

"Not really, I only had two other ideas, you produced loads of weird names."

"Trying to be helpful."

"By suggesting Jezebel?"

Jen sniggered. "You didn't, seriously?"

"Why not, it sounds pretty?"

"The poor kid would have been bullied at school as soon as they found out what it meant."

"What does it mean then?"

"Please Martin, not again. We went through all this before. She's Aisling and she's lovely." Lucy leant back and closed her eyes. Jen stood up.

"I'll go, and let you get a rest." She leant forward and kissed Lucy, an unusual gesture from an old classmate, but one that Lucy suddenly felt very glad of. "Bye. Bye Martin."

"Bye." Martin moved further up the bed till he was sitting at Lucy's hips. She shunted a little further over, to release the tension of the blanket pulling her down. "I've some great news, Lucy. Our lives are going to change!"

"Yes, everyone has told me. A baby changes everything."

"No, not that. I've signed on for a new course in jewellery making. Starts in September."

"What?" Lucy opened her eyes and looked at him. Martin was smiling at her. "An evening course?"

"Of sorts. It's a full time evening course. Leads to a diploma. It's handy - the new College in Donnybrook - so I can go straight to the course after work each evening. And it's some weekends. Pretty intensive, must be good. Their brochure is very impressive."

"What are you talking about? Since when did you want to make jewellery?"

"Since he envied you when you came back as Alessia from Malatos with the gold pin for your mother and he saw how she looked at you with admiration and respect," Roki said from the end of the bed, *"and this time he's going to do it."*

"I don't think it's going to work, not in the short term," Trynor answered, *"Watch."*

Lucy pulled herself up in the bed, so that her eyes were level with Martin's. "Please explain."

"I told you," Martin said, "I'm going to take this new course, become a jeweller. You can charge good prices for unique items in precious metals. We'll be rich!"

"And in the meanwhile?"

"Well, I'll keep my job during the course. It runs weekdays, six till nine. And one Saturday a month, unless we ask for more."

"So I'm going to be on my own, nearly all the time. With a tiny baby. You said you were going to be supportive; I don't think I'll feel supported. And how much does it cost?"

276

Martin looked at his hands. "Not too much. The savings account covered the first term."

"What do you mean, the savings, and 'covered'?" Lucy was worried now.

"I took out the money from our account and paid the deposit for the course with it. Simple."

"That was our money, Martin. More than half of it was mine. You should have asked. We should have discussed this. We had all sorts of plans for that money. Including a decent couch. A new cooker. Not a pipe dream. And now it's gone. We're stuck with a couch that should be in a skip. A cooker that doesn't always come on. You'll have to start saving again, harder."

"Oh, I won't be saving for a while. I have the two other terms to pay for."

"How much?" When Martin told her, Lucy winced. "But that won't leave us enough for the mortgage. Never mind the bills." Tears began to creep down her cheeks.

"But you have a good job. We'll be fine." Martin put out a hand and rubbed Lucy's shoulder. "My girl is great, a real Liberated Woman!"

"He's doing it again, Roki," said Trynor, "Having his own life at her expense. Stole her job last time, stealing her freedom and choices this time. You should stop him."

"It doesn't feel liberated, to be sitting here with a new baby, being told I've been robbed. That I'm going to have to go on working full time. That my baby is going to have to have a minder."

"It's only for a year. Then I'll be working with gold and precious stones and we'll be in clover. Come on, Lucy, give me a smile. I'll make something beautiful for you first. You should be pleased you have a husband with get up and go."

"I was pleased to have a husband with a secure job. Plenty of people don't. Jen's Peter was made redundant last week."

There was a tentative knock at the door. "Can we come in?" Betty Browne put her head round the door and went straight over to the little cot, smiling down at it and stroking the baby's hand. Robert came to the bed and leant past Martin to kiss Lucy.

"So, how's my girl? And my other girl?"

"I'm fine, Dad. And Aisling is great. The feeding is going really well." She smiled and looked over at her mother, who now had

Aisling in her arms and was crooning softly to her. Lucy hoped the tears would not show on her face. She didn't feel up to explanations just now. Or having to stand up for Martin. She needed to get used to the way life was going to be now. Busy. Working full time, if she could get the hours; minding the baby on her own in the evenings. Oh, please, she thought, let him just do the course but stay in his job afterwards. Then we can get back to normal. Maybe he could make his jewellery in the evenings, as a hobby. It would be a good hobby, maybe I can get him to teach me. I wouldn't mind having a go. I wonder would I be any good?

"You would be spectacular, my darling. But there is no point. You have done that, in Crete, in ancient Rome, one of the times in China, when you weren't making the fabulous pottery and once I think in Germany. Enough. Time to do something else. Just enjoy wearing the jewellery this time."

Chapter 43
Late 1987

"You're a selfish bastard, d'you know?" Kathleen slammed a plate down in front of David, so that the piece of battered fish on it jumped. "You completely ignore what I want, don't do anything I ask, even when it's for a really good reason, and I'm here sorting out everything about the house for you." Kathleen's speech was very slightly slurred and David looked at her more closely.

"Have you been drinking again?"

"There you go again. Nothing I say is valid. Always blamed on drink, or PMT, or something. Never on you. Bollocks." She sat down and rested her head on her hand, staring at him angrily. David looked back at her, partly glad that the girls were away at a friend's house, but mostly wishing they were here, to defuse Kathleen's wrath. Maybe she wouldn't be drunk if they had been here.

"What have I done to upset you, Kay?"

"Still the same. No change. Still argue about everything I want. Never come home and offer that we'll go away somewhere, I always have to ask."

"How could I offer? When would I get the chance? You're nagging at me about it all the time."

"Well, if you suggested it first, it would be nice."

"I'd have to suggest on the second day of a holiday that we'd go somewhere else. That's when you start nagging."

"That's a lie. I love our holidays. Why else would I want to go?"

David reached for the ketchup. "I don't know why you want to go, love. I know you love it the first day. I've said that before, I love you the first days. Then you change back and push me away."

"I told you, years ago, no vasectomy, no touch."

"Not that again? You seemed to get over that idea, actually, you were quite friendly for a few months after that," David reached out for Kathleen's hand. "Let's try to recreate that. How did we do it?"

"Haliken did it, David," said Jotin, "we needed you off that hook and he pulled out the stops, got Kathleen to feel more sexy. Couldn't keep it up, though, sorry."

"I don't remember how I felt. I only know you are always on at me."

"Oh, Kay," David sighed, "I don't think expecting to make love to your wife is abnormal, you know. I think most men do it."

"Maybe they've all done what their wives asked."

"You're not trying to tell me you think every other man out there has had an operation?"

"Sandra's husband has," Kathleen sniffed, "so she feels respected. Not just used."

David stared at her. His friend Ken had been home this summer and had confessed that he had had 'the snip' as he called it. But he had five children, so he had to 'do something drastic', as he had said. His wife had had to have a section for her last delivery, twins who had been lying the wrong way. "And we only have to look at each other, and she's pregnant," he had boasted. "You're lucky, just the one set of twins, and then freedom!" David thought back over all this and wondered if Ken had done it as a gesture of respect to his wife. Seemed a bit cold. The way he had nudged David and winked didn't seem cold at all. Quite the opposite. Kathleen's angry voice called him back to the present.

"Why are you staring at me like that?"

"I'm sorry, I was thinking. Ken had a vasectomy."

"First good thing I've heard about Ken, then. He has some sense." She got up and went over to the counter, where a heap of papers languished, waiting to be dealt with. She rummaged through them and pulled out a coloured leaflet, which she slapped down on the table in front of David. He picked it up. 'Family Planning Services', it was headed, and then, 'Vasectomy'. He read through it and looked at Kathleen again, his fish growing cold on the plate between them.

"Why now, Kay? You haven't mentioned this for ages. Are you feeling like being cuddlier for some reason?"

"You want me in that way. That's the deal. Or no more at all."

"Not even on holidays?" David tried to keep the mood light, but found he was struggling.

"Not even then."

"Oh, Kay. You don't leave me much choice, do you?"

Yes. You always have choices, Davy. Leave her. For goodness sake, you'd get more sex if you did! We'll watch you, keep you safe till Lucy leaves Martin. Once little Aisling is a bit bigger, once Martin has finished his course, we reckon she'll see sense and run.

Come on, no operations now. Dawn is waiting for you to be ready for her."

David sat woodenly and stared ahead of him. He couldn't work out why this suggestion bothered him so much.

"My fault. I'm saying too much. NO VASECTOMY! Leave her!"

"I'll leave the choice to you, Kay." Jotin screeched softly in frustration and then said "No, trust me, David, trust."

"I'll trust you. You make an appointment for this first visit and we'll follow it up."

"What do you mean, you'll trust me?"

"Did I say that? I suppose I'll trust you that things will improve, once this is done. That you'll relax."

"Of course I will," Kathleen leant over the table and kissed him. He put up a hand to her head and stroked what she had left of the thick curtain of hair he had fallen in love with. It was still thick and slightly curled now, but it had lost a lot of its old sheen. Maybe that would return if they could rediscover what they had lost.

"Don't count on it."

"I've a terrible confession to make, Trynor," Jotin was sitting hunched, protecting his energies from passing guides and other spirits. I tried as hard as I could, but I didn't succeed. He's having the operation this morning. Misunderstood everything I said to him. So unless we can get him together with Lucy in the next few months, before the sperm die off, we're out of time. Sorry."

Trynor sat down and put out a hand to Jotin. "Don't take all the blame. It was me who made the biggest mistake here." He stood up and paced up and down a little, his energies circling his head as they wove patterns of thought. At last he sat down again.

"I don't know that you need to be too hard on yourself, really. I mean, I can't be sure I'll get her away from Martin at all. She's really busy now, he's doing that course and she is so busy with her work and the baby, she just doesn't hear me at all."

"What a change," Jotin's tone was sarcastic, "when do they ever?"

"I know. We're not really getting through, are we? Maybe we need some more training, before their next lives. We have to get this sorted next time."

"You feel we've had it, this time round?" Jotin was jiggling his *energies, as though trying to keep himself warm.*

"Well, let's look at the facts," Trynor said in a voice that began to bubble with amusement, "they are both, possibly irretrievably, married to other people and he now can't get anyone pregnant. Good material for making a baby, which is the whole point." He sat down and his energies began to subside, in a way that would have reminded a human watcher of a pressure cooker after it was taken off the heat.

"Well, all's not lost."

"We know that, really. In what way in particular?"

"They have a lot to learn, all of them. Patience, forbearance, tolerance. They can do all of that."

"Don't forget enjoying life. They need to do that too. That's what we should do. Help them to enjoy. And try to practise getting them to hear us."

"Yes. We'll have lots of time for that," Jotin stood up and stretched, "But first I have to check on some of my other humans. They've been a bit neglected recently. See you round."

David looked over at Kathleen, who was sitting hunched over an atlas, turning a strand of hair through her fingers. He noticed again the deep furrow between her eyes and the pinched look to her mouth. She had used to smile all the time before they got married, in fact that was one of the things that had attracted him to her. Now she looked permanently cross and worried. Poor Kay, he thought. We'll never be able to fit in enough away time for her to be able to cope when we're here. I can't afford the time, or the money. He thought back to their last holiday, with the girls, when they had gone to Spain on a package trip. That was fun, playing in the Mediterranean with them, three of them squeezing onto one pedalo, the girls giggling and pushing. Better than the Irish Sea any day, it was no wonder that Kathleen wanted to go. But then David remembered that it had been him playing with the girls, while Kathleen lay on her sunlounger reading. She hadn't joined in, not once. She had wanted to go on the supplementary coach trips and had enjoyed the one they did manage, but it wasn't enough. Kathleen just had wanderlust and it was carving a trough down her forehead. The vasectomy hadn't made any difference, not in the long run. She was still happy and sexy on the first day of the holiday and gradually less friendly after that magical day. She didn't actually refuse him now, when he approached her in bed, but she didn't respond, just lay there and waited politely for him to finish. He had thrown away his precious picture of 'Clothilde' after she had fulfilled her purpose of emptying his tubes after the vasectomy, thinking he would not be needing her again. But he had had to buy another magazine. No Clothilde:- he fleetingly hoped she had moved on to a better job, as he transferred his attentions to Paulette, a busty blonde. She's not much less responsive than Kathleen, he thought, smiling behind his hand and she never sighs.

"Kath?" said David, surprising himself. He didn't usually start conversations these days, in the hope that peace would reign for longer and Kathleen might become more content.

"What?" Kathleen's voice was dull and uninterested.

"Have you ever thought of getting a job involving travel?" Now where did that come from, David thought.

"Me. Someone has to keep trying round here. Get her out of your hair for a while and find out who you are for a change. Stop all these trips and save up for that piano you want." Jotin was sitting on the sofa beside David, watching the television. He enjoyed good plays. *Unfortunately, this was not a good play, so he was trying a bit of manipulation again. Probably won't work this time either, he thought. This is one tough assignment. Wretched Trynor, if he'd got it right those two would need almost no minding at all, they'd be doing it themselves.*

"Want to get rid of me, do you?" said Kathleen.

"Yes" said Jotin.

"No, of course not" said David.

"Coward" said Jotin. "Why don't you just say yes and get it over with?"

David continued. "I just thought, you're always so unhappy here, always wanting to go somewhere, that maybe if you could be, I dunno, a tour guide or something, that you might be happier. And it wouldn't cost anything."

"How could I be a tour guide? I don't speak any languages well enough. And I'm too old to start being an air hostess, in case that was your next smart suggestion, trying to get me killed off in an air crash."

"You're not afraid of dying in an air crash when we've bought the

283

tickets, why should you if you're being paid?" David sat back and tried to think of some other job Kathleen could do. "How about presenting travel programmes? You'd have to get into RTE first, I suppose. How about improving your French, or learning a new language? An unusual one, so you'd be in demand? What about writing a travel guide? You know most of Europe inside out already. Just find an angle."

"You write the bloody book. You present the programmes. You learn a language. Leave me alone!" Kathleen threw the atlas on the floor and ran out of the room, taking huge gulping breaths as she went. David closed his eyes. Up to bed, under the covers and cry, up two hours later and stamp into the bathroom for a hot bath, cucumber slices on the eyes and a demand for hot chocolate and an apology. The same every time. And I apologise. Every time. But what exactly have I done wrong? Just opened a discussion point. Idiot. Why didn't I remember, Kathleen doesn't discuss, Kathleen states. That's it. No more discussions. Just ignore her as best I can from now on, do what she wants when I must. Trying to solve things is just too tiring.

Chapter 44
Spring 1991

David let himself into the house. He stood for a moment and listened. He was sure he was on his own. What a luxury, he thought, a few minutes to draw breath before the onslaught. In the kitchen, he filled the kettle and switched it on, then leaned over the counter to look out of the window. There was a bit more light in the sky every day now. Soon the grass would need cutting again. Soon the summer travel brochures would appear again and his sheets of calculations would have to start.

The water hissed and a cloud of steam engulfed him. David got out a mug and spoon and reached for the jar of coffee. Propped against it was an envelope, 'David' starkly on it. He took it and sat down, a million thoughts tumbling simultaneously through his mind, some bad, some good, but none of them simple. It was Kathleen's writing, looking rushed, as always. Open it, you idiot, stop trying to guess. You'd never keep up with her anyway.

"Dear David, I've gone. I can't stay here any more. It was a big mistake, me trying to be with you. I always have wanted to be somewhere else, but then when we go somewhere, that's not right either-

"You can say that again" said David aloud, his voice startling the room. "You always were a discontented bitch."

-so I think it must be us that's the problem. So I'm going, don't bother to track me down, I'll be moving around. I've taken the money. Maybe I'll get a divorce if I pass through Las Vegas. I'll let you know. Kathleen"

David read it again and again. The light slowly faded while he tried to decide what to think, even what to feel. He wouldn't miss her, though he'd certainly notice her absence. The girls would keep him busy. The girls. What will they think, has Kathleen explained to them? His thoughts, now only in thousands, whirled round and round, circling and dodging, refusing to settle. I tried, oh God, how I tried, he thought. And this is the end of it. I wasn't good enough.

She wants so much and it's not what I want, or what I have to give. We really weren't partners at all, just spouses. But I thought it would be me that would crack and now it's happened, but it's on her terms. The money. She says she's taken 'the money'. What money? She can't have! He got up and went into the back room to search the sideboard for the building society book. The rainy day money, not much but growing slowly, they'd both agreed to pretend it wasn't there, so that the girls could go to college, or have slap-up weddings one day. They would be dipping into it this autumn, for the college fees. It was gone.

"So, in the end, the girls are taking second place to Miss Whinge. Again.   But I really didn't think you'd go so low, Kay, I really thought that was sacrosanct. I didn't realise before, but I was right just now. You really are a bitch."

"Who's a bitch, Dad?" Caroline was behind him and her arms snaked round his waist. "Not me?"

"Wouldn't be surprised" said Clare. "Worms can turn."

"No, not either of you." David stopped and looked at them, these beautiful young women he had worked so hard for and put up with so much for, and wondered what to say to them. Could he bad-mouth their mother? Could he lie and pretend he and Kay had parted amicably? What would be the best? Nothing would be good and in the end he decided the truth was easiest for everyone. No trying to remember the story, for one thing. So he told them, just the bald facts, and showed them their mother's letter. They stood quietly together, their long hair hanging like two glossy brown curtains, one smooth, one wavy, as they read the short message and then four wide eyes turned to him.

"Is that all?" said Clare. "She didn't say anything about us?"

Caroline was running up the stairs. Her feet pounded around above their heads for a few minutes and then she was down, her eyes glistening.

"Nothing. No notes for us. Nothing." And she started to cry. Clare put an arm around her and sniffed.

They sat around the table later, over a scratch meal of rashers and baked beans. The girls were very quiet, their eyes red rimmed. David felt disloyal, because within him was no grief, just a feeling of relief. At last there was a change; he wouldn't have to struggle to finance yet another trip and field the complaints when the trip was a disappointment.

"Why are you smiling, Dad? Is there a joke?" Caroline's voice was sharp. David sighed.

"It's really hard to explain. I don't think anyone will understand. I don't really understand myself, yet." He looked at the girls, pleading silently with them to at least withhold judgement. "I'm sorry, loves. I'm really sorry this happened."

"Why are you sorry, Dad? It's not you that's walked out," said Clare.

"Your mother was really hard work..."

"Yea, high maintenance, it's called. We noticed." Clare slumped in her chair and pushed her plate away.

" ...so I suppose I'm smiling at the irony of it. That I struggled for years to keep her happy, not to walk out like I've been advised; and in the end she walks out and saves me the bother. I'm sorry girls, but there it is. Maybe I can relax a bit now. Though I have to start the rainy day fund over again."

"I don't care about your rainy day fund. I'm just going to miss Mum," Caroline was crying again. "We don't even know where she is. Or if she's safe."

"Probably once she's got somewhere and got over the shock and excitement of leaving, she'll let us know. Let you know, anyway. She'll be fine, she's very competent, your mother, underneath."

"I'll get on to Haliken and make sure Kathleen keeps in touch with the girls. Don't worry, this is much more how it ought to have been, years ago. Relax. It'll work out, now. If Trynor and I have anything to do with it." Jotin stroked his hand over David's head and David sagged in his chair, his eyes closing.

"Dad, you're knackered. Go on up to bed. Me'n Caro will tidy up. Seeya tomorrow."

Jotin rushed through the crowds of gossiping guides and angels, looking for Haliken. He was excited, his energies whirling around him in flashes of bright colours. Where was Haliken? Surely he hadn't taken all his energy to Earth to go with Kathleen?

"Haliken, Haliken, over here!!" Jotin panted up to Haliken and frowned at him. "What d'you think you're up to, doing that without warning me? It took me totally by surprise, I didn't get to David for ages, I didn't know he needed help. Never mind the

girls."

"Steady on there. I didn't know either. The first I heard was a call from the airport, about the difficulty of getting a flight to somewhere interesting at short notice."

"You mean Kathleen just up and left? On her own? Without you prodding her? After all this time, why now?"

"I have no idea. I've been trying to get her out for years, reminding her how independent she used to be, how the ability to cope on her own was still deep inside her. I'm fed up telling her she would be better off using her energies to organise herself instead of bullying David. Maybe eventually all my persuasion hit critical mass. Anyway, yes, she just up and left. With no plan. And no ticket. So I hear, 'oh come on, somebody, get me out of here!' so I got her out of there."

"So where's she gone?"

"Paris. It was the next flight we could get. And she has a little French."

"And then what? It's a big place, easy to get lost, or into trouble."

"I'll do my best to keep her out of trouble and trying to make herself understood will calm her for a few days, at least. I think she has an old school friend there. I'll remind her. Or there are plenty of trains and planes out. She has a passport!"

"Don't we know it. Well, I really came after you to say, get her to contact the girls. I know she's not interested in them, but there's no point in them finding out and if they're happy, my David can be happy and I can get on with the real work. She didn't leave them any sort of note and they're very upset."

"Did she leave David a note?"

"Yes, not a very nice one, just saying she might get a divorce and that she's taken the money."

"Okay. I'll get her to spend a little of it as soon as the shops open. If you need me, just shout." Haliken stood back a bit and he and Jotin regarded each other solemnly. They had worked together for eighteen years longer than they had expected originally, but were surprised by the sudden ending of their close alliance. It would seem strange, suddenly being apart, maybe even on different continents.

"Let me know if she does get a divorce. Try to get her to send *enough information to stop the family worrying. I hope she finds something to ease her pain, till her body is ready to let her go Home."*

"Will do." Haliken and Jotin threw their energy around each other, in a gesture badly mimicked by the human hug and were quiet together for a moment. Then Haliken was gone.

A few days later, there was a ring at the door just as David and the girls were getting ready to go out and the postman handed in a parcel. In it were two beautiful scarves and a few postcards of Paris.

"So, what do you think, Jotin? Is there any point in trying?" Trynor was lounging on some grass, in a beautiful garden made for him to think in. "I mean, the whole point was that they could have a baby together, and allow Moonsong, Dawn, to spend a life with them." He rolled onto his back and looked at the sunlight, shining out of a clear sky above him. Really, his friend was very skilled at making Earth facsimiles. This one was quite like France. He closed his eyes and listened. Yes, he could even just hear the hum of insects. Clever.

"I don't know, really. David is available and still very interested in women. I mean, he's only forty-one. But that vasectomy does seem to spoil it all. Lucy is hardly going to go for a man who can't give her a baby, is she? Or is she happy to stop at one?"

"Two. Did I not tell you, she had a son too, just over two years later. He's one and a half now, a cute little thing. She still has quite an urge to have another, but she's uncertain about it. She thinks it's because she has to work so many hours, but it's really because her soul knows she's not meant to have them with Martin. Her Aisling and Robbie are both good kids. Souls she knew already, so they can work through some small issues together."

"Did they know Martin?"

"No. Roki says children were 'surplus to requirements' this time, so we used souls who knew Lucy. None of the ones who knew Martin were free, he wasn't really meant to have any children this time."

"Did Roki say what he is meant to be doing?"

"Learning honour and self-reliance, apparently." The two guides sat quietly after this, for a long time. Then Jotin caught

Trynor's eye and asked "Did he say how he was doing?" and they both burst into peals of laughter. Bits of energy broke free from them as they laughed and floated up, shimmering in the sunlight, before drifting back down to coalesce again with them, as they lay on the grass, holding their sides. Trynor was hiccoughing.

"Oh dear, it would be funny if it wasn't so tragic!"

"They have some good sayings, the humans, don't they?"

"Yes, it's a good school, Earth." They lay quietly again. Trynor broke the silence.

"She's twenty-nine. That is young these days, apparently. Plenty of time to meet another man and have a good relationship. David isn't too old, either."

"I wonder what Mohmi thinks?"

"I think you should go for it," said Mohmi, joining them on the grass.

"Mohmi! Welcome. Were you listening to all that?"

"No, only the last sentence. But I assume 'what Mohmi thinks' is about getting David and Lucy together?" The two others nodded. "Because I have had an idea. And I have talked out my idea with Dawn and a couple of other guides and we think we have a plan. Care to hear it?"

The two guides nodded, very enthusiastically and Mohmi started to explain. After a few minutes, she sat back and looked at the others, a slightly smug expression on her face. "So, what do you think?"

"And you say Dawn is happy with this idea?" Trynor asked, "Because if everyone is in agreement, I can't see any reason to hold back. It would work." He got to his feet and did a little dance of hope and triumph, then found his feet tracing some ancient moves across the grass. Jotin joined him and together they dipped and circled in the old moves of the earth walk, which they had danced so often beside Alessia and Danthys. They smiled at each other, hopeful that they might soon dance again together with their beloved people.

"Well, it's over to you, really, Trynor," said Jotin as the dance ended. "We're ready, we're free. I can be wherever you say, just keep the flowers handy for her breast."

"Yes," Trynor said, sitting down heavily, "but I still have to get her to see that she shouldn't be with Martin. I wonder would Roki get Martin to leave, like Kathleen did."

"We won't be lucky twice, I don't think. If you can't get it through to her, we can just try the more dramatic way and throw David into her arms. He'll get her away from Martin if you can't. Sometimes humans are better at these jobs than we are."

"More persuasive, more sexy, more cruel, more passionate. It's hard to be as passionate about things when you know you have eternity to get it right," Mohmi interjected, "that's why it's so useful having lives. Puts a sense of urgency on things. Well, usually. I wonder about that sometimes, when I think back over my three lives in a row in a monastery. I got rather too static there. But most people these days seem to be in a rush about everything. Go for it, Trynor. I'll back you up, if necessary."

Chapter 45

"Put on the kettle there, Caro. I think we need to sit down and have a think. Where's Clare?" David got out three mugs and put them on the table. Then he opened a paper bag and lifted three custard slices carefully onto a plate.

"Oh, Dad!" squeaked Caroline, "you shouldn't! Those are absolutely loaded with calories."

"That's why I got them. Fuel for our extraordinary meeting. Oh, Clare, hi. Tea or coffee?"

"Coffee. I'll do it, you sit down. Oh wow, I love those! What's the occasion?"

"Just an important discussion." David sat at the table and watched his daughters as they made the hot drinks and shared out the cakes onto three plates. They're so precious, he thought. Worth every moment of the misery. Look at them, so beautiful. I'm glad they got their Mum's hair, instead of my mousy stuff.

"You're blond, David, not mousy. I have it on good authority."

So clever, too. Going to do well in their Leavings, maybe go to college, support their Dad in his dotage. He smiled.

"Nice discussion, obviously," Clare sat down at the table and stirred her coffee.

"Not really. We have to discuss money and how best to arrange things between us."

"Why? There's always been enough, hasn't there?" Caroline forgot for a moment about calories and took a big bite out of her custard slice.

"Just. All those holidays and trips stopped me saving much. We just had the rainy-day fund, when you were born I put that aside. Your Mum and I agreed to pay into it every month, but otherwise to pretend it didn't exist. I hadn't even had the book updated recently, I didn't know exactly how much was in it until I dropped into the building society and asked them. Not that it matters now, it's gone."

"Well, what do we need it for?" Caroline had the confidence of youth.

"Our fees, that's it, isn't it, Dad? If we go to college?" Clare had always been the cautious one.

"To an extent. Your school fees will be finished of course, but I do have something outstanding on the loan for them. I can probably manage one set of college fees straight away, without taking out another loan."

"Then one of us will defer and get a job and save up. I don't mind waiting." That was Clare, as always being sensible.

"No, I'll wait. What a good excuse to get a job straight away, not have to go to fusty old college," Caroline's eyes shone, "and no-one could object. Actually Grandpa Clonskeagh will be positively joyful, he doesn't approve of college. You go Clare, you know what you want to study. Maybe I'll find out later what I want."

The conversation went on for two hours and in that time David felt his daughters, officially adults since their birthday in January, truly grew up. He was able to share with them at last, a little of the difficulties he had had over the years, keeping things going despite the constant financial drain of so many holidays and trips. He tried to keep it factual, to avoid emotions and blame, but Clare was too cute.

"But Dad, if you knew it was costing too much, why did you pay? Why didn't you just say no?"

David felt bewildered. It was a question he had often asked himself. He had tried, once or twice, but the storm of tears that resulted was just too wearing. And of course, he couldn't confess to Clare that he only had sex on the first day of any trip. That was just too odd.

"I'm not sure, darlings. Your Mum cried a lot. I tried to fix her," a bit of the impatience he had felt for eighteen years came jumping to the surface, "but it was never enough. I don't know what more I could have done."

Caroline patted his arm. "I think you were fine, Dad. I overheard Granny Clonskeagh once, saying you were 'too patient by half' with Mum. And she's Mum's mum. What does she think of Mum going off?"

"Bet she'll be cross," Clare got up and put the kettle back on.

"But Granny Howth will be crosser. She always is."

"There you are Dad," said Clare as she spooned coffee into the mugs, "that's why it happened. You were brought up by Gran Howth, who's very firm and organised, so you learnt to be good, but Mum got Gran Clonskeagh, who's a softie, so she learnt to cry for what she wanted. Blame the Grannies!"

"I don't think you need to do psychology in college, love, you have it sorted already." David leant back and looked at her and her sister. Maybe she was right and it was that simple.

"That would save all the fees if I didn't. But don't worry, Dad, like we said, whichever one of us goes to college will get a part-time job, so you don't have to worry about expenses. I could maybe do a bit more baby-sitting, it's good, you can get a bit of study done."

"I know of some children called Aisling and Robbie whose Mum would love to meet you," Shelta, Clare's guide, mused. "Do you think they'd be too far away?"

Jotin smiled. "I hadn't really been thinking. I've almost given up, really. But maybe we should work on it. Put out a query for connections, see can we work out an introduction somehow."

"And we won't go on any holidays. So I think it will be fine. Me and Clare will help with the house, and the cooking."

"Yes," said Clare, all business, "let's make a shopping list." She got up to fetch a pen and the scratch pad.

"Oh no, oh no!" David put his hands to his head in mock horror. "The first action of the new regime is to plan more spending. Help!" Clare laughed and flung her arms round him.

"I love you, Dad. You're the best!"

Chapter 46
Autumn 1991

Lucy herded the two children up the stairs despite their protests that it was too early for bed. She wanted them settled before Martin took over, or they could be up all evening. Martin was due back at seven, to let her go out to the practice meeting. This one would include a demonstration of some new equipment, so she wanted to be there in plenty of time, to be relaxed and able to concentrate.

"Can we have a bath? Mummy, please?" Aisling, at four, was at her most winsome, smiling coyly.

"Baff. Baff. Bubbles!" said Robbie.

"No, no time tonight. You'll just have to be dirty tonight. Come on and we'll do a lick and promise, then your teeth."

"I Want Baff. I Need Baff," shouted Robbie, struggling to get out of his clothes.

"Sorry, no bath. Just strawberry toothpaste." Lucy wiped Robbie's face and set about the struggle to brush teeth in two firmly shut little mouths.

At five to seven Lucy escaped from the bedtime ritual and started her own very hurried preparations.

At ten past seven David walked into the lounge of the Grafton Hotel. He would just have a glass of water to settle him before the others arrived. This was an important dinner, to celebrate the deal done earlier today with their Italian suppliers, but it didn't explain the nervousness he was feeling. He should feel relaxed, he had been the one to negotiate the discount for bulk, the one who had been praised by all sides, by the Irish for getting the discount, by the Italians for placing such a large order. Because he had thought of going round the country to nursing homes, checking on whether they needed more equipment. One sterilizer to nearly every home made up a big order, no need to persuade those suave hospital managers. He felt pleased. More relaxed at home than he could remember ever before, now that Kathleen had gone and the litany of requests for holidays had been turned off. It's like a holiday all the time now, at home. And this order will go most of the way to paying at least one of the girls' fees for this year, assuming we don't go away on a big holiday. He sighed and closed his eyes for a moment. Never again, if he didn't want to. No more demands that he go to a beach, or on a train, or on yet another coach excursion. He remembered steeling himself to cope with yet another beach, to avoid the coach trips. Stay here, chill out. So why do I feel so jumpy?

"Because you're meeting Lucy tonight. It's all perfect. She's cross enough with Martin to look at you and you know you're ready to forget Kathleen. And here you are in a comfy lounge, looking good, and she'll be done up too, so apart from admiring the flowers, I hope Trynor has remembered the flowers, all you need to do is smile, remember?" said Jotin. "Smile, just keep on smiling."

David stood up, smiling broadly and held out his hand to greet the Italians, who had been ushered in by his colleague, William O'Connor. He ushered them to chairs and took orders for pre-dinner drinks, while O'Connor went to let the dining room know they had arrived. The party at the next table was getting large and cheerful. Young professional men and women were greeting each other happily and exchanging gossip about their work and families.

Jotin came into the living-room where Trynor was waiting with Lucy. Lucy was pacing, looking at her watch and at the phone.

"Martin, where are you?" said Lucy, "I'm late already, I'm going to miss the pre-meeting drinks and just have the solemn bit of the evening. You knew I was going out. Come on."

"Where is he, Trynor? I thought you said this one was a dead cert."

Trynor shrugged. "I don't know. He should be here. We should be on our way. Go and check with Roki."

"Keep her calm. She has to make David smile so she'll know him, after all. Hang on." Jotin disappeared. Trynor went over to Lucy and stroked his hands through her aura.

"Calm, little one, calm. It's not long now, then the excitement can start. Oh boy, are we all going to have some fun! And about time, too."

Lucy shivered. Goose walking over my grave. She sat down,

closed her eyes and tried to breathe down into her abdomen like in the yoga class. Deep breathing is calming, I will be calm, I will not let him get under my skin one more time. The bastard, how dare he, he knew it was my turn to go out, if he wanted to be out too he should have arranged a sitter. Why is it always my responsibility to sort out babysitting? The selfish, mean-minded.."

"Deep breaths, Lucy"

"...something must have happened. In 1-2-3-4, out 1-2-3-4-5-," Lucy tried to keep her mind empty.

Jotin came back, eyes flashing. "They'd stopped off for a drink. Martin was telling his pal that Lucy has "a little girls' do tonight" and that there was no rush and Roki was just sitting there, telling me it's important for Martin to keep up with his friends. I told him what I thought. He's coming, now. That Roki can be a real nuisance." Jotin looked at Lucy. "How's she doing? Looks okay now, keep it up. Love the flowered top, should do the trick perfectly. I'll go and keep my side of things calm and ready. See you for the fun!"

Fifteen minutes later, Lucy heard the car in the drive and went out to the hall, as Martin came in calmly, as though nothing had happened.

"Where were you?" Lucy shoved her arm into her coat sleeve, pushing the ripped lining through so that it dangled. "Oh damn." She pulled the lining back up the sleeve and held it at the shoulder while she manoeuvred more carefully this time. She buttoned herself up and pulled on a hat. She looked at Martin.

"Well?"

"Looks like you could do with a new coat," said Martin, "that one is shot."

"I know I could. And shoes. And just about everything. What are you going to do about it? You haven't earned a penny for four years." She searched through her bag for her keys and went to the door. "Aisling is asleep, but I'm not sure about Robbie. Over to you." Lucy let herself out into the frosty evening and got into the car.

The restaurant manager came over to David and William.

"Your table is ready, sir. Would you like to order here, or come through?"

"Order here, please order here. She'll be here soon. Remember, David? You've got an important meeting here any minute" *Jotin pleaded.*

"We've an important meeting..." said David and faltered.

"Yes, in the morning," said William. "We don't want to be up too late. I think we'll come through in a moment."

"Thank you sir. When you're ready"

Lucy drove into the underground car-park and started the zigzagging process of finding a place.

"Just get out and run, you've taken long enough getting here as it is. Never mind parking. Come on." Trynor was exasperated. Everything took so long. He and Jotin had put such a lot of work into setting up this evening. He was tired. Tired made mistakes. Careful, that's why you're in this situation, lapse of concentration about forty years ago and she was born too late. Now she might arrive too late again. No, here's a place. Well done. Now on we go."

Lucy stepped out of the lift and looked around for the lounge. She walked down the corridor to her left, following a buzz of conversation and found herself at 'Barnacle's Bar'. She pushed through the throng in search of her group, *Trynor at her heels, shouting unhappily, "No, No, not in here, you're wasting time."*

"Can I help you?" The floor waitress was young and perky.

"I'm looking for a group. From the Earlsfort Clinic."

"Did you try the lounge? Past reception and straight on."

"Thanks," Lucy pushed her way back out of the bar and hurried along the corridor. Why do I feel so worried? It's only a work meeting. Same old faces. Same old jokes. She came into the lounge and caught sight of her colleagues, squeezed around a rather small table. A group of business men were just standing up from the next table along and moving away.

"Hi, Lucy. Was the traffic awful?" Her colleagues spread out to take over the table recently vacated and made room for her. "We've a few more minutes before the meeting, would you like a drink?"

Lucy looked around vacantly. She felt terrible, as though she had just been robbed. She checked for her bag at her feet.

"No, it's all right, the drinks are on the company. What'll you have?" Gemma was getting to her feet.

300

"I don't know, I'm driving." A wave of despair ran through her.

"I'll go now, Lucy. You don't know what you've just lost. I'm making you feel bad. I'll see what we can do. Maybe he'll be around later, after your meeting. Have a drink."

"On second thoughts, I'll have a G and T. It'll have worn off by the time I leave. Might as well." Lucy leaned back and smiled. She was glad she had moved from the hospital to the private clinic, apart from the small rise in salary. She had a little autonomy, was able to try out some of her own ideas. These were good people. She felt at home with them.

David looked at the menu without interest. There didn't seem to be anything he really fancied, though he felt really hungry, empty even. Yes, there was a huge hole in his stomach, the toast he'd had before coming out must have gone down really quickly. Better have something filling.

"We'd better sort a more foolproof plan the next time and quickly," Jotin was talking to Trynor in the hall between the lounge and the dining room, "or David will get so heavy Lucy won't look twice at him, if he's going to try to fill his emotional void with food."

"And Lucy is going to get drunk. Oh, Jo, what are we going to do? We have to be more sure things will work and stop them feeling our panic and disappointment. It's not fair to them, we got them in this mess and we're not helping them feel good."

"Well, you have to work on Lucy, to make sure she leaves Martin. Is she anywhere near, yet?"

"Not really."

"Well, why don't we talk to all her colleagues' guides and fill them in? Then some of them could say some things that would make her think?"

"Good idea."

So Jotin and Trynor went back into the lounge and talked quietly and intensely to the guides who were gathered loosely around and who had thought they were more or less off duty for the evening. Many of them nodded and said 'see what I can do' and 'well, maybe not tonight, but I'll try'. One of them leaned forward and whispered in a woman's ear. Elaine turned to Lucy and asked

"So, are you going to go on the job-share scheme when they bring it in next year? I think it's a great idea. I'd love to share with you, I know we'd get on really well, be able to work it out between us to suit us both."

"No, I can't," said Lucy, feeling embarrassed.

"Why not? Your kids are little, aren't they, like mine? I mean, it cuts down on child-minding. After paying that and the tax, it's hardly worth our while working. I got almost nothing last month. Just do it to get me out of the house."

"I need the money at the moment. I can't afford to do fewer hours, ideally I should do more. This is really only a big part-time job anyway. I can't afford full time child-minding at all. I just juggle things with my Mum and sitters." Lucy didn't mention that Martin did not help. Elaine wouldn't expect him to. Husbands seemed to be creatures whose salaries pushed their wives' earnings into the higher tax bracket, not people who helped at home. Lucy wondered what Elaine's husband earned. She plucked up her courage and asked. When Elaine told her, she felt even more embarrassed.

"Why, what does yours earn?" Elaine was on her third drink; the speaker had been delayed.

"Oh, Martin is setting up a business. It isn't making anything just yet."

"What does he do?"

"He's selling equipment to manufacturing jewellers. He did a course in jewellery-making a while ago, found it wasn't something he wanted to do,"

"Hadn't any talent."

"and decided to go into supply instead. He used to be in Sales, so he knows the ropes."

"Oh, he'll do well, so." Elaine took another slug of her wine.

"You weren't meant to say that bit!"

"Maybe I'll wait and do the job-share with you when he gets going? Or if you don't want to, I'll ask Clodagh."

"I think maybe you should ask Clodagh," said Lucy, in a small voice.

Chapter 47
Spring 1994

"Oh, for God's sake, would somebody please find me a parking space, quickly?"

Trynor leapt to his feet. "Alert! Alert!" he shouted. "I've a chance to Get Through! Everyone with a car on St Stephen's Green check their person please. Wheewhoo, wheewhoo!!"

Jotin had been chatting with a group nearby. He came over when Trynor started his emergency vehicle noises.

"What's the fuss, Try? Lucy sick?"

"No," said Trynor, "she wants a parking space, to get to some sort of class on time and this time she actually asked 'somebody' for one. So if we're quick, I can make contact. David parked on the Green?"

"No, I can't help directly. He's in work, went in by bus. But he's doing routine stuff, doesn't need me just now, that's why I'm here gossiping. I'll come and help."

Lucy was on her second circuit of the green, wondering if she would be lucky, or if she should try further away. But with the amount of time she had to get to the class and the state of her puff, she'd never run back in time. *I should take up some exercise, go back to my badminton, do a keep fit class. Or a get fit class. Maybe I'd get a parking space easier if I was trying to do something really useful, instead of just amusing myself with 'art therapy', whatever that is. But maybe I need therapy. I certainly need something therapeutic, something has to change about me, I can't go on like this. Oh, wait, there's a woman coming to her car.*

Lucy slowed down and pulled in just behind the woman, who was putting several large bags into her boot. Lucy tried to catch her eye, to smile an 'are you leaving?' at her, but the woman, aware of Lucy's presence, turned away feigning not to have noticed and walked back towards the shops.

"Bitch," said Lucy, "you could have at least looked at me." She thumped the steering wheel with her fist. "Oh come on," she said, "somebody, if there is anybody, get me somewhere to leave this car!

Or I'm just going to go home and not do the wretched class. Such a waste, after organising Jen to mind the kids. Or maybe I'm not meant to do the class, maybe I'm just meant to sit at home the whole time I'm not working."

Trynor was running down Grafton Street calling out "parking alert, parking alert, any cars on the Green? Quick response please?"

An elderly guide put his head out of a burger shop. "Your person have to get somewhere?" he asked, "or are you Getting Through?"

"Getting Through, if we're quick," Trynor panted, "can you help?"

"I'll try. Maybe we can get this 'to go' instead of sitting down. Carry on with others, though. It mightn't work." He turned back into the shop and Trynor heard him urging the young man at the counter to order to take away - 'your meter's nearly up, you'll get fined. It's not worth waiting. Come on, go home quickly...'

Jotin was just inside the door of Switzer's. He raised his voice:

"Anyone parked on the Green, ready to go, NOW? My pal can Get Through if you move." There was a general low muttering and in three sections of the shop two women and a man looked at their watches and headed towards the door. As the first woman went out into the street, a young man carrying a MacDonald's bag collided with her.

"Oh, I'm sorry" he said. "Are you OK?"

"Yes, I'm fine" she said.

"Tell her about your meter," said a voice at his shoulder.

"Oh good, sorry about that. I've just realised my meter's nearly up. I wasn't thinking," and he dashed off. The woman looked at her watch again, muttered 'Blast' and set off quickly towards Stephen's Green. Behind her, the other woman, who had left the perfume counter in the middle of trying to decide between two fragrances, stood in the doorway feeling puzzled. Why did I come out here, she thought.

"Because you overheard someone else's guide talking. You ought to listen to me more and other peoples' guides less, my scatterbrain. Go on back, we can't help on this one. Go back and buy perfume." She turned back into the shop, still puzzled and returned to the perfume counter. "Sorry, I don't know what came

over me. I suddenly thought I should move my car, but I didn't bring the car today! Ridiculous, isn't it? The early Alzheimer's again!" She picked up a tester bottle and sprayed the inside of her wrist.

Lucy was driving slowly, wondering whether to go around again, or to go off down a side street and risk getting stuck in the one-way system and maybe still finding nowhere to park. Maybe just one more turn, she thought, and pulled out into the right hand lane to go round the corner. The lights turned red and she was stopped behind three other cars. She watched, feeling helpless as a stream of traffic entered the Green from her left. Probably all going to park in my place, she thought bitterly.

"No, I think we have it sorted. Just get over to the right as soon as you get round the corner." Trynor looked over to the parking spaces, where Jotin was standing, beckoning towards the group of guides who were ushering their people up the street.

The lights changed and Lucy moved slowly around the corner. As she did, three people reached their cars and realised they were all slightly early, there was time left on their meters. But moments later, three cars moved slowly out into the traffic.

"Wow," said Lucy. She pulled up beside the first car and waited. The young man grinned at her as he passed slowly by and waved her into his space with a hamburger. Lucy moved past the space, indicating to back in.

Trynor stood guard on the other side of the space, grinning, arms akimbo, saying to any friends he saw "Parking Angel, hands off this space!"

Another car pulled up and waited for Lucy to park. As she put on her handbrake and turned off her engine, she said "I don't know if it's just coincidence, but if anyone just arranged that, thanks."

"You're very welcome, my love," said Trynor. "It worked, Jotin, it worked! And she said thank you! I'm through!"

"No you're not, not by a long chalk. You've started and that's great. But you're going to have to be very interactive for a long time before she'll realise you're there. Took me forty two years to get through to the last one I managed to contact. Mostly they don't ever realise. David's nowhere near."

"So I'm ahead of you on this. Don't rain on my parade. I'm going to enjoy it, starting with going to listen to her tell everyone

about me," Trynor jumped across the road and followed Lucy into the building.

"Best of luck, Trynor" said Jotin.

Lucy followed a hand-painted notice indicating 'Art Therapy, two flights up, on your right' and creaked up the old stairs. She mused for a moment on the changes these stairs must have seen since they were built in the reign of King George-whenever exactly that was. Must look it up, she thought. Live in a city built by the Georgians and don't even know when they lived. Though I'm not as bad as that woman who wrote to the Irish Times once who seemed to think that Dublin was built by people from Georgia in the USSR. I hope she was joking.

Lucy was smiling to herself as she reached the first floor and entered the room labelled Art Therapy. A plump woman of about fifty bustled over to her.

"Come in, come in! You're welcome to playtime. And you are?" she ran her finger down a list on her scruffy clipboard.

"Lucy Fitzger - No. Lucy Browne. You probably have my old name."

"Good girl Lucy Browne. Welcome back. Stick with it kid."

"I've a Lucy Fitzgerald here, is that you?"

"It was," said Lucy. She couldn't think of anything else to say. She'd just shocked herself to the core. What would Martin think?

"So I'll change you to Browne, will I? With or without the E?"

"With, please," said Lucy Browne. She stood looking through the woman and her clipboard, realising she had just taken a step to somewhere. The woman was talking again. "So just pick your cushion in the circle, we're waiting for two more, I think, then we'll introduce ourselves."

Lucy walked over to the circle and picked a large purple cushion beside a younger woman with dyed red hair and huge earrings. She sat down, crossed her legs and tried to quiet herself inside, taking breaths deep into her tummy as instructed by her yoga teacher.

"Hi, I'm Ciara. I'm really excited about this course, are you? I think it's great to sort of get to the real you through painting, y'know? I do a bit at home, but, like, I never seem to really reach myself, y'know? What d'you suppose got Miriam into this, doesn't really look the type?" Lucy looked over at the woman with the clipboard.

"Is that her name? What should an art therapy teacher look like, I wonder?"

"Well, more interesting, I suppose? She looks kinda ordinary, don't you think?"

"Yes, nice and ordinary." Reassuring, thought Lucy. Not so individual as Ciara, anyway, imagine being able to wear flipflops in March.

"I'm ordinary, too. Lucy, by the way."

"You can't be too ordinary," said Ciara "or you wouldn't be here. The ordinary people are all learning Spanish, or beginner's computing."

Lucy laughed. Ciara was right, it was a bit unusual to give up your Saturday to paint just to find out who you were. Maybe the ordinary people know already, or maybe they're all content with their lives and don't care. Anyway, I'm obviously meant to be here, or I wouldn't have got that space.

"I'm meant to be here," said Lucy. Why had she said that? Wasn't ordinary good enough?

"Sure, we all are," said Ciara. "but how do you know?"

"Well, I stupidly came in the car and then I couldn't find a space, but I went round the Green again and there were three cars just leaving and I got a space just opposite, so I reckon someone arranged for me to be here." Ciara nodded knowingly.

"Yes, your angel knows what's best for you. It'll be a great day for you, just wait and see."

Trynor sighed. Jotin was right, he thought. I don't think it matters whether Lucy is here or not. They've got the wrong end of the stick entirely.

"I only did it so that you'd realise you've got 'an angel', Lucy. So that you'd listen to me more and pay attention when you do hear me."

"Isn't that the truth," Ciara's guide piped up. "This kid is the pits. Dear sweet well meaning thing, spends hours choosing crystals and wafting incense around - just as well I'm not allergic now like I was when I last had a body - but she never really listens. Just makes up her mind to the most romantic alternative and goes with it. I've struggled with packs of Tarot cards and tea leaves, I've enlisted help from the guides of suggestible fortune-tellers, but none of my real messages seem to get through. It's exhausting

sometimes, but you have to keep trying. At least your girl seems to stay quiet sometimes. Ciara never shuts up."

"What do you need her to know?" asked Trynor. "Maybe Lucy and I can help."

"I need her to stick at something. To stay in her job. She feels edgy and keeps moving to 'something better', but actually, if she could stay where she is for long enough, she'll be noticed and trained for public relations work. She's a natural, look how quickly she made your Lucy laugh, but she doesn't know it yet. And she's thinking of resigning this week."

"So we need to stop her. That's the hardest, isn't it? Let me think about it."

Miriam was ushering the final two participants to their places in the circle. She sat down herself and smiled brightly.

"Welcome, everybody, to the first day of this Art Therapy course. I'm Miriam Collins, and I'm a member of the Round the Corner centre for life enhancement." She went on to describe her qualifications as an art therapist and then after asking each person to introduce themselves and say why they had come, she handed out sheets of paper and put big pots of coloured paint and large brushes at each place.

"Art therapy is not about painting beautiful pictures, but about unlocking something within ourselves and listening with new ears to our inner voice."

"Sometimes that's me, Lucy," said Trynor.

"So now, choose a colour and paint an animal on your sheet. Don't talk, this is in silence." Lucy chose brown and tried to produce a reindeer on her piece of paper. It looked nothing like one, more like a culinary accident, she thought.

"Now stop. Put your brush back. Now everyone stand up and move one place to their right. No, Peter, leave your paper- it's not yours anymore." There were squeals of protest and of mock embarrassment that private attempts were now public property.

"OK? Now, no talking, no telling what it's meant to be. The art speaks for itself. Choose another colour and add something to the picture in front of you." Lucy looked at Ciara's work. Probably a kangaroo, she thought, despite being blue. She chose green and started to paint a gum tree. Eight paintings and a lot of laughter later, she got back to her own deer, now nearly obliterated by everyone else's additions and improvements.

"Who put a tree beside my dolphin?" said Ciara.

"Maybe it's seaweed," said Lucy, deciding not to confess. "It's hard to tell what other people mean things to be, isn't it?"

"It was a perfectly good dolphin," said Ciara, "The right colour and everything."

"Are dolphins blue? I thought they were black," said Lucy. *Trynor whispered in her ear.* "It was moving on so fast that was the problem. It would have been easy to tell if you'd been there long enough to put a fish in with it. We didn't have enough time to make it a proper picture. Look at my reindeer. I don't know what Brendan thought it was."

"So, anyone any thoughts about that?" asked Miriam.

"Everyone has hugely different eyes," said Lucy a bit timidly, "they see what I didn't paint."

Everyone laughed. "Yes, if you want your picture to end up your picture, you've got to stick with it," said someone, "this way, you lose control."

"Same with life," said another voice.

"If you had it just a little longer it might work," said Lucy. "If I'd had time to put Santa in Brendan would have known what it was."

"But it doesn't matter, does it?" asked Miriam "The pictures are all interesting."

"But meaningless," said Brendan, "I mean. It's OK for a painting course, but you wouldn't want to go on like that all the time, would you?" Ciara was looking thoughtful. "Yea," she said slowly "we really were rolling stones, weren't we?"

"I think that's enough," said Ciara's guide, "to be going on with, anyway. Thanks Trynor. Let me know if we can return the compliment."

At half five Lucy was crossing the road to her car with an armload of rolled paper and a lump of clay. Great to be parked so close, not to have to lug all my masterpieces and sculpture half way round town. She put them on the back seat and sat back into the driver's seat, taking a moment out before heading out into the traffic. Well, Lucy Browne, pleased to meet you. Long time no see. Can I let you out more often, I wonder? Lucy Browne does fun things anyway, not like Lucy Fitzgerald. She just does the dull stuff. Like survive. Like earn the money for Lucy Browne to squander on courses. Not squander, why shouldn't I do pointless stuff? It was fun and the visualisation was great, imagine Nelson Mandela giving me three oranges. But the painting of it is silly. Looks like a pawnbroker's sign. Still, it means something to me, isn't that what Miriam said was important? Lucy started up the car and edged carefully out into the evening traffic.

Chapter 48
October 1994

Lucy came out of the building society with a small feeling of satisfaction. She was keeping up with the monthly repayments and had at last cleared the debt left by nearly a year of paying nothing when Martin had been doing the course. The manager had been really decent about it, allowing such a long gap with no threat of repossession. She walked back home slowly, not in any hurry to get there, trying to take pleasure in the soft autumn sunshine and the stiff breeze detaching the first brown leaves from the little trees in the front gardens. All the self-help books suggested finding pleasure in small things, making each day good, not worrying about the bigger picture. That was obviously the answer, everybody else must find it easier. Maybe I'm just an ungrateful wretch. Look at all I have, two great kids, bright and not ever sick. A husband. Maybe it's not his fault everything has always gone wrong for him, he is trying. A house that I can nearly afford. A car.

"Oh, hello Brian. How's the garden?" Lucy walked a couple of paces into Brian's garden and looked round. "Are you planting more bulbs? I wouldn't have thought you needed to. Your daffodils were lovely in the spring."

"Thanks, Lucy. They did well this year. I'm adding in some extra narcissi. Fancy ones, with double centres. And some crocuses. How're things in your garden? Martin should plant those tulips I suggested, if he hasn't already. Here, have a narcissus, he can put it in with the tulips," Brian handed Lucy a bulb. "How is Martin keeping? Difficult times for a business, have to keep busy, I suppose. Don't see him round much these days, always rushing off somewhere?"

"Yes," said Lucy, "always busy."

"Well, that's good to see. A man has to get out in the big world, hunt the mammoth, bring it home to the cave." He struck a pose. "Man's gotta do what a man's gotta do!"

"That's what they say," said Lucy.

"Hear you're keeping up the little job, too. That's great, Lucy.

Keep your hand in, don't get rusty. Shame to see women wasting good qualifications. Lovely to see you getting to do good, helping people."

"Yes" said Lucy "the pay is nice, too."

"But in your situation, the money can't be important. Surely it's more for the interest of it?" Brian stuck his spade into the ground and leant back against his car, smiling at her.

Complacent bastard, thought Lucy. The whole world works according to how it's worked out for you. Your wife never had to go out to work. You probably wouldn't let her, it would have made you look small. You didn't have a difficult spouse to deal with. You didn't have to walk the world in a foreign language, everyone was speaking the same settled family-values speak that you are. You got recognition for what you achieved. You didn't have to smile sweetly and pretend it was Marie who made all your money, paid for your life. You got support from everyone. Dammit, you were a man with an at-home wife. Standard issue. Nothing to explain. Just weed your bloody garden again and go in for tea. Oh shit.

Lucy looked at Brian. She saw a nice, gentle, well-meaning man. He didn't mean it to hurt. None of them meant anything to hurt so much. Maybe not even Martin, he just doesn't ever think about anything outside himself. The World According To Martin, that's what I'm living in. And this is a subsection, the world as seen through Brian's eyes. Well, here goes, let's introduce just one of them to the world as experienced by Lucy. I can't be part of this lie any more.

"Well, not really, Brian," said Lucy, "the money is vital. I'm paying the mortgage, the bills, the school 'voluntary contribution' and extras and for the admittedly very small mammoth," She raised the hand holding a supermarket bag. "So I don't have much time to wonder whether I'm interested in my job, or helping anyone. Just my kids. Better go and cook the mammoth. Thank you for the bulb." She smiled what she hoped was a hugely confident smile and set off up the road home, pretending not to notice Brian's puzzled face.

It was a lie I was helping to propagate. I've been being dishonest to myself too, by doing it. But I wonder, will being honest make things work out any easier. Do I have the energy for honesty all the

312

time? It's easier just to go with the flow.

"No, Lucy, going with the flow is only easy in that you don't have to paddle. But you're more likely to hit rocks, or be overturned. If you can't get ashore, at least steer."

Maybe I'll just take it one step at a time. Give myself credit for achieving what I do. Lucy stopped walking, as a momentous thought came to her. "Oh God," she whispered "help Martin realise how much I do." Lucy rummaged in her bag for a tissue, and blew her nose.

"What were you asking the Boss about? I wish you wouldn't close me out of those communications. I could talk to Roki about Martin, he might be able to help. Though on second thoughts, he's never shown enough maturity to help about anything else I asked for. He even enjoys the tipsy phases. Says it's fun."

Lucy let herself into the house and put down the shopping while she enjoyed the onslaught from Fuzz. Fuzz had really kept up her side of the bargain after being adopted from dog rescue last year, as Lucy said to herself, 'to be enthusiastic about me'. Other people were told that she had been adopted 'for the children.' Fuzz ran to and fro on the sofa yipping; then threw herself around the room, rushing at random, occasionally jumping up at Lucy, but rushing away if Lucy tried to touch her. After a minute of this, she sat on her favourite cushion and panted, looking at Lucy with dark round eyes. Lucy sat down beside her and keeping her hands away, leant over to look into Fuzz's face.

"Hiya Fuzzles! You a good girl? Yea, you are. Good Fuzz, good girl."

Fuzz licked Lucy's cheek and the ritual was over.

"Come on, out you go. You've minded the house beautifully, now go and check out the garden." Lucy opened the back door to let Fuzz out and started unpacking her shopping. Lucy was an imaginative cook, a skill she had learnt from an old great-aunt, to whom she was eternally grateful. It meant they ate well, no one would guess how little she needed to spend. Today Aisling and Robbie wouldn't eat much, they'd be full of sausages and ice-cream. So a stir-fry would be perfect, the portions could vary to suit the appetites. Lucy rooted through the cupboards for a piece of fresh ginger, cut a slice, and started making tiny dice. For Lucy, cooking was relaxing and creative and her mind could wander.

She was putting the lid on a fragrant sweet and sour creation, when Fuzz barked and then rushed to the front door, her tail pumping, as Robbie came rushing in, followed by a rather more dignified Aisling.

"There was a magician! I got to help him! And the wand kept breaking! And I had to guess a card; and he had a real fluffy rabbit and I had to hold her and make sure she didn't pee!" Robbie was triumphant and high from the party food.

"Robbie's sugar-hyper again," said Aisling, with all the certainty of her seven years. "He had four Cokes. His teeth will fall out, I told him."

"No they won't," Robbie protested. "Anyway, you had some too. And Dad had wine."

"When?" asked Lucy, as she measured out rice.

"After the party. The collecting Dads got wine and stood about and talked about a football match. Not rugby, so Dad didn't say much, just drank the wine."

"Martin, did you drink and drive?" said Lucy, as Martin came into the room, carrying a bag of peat moss. He dumped it down with exaggerated grunting and grinned.

"Only had a little, to be sociable. It's not far away. You never know who you might meet at these things, you can't just rush away. It's called networking. Might be potential customers." He opened the back door and carried the peat moss outside, leaving the door open.

It sounds reasonable, thought Lucy, as she stirred the sweet and sour. I don't know the first thing about business. Maybe that's how it's done. In my business you just wait for customers, it'd be undignified to go hustling. But Big Business is different. Advertising everywhere.

"Big business makes money, Lucy. What about that?"

But Martin doesn't ever seem to bring any money home. I earn money, for all I don't hustle, or 'network'. I just have a job. My way is working, at least a bit. She smiled. My mammoth smells good!

"What's the joke?" Martin was back in the kitchen.

"I wish it was a joke," said Lucy. "I was talking to Brian on the way back from the shops. He was asking about you. How things were going with your work, how busy you must be."

"He'd know. He ran that firm for years. He knows how it is."

314

"And do you know, Martin? Do you have any idea how it is? When you're going to bring home any money? Any contribution? Any mammoth, as Brian called it? Or am I going to have to share my mammoth with you for ever?"

"Of course not, it won't be long before I'm in profit," said Martin

"How long?" said Lucy.

"That varies, of course. After all, this is capital equipment I'm selling. Firms don't make up their minds just like that. It's not like selling cheese, you know!"

"I wish you did sell cheese, then people might buy something. If you'd start selling something they actually want. Which part of 'we don't want any, thanks' do you not get? Those gadgets you were selling last year were meant to be like hot cakes."

"Oh for God's sake Lucy, will you lay off! I know what I'm doing, but if you keep going on at me it doesn't help." He took a deep patient breath. "Those great gadgets, as you call them, were too like the competition. And anyway, they didn't have a great mark-up on them. I've new ones now, far better, more expensive. When I get this order from Blake's, I'll be banking ten grand for us. No more grotty camping holidays, we're off to the Caribbean!"

"What was wrong with our holiday? I thought you enjoyed France?" Lucy's mind ran back through her memories of their last and most exciting holiday, trying to remember Martin's moods. But all she could dredge up was the image of Martin lying on their folding sun chair with a book over his face.

"France is okay," said Martin, "but it won't be a patch on what Dad will arrange." This last comment was directed at Aisling, who had just come in. He grabbed her hands and whirled her around.

"Dad!" squealed Aisling. "What are you going to arrange?"

"A really posh holiday. Where would you like? Jamaica?"

"The Maldives. Before they sink. The ice caps are melting and we'll all be flooded, but the Maldives are flattest, they'll disappear first. Unless we all stop being selfish and burning fossil fuels and using sprays," Aisling paused in her recitation, "We did it in school."

"Well," said Martin, "we'd better arrange the CFC free holiday then. Life on the beach, palm trees, surf, cocktails at dusk. Nothing's too good for my girls. Go and look out your togs!"

"No, Aisling," said Lucy, as Aisling, eyes shining with expectation, was heading out the door with plans of rooting through the cupboards for her flippers. "No, Dad doesn't mean now, love. It's just a daydream. We can't afford the Maldives yet. Maybe France."

"Oh Mum, don't be a spoilsport. Why won't you let Dad bring us to the Maldives? You'd love it too!"

"Of course I'd love it. I just wouldn't love paying the bills for it when we got home. Your Dad hasn't the money for it just now, he's just encouraging himself by telling us all fairy stories."

"Stop throwing cold water, Lucy," said Martin "you always undermine my efforts. What's wrong with looking ahead to the good times?"

"Nothing. Not if there really are good times ahead. And it's OK to fantasise too, but you get the two mixed up and the result is a lie."

"Don't be ridiculous." Martin walked out of the room. Lucy blinked hard and got out the plates. Aisling stood uncertainly, leaning against the table.

"Your Mum needs some love now. Give her a hug or something" Lekna was sitting at the table beside Aisling. "It'll help you too. You support her and she'll have more strength to keep going. You need your Mum well. Go on."

"Mum, I really liked France. Specially the campsites with swimming pools. I'm not that keen on swimming in the sea really. Can we go to that site with the diving board again this year?"

"Good girl, that's the way."

Lucy wiped her eyes with the back of her hand, came over and swept Aisling into a hug, burying her face in her daughter's hair. After a while she looked up, quietly took a deep breath and smiled at Aisling.

"I'll do my best. I don't know if we can go for long this year, but we'll manage something. Now, how about setting the table and telling Robbie to wash his hands. It would do him good to sit still for a few minutes, even if he isn't hungry."

Lucy looked at her two children as they sat, increasingly quietly as the excitement of the party wore off, eating the little portions of food she put in front of them. Her heart filled with pride when she watched them, Aisling being so grown up and aware of the world, at not quite eight,

"She's an old soul, Lucy. Lots of experience. That's why she's here, for you. She almost always hears Lekna, too."

and Robbie, trying desperately to keep up with his adored older sister. He was an exuberant child, inclined to rush into things, to see the best in everything. She was glad she had held him back a year, so he was only in the first term of Junior Infants, even though it had meant an extra year of Montessori. It was worth the fees, for this self-confidence. Just gone five, with the energy of five children, only now beginning to droop. Fuzz was standing on her hind legs next to Robbie, her front paws on his leg, pawing at him occasionally. Fuzz knew Robbie was a soft touch. He took after his namesake Grandad, he was caring too.

Martin was finishing his food. He was always finished first, shovelled it in in great scoops. Rarely made any comment. "Food is fuel" he'd said once, after Lucy had spent all afternoon making an elaborate meal for Jen and Peter, "I don't know why you bother."

"Because I think food is interesting. It's relaxing to prepare and enjoyable to eat. It's not just to fill you up." Martin had said he would prefer a pint.

"I'm going out," Martin pushed his chair back and stood up. "I've a person to see."

"What about?"

"The business. I talked to a man on the phone yesterday who said he had a contact in Blodwen's, you know, that chain of shops?"

"Yes, the really cheap and tatty jewellery."

"That's them. But anyway, he can get me an introduction there and if I get in with them, I'll be selling display cabinets all over Ireland. North and South. Told you, it's only a matter of time."

"Why can't you meet him in office hours?"

"Not how it works," Martin tapped the side of his nose. Lucy wondered what that meant, wondered if Martin knew what it meant either. "It's who you know. See you." He swung on his heel and went out.

"Daddy!" Robbie was out of his chair running after his father, "Night night?"

"Oh, yes, sorry, Rob. Night night." Martin bent down and kissed the top of Robbie's head. "Night, Ash." He was gone.

Chapter 49
November 1994

Lucy struggled her full trolley out of the supermarket. She was trying to push it and it was more or less in front of her, but it seemed to have ambitions to be a racehorse and lead with one shoulder. Certainly it wasn't going forward. She gave an exasperated tug and the wheels locked, dragging her sideways into the line of parked trolleys. She stopped, wrestled her trolley free and then leant on it to catch her breath. She looked up and across the car-park. The late-afternoon light was heavy, it had a solid quality, a translucent grey hung in the air between Lucy and the world. She felt a smile grow on her face as she watched the other shoppers come and go in the gathering gloom. A germ of triumph sprouted, somewhere deep inside her and bubbled its way up to her throat. It's beautiful, she thought, and maybe I'm the only person here who knows it. Look at them all, scurrying in out of the dusk, out of the horrible dark night. But it's not horrible and actually, not really dark yet either. You could cut that air up like snow, she thought, and make an igloo out of it. She laughed, a short surprised sound, muffled by the silent air. But her eyes still glowed and she tugged her shopping between the rows of patient cars. Who'd have thought a dark evening could lift my heart? Maybe I'm losing my mind totally. The strain is getting to me. She stopped behind her own car and let the trolley go, so that it turned as though on one wheel and sagged against the boot she was trying to open.

"Oh, for goodness sake! Who invented these stupid things?" Lucy pulled the trolley clear, opened the boot and began to lift the heavy bags in. On my own again, she thought. Always on my own, or with the kids. It's great they're safe down the road at Marge's. It's easier to shop without them wanting stuff all the time. Them and Martin, the odd time he bothers to come, throwing in treats we can't afford. She finished loading the boot and slammed the lid with a satisfactory thud, pulling the trolley clear and trotting with it over to the trolley bay. On the way back, contemplating the chances of someone stealing all the groceries in the time it took to park a trolley and wondering if one really ought to lock the car, she stopped again to look around. The air had darkened and the mystical half-light had been swallowed by the night. Like me, thought Lucy, as she sat into the car and groped with the key for the ignition, I think I'm being swallowed too. What can I do about it? Have I the energy to do anything about it? I feel as if I am just lurching from week to week. Hey, you who does parking spaces, do you sort other stuff too? I could do with some help here.

"Leave him, Lucy. He is exhausting you. You would be better off even on your own. But you won't be on your own, not for long."

I'm exhausted. I'm on my own, really.

"Apart from me, of course. Try and remember I'm here. I'm on your side."

Lucy backed out of the space and turned the car towards home. She drove the short distance automatically, her mind elsewhere and nowhere. Back at home, she lugged the shopping into the kitchen, carefully avoiding stepping on Fuzz who was doing her usual greeting dance. Lucy stuffed the frozen things into the freezer compartment and put on the kettle. She would just have time to relax before Aisling and Robbie would erupt into the house and distract her.

She took her mug into the sitting room and flopped onto the couch. Fuzz jumped up and climbed up onto Lucy, hoping for more attention. The phone shrilled and she startled, catapulting Fuzz onto the floor and spilling tea onto her leg.

"Hello? Oh, hi Jen, just a sec," Lucy put down the receiver and the tea and went for a cloth to mop herself down. "Yes, sorry, I leapt a mile when you rang, I've drowned myself in tea. No, it's okay now. No, only old slacks, not important. I don't have any that are, really."

Jen chattered, about her son, about Peter's promotion and her mother-in-law's hospital investigations. Lucy listened, feeling out of it. No promotion for Martin, how could he, with no job. He's a one-man outfit since he fell out with his brother three years ago. So he doesn't see his family anymore because he refused to speak to anyone who didn't take his side. He hangs out of me, makes me agree with him about everything or he gets angry and sulks. Of course, I have my own family, but they don't like Martin, never did. Maybe they were right. Her thoughts stopped, her mind on hold. After a while she became aware of Jen's voice squeaking down the wire, "Luce, Luce are you still there?"

"Yes Jen, I'm here. Sorry, my mind wandered and I realised: I think my marriage is over."

"Yes."

"What? What do you mean?"

"You've noticed. That's great." Jen stayed silent and Lucy's thoughts whirled around her.

"How did you know? When?"

"Oh, Luce, it's been as plain as, as whatever things are as plain as, for ages. I mean, I've watched you, trying to make things work with that eejit hanging out of you. You're exhausted. We can all see it."

"You're right. I am. It's like living beside an open fridge or something, every bit of happiness I create just gets sucked away. I have to be richer than I can manage, happier than I feel, just to stay on the spot. But now what? I'm stuck, I can't do anything about it really. Martin says his business will get off the ground this winter, with the Christmas sales and then I can cut back and work less and have more time with the kids and.."

"Whoa," Jen cut across her, "Take it easy. One thing at a time. For now why don't you just get used to the idea and not change anything. Maybe it will come clearer later. Just do something to look after yourself."

"Well, I do yoga and I'm still going to the art therapy sometimes. I think that was a huge help. Did I tell you about the parking space?"

"Yes, several times. Why don't you ask whoever was getting you a parking place to help you now?" Jen laughed. "He must be at a loose end, now that you aren't in a car!"

"Don't mock."

"Don't mock, Jen. I really think something was helping me. I did try talking to him, earlier. Didn't get any reply." *Trynor sighed.* "But I think you're right. I'll ask again."

"No point, darling. I'm already trying my best. But she's right, your friend. Look after things one at a time."

"I'd better go, Jen. Lots to do. How come you aren't making dinner, which is what I have to do now?" She listened, as Jen explained that Peter was bringing home Chinese take-away, as he did whenever he decreed that Jen deserved a day off; then sighing

321

internally, Lucy said goodbye to her friend and hung up. She scooped up Fuzz and hugged her, burying her face in the soft fur, feeling the hot skin with the end of her nose. It's so simple for Fuzz, she thought, she's so lucky. She just loves me and she's with me and that's it. No worries, just happy for now. Maybe I can copy her.

In a similar house a little way down the street Marge was distracted and busy. She had just got home and was being bombarded by demands from her three children. Her baby-sitter in contrast was calm and unflustered.

"I'll walk Aisling and Robbie home, Marge. They tell me it's only a little way. I'll come back for my bike."

"Thanks, Clare. That would be great, it's dark out. It was really good of you to help out, when you had to come so far. Yes, Jamie, I'm looking, it's gorgeous, clever boy," she said to her three year old who was dancing on the spot just in front of her, holding up a Duplo construction to be admired, "now, hold on while I find my purse. Three hours, wasn't it?"

"Yes. Do ring me again if you're stuck. It's not that far really, my bike is pretty good. And I have different lecture times from Mandy, so if she can't make it, maybe I can. Thanks." Clare pocketed the money and wrapped her scarf snugly round her neck. "Come on, Robbie, Aisling, coats! Hurry up, Marge is busy now."

"I'm sorry for inflicting neighbour children on you, as well as my own," Marge was unwrapping Jamie from her leg and trying to take off her coat.

"It was really no trouble. Aisling and I got on really well, didn't we? And Robbie just mucked in. It made no difference." Clare took Robbie's hand and they moved towards the door.

"Clare has twins," Robbie announced solemnly.

"Is a twin, silly," Aisling was knowledgeable. "She's called Caroline and she has the same hair but straight. They don't know which one is older."

"Why not?" Marge was momentarily interested.

"Because my parents couldn't decide which of us was which, until after they'd taken our identity bracelets off and then they couldn't remember. It doesn't matter really; actually we think it's better."

"No fights? Just as well you aren't royalty and needing to know,"

Marge opened the door. "Thanks again, Bye now."

Aisling and Robbie walked slowly up the street with Clare. It was only a few hundred yards and Aisling suddenly found she didn't want to say goodbye to this new friend.

"Can you come and babysit us? I'll ask Mum, I'm sure she wouldn't mind changing." She reached up and rang the bell, then hopped from foot to foot. "Mum? This is Clare, she's Trish Jamie and Conor's sitter and we'd like her to be ours, is that all right?"

"Good idea, Aisling," said Selta, who had accompanied Clare on this new job, "Hey, TRYNOR! Are you there? Look what we've got here!"

"Brilliant!" said Trynor, "Come on Lucy, say yes. It'll work out just fine, her Dad can collect her one night and then you'll meet and Bob's your uncle, as you say."

"Hello, Clare," Lucy looked at this young woman and felt she had met her before. "Do I know you from somewhere?"

"I don't think so, Mrs Fitzgerald. I don't live locally."

"Oh, that's a pity. Though we already have two girls who sit for us. They're both nearby."

"That's okay, I didn't come to ask for a job, that was Aisling's idea. I was just helping Marge out, my friend normally sits for her. But we both have Finals coming up, so we don't do as much as we used. But if you're stuck, Marge has my number. Bye now, bye Ash, Bye Rob."

Aisling watched Clare walk down the short drive.

"I'll ask Marge for her number tomorrow, Mum."

"Why?"

"Because we'll need her and Marge will be out and then we'll have lost our chance."

"You make it sound like winning the Lotto! Our chance of what?"

Aisling thought about this as she took off her coat. "Of being friends with Clare. Seeing her twin sometime."

"Well, it sounds like she's really busy, if she has her Finals. Those are really important exams. She's a bit old for baby-sitting."

"She's nice," Aisling was pouting, "she can tell stories and knows how to do hair and she can draw. I'd like a sister like her."

"I'd like a brother," said Robbie.

"Dad, you should get a girlfriend. It's not right, being here all on your own."

"I have you and Caro. That's enough for the moment." And Paulette on page thirty-one, he thought, a bit guiltily. Very flat and unresponsive, but not demanding anything. A very cheap date. "I don't think I have the energy to get to know anyone. It's a lot of work. Learning if they prefer tea to coffee, and if they take milk, or want ice in their gin, or if it's vodka." David sat down and opened the paper.

"But if it was someone you clicked with, Dad, it would be easy. Look at Caro and Declan. Just as well she went to work in the bank, instead of college, they're meant to be together, anyone can see that."

"And look at you and that Luke. Anyone could see you weren't, except you. Took you three years to cop on."

"Yeah," Clare hugged her knees, "He was a waste of space. You should have pointed it out sooner. I'll help you with girlfriends."

"You think I'd listen, when you didn't? Caroline and I were blue in the face trying to point out to you that Luke was using you. But you didn't hear a thing. Why should I?"

"You're older. More sensible."

"I don't think that's a given. I might make appalling mistakes. The world isn't like that film you dragged me to last year, where everything worked out. Life isn't like that. If I flew to the Empire State building to meet someone at the top on Valentine's Day, it would be closed for maintenance."

"You loved that film. Have some faith Dad,"

"She's right, David. Listen to Clare."

"If you don't go out there, you'll never find out. Even after Luke, I haven't given up. I still go out and meet people."

"You're twenty-one. You're meant to meet people. I was twenty-one when I met your mum."

"You're only forty-four now. Hardly antique. And you're going to be on your own in a year or two. Caroline is going to be with Declan and I'll be away working, probably. Or trying to do post-grad. You don't have to marry anyone, Dad. Just have a friend."

"I can't marry anyone. I don't think the Irish law recognises foreign divorces, so that paper your mum sent from America is no use to me."

"We'll all vote for divorce when they have the referendum. It'll go

324

through, all my friends think so."

"You're in Trinity and you live in south Dublin. I don't think it's so certain in other parts of the country."

"By the time you know anyone well enough to marry them, it'll be possible."

"Oh, I'm meeting the love of my life when I'm ninety, am I?"

"Dad! You have no faith. Go out there and meet someone. Take up dancing. They're always short of men at dancing classes."

David was silent. I'd love to dance properly, he thought. I've always enjoyed moving to music, it would be good to know the steps.

"Go for it! You'll be good, you have a sense of rhythm. Now all we have to do is get Lucy to the same class. You choose where, I'll do my best. And we'll work on the divorce scenario. A lot of us are plugging away, trying to make sure our people vote for it. Too many of us are guides to people in bad situations. You're lucky compared to some, at least Kathleen got sense and moved away. Lots of them hang on to the sinking ship. Oh, listen to me, no wonder you never understand me, when I gabble like this. Dancing classes. Dancing classes, Dancing classes!"

"How will I find a class?"

"Good for you, Dad. That's the spirit. I expect the new terms start in January. We'll have time to ask around."

Chapter 50
Spring 1995

As Lucy put the receiver back it rattled, missed the cradle and clattered to the floor. She pulled it up by its cord with trembling hands and replaced it more carefully. Then she sat and looked at the phone and the piece of paper where she had written confidently only a moment before, '10th March, 4.30, Marian'. So easy, to ring the marriage counselling people and ask for an appointment. So difficult to tell Martin. I don't know how to put it. He thinks everything is fine, at least I think he does. How can he think we have a normal marriage? No sex unless he's drunk. Neither of us properly working, or properly at home. No discussions. And now, when I want to make things better, I'm scared to even say it to him. Have to be so careful every time I say anything he mightn't like, or he sulks.

"Why does it matter to you that he sulks, Lucy?" Marian, the counsellor, was sitting opposite Lucy, listening carefully to the whole story. Martin had refused to come.

"He makes me feel wrong. As though I'm in charge of his happiness and I've spoiled it. Failed him somehow."

"It sounds like you are having difficulties communicating properly. It would really help if Martin would come next time, but if he doesn't, I can still help you to cope with the situation."

"Don't do that," Trynor said to Marian's guide, "We don't want her to cope. We want her out. Can Marian do that?"

"She won't always do it directly," said Marian's guide, who was sitting on the floor beside Marian, "but it often happens, when people realise what's actually going on in their lives. Get your girl to keep coming, even if her husband won't. After all, you only have to worry about her, you know."

"You sound like a counsellor yourself."

"Yes, don't I? After all, I did go to nearly all the lectures on the counselling course. I could have passed the exams. Pity I can't practise, just sit here trying to get across to people. Marian sometimes hears me, that's fun."

"Well, can you work on her hearing you and tell her to help Lucy realise what's going on?"

"You sure you want her out?"

"Never surer."

Lucy walked slowly up Grafton Street, thinking over what Marian had said and what she should do next. Three more visits on my own with Marian and then ask Martin again if he'll come. I really don't want this to fail, she thought. I have to have another baby. My gosh, what am I saying? Another baby? What on earth for? I have my girl and my boy - the gentleman's family, they say. We can't afford another, well I can't afford another, not to mention taking time off to have it. And when would we conceive it anyway? He's interested in me once every two months if I'm lucky. Or unlucky, seeing as it's always for him and never for me, those drunken fumblings. But I have to try. I can't just give up without trying.

"Don't see why not. Plenty of people do, why should you have such high standards? Ruddy nuisance, you are, wanting to do your best all the time. Cut and run, Lucy, cut and run."

Lucy broke into a trot and jogged her way up the street, weaving between the ambling crowds. At Stephen's Green she stopped, a little puffed, and wondered why she was in a hurry. She walked more sedately across the road and went into the Green, passing the duck-pond on her way across to Earlsfort Terrace and the clinic, where Clodagh was holding the fort. As she did with Fuzz, Lucy envied the ducks their unconcern, their absorbing interest in the moment, as they upended in the endless search, as Beatrix Potter had put it, for their lost clothes. She smiled, remembering the picture of the guilty kittens being ticked off by their mother and then stopped smiling as she realised that that was the expression Martin had adopted when she had asked him to come to the counselling.

"I think he treats me like his mother. I realised last week, when I saw the ducks." Lucy looked at Marian, glad she had explained. Marian looked a bit bewildered, not making any quick connection between ducks and filial piety.

"Tell me more about that," she asked. So Lucy talked and as she

328

did she began to realise things about herself as well as about Martin. How she had allowed herself to become the bread winner, 'because I always want things to be right, and after all, I could earn money'. How she for reasons she could not explain, wanted to have another baby.

"But that is crazy. My marriage is terrible and I'm talking about babies. How can I even think it?"

"Maybe we will get your marriage better and Martin will get a better job and then you can have the time to have one. Let's wait and see. You aren't old, you have time to spare."

"But if Martin won't come to see you, how can it improve? He just looked hangdog at me when I said I'd been here and then talked about something else. I'll try again, but I don't know."

"So, I thought I'd better come and put you straight." Martin sat back in his chair and looked at Marian. He had been talking for twenty minutes, ever since the start of the session. Lucy had said nothing, while Martin explained to Marian, as though to a stupid child, exactly why his business was not yet making any money, why he had needed to go with his friends to rugby matches in Wales, Scotland and Italy this year, as well as attending local matches nearly weekly. He had told her what a wife's duties were and how he had agreed to let Lucy work – 'I'm a feminist really, wouldn't force my wife to stay at home' - and how he bathed the children at weekends, 'rugby permitting of course.' Then he explained how his brother and sister had fallen out with him and how that was affecting his ability to concentrate and had reduced his self-confidence so badly his work might suffer if he did not have a secure family background.

Marian smiled at him, so calmly that Lucy was amazed and had to hide her own amusement, then announced that they would now work through his points one at a time and that she would ask Martin to stay quiet while he listened to Lucy's comments.

"Good for you, if you can achieve that," Roki said, *from his place on the windowsill, "He talks a lot. I mean, I don't ask much of him, just to listen occasionally, but he talks through me every time. You hear, Marty? Listen to these women now, just for practice."*

"Let's go for coffee and I'll tell you what that Marian needs to

329

learn," Martin was in full flow again, "come on, I'm buying."

"What an offer. I can't resist," said Lucy as she followed him into Bewley's and prepared to be told in full what was wrong with this experienced counsellor.

David let himself into the house, humming under his breath. He felt energised by the evening, as he always did, moving to music was a good idea. Trust Clare to think of something useful. But the Samba this evening had been a bit of a disaster in dancing terms. He had discovered his third foot and put it everywhere he shouldn't. His partner had been highly amused, 'in hysterics' she had said, wiping her eyes. It was her third year of dancing classes and she knew what to do. I'll get the hang of it, David said to himself, like I did with the other dances. Eventually. He went into the livingroom, sat down at his piano and stroked the smooth wood before lifting the cover and starting to play a waltz, one he had danced to earlier that evening. So wonderful to have a piano at last. Unlike those holidays, I have it every day, it's not just a memory. His body swayed with the rhythm of the tune and he didn't hear the door opening. Clare came in quietly and sat on the couch. The waltz ended and David sat still, the last notes dying away.

"That was lovely, Dad."

David spun around, gasping.

"Clare, you put the heart across me! Don't creep up on me like that!"

"I'm sorry. I didn't actually creep. You were too absorbed to notice. Good class? Any girls yet?"

"Why do you want me to meet a 'girl'? There's lots of women there. All very nice. Thought my samba was a riot."

"Wow, you learning the samba? I'd like to see that! Why was it a riot?"

"My first time, I don't know the steps, got them wrong, nearly fell over. Carmel was in hysterics."

"Oh, 'Carmel'? My idea is working, then? First name terms?"

"Carmel is over seventy. She always grabs me as a partner, says I remind her of her nephew. She dances well, so I don't object."

"But you should object, Dad. I sent you to the class to meet a girlfriend, not a granny. Dance with someone else next week."

"No, not after all my hard work getting Carmel to monopolise

330

you. Just learn to dance. We're working on Lucy." Jotin was sitting on the piano, where he had been enjoying the vibrations from the music.

"Well, I do try. There is a shortage of men, like you said. None of the women stands out. I'm happy enough for the moment, it gets me out of the house and back into the music. I missed the music, all the time you were small." He turned back to the piano and started to play again, very quietly. Soft notes escaped gently from the wooden case and gathered around him and he escaped from the moment, *back across the years to the lyre and the fiddle and the many other instruments he had mastered, tunes he had loved and lovers he had wooed with them*, to a gentle place within himself where he was totally at peace.

"Hi Lucy, how was the holiday? We had a great one, loads to tell you," Jen was in full flow on the phone, "We all got so brown, and that hotel was just great. You should go next year."

"Maybe I will. Ours was okay. We got half way down France and stopped in a really nice campsite with a pool. The kids were in heaven. Robbie can almost dive, Ash can swim the whole length of the pool underwater. And she tried eating a snail! It was good to be away from the clinic and the house. But I've a huge Visa bill now, it'll take me till Christmas to clear it. I'm trying not to think about it, not to lose what I've gained."

"Did you gain, Lucy? Was it good for you?"

"It was fine. It's great watching the kids have fun and they encourage me. I mean, I'd never have played mini-golf except I was bullied into it and it was a laugh. Robbie won, because we gave him such a big handicap and he cheated."

"And you and Martin?" Jen was hesitant, "how did that side of things go? Did any of the counsellor's tips work?"

"We didn't actually fight. But we didn't miss having no baby-sitter, if you know what I mean. The kids are a great buffer."

"Poor kids. Did they notice?"

"I'm not sure. They didn't say."

"Of course they didn't say, Lucy. They don't really understand what they're seeing. But they do know things could be different. They've been in Marge's house, after all."

"Well, are you free to come over at the weekend? We'd love to

331

show you our photos and we brought home a bottle of the most amazing hooch, you have to try it. It stops all pain."

"I could do with that. But do you mind if I come on my own? It's hard at the moment, Martin is inclined to tell everyone we meet about the counsellor and what an idiot she is. He nabbed some unfortunate English people on the campsite and went on and on about it to them. Funny really, it turned out the man was a clinical psychologist. I'd love to know what he actually thought of Martin's lecture!"

"No, you come. You're my friend, Lucy, it's you I want to see, really. You bring whoever you want."

"Just me."

"This time."

"Half seven Saturday okay? Okay, seeya."

David was sitting on a sun-lounger in the back garden, with a beer on the stool beside him. He had spent a couple of hours dead-heading the roses, generally tidying up the messy growth and was feeling a little tired but quite happy. The sun was warm on his skin and small birds were twittering nearby, giving him the illusion of being in the countryside. The fifth summer in a row that I haven't been away anywhere. The peace of it. I wonder how long it will take, before I want to go away again? No more beaches, ever again, if I don't want and at the moment, I certainly don't want. What is it with beaches, everyone else seems to be addicted to them and I can't be bothered. And barbeques. It's great living in a climate where you don't have to have barbeques all the time. They never light properly, you spend ages fussing round them, burning your fingers on the matches and in the end, you've got a petrol flavoured burger. Crazy.

"Only because you're still nervous of open flames. No need to have barbeques, stick with the grill. Why revisit the scenes of your deaths? Though it really is curious why you are all so fussed about how you died, when you know perfectly well when you're on this side that being dead is not the problem. I mean, neither the wave nor the fire actually hurt you, it was so quick. I'm so glad I put you to sleep on that train. It would have been a pest if you'd been afraid to get on a train this time round, with all those trips."

And no more train trips, coach trips, plane trips even. Nothing.

Just sit here and get old.

The phone rang inside the house. David grumbled a bit, but got up and trotted inside, assuming it would be one of the twins. It was Carmel.

"Hello, David? Hope you're enjoying the sunshine, isn't it lovely? Well, some of us are missing the classes and we're getting a group together to go to the tea dance next Sunday in the Grantham hotel. We'd love you to come." She reeled off the list of participants and David could see why he was needed. There was only one other man.

"I'd be delighted, Carmel. So long as it isn't another gorgeous day, I wouldn't like to be indoors on an afternoon like this."

"It won't be. When do we ever get two good weekends in a row? So will we see you there? It's at four o'clock."

David enjoyed the tea dance, it was good to move with the music again after a couple of months of holidays and even his samba wasn't too bad, just a little rusty. Over the tea, Carmel started to quiz him. How such a nice young man was out without a wife. David explained, leaving out anything that made him sound too sour, just the bare facts.

"She just up and left? The hussy!" Carmel's views on the world were straightforward. "Did she have another man?"

"No, just realised that her wanderlust was too strong."

"She'll come back, so, when she gets it out of her system. Can she dance?"

David explained that Kathleen would not come back and that if she did, he would not want her to live with him. He told her about the divorce papers from America.

"Don't worry, David, she can't get rid of you like that. There's no divorce here and that's how it should stay," Carmel patted his hand.

"I'd like to be divorced properly," said David, "I have a legal separation, but it doesn't feel finished. The American divorce is no use here. If I wanted to remarry, it wouldn't count."

"Would you want to remarry?" Carmel's voice rose to an indignant squeak.

"Yes, if I met the right woman," David looked at Carmel, who was staring at him, astonished, "I don't think I know what it feels like to be married, not really. I'd like a chance to."

"Are you proposing?" Carmel was trying to cover her confusion.

"I think I'm too young for you, you know."

"I'll wait for you," David said gallantly, "in the meanwhile, I'm going to vote for divorce in the referendum and pray that enough other people see the light."

"Have you any children? What about them, how do they feel?"

"Twin girls, they're twenty-two. They know why their mother left. They remember being dragged on all those holidays, trip after trip. They're a bit like me now, happy to stay here. It was Clare who made me take up the dancing, she wants me to meet someone new."

"Did she? Goodness. Is she not worried that someone new would displace her mother?"

"From what? She has heard twice from her mother in five years. Her mother isn't a big issue in her life at the moment. She's looking for a man for herself, but she worries that I'll be all on my own, if she settles down, like her sister's going to."

"I never met anyone with a story like this before," Carmel was quiet, "I can see how you would vote 'yes'," she patted his hand again, "do you know, I think I might vote yes myself, to give you a chance. You deserve it. I had mine, my Con was the best man you could meet, kind and gentle and funny. I never thought I was lucky, just reckoned I got what I deserved. But now I see, I was very lucky, even though he died on me three years ago, the wretch. We had six beautiful children, they look out for me and we have good memories of the old days."

"The children could vote yes too."

"And maybe I'll tell my children about you and we can swing the vote!"

"You're very kind, Carmel," David was moved. He guessed what kind of background Carmel had come from and knew what a big gesture she was making on his behalf. If she made it when she got into the booth.

"She'll stick to her word. We'll remind her."

David stood up. He could hear music again from the ballroom. "May I have the honour of this dance, Madame?" Carmel took his arm and smiled up at him. "Delighted, Monsieur! Until I can find you a young one to take my place!"

Chapter 51
Autumn 1995

Lucy swung into the driveway in an elderly baby Fiat, looking forward to showing off to the children and to Martin, that she had managed at last to make them a two car family. She had bought their other car several years earlier, but Martin insisted on using it most of the time, so Lucy was left feeling stranded. And not just feeling, she thought, really stranded more than once. Those business meetings of Martin's give me the pip, the way they have to come first. But not anymore.

She let herself into the house and shouted "Hi! Anyone here?" A distant mumble came from the kitchen.

"Guess what I've got?" said Lucy as she went into the room, where Aisling was sitting at the table doing homework, still in her school uniform. Susan the baby-sitter was sitting at the other end of the table, her head down, working on problems from past exam papers. She never reacted to much.

"Where's Robbie?" asked Aisling, looking up. She was eating a chocolate biscuit and showering crumbs down her school jumper. Fuzz was under the table, fielding the crumbs and hoping for larger accidents.

"If he didn't come home from Marge's, I suppose he's still there. I came straight home," said Lucy, "Did you check, Susan?" Susan shrugged.

"No. Ash got here as usual just after I arrived. Robbie didn't come. I suppose he must be still there."

"I thought he was with you, like always," Aisling looked up at Lucy and frowned. "Didn't you collect him?"

"No, I told him to come home with Marge today, stay there till you'd be home and then ring here for Susan to fetch him. He's probably still playing with Jamie." She went to the phone and talked to Marge's sitter. Her heart began to pound.

"You mean he didn't come home with Marge? You haven't seen him at all?" Lucy sat down heavily and looked at Aisling's wide eyes staring back at her. "Oh God, no. Oh please. Where is he?" She picked up the phone book and searched frantically for numbers.

Twenty minutes later, she had found the school closed and unanswering, Marge in a meeting and unable to come to the phone, Robbie's best friend Greg safely at home and unable to say where Robbie was; his other friend, also at home, was able to tell her that he had seen Robbie waiting outside the school.

"Maybe he walked home. I don't think he's got lost, Mrs Fitzgerald, it's not far enough."

"No, thank you Marcus, I'm sure he's not lost. But he's not allowed to walk home. Did he say anything to you about who was collecting him?" Lucy's mind whirled through the possibilities. Gradually she became a complete blank, as each phone call achieved nothing and she numbly realised that each hope was vain.

"If we'd a car we could go and search," said Aisling.

"We have, come on! Please stay here, Susan, in case Robbie comes back," and Lucy was out the door, Aisling right behind her, full of excitement when she saw the car, - "you bought it just the right day, Mum!"

"If I hadn't bought it, I'd have been at the school to walk home with Robbie and he wouldn't have gone off like this," Lucy cursed herself inwardly. Why had she gone off like that to surprise everyone? It would have been better to tell them, maybe even bring them to fetch it. She was being punished for trying to have fun, trying to make life easier. Oh please, help me find Robbie. Quickly.

"It's all right, he's safe. Don't get in a fuss."

Lucy reversed carefully out of the drive and considered which way to go first. Up to the school and retrace his steps. No, that didn't seem right. How did you start a search, when Robbie probably wouldn't be on the street, but safe inside some as yet unknown friend's house - I'll kill the woman who didn't make him ring home - and if he is hurt somewhere I won't see him. Lucy's shoulders started to shake and she put her head down onto her hands where they gripped her new steering wheel.

"Don't cry, he'll be home soon," said Trynor. "Come on, listen. Make yourself feel better, go for a drive, the car is great."

"Aisling, Robbie is OK, but your Mum isn't. Be a distraction. Be annoying," Lekna gave Aisling a poke in the chest.

"Ow! Mum, this seat belt is too tight, it's cutting into me. Are we going anywhere or just sitting here, 'cos I don't want to be cut in two for no reason."

"We'll go around a bit and see what we see," said Lucy. "The seatbelt is fine, just ease it out a little."

An hour later, Lucy was crabby and on the verge of tears. They had driven around the whole area twice, crisscrossing their path several times. They had called to the Garda station and reported Robbie missing; a laconic Guard had taken details but had failed to give any sense of alarm.

"We'll let the cars know, Ma'am. They'll be watching out. Did he not go with his father?"

"No, my husband left early this morning to do some business in Athlone."

The Guard was calm, but not calming. It seemed Robbie was not missing long enough to cause worry and he thought half three in the afternoon was not dangerous. "Let us know, Ma'am, if he doesn't come home for his tea. They mostly do," was his encouraging suggestion. They had called back into the house three times to see if Robbie had arrived, but could tell each time by Fuzz's ecstatic welcome and Susan's casual "No, not yet," that there was no good news. They came home again in silence to let Susan go home. Aisling's grizzling about the discomfort of the whole episode was silenced by the seriousness of a visit to the police station. Once again, Fuzz greeted them, full of joy that her people were home.

"Trouble with you, Fuzz, is that you can't count. There should be three of us," said Lucy.

"Four," said Aisling, "shouldn't Dad be back? He sometimes is by now."

"Should he? Even from Athlone? What time is it?"

"It's nearly half six." Aisling went over to the television and switched it on. "Let's see if there're any accidents on the news, then you can ring the hospital."

Lucy sat down heavily. It was said that bad news travels fast and no news is good news, but supposing that was wrong and like her Dad said, the world had ended and no-one had remembered to tell her? I never hear anything unless I ask specifically, she thought. I wouldn't make a reporter, I can't ferret out gossip. And now I don't even know where my own boy is. What sort of mother does that make me?

"I'm not going to ring hospitals just yet, I'm going to ring Jen. I need to talk to someone who'll say something encouraging, not depress me worse." She reached out to the phone and as she touched the receiver, it shrilled. Lucy grabbed for the phone, but it slipped and fell onto the carpet, where it squeaked "Mum? Mum?"

"Robbie? Where are you? Why didn't you ring? Are you all right? Where are you?"

"We won, it was great, they were beating us at half time, but then we got a cool try and beat them by 3 points!"

"Who's 'we' Robbie?" Lucy was trying to be calm, now that Robbie was obviously all right. Now he would have to be fetched and reprimanded.

"Old St Christopher's of course. We were playing Howth College."

A new anger began to grow in Lucy: "Are you with your Dad?"

"Yes. We're in O'B s now having a jar. Well Dad is and I'm having a Coke and crisps. Dad sent me to ring you and say we'd be home later."

"Get Dad to the phone please, Rob."

"Okay." Lucy heard a crash as the receiver at the other end was dropped and then just a distant hubbub. She waited, but no-one came. After a minute or two, the line went dead. Lucy hung up and stared at the phone. Thank God Robbie is okay.

"OK then Aisling, dinner to make." Lucy was all business. They'd be home soon, explanations and apologies would be given, dinner eaten, normality restored. She got out an onion and started to peel it. She had no idea what dinner would be, but she'd get an idea while chopping.

At half-eight Robbie and Martin still weren't home. Lucy and Aisling had finished dinner and left enough for microwaving later. Lucy was having a cup of coffee and trying to read an article in her professional journal, but she couldn't concentrate. She read the words and each one made perfect sense, but she had no idea what the author was actually saying. It might as well be in Russian, she thought, Cyrillic wouldn't be any less meaningful. She put the magazine down and looked into her coffee. There must be a reason, he's met someone who can give business advice, that's half the point of going to the club, to keep in touch and make new contacts. I haven't many contacts, not business ones, just Jen and Gina. And the people at work. And Alison. Actually, that's quite a lot really. And all those people that we know as a couple, but they don't count in this tally because Martin knows them too and he has loads of friends I never get to see. Which is crazy, because I like going to matches too, but I never seem to get the chance. Could have gone today, though, if I'd known about it; we could all have gone and been a family again. And we could have come home together at a better time for Robbie's bedtime. Lucy looked at her watch, it was nine o'clock. She felt so trapped, sitting at home waiting, unable to do anything, until she remembered the car. Her freedom was sitting in the drive waiting for her.

"Aisling, come on, we're going to Donnybrook to get Robbie." Aisling grumbled about having to go out again, but complied. She waited in the car on double yellow lines outside O'Bs, to explain to curious policemen or irate motorists that her mother was rescuing her six year old brother from the pub. Inside the pub it was crowded and smoky and Lucy had to push through the groups of men, as she looked for Martin. Eventually she saw Robbie, slumped back on a seat, his eyes shut. Martin was a few yards away, gesticulating excitedly with his friends, but he glanced over at Lucy.

"Hi guys," Lucy raised her voice to be heard, "I'm taking Robbie home now."

"Hi Lucy, have a drink, help us celebrate! Ah, come on, what'll it be?"

"No, Martin, he should be in bed."

"Don't ruin the party, sit down." Martin pushed a hand into Lucy's chest and she staggered back a pace. Colm, one of Martin's friends, put out a hand to steady her and Martin came closer.

"You are making a show of me, Lucy. Now have a bloody drink," Martin spat the words into her ear. She shook her head. Martin took a ten pound note out of his pocket and thrust it at her. "You always say I don't pay," he muttered, "so now buy yourself a gin and stop being ridiculous." He turned away and was soon shouting about the winning try. Lucy reached for Robbie and pulled him up.

"Come on, sausage," she whispered to him, as she put her arm round his drooping shoulders. Colm made a space for her through the crowd and she smiled at him.

"Thanks. Tell Martin I've gone when he stops talking, will you?"

Robbie, when he came out with Lucy, was tired and fractious. He protested several times that it was not his fault.

"Was too. You were meant to come home with Marge after school," Aisling was smug. It was good not to be in trouble.

"I was waiting for her, but Dad came, and I went with him. But we didn't come home, we went to the match."

"You should have come home first and told me, then I could have told Mum. Then I wouldn't be out again looking for you."

"That's enough, Aisling. It's not Robbie's fault. I'm sorry for being so cross, Rob. I was just worried."

"Okay. Whose car is this?" When Robbie found out that the car was here to stay he perked up and started planning trips. He fell silent, thinking, and by the time they reached home he was asleep. Lucy carried him up to bed and put him under his duvet. Then, after remembering to phone the Garda station to let them know Robbie was safe, she went to bed herself, feeling that the day had been long enough.

Someone was shining a light in her eyes, shouting at her 'where is your son? Where is he? Where did you leave him?' She began to protest that it was not her fault and then she woke up. Martin was in the room and had turned on the light.

"I was asleep."

"I'm not. And I can't see in the dark," Martin lurched towards the bed, "and I'd like to see my wife, because I'm feeling good and a man needs a wife when he'sh feeling good." Martin sat down heavily onto Lucy's feet and put a hand on the curve of her hip.

"Well, I'm not feeling good, Martin. Actually, I'm feeling about as bad as I can. I'm very angry with you."

"Why? Did nothing wrong. Good guy. Try hard, gave you ten quid. Good father, had a good time. Won match."

"You are not a good father. And you are a lousy husband. You took Robbie from school without telling anyone. I thought you were in Athlone, it never crossed my mind you'd collected him. It would only have taken you a minute to call home and leave a message, or ring work and tell me. But no, you went off gallivanting and left me worried sick."

"Not sick now. Looking beautiful. Give me a kiss," Martin leant forward and breathed yeasty fumes at Lucy. She leant away.

"Not now, Martin. I don't feel loving towards you. You don't care for me, how can I?"

"My wife. Have to love me - make love to me. Your job." Martin's hand was working its way in under the duvet and onto Lucy's thigh. "Come on, Luce, 'tsa a great day, won the match, good time with the lads, wanta finish it properly." His fingers walked over her leg towards her groin and he pulled her leg towards him, his hand searching. He was up on one elbow now, leaning towards her, pushing her back onto the pillows with his shoulder, his breath fast and ragged. Lucy felt his knee pushing between hers and she struggled from him.

"No, Martin, stop!"

"Won't." Martin laughed and grabbed her arm, pushing her down. Lucy put her hand over his and gripped.

"That's the girl. A bit of spirit." Martin's knee forced between hers again and Lucy jerked her leg up to get away. Then her head shot back as Martin's first slap hit her face. The second connected with her nose.

"Bitch!" he snarled, "going for the balls isn't fair."

Lucy gaped at him. Fair? Her nose was throbbing and she felt tears starting. She took a deep breath and rolled towards his pinioning hand, pulling her leg free and kicking towards him. Martin grunted and let go. She hit the floor with her knees and in moments had grabbed her dressing-gown and was out of the room and running across the landing into the bathroom. She slammed the door and shot the inadequate little bolt she had screwed on at the very top after taking the key away so that the children would not get locked in by accident. She hoped it would hold. As Martin swore and banged on the door she threw her weight against it, bracing her feet against the bath. The door bulged and vibrated behind her as he thumped. After a minute there was silence and she heard his feet going back to the bedroom. She sagged onto the toilet, tears streamed down her face and blood trickled onto her lip.

"He's gone mad! Drunk, but he's been drunk before. This time he's mad!"

"No, not actually mad. Just telling the truth. In vino veritas, they say. That is how he thinks. How he has always thought. You should not have married him, I told you." Trynor was perched on the side of the bath. "Now, come on, wash your face and go and find somewhere to sleep. You can't talk to him tonight, he's past it."

Lucy splashed her face with cold water and looked at herself in the mirror, her eyes red-rimmed, her hair spiky, a bruise beginning under one eye. There was a tentative tap on the door.

"Go away!"

"Mummy?"

Lucy opened the door. Aisling was on the landing, her eyes big in her face, her hair sticking up round her face like a halo. She was clutching Teddo, who had only this year been allowed to stay in bed all day and not accompany her everywhere.

"What's the noise? Is Daddy angry?"

"Daddy got very excited at his match and then he had lots of beer. He's gone to sleep now," I hope, added Lucy under her breath. I wouldn't be able for him if he came at me now. "And you should go back to bed." She led Aisling back into her room and lifted the duvet, encouraging Aisling to settle Teddo in his place on the pillow and cuddle beside him. She stroked her daughter's shoulder and sang softly almost under her breath, watching the child's breathing slow, becoming even and calm. So much for my little triumph, my new car. Just another bad day. More struggle. More keeping it normal for the kids. Covering up. Hiding the problems.

"No, Lucy, not more of the same. Time to change. Listen to me. Time to change."

But if he thinks I'm going to go on like this, keeping the whole household going, so he can go off to matches on a weekday, steal my son and not tell me where he is, he can think again.

"I don't like Daddy shouting," Aisling was looking up at Lucy, "if he goes on he should stand in the Naughty Square, like in Robbie's classroom." She closed her eyes. Lucy looked down at her and her eyes filled up. Out of the mouths of babes, she thought, she is right. And I don't think the naughty square is anywhere in this house. She leant over and kissed Aisling on the forehead, quietly tiptoed out of the room and crept across the landing. Martin was snoring. Lucy eased into the bedroom and opened the wardrobe, pulling out the single duvet that was there for visitors. Then she went downstairs and rolled herself up in it on the couch in the living room and fell into a heavy sleep. *Trynor tried to make sure she didn't dream.*

342

Chapter 52

Trynor was excited and went in a flurry of energies to discuss this development with Jotin and Mohmi. They were waiting for him, with a table laid with a white cloth, holding several dishes. Jotin called over to him.

"Look! Mohmi's told me she's able to make food! I've tasted some. Not quite as good as the real stuff on earth, but worth trying. It might save you a return trip."

Mohmi waved a hand towards the table.

"Guten Appetit! I've been trying for ages to create a strudel. You can tell me how successful I've been. And I've done latkes, though I can't seem to get them properly crisp, and some weisswurst- those are easier, they have almost no taste anyway. Try them."

"Did you make any mustard?"

"Sorry, I forgot. That would be tricky."

"Mmm, the latkes aren't bad," Trynor was talking with his mouth full, "maybe need a bit of salt." Mohmi closed her eyes and waved her hands with great concentration. Trynor took another bite. "Yes, well done. You've been practising this, I think?"

"For hundreds of years. Haven't done these exact recipes before."

"Did you know we had reason to celebrate? That Lucy eventually realised she can't stay with Martin?"

"Yes, we'd heard. How is it going?"

"Not bad. There was a great row one morning, Martin was hung over and made things worse by trying to defend himself. Lucy said she was never going to sleep with him again and that he could set up a camp bed in the garden shed. And he said he had more sense than that and that he would go to Colm's. So he did. He's there now and Roki is furious, because there is a big row there now, Colm's wife is not as keen on Martin as Colm is."

"How are Lucy and the children?"

"Lucy is stunned at how easy it was. Aisling saw how upsetting Martin's behaviour was and understands a little. Robbie is less sure, but Lucy has told him he can see his Dad whenever he wants, so long as he lets her know, so he's calm at the moment. Lucy is organising for the two of them to go to 'Rainbows' groups for some support. And she has made an appointment with a solicitor. So full steam ahead on the meeting!"

"Haven't you forgotten, it mightn't be plain sailing?" Jotin was speaking softly. "Mohmi's alternative idea might not work out and there's not as much point getting them to meet if they can't have the baby. It's Moonsong insisting on having them as parents again. Maybe, once she's an adult and can cope on her own we should move them on to another life quickly and make them both the same sex - and straight - so they can notice their abilities and get on with inventing something!"

"No, I want to watch them grow old together, after all this. If something comes up later we can re-think on that and get them out of here quickly. Car accidents are ten a penny. But for now we should let them have some fun," Trynor was on to the strudel now, "like I'm having now, this is great. Not quite as good as the real thing, but not half bad at all. Well done, Mohmi."

"Thank you. Pleased to be of assistance. I've been talking to Moonsong again, about how to manage this time round. And she's happy whatever we can arrange. So I'm fine tuning my plan now, looking for actual people and guides to help. We have a few years, if they aren't actually together yet."

"No, we have to work on that," Jotin said "For a start, you have to get her into the right dancing class. There's David, learning the waltz and the cha-cha and being madly popular with all the wrong women; I'm on my toes keeping him from getting too tightly embroiled with any of them. Carmel is a great help, keeping him away from most of the younger ones and that had a good spin off value, she voted for divorce and so did a lot of her friends. She's a persuasive woman and she's so fond of our David she wanted the best for him. And enough others like us were obviously working too, a lot of Davids and Lucys out there and a few Carmels, so the law is changed. But there is our Lucy, learning to dance her chakras! What possessed you to let her join that class?"

"She heard about it at art therapy. Actually, I think it helped her to centre her energies and realise what was going on, how much energy she was losing to Martin. He was doing fine and she was becoming exhausted."

"Well, thankful for small mercies, I suppose. Nothing wasted, even if you didn't plan it."

"It did cross my mind. I'm not a totally useless guide!"

"I didn't suggest you were. So which of them should move? We'd better be clear about it, or they'll both move and we'll be no better off."

"Good plan," said Trynor, "perhaps we should write a list, like Lucy does?"

"Next time round, I certainly think so. Or call in some older guides to keep an eye on us. This time, I think Lucy should move class. The ballroom dancing is sociable, so I can't see how I'd get David out of it. And if she learnt the steps, they could dance together again, like they have before and you remember where that led, every time!" Jotin's eyes twinkled.

"You're right. I'll get working on it. You keep David safe in the meanwhile. Apart from Carmel, is he interested in anyone at the moment?"

"Mildly. He's had coffee after the class a few times with a woman called Mary. She's pleasant, separated like him, but it's not very intense. The minute he sees Lucy it'll be goodbye Mary."

"Have you pushed him to go for a divorce? He'll qualify when it comes in next year, Kathleen has been gone for four years already, that's long enough. Not that they have to be married to have a baby, not these days."

"You've forgotten, we had a vasectomy. It'll take him a while to realise he should think of getting it reversed. If that even works; I don't think we can be sure of it. But he has thought of divorce, he had several drinks to celebrate when the referendum was passed. He told the girls that it was probably the three of them and Carmel that swung it!"

"Work on them both to get divorced," Mohmi broke in, "My idea depends on it."

"How are things going with your idea?" Trynor was still a bit excited, everything had changed for Lucy so recently.

"I'm still working on the details. Be patient, there's no rush."

"No. And I think Lucy shouldn't meet David just yet. She is too sensible to allow herself to fall for anyone she meets on the rebound. That's why she stayed so long with Martin."

"Why?" Jotin was puzzled, "What rebound was she on?"

345

"No, I mean she is sensible. Prides herself on it. Always makes her head rule her heart, she's been shouting me down for years, only just started listening. If she'd listened sooner, she'd never have got involved with that wastrel in the first place. Down with sensible! Long live listening!"

"Hear, Hear," said Jotin and Mohmi, and they all laughed.

Chapter 53

"So, can we do it this life, do you think?" Jotin was lounging on some soft grass, looking up at Trynor and Mohmi, who were sitting on a bench eating strudel with whipped cream. "Can we actually get them together? They're both single at last, we had better get on with it quickly. Your Lucy is a beautiful young woman still, someone else might grab her. Get her into flowered shirts and I'll get David into her vicinity, then we can relax. I hope."

Trynor wiped cream off his mouth. "Your idea working out, Mohmi?"

"Yes, it's all systems go, as they say on earth. I'll explain when you've got them together. Just don't worry about Dawn, Moonsong, she'll be able to join them eventually." Mohmi finished the strudel and got up. "I'm going to learn how to create flowers next. Not so tasty, but beautiful. I'm starting with snowdrops. See you."

"Okay, so you need to get Lucy to the next tea dance. They have a few through the summer and David usually goes. Carmel will help get them together, I reckon, she's almost adopted him!"

Lucy was looking in her wardrobe in despair. In a moment of madness she had promised Jen that she would go to a tea-dance with her and Peter on Saturday, but she had nothing that vaguely resembled a dancing outfit. I've only jeans, tracksuits and tee-shirts. And work clothes, but I'm not going to a dance in navy slacks and a white tunic. No skirts to speak of, just that one mini that I bought in a sale in another mad moment. I'm not wearing that anywhere, it might have even worse results than the time I wore it to go out with Martin, that time he put his hand up it and refused to take it down and everyone noticed. She pulled the miniskirt off the hanger and threw it in the waste basket.

"Shame, David would have liked that skirt." Lucy stood and looked down into the basket, at the skirt lying crumpled among used tissues. She thought of retrieving it, but resisted and looked again at her cupboard.

"Okay, so I can't convince you. In that case let's go shopping."

I'll have to buy something. And I'll have to bring the kids, we'll have to go now, I only have the one free afternoon between now and the weekend. Though I could go on Saturday morning after Martin collects them. But that's cutting it fine. Suppose Dunnes' has nothing and I have to go into town?

"Aisling, Robbie, into the car please, we're going to Cornelscourt."

"Oh no, why?" There was a chorus of groans.

"Because I'm going out with Jen on Saturday and I have nothing to wear."

"I need some things too, Mum," Aisling stopped groaning and was winsome.

"Is there a toyshop?" Robbie also switched on the charm.

"No. We are just going to get something for me, so I don't make a show of myself at a dance. I can't afford to buy something for everybody."

The children grumbled a bit more, but got into the car and put on their seatbelts. They chugged carefully to the shopping centre. This car had been hers for less than a year, but it had been old long before she got it and needed careful handling. Its huge advantage was that it was so tiny, so she could fit in the smallest parking space.

The clothes shop was almost deserted. Everyone with sense is out in the sunshine, thought Lucy, not trying to buy a skirt to go to a dance that probably only geriatrics will be at. Jen thinks it'll be 'a laugh'. But she has Peter, to save her from the wheezing fat old men who'll want to dance with us. I see enough of those at work, I don't want to have to be charming to them socially as well. The only reason I'm going, is because I like dancing and haven't done it for years. Can only waltz, really and then only if my partner is really good. Must learn the other dances sometime.

"Yes, learn to dance. Soon. Oh look, here are some great blouses, see, all flowers? Buy one of these, we need flowers."

"No, Mum, they look like wallpaper. Yuck." Aisling was dismissive. "You need something elegant." She was off, rummaging along the racks. Why did I think I should come on my own, thought Lucy, she's more interested in this than I am, as Aisling pulled out one thing after another, passing judgement on each. The pile deemed suitable to try on grew slowly. Robbie grew bored and began to whine.

"Okay, Ash, that's enough. I'll try these on and something will have to do."

They went into the changing rooms and Aisling was put in charge of Robbie while Lucy struggled into and out of clothes. At last she reluctantly chose an ankle length skirt and a short sleeved blouse with a lowish neckline. They'll do, she thought and I could wear them for other occasions too.

"They'll be fine. But we still need a flower." Trynor wondered what to do and talked to Aisling and Robbie's guides.

Lucy led the way across the shop to the sign saying 'Pay Here', paying no further attention to the racks of clothes. They walked through the children's section to get to the till and as they queued up, Robbie delved into a sale bin and came out with a tee-shirt, which he thrust at Lucy.

"I'd like that," he said very firmly. Lucy looked at the bin. All at forty pence, well he wasn't asking for much. She looked at the shirt. It had a large sunflower on it.

"Do you really want to wear a flower?" Robbie looked puzzled, looked at the flower and shrugged. "I suppose." *"Good boy," said his guide.*

"Don't be sexist, Mum. If he wants a flower, why shouldn't he have one?"

"Okay, my little women's libber. Give it here." Lucy handed the tee-shirt to the cashier with her skirt and blouse.

"Thanks guys," said Trynor to the children's guides.

At home, Lucy put on her new outfit again and turned this way and that in front of the mirror. It looked quite good, more feminine than she had been wearing recently. The skirt would twirl a little. Robbie came into the room, followed by a giggly Aisling. He had the flowered teeshirt on and it reached nearly to his knees.

"Look at Rob's dance dress!" laughed Aisling. Lucy looked at it, surprised.

"Why didn't we notice in the shop it was huge? What size does it say on it?"

Aisling pulled the neck of the shirt out and peered down. "I think it's a ten. Is that your size, Mum?" Robbie pulled the shirt off and threw it on the bed. "I got it for you Mum, really," he said.

"You did not, you liar!" Aisling advanced on him, making I'm going to tickle you movements with her fingers and the two of them ran squealing from the room. Lucy picked up the tee-shirt and held it up against herself. It would probably be tight, she really needed a twelve. But the flower was huge and bright and cheering. Deciding she could probably wear it sometime, she stuffed it in a drawer.

David's phone rang, jolting him awake. He wondered for a moment where he was, he had been running through a field full of flowers, pursued by a purple pig and a cow with neon horns. He sat up and swung his legs out of bed, wondering who could have anything urgent to say to him on a Saturday morning at the crack of dawn. Suddenly curious, he went down the stairs two at a time,and lifted the phone with a breathless "Yes?"

"Hello, is that David Hyland?"

"Mmm"

"I'm so sorry to bother you, you don't know me, my name is Eileen Sweeney. Carmel's daughter."

"?"

"My mother goes to the dance class with you."

"Oh, yes, I'm sorry. I wasn't with you for a minute. Is there a problem?" David sat down on the little stool beside the phone, feeling suddenly cold and wishing he had stopped for his dressing gown.

"I'm phoning from St Matthew's. Mum has been brought into Casualty. She asked me to ring you to say she probably won't be at the dance this afternoon."

David looked at his watch. The 'crack of dawn' turned out to be half-ten.

"I'm sorry to hear that. Is she seriously ill?"

Eileen Sweeney described the symptoms and her worries. From his contact with nursing homes and hospitals down the years, David guessed that indeed, Carmel would not be at the dance. He said he would call in and see her later in the morning. "They might still know me there, a little. They'll probably let me in. Give your Mum my love." He rang off, fetched his dressing gown and went into the kitchen to put on the kettle. Poor Carmel. He hoped it was not her heart, but feared it might be. I'll miss her at the dancing. There's no-one else there that I go to see, really. Mary is pleasant, I'll have to

350

get to know her better.

"Don't bother about Mary. Unless you want to ring her to go to the tea-dance. Or were you going to be brave and go on your own? That would be best. Saves Mary from having to make her own way home."

David greeted the porter at the door of St Matthew's Casualty Department, then squeezed past the waiting crowds to the nurses' station. He recognised only one of the nurses on duty, but that was enough.

"Hello, Brenda! You still in charge of this madhouse? Well organised chaos as usual."

"Mr Hyland, it's a long time since you were going the rounds. I barely remember you and your brochures. What has you here today? I don't suppose you've come to hand out free pens?"

"You're right there. When you're in management you never get your hands on anything. They only trust me with the one company biro for my own use. No, I've a friend in, I'm told. Carmel Sweeney."

"Oh yes, she's being transferred to Coronary Care for observation. I think she's still in cubicle nine."

David went over to the curtained cubicle and announced himself. "Knock knock? David here." He peeked in and saw Carmel, attached to a monitor and with a drip in her arm, lying back on the pillows looking pale but still with a glint in her eye. She raised her unattached arm and beckoned him in.

"What did Eileen go and spoil your morning for, telling you I was here?"

"You asked me to, Mam. Do you not remember?"

"They've pulled me and pushed me so much since I got into this bed it's a wonder I remember my own name. But I'm fine now, David and I don't want you fussing about me. You're to go off to that dance anyway. It's important."

David took Carmel's hand. "Why is it important? I go to dance with you and I don't think you'll be dancing today."

"I don't know why, but I have a feeling. You go and dance," she shook her head and closed her eyes for a moment. "I don't know what I was thinking, telling her to say I was here. You're not to let it stop you. You go, d'you hear?" She closed her eyes again. "I'll be still here tomorrow. Come and tell me all about it, all the news."

Davis smiled. The news, indeed. The tea-dances were the most unexciting events he had ever been at. Pleasant, but not newsworthy. And now his friend would not be there and he'd be worried about her.

"But aren't you always the news, Carmel? Why would I go there, when my pal is here?"

Carmel tried to lift herself up in the bed. "You go to that dance. You do it for me. I voted for you, so now, don't be wasting my effort and putting my soul at risk for nothing." She sagged back, exhausted. David looked at her and wondered. Did she know something? Maybe I should go and be nice to Mary. I'll try it.

"Okay, Carmel, I'll go. You rest now and don't fuss. I'll come and see you tomorrow."

Robbie was standing on the armchair, leaning on the back of it, looking out the window. He was hoping to be the first to see Martin arrive. Martin had been on the phone during the week, telling Robbie what they would do this Saturday and how he expected to have a new car by then. So Robbie was in a fever of excitement each time a car passed, thinking each one was his Dad. But so far none had stopped.

"It's only half ten, Rob. Dad never gets here before eleven." Aisling was ever the older sister, calm and knowledgeable. She wanted to see her Dad again too, though she was cautious. After all, she had heard the Big Fight, as she called it to herself.

"I wish he would come sooner, like he said," said Lucy, "and bring you back at a sensible hour. I seem to spend my Saturdays waiting around for him. It's worse than going on a date, all this anxious waiting."

"I don't think he means to be late, Mum," Aisling was thoughtful, "I just think he's surprised by things a lot."

Aren't you right there, thought Lucy, looking at her little girl in amazement. So young and so perceptive. Martin goes through life in a constant state of astonishment. Never predicts bad traffic and is caught in it. Forgets that if you have four pints, you end up drunk. Wonders that he gets cold when he goes outside without a coat in January. Is amazed that the people who collect car tax actually want him to pay it. Tries to rape his wife in a drunken stupor and is puzzled that she is cross about it. Oh feck, she said to herself, why am I thinking about Martin again? Wasting my energy trying to work things out. I'll go and wash my hair, he'll hardly come before I'm finished.

She came downstairs again with a towel round her head, to find Robbie sulking in the chair and Aisling glued to a children's news programme.

"Look Mum, aren't they sweet? They're Chinese."

Lucy looked at the screen. A group of English couples were in some sort of waiting area and some women in airline uniforms were handing them babies. There were lots of tears, but it was not the babies who were crying.

"They've come by plane from China. To be adopted, in England. Aren't they lovely?" Aisling had gone misty, as she did whenever there was a baby around. Lucy sometimes wondered if she would have to lock Aisling up when she got into her teens, to stop her producing her own baby. A pity I can't have a baby, Ash would love it and it would be good for Rob too.

"We're working on you having a baby. At least, Mohmi is. I hope her plan works out, otherwise we'll have to find an expert in vasectomy reversal. Don't give up on the baby idea. Today's the day you meet its father! I'm so excited!" Trynor did a little dance around the room, bumping into the children's guides who laughed and pushed him away.

Lucy felt fidgety and went back upstairs to comb out her hair and try to blow dry it. She was still in her dressing gown, but thought better of it and pulled on jeans and Robbie's sunflower tee-shirt. It felt a bit tight, but it was clean and cheerful. It would do until she had to change for the dance. Downstairs, she pulled the ironing board from the cupboard under the stairs, fetched the basket of clothes and the iron and set herself up in front of the television, so that she could chat to the children while she did her least favourite job.

Finally she finished the ironing and put the last folded little shirt on the heap in the armchair with a satisfied 'there!' and looked round. Robbie was looking very glum.

"Daddy isn't coming, Mummy."

"I'm sure he'll be here in a minute," Lucy lifted the heap of clothes, "He's often a bit late."

"But Mum," added Aisling, "it's after half twelve."

353

"Is it?" Lucy put the ironing down and looked at her watch. Aisling was right. Martin was always late and twice had been very late. He might yet appear, all bonhomie and cheer for the children and 'this isn't necessary, you know,' for Lucy, as he again told her in an undertone that he was prepared to come back and forgive her for throwing him out. He didn't understand that she was unlikely to forgive him.

"I'll phone your Dad, something has kept him." Lucy dialled Colm's number and spoke with Colm's wife. As she listened, she sat slowly down onto the couch and when she hung up, it was very gently. She looked at Aisling and Robbie.

"Your Dad is in London. She's not sure for how long, but probably two weeks. I'm sorry."

"Why didn't he tell us?" Robbie was standing up, his hands clenched at his sides. "I hate you, you made him leave, he would be here now if you hadn't." He ran from the room, slamming the door.

"I don't know why he didn't tell you, Ash. I'm sorry. I'm sorry."

"I don't think it's your fault that he went to London, Mum. Robbie doesn't understand as much as me. I'm older." Aisling was looking at Lucy through tears. Lucy put her arms around her little daughter and hugged her hard.

"You don't have to understand, Ash. No-one should have to understand this stuff, not even me and I'm ancient. It's all right for you to be upset with me and your Dad. We'll do something this afternoon to try to cheer ourselves up." She kissed Aisling on the head and then went upstairs to comfort Robbie.

David went into the kitchen to see what there was for lunch and stood despondently in front of the open fridge, looking at a small piece of red cheddar and two eggs. He shut the fridge again and looked out the window at the summer garden, the overgrown grass that he should have mown, the straggly annuals that Clare had planted in the one clear bed. There was a slight haze of blue from a patch of cornflowers. The plastic table glared in the sun. Now, if I had some lettuce and several other things, and some enthusiasm, I could make an elegant salad and eat it al fresco, he thought as he wondered what to do with the meagre offerings in the fridge. I love good food, why do I forget to buy any? Maybe I'll skip lunch and go to that tea-dance. They do good sandwiches there.

"Dad?" A voice called from the hall and Clare brought a scent of sunshine into the room. "Lunchtime? What is it?"

"I didn't expect you back, you said you would be out all day."

"Yea. Change of plan. Boring story." She opened the fridge and looked in. "We've let this run down. Needs shopping. Let's go after lunch." She took out the cheese and the eggs and fished the sandwich toaster out of the cupboard. "Set the table, then I'll sort you out." David did what he was told, wondering not for the first time where Clare had got her facility with cooking. Not from him, or her mother. He watched as she worked, creating a tasty meal from odds and ends.

"If things had gone right, you'd have said Lucy taught her," said Jotin, wishing he could join in and taste the egg cheese and onion toasted sandwiches that were now sizzling in the machine, "but really they both learned in France, in that kitchen in Merillac."

Over lunch, David told Clare about Carmel and the tea dance, and tried to persuade Clare to go with him. But Clare refused, insisting they needed to go to the supermarket. She was not impressed by Carmel's hunch that David should go to the dance, pointing out that Carmel was a 'romantic old lady who's having a heart attack' and giving her opinion that as such, she was unlikely to be reliable.

"Oh, she was reliable, for the situation as it was a few hours ago. We were feeding her all the right cues," Jotin laughed and Clare's guide joined in.

"Yes," she said, "and now we're feeding you. You're the easiest of the lot to guide, my pet. You actually hear me, even if you are a bit of a cynic. And you are right, the supermarket is a great idea, even though you did think of it yourself. I'll go and talk to Trynor." And she was gone.

"Come on, Dad. Let's make a list."

Lucy had asked the children what they would like to do for the afternoon and they had tried to guess what Martin had planned for them, 'so we don't miss it' as Robbie explained solemnly. He had cheered up once an outing was promised. Good thing, thought Lucy, not to always be the boring 'go to school, time for bed' parent and get a chance to be the 'where would you like to go' one. They had a discussion of fun places and places they had never tried and old favourites. Lekna was busy, talking to Aisling. She had had an exciting visit from Clare's guide..

"How about the Natural History Museum, Mum? I like that."

"What's that?" Robbie had forgotten their visit there last year.

"You know, Robbie," said Aisling, "the Dead Zoo."

"Oh, yes! Whale bones!"

So it was decided. They would go into town, but on the way back they would stop off at the Merrion shopping centre and get some groceries. Robbie and Aisling would be allowed to choose what tonight's dinner would be. I hope I don't have to bribe them into happiness every weekend, thought Lucy. I hope Martin comes back and sees them again. Better phone Jen and tell her I can't go to the tea-dance.

"But they could come here, my Mum is coming to sit with our kids." Jen was insistent. For a moment Lucy weakened, after all, she had bought an outfit specially to go out in. But when she thought about it she remembered Robbie's face and she knew where she wanted to be.

"No, I've promised them a trip to the Natural History Museum. I can't just dump them with no warning. Maybe next weekend?"

The children enjoyed the whale skeleton and the stuffed animals; they were lucky and were allowed to see the glass replicas of microscopic creatures, while the curator explained to them how tiny the actual creatures are. Robbie was more impressed by the size of the whale, but Aisling was enthralled by being able to 'see' such tiny creatures. They came out into the sunshine and with promises of ice-cream, made their way to where they had parked on Baggot Street, talking all the way about the animals they had seen and agreeing that next time, maybe they should go to the real Zoo, to see some of them 'with their own insides and eyes' as Robbie put it.

Aisling and Robbie fought for the right to control the trolley and with Lucy behind them keeping peace and steering, they made their way into the supermarket. They started in the vegetable section and Lucy was choosing carrots when Aisling gave a squeak- 'Clare!' Lucy looked round.

"Look, Mum, over there, it's Clare!"

"Who?"

"Remember, Clare who babysat for Marge once, when we were there. She walked us home. She was nice."

"Oh yes, I remember vaguely," Lucy looked round and at the end of the next aisle saw a young woman with beautiful auburn hair and a full trolley, talking to an older man. He was taking jars off the shelf and studying them and then turning to Clare to ask her opinion. Clare said something, the man smiled and Lucy caught her breath.

"Will I go and say hello?" Aisling asked and Lucy nodded.

"Hello, Clare! Do you remember me? I'm Aisling and there's Robbie," she pointed, "And you met my Mum!" Aisling fell silent, suddenly dumbstruck. Lucy stood and smiled uncertainly at Clare. What on earth was she thinking, they had barely met once, nearly two years ago. Clare was too old to babysit then, she would be well out of that now. What would they have to talk about?

"Oh, hello, Mrs Fitzgerald!" said Clare.

Lekna kicked Aisling on the shin. Aisling yelped. Clare looked at her, her face a question.

"Mum doesn't call herself Mrs any more. Not since Daddy left. She's 'Ms' Browne now." She rubbed her shin and glared at Robbie, who stuck out his tongue at her.

"That's the girl, Aisling. We're nearly there." All their guides were gathered quietly around. If they had needed to breathe they would have been holding their breaths. They were holding a ring of energy around the little group and waiting. Selta whispered to Clare.

"Oh, I'm sorry to hear that, Ms Browne. Anyway, this is my Dad," she indicated the tall man beside her. Lucy looked at him again and he lifted his eyes to meet hers as he put out his hand to her.

"David Hyland," he said and his eyes lowered again. Lucy looked at them, followed their path and felt a giggle beginning to form deep inside her. This gorgeous man was checking her out. Me, she thought, me of the tiny boobs and here is a lovely guy, looking straight at them. First time that ever happened to me. Maybe it's the too tight tee-shirt.

"No, the flower."

She grinned, as she said "Lucy Browne" and looked David straight in the eye. She knew him from somewhere, she was sure of it. Her face still wore the delighted grin and David's began to match it, his mouth widening and his eyes crinkling. They stared at each other, still holding hands in a handshake that had never got off the ground. Clare looked from her father to this pretty woman and then at the two children, who were staring at their mother, wide-eyed.

"Aisling and Robbie," she said softly, bending down to them, "I think we should go and check out the sweets aisle for a minute, don't you?" She held out her hands to them and the three of them moved away, discussing the relative merits of Smarties and Skittles. Aisling looked back and saw her mother still holding hands with Clare's father. She thought she ought to be bothered, but she wasn't.

"I'm sure we've met before," said David.

"You bet!" chorused the five guides, "Come on, get on with it, we've got rid of the kids." The children's guides had stayed behind to watch, knowing not much could go wrong in the sweets aisle.

"Yes, it feels like that to me, too," said Lucy and she looked down at their linked hands. "So maybe that's why it doesn't feel odd to be holding hands with a total stranger?" Now why did I say that, she wondered, drawing attention to something embarrassing. But she wasn't embarrassed. And she still wasn't embarrassed when David raised her hand to his lips and bowed exaggeratedly over it, brushing the back of it with his lips and staring again at her breasts.

"Madame," he breathed, as he raised his eyes and looked into hers.

"Monsieur," Lucy answered, wondering only for the tiniest of moments had she gone mad, as she looked back into his eyes, captured by their depths.

"How about going for a coffee?" said David, returning to the modern day, "there's a café just outside. Leave the trolleys here, Clare will find them. Come on." He turned, still holding Lucy's hand and they moved together towards the café. They were both still smiling and looking at each other as they walked.

The guides began to relax, they looked round at each other and smiled. Then Jotin raised his arms in the air and began to shout,

"Yes! Yes! We did it!" He held his hand towards Trynor's and they copied the humans' 'high five', beginning to dance together, circling and weaving. The children's guides joined in, happy that all was at last working to plan and they began to sing a song of hope and triumph. Other guides, passing with their Saturday afternoon frazzled humans, asked what was going on and when it was explained they began to smile too, joining in the clapping and

dancing, so that very soon, the shop was full of dancing and circling guides, singing in triumph and all over the shop, people found themselves tossing wine, fillet steak, cakes and all manner of unnecessary treats into their trolleys and beginning to sing snatches of happy songs.

Over in the little café, David pulled out the chair for Lucy and as he leant over to push it in for her, he breathed in the scent from her hair.

Chapter 54
Four years later, China

She woke in the dark, with an aching damp between her legs, and as she remembered her cheeks became damp too, but the ache was deeper. For a moment she had been so happy, as she had heard her son's first cry. Then they had told her– it is only a girl. TieJuan looked down now, into the little crib and could just make out the form of her sleeping daughter, her tiny hands curling against her face. I will fight for you, she thought, I will fight for your survival, my pretty one. Yesterday had been loud, first the noise and excitement of the birth, but then the recriminations had filled the farmhouse. The tests had said it was a boy, so he had survived and would have been protected, to work the farm. But the tests were wrong and according to her husband's mother, it was TieJuan's fault, maybe she had even lied. She was accused of ingratitude, of theft, of cheating. She was tired now, tired of defending herself, and knew she would need all her energy to defend her daughter. My little one, she thought, my blood, my tears. Not unwanted, not at all. Even your father wants you and wants to love you, though he dares not admit it. His mother is too strong, has survived too much adversity, to accept defeat. If she wants a grandson, she will get a grandson. In horror and dread, TieJuan had heard through the door as it was explained how that might be possible, what fate might await this precious scrap of babyhood; she had clutched the baby tight to her and screamed defiance when the deceitful grandmotherly arms reached out.

Now in the dark she knew it could not be as she dreamed. She could not hide the baby all day and all night, she must work, in the house and in the fields. One day, there would be an accident. And then she would be free to have a son. A son she would love, of course, but bought with his sister's blood. No. Her mother-in-law was a forceful woman, but TieJuan would show her what real strength was. She eased herself slowly from the bed and though her husband sighed and turned over, he did not wake. Treading as softly as she could, she dressed warmly, for the nights were bitter in the winter. Then she gathered up the baby's clothes and put them in a small bag, which she wrapped with her daughter inside two little blankets and a quilt. She lifted the bundle and eased herself out of the room and into the kitchen. Laying the baby on the packed earth floor, she reached up to the decorated box in its place on a high shelf and helped herself to a small sum of money, not enough to attract attention. Then with the baby once more in her arms, she tiptoed out of the house.

The chilly air outside made her gasp and for a moment she felt faint, but she took a deep breath, even as she pulled the quilt over the baby's face. As the cold air hit her lungs, she felt her strength return and her resolve strengthen. She murmured reassurance to the dog, whose tail wagged twice before he drifted back to sleep. Then she was out of the farm, onto the track leading towards the village. TieJuan set herself a steady pace, not too fast, so that she would be able to keep it up and not become exhausted. Luckily the birth yesterday had not been particularly difficult, she was not too tired or sore. She trudged on, walking more gently when she reached the village and avoiding the gateways where she knew there were good guard dogs. One did smell her and stood up, stretching, his chain rattling, but she was soon past and no one was alerted. She almost smiled at the idea of someone stopping her. After all, she was solving the problem for her family, not committing a crime.

She walked on and on. The night was dark and overcast and it took all her concentration to keep to the road as it wound through the fields. After two or three hours she came to the bigger road, which ran straighter, between the two big towns. She hesitated, wondering which way to go, which town would be safer, or better. She had never been to either, as far as she knew. There was nothing to help her decide. She looked into the bundle in her arms and whispered "where would you like to live, my little one?" and after a moment was surprised when the baby turned her head and opened her eyes. TieJuan could just make out their gleam, as though she was looking towards the east, to the right. So TieJuan set her face that way, whispering again, "I hope you're right, my precious little one."

"Oh, she's right," said Mohmi. "I told her. We know what we're doing here. You would have forgotten even if we had been able to tell you." Mohmi smiled at TieJuan's guide, who was so close he was almost surrounding her. He smiled back and blew a kiss onto

TieJuan's head. TieJuan strode confidently along the road, her second last decision made. She was careful not to think too far ahead, she was just enjoying the feel of the bundle in her arms and the scratch of the cold air in her nostrils.

The baby began to wriggle and fuss, so TieJuan, glad of an excuse to stop for a while, moved to the side of the road and sat down, unwrapping the baby a little and loosening her own clothing so she could offer a breast. This was only the third time she had done this and it was still a wonderful novelty. She felt the baby's mouth searching and helped her, then they both settled to the suckling. It was over soon, there was no milk yet. As TieJuan prepared to turn the baby and offer the other breast, the clouds above parted and a sudden flood of silvery light engulfed them. The baby looked up at the white disc above and gave a little cooing sound, her first utterance that was not a cry. TieJuan laughed and kissed her.

"You have named yourself, little one" she said, looking down at the beautiful face with unusually pale brown eyes fringed with thick lashes, eyes that were still looking up at the moon. "You are ShengYue, Song of the Moon. I have nothing else to give you, but I can give you a name."

"So we come full circle, my friend" said Mohmi, "Even your name is right!" The baby gurgled and Mohmi could hear her thoughts clearly–'yes, but a lot could still go wrong'. Mohmi answered soothingly, "It won't, it's all going fine. Relax." The baby closed her eyes and concentrated again on feeding.

The winter dawn was just breaking as TieJuan carried ShengYue into the outskirts of the town. People were stirring but the streets were still quiet. On one corner a noodle seller was setting up his stall and TieJuan realised she was hungry. Even more, she was thirsty. She had not thought to bring any water with her as she crept away from the farm. She approached the man, feeling for her money.

"Can I buy some water?" She felt suddenly very tired, now that she was standing still and she swayed. The noodle seller indicated a crate. "Sit down and rest. In a few minutes I can sell you some tea." He looked at her, his shrewd eyes taking it all in. "You have come a long way, so early." He did not seem to need a response, so TieJuan stayed silent. "And the baby's mother?" TieJuan hesitated. "Dead, I suppose. Terrible. It happens and then the baby must go to the baby home. Such a shame. So many girls with no mothers." He handed TieJuan a cup and she bent her head, allowing the delicious familiar smell soothe her fraying mind. He knows, she thought, I am not the first. Other women have had to do what I must do. The idea was comforting for a moment and then the scale of the tragedy seemed so huge she could not stop the tears of fear and loss that streamed down her face. She tried to wipe them away on her sleeve and looked up at the noodle seller, who was sipping hot stock off a spoon, checking its flavour.

"Her name is ShengYue." The noodle seller looked down, surprised.

"A pretty name. Her mother's choice for her?"

"No" said TieJuan "she chose it herself, when she sang to the moon."

"They might change it, in the baby home, unless you tell them. How will they know?" He looked at her kindly and then rummaged through his things. He pulled out a piece of paper, the label from a sack of noodles, which had a fairly clean blank side and the stub of a pencil. "Here– write it for her."

TieJuan was embarrassed. "I do not know all those characters," she said. "Do you?"

"I think so. I'll try." He licked the tip of the pencil and wrote carefully, his tongue protruding from between his teeth as he formed the shapes.

"There. I think it says 'my name is ShengYue'" he said as he handed her the paper. She opened the quilt bundle and tucked the paper against ShengYue's tiny chest.

"Thank you," she said to the noodle seller, "it will make it easier for me. It is a tiny thing, all I can give her."

The noodle seller looked thoughtful and said nothing for a moment.

"Her guide looks more upset than they usually do and I've seen some," said the noodle seller's guide to Mohmi, nodding towards TieJuan's guide, who was wrapped round TieJuan, stroking her hair and murmuring to her.

"Yes, it's a slightly different story," said Mohmi, "TieJuan had agreed in spirit that she would take a life where her baby could die, that she wanted to experience a severe loss. But we discovered

recently that we need a baby, so her guide agreed on her behalf that she would give this baby away, rather than let it die. Harder for her, much harder. A dead baby's story is finished, an absent living one could haunt her always. Her guide feels it will be an even more useful experience for TieJuan, but I think he's feeling guilty just now, for putting her through this. I'm glad you're here."

"We're always here, or somewhere like this. My man hears me pretty accurately now, he's such an old soul. He's just in this life now to help others. It's fun to watch him, after millennia of having to get him out of tight corners." The noodle seller's guide glowed the soft deep purple of a wise old soul and he leant forward to whisper to his human. The noodle seller looked at TieJuan and his crinkled eyes were unnaturally bright. He opened his mouth to speak, closed it and then reconsidered.

"It seems to me that you are giving her more than that. A lot more. Forgive me if I am wrong, but I think you are giving her life. Twice." He turned back to his pot of bubbling stock and stirred it, avoiding TieJuan's eyes. She watched, her mind empty.

"In my day, we could have all the children we wanted. I have two daughters and a son," said the noodle seller. "I love them all." He scooped up a handful of dry noodles and dropped them into the stock, along with two pieces of chicken. TieJuan watched as the pot bubbled and the noodles rolled to the surface. She watched blankly as he scooped them out and into a bowl which he handed to her. She looked at the noodles and meat in the fragrant broth and thought it was the most wonderful meal she had ever been given. Her hunger overcame her and she ate quickly, draining the bowl and handing it back as she fumbled for her money. The noodle seller waved her hands away.

"No. No charge. It is my gift. And here is some water for later." He handed her a small plastic bottle. "If you pass later in the day, come back. There are always noodles." He smiled at her and at the baby. "Goodbye, ShengYue. May you always be as lucky in life as when you chose this mother." He turned away abruptly and TieJuan found herself thanking his back as he started to deal with his first customers.

TieJuan walked away through the streets. There were more people about now, all busy, pushing this way and that. She had no idea where to go. She walked on, putting some distance between herself and the noodle seller, feeling it was safer not to leave too clear a trail. Not that anyone will want to follow, she thought sadly. No, my husband will want to, but will not try to. He is too obedient. He will wait for his son. She was struck by a terrible thought. Would she have to make this journey again, with another daughter? Would she have the courage, twice? Oh, please, no, she thought, please let me have a boy next and enjoy his little hands and his searching mouth.

"You will, do not worry. And Mohmi will watch this baby for you. It will be all right." Her guide again wrapped his energy around her and held her tight. "Now forget that thought and go on."

TieJuan went up to an old woman who was sweeping her doorway and asked for directions to the baby home. This time there was no interest, no sympathy, but a fairly clear set of instructions. It was not too far.

The sun was shining feebly onto the low walls of the orphanage when TieJuan rounded the corner opposite. She could hear babies crying and childish voices talking shrilly. Through an open door she could see a line of tiny children sitting on a bench, waiting for something. They looked well fed and not unhappy. Still, she hesitated, wondering what exactly to do next. Then, one of the tiny girls saw her and toddled down the passageway towards her, saying 'Baby?' and pointing at ShengYue.

"Yes" said TieJuan, with more resolve in her voice than in her heart. "A baby for you," and she kissed her daughter and laid the bundle just inside the open doorway, at the toddler's feet. She turned and walked away quickly, trying not to look back, but at the corner she turned and saw that the little girl had squatted down and was stroking the quilt, squeaking 'My baby! My baby!' until a woman came to the door and picked up the bundle. She looked out of the door, up and down the street, but TieJuan moved out of sight, watching with just one eye until the nurse carried ShengYue into the darkness of the house. Then TieJuan walked away, starting the long trek back to her village and saying to herself over and over, "I am going to have a baby, I am going to have a son," hoping that the repetition would make it true.

Chapter 55

The heat in the nursery of the orphanage was oppressive on this summer afternoon. Many babies lay listlessly in their cots, their little heads sweaty. Some of the older ones were sitting up looking around and one or two had toys that they were waving in the air, delighting in the noise when their unplanned movements caused a crash against the bars of the cots.

"Look at you ShengYue! Are you trying to beat your way out?" A nurse had come into the room with a pile of washed laundry which she was now putting on shelves. She smiled at the babies and the little girl she had addressed waved her arms again and grinned.

"You are happy today! Maybe today is your lucky day!" The nurse bent down and kissed the little head, which had a mop of slightly wavy hair. Then she moved on, talking in turn to the other babies.

"She's right, ShengYue. It is your 'lucky' day- or will be if you keep smiling!" Mohmi was there beside the cot, playing with the baby, waving her arms, encouraging ShengYue to copy her. When the baby mimicked her correctly she congratulated her with great enthusiasm and ShengYue cooed and gurgled.

"My, you are cheerful today," said the nurse.

"We both are, we have high hopes!" said Mohmi. The other babies' guides were quiet, knowing nothing was planned for them today, but enjoying Mohmi and Moonsong's happiness.

"Well, let's get you all cleaned up before the visitors arrive," said the nurse, as she started to undress and change one of the babies. She worked steadily, changing each child, talking a little to each one, but efficient and almost brusque all the same. She was just putting the last baby back into its cot and was leaving the room to start preparing the next feeds, when she heard a car pull up outside. She scampered off down the stairs. *Mohmi followed* and ShengYue strained to see where she had gone, feeling suddenly alone. Her little mouth began to pucker and her lip to tremble. *Then Mohmi was back and with her was an old friend.*

"They are on their way. They are looking for you. Remember what we discussed," said Trynor and he was gone again. ShengYue looked at the doorway, at the other side of the room, with two cots between her and it. She looked at Mohmi, uncertain. There were footsteps on the stairs and then they could hear a woman's voice, speaking a language that was unfamiliar.

"Oh, David, I'm nervous. Or excited." There was an answering mutter in a deeper voice. Then a group of people came into the room. The director of the orphanage, carrying a big file, an unfamiliar woman who was talking to the director and then the two strangers. Strangers with light hair and big noses. ShengYue looked at them and began to smile tentatively. Lucy and David stood just inside the door, looking around at all the little cots, only half listening as the director explained the wonders of the orphanage and was translated. They were holding hands, squeezing each other as they prepared to make a momentous decision.

"All these babies suitable for you," said the translator, "we can give you detail of each one. Which one you like to start with?"

"We want a very young baby, don't we, David?" asked Lucy, "so that he or she is really ours." David nodded and the translator talked to the director for a moment. Then she pointed to the cot near the window.

"This little girl just three weeks old," she said. "You want to hold her?" Lucy moved to the cot and looked in. The baby looked around with uncoordinated eyes. Lucy put down a finger and touched the little head. The fine downy hair was soft.

"She's lovely."

"Or this one is five weeks. Bigger. Stronger girl when older." This baby's eyes were beginning to focus and she seemed to look at Lucy with a solemn stare.

"Hello, beautiful" said Lucy. David, beside her, said nothing, but reached out to the baby's hand. The little fingers grasped David's and he was plunged back through the years, remembering his twins and all the difficulties of those times. He shook himself, trying to return to the present.

"Here another little baby. Not sure but think one month old. Good health."

"Are they not all in good health?" Lucy was alarmed.

"Oh yes. Very good. Good food, clean, all injections. Is all on papers." She indicated the file in the director's arms.

"Oh, David, how do we choose? How can we say come with us to one and leave all the others? What will happen to them?"

"I don't know, love. But I'm sure it's not like the Cat and Dog's home. They aren't going to put them down." He was trying to stay light, but privately he agreed with Lucy. How could they choose?

"Come on David," said Jotin. "We've got you this far, don't go forgetting on us now. You're here for a special baby, not just any baby. Look around."

"Maybe if we spend some time and just talk to each one, something will come clear," said David, beginning to walk between the lines of cots. Lucy followed, looking at each child, thinking how beautiful they were, with their dark almond eyes and black hair. How could their mothers bear to part with them? She turned to the translator to ask this, but the translator either did not understand her, or chose not to.

"No mothers. No fathers. Orphans. Most left at doorway. Some with some clothes. Some wrapped in paper."

Lucy felt worse than ever. Her Aisling and Robbie had been so lucky, she thought. And David's girls.

"And one of these. Come on, girl. She's here. Look for her." Trynor was nearly dancing with frustration. He turned to Jotin. "They are still so deaf! They want her, they've come all this way for her and now they decide they want an infant and get all worked up about the others, who are nothing to do with us at all!"

"No, but they don't know that. And they are good people, full of compassion. That is how it should be. There is no learning if they know too clearly. Now, come on, what can we do?" Jotin, Trynor and Mohmi came together for a moment, and then, smiling at each other, each went back to his own person. Trynor nudged Lucy. Lucy turned and walked away from the cribs with the tiny babies. She thought she would clear her head by looking at some of the older ones, seeing what condition they were in. She looked around and noticed a baby sitting up, looking solemnly towards her. Lucy moved towards her, noticing a slight wave in her fine baby hair and eyes that were more brown than black. *Mohmi stepped between ShengYue and Lucy.*

"Now my little one," she said, holding out her arms to ShengYue, "now is the time you raise your arms to me and smile.

Everything is wonderful!" and she smiled and laughed at the baby, making faces at her. In response ShengYue giggled and raised her arms. Lucy stepped right up to the cot and lifted the baby up, kissing her nose. ShengYue giggled again and waved her little arms. In her baby mind she felt this woman was just right. Lucy turned to the translator.

"Can you ask what was left with this baby?" The director consulted her file.

"Two little blankets, a few clothes, a quilt. And a piece of paper saying 'my name is ShengYue'," said the translator.

"Does ShengYue mean anything?"

"Yes. It mean Song of the Moon."

"Song of the Moon. Moonsong." Lucy felt a prickle down her spine. "How beautiful. I wonder why she got that name? It must have been important, or the note wouldn't have been left with her. Moonsong. I wonder is there an English name for that? David, what will we call her in English?" Lucy turned to him, holding their new daughter and he came over and put a hand on each of them.

"So we have chosen you, have we?" The baby smiled at him and waved her arms again.

Mohmi, Trynor and Jotin stood together, watching. Their energies were soft and relaxed, exuding happiness and relief. The other guides in the room smiled too.

"So we start from seven months now. They can bring her home and bring her up. She will be well," said Mohmi, happy to be released from the need to constantly guard her child, now that she had found her parents.

"Mm. It will be good to have a simple existence again," said Jotin, as they watched the family getting to know each other again. "There is nothing else to learn for the moment. Just to enjoy the world and each other. Nothing to go wrong this time."

"No" said Trynor "what could possibly go wrong?"

There was a long silence. They smiled a little sheepishly at each other. Then for a moment, Mohmi was gone. She came back, looking satisfied.

"I visited TieJuan, the baby's mother and had a word with her guide. She is well and expecting her son. She was napping, so we sent her a dream of this scene. When she wakes she will know her

370

daughter is safe." Mohmi indicated the new family and went over and whispered to Sheng Yue.

A wonderful chuckle of baby laughter echoed through the room.

~~~~ ~~~~

Author's Note

"Despite the Angels" is entirely a work of fiction. It is not necessary to believe in reincarnation, guardian angels, or spirit guides to enjoy it. None of the characters are based on, or intended to represent, real people living or dead, and similarities are purely coincidental, with one small exception, see 'Dundee' below. However, I have used some historical places and events on which to hang my story.

Crete. Tylissos was an actual Minoan village, and there is a modern town of the same name. The sanctuaries were actually on the top of the high mountains which surround the town, but I have invented one on a lower hill, maybe the site of the modern church, as Alessia could not run up such high mountains in the time available.

Bull dancing did happen in Minoan Crete, there are frescoes showing it (and showing the breast-baring bodices) but the religion in the story is my invention. Diktynna was a name used for the mother-goddess around this period. Double headed axes were a commonly used symbol.

I have re-named the palace of Malia as Malatos to distance the reader from the modern pie-and-chips resort. A sword with a crystal pommel may be seen in the museum in Heraklion. A pendant in the shape of two bees was found between the Malia palace and the sea, dating from earlier than this story. It is my fancy that it was made by an ancestor of Mikolos, and the symbol remained in the family. I made the name Armishamai from the words for song and moon in one of the ancient languages.

The Diktean cave on the Lassithi plain can still be visited, and was used by the Minoans as a sanctuary. Various offerings were found at the base of the stalactites.

Recent evidence suggests that there may have been some human sacrifice in Minoan Crete. My own instinct about this is that it is more likely to have occurred in the post-tsunami era, when the society was crumbling, and fear and insecurity would have been more prevalent. It is unlikely to have been found necessary in the peaceful matriarchal pre-tsunami society, so that is why Jotin reassures Trynor that he is safe.

In the Médoc, I have invented the Château of Merillac, and have placed it on a piece of land I have risen from the salt marsh somewhere north of Jau-et-Dignac, near the modern village of Talais. The church of Notre Dame du Fin du Terre at Soulac-sur-Mer is still there, now dug out of the sand. (Soulac was rebuilt as a seaside resort in the early 1900s.) Salt gathered from the marshes was a major source of income. Many châteaux and large farms were burnt out in the summer of 1789, by peasants who were panicky about the slow progress of the revolution. The name deVrac is an invention (by Daniel's great grandfather, who had a sense of irony) – 'vin en vrac' means wholesale wine.

Dundee did suffer from the dreadful Tay Bridge Disaster, much as described. None of the people mentioned is based on any actual person involved, with the unavoidable, and I hope harmless, exception of the kindly station-master, who did send the relatives home when he heard the bad news, hoping to save them a sleepless night. I hope his relatives will forgive me for putting words into his mouth. The exact number of casualties cannot be told, though there are estimates of around ninety. Babies would not have been recorded, as they did not need tickets. 'High Girders' by John Prebble gives most of the known facts.

A whale was towed ashore as described; and chips (French fries) were introduced to Dundee in the 1870s by Edward de Gernier from Belgium.

China has a one-child policy, but in fact a real TieJuan would be allowed a second baby as she is from a farming family, and her first child is a girl. But her mother-in-law is an unpleasant woman, who does not want to waste money rearing a girl, who will belong to her husband's family when she marries, and be of no further financial value to her birth family. My thanks to Dr XeiMei (Anna) Lee for help in naming TieJuan and ShengYue. Tie-Juan means iron-flower, so this name suits a strong country girl. Chinese parents often choose names which represent their hopes for their children. TieJuan's parents certainly got a strong daughter.

The spirit world. This information comes from my own personal and professional experience, but mostly from my imagination. I have also borrowed loosely and inaccurately from the works of Dr Brian Wiess and Dr Michael Newton.

For those who have not noticed: Hetrion in Crete re-incarnates as Etienne in the Médoc, and possibly as Edward McIntyre in Cupar. Rasifi in Crete becomes Rosemarie in France, and then Dorothy's mother Rose in Cupar. None of these characters has taken a life in the Dublin story. It is also completely unnecessary for souls to take names (or bodies) that resemble those they have had in other lives. I did it this way to make it easier for the reader to see who was who.

A note for my readers in America.

My spellings are all UK/Irish, and are correct (unless they get tangled during the publishing process!). As the story is set in Ireland it is appropriate that the language should be Irish, and I hope you will get used to it, as I have got (gotten!) used to American usage when reading books set in America. In case the meanings of all the words have not been clear, here are some 'translations': All through the story 'eejit' appears, this is the Irish form of 'idiot'. In Chapter 1 a 'choc-ice' is a bar of ice cream on a stick, covered with a thin layer of chocolate. Chapter 11 has 'willie', a colloquial term for penis, and 'hooer', which is a Dublin pronunciation of 'whore'; on the other hand 'feck' is not an Irish spelling of the usual swear word, but a separate word in common use, which is not considered vulgar, it is rather like 'heck'. In Chapter 12 hair is like a 'conker' which is a horse-chestnut, which are a beautiful shade of rust brown. Chapter 15 mentions David's 'C.V.', this is a 'resumé' or 'curriculum vitae'. The 'fish fingers' in Chapter 38 are called 'fish sticks' in America, I think. In Ireland and the UK we 'hoover' our carpets with a vacuum cleaner, (Chapter 41). In Chapter 45 'Clare was too cute' means she was canny, not adorable! Chapter 49 has Lucy struggling with the 'boot' of her car. This is called the 'trunk' in America. And finally, 'having a jar' (Chapter 51) means having a drink, usually a pint of beer.

My grateful thanks are also due to:

My father, Dick Stringer, who told me during his final illness that his big regret in leaving this world was that he had not 'written a novel or designed a cathedral'. Well, Dad, I couldn't manage the cathedral, but this book is for you.

My husband George Gogan, who put a line through a whole day per week in my appointment book and insisted that I 'get that book finished'. This is for you, too.

Gerry Clabby who, when we were on a story-telling course together, asked me 'How long have you been a writer?' which gave me the courage to start.

Mme Micheline Cassou-Mounat of Bordeaux University, who gave me very useful information about the economic situation in the Médoc at the end of the 18th century.

Members of the Dalkey Writers' Workshop; of the 'BeCreative' e-publishing course; of the Facebook groups Indie Writers Unite and especially of the Alliance of Independent Authors for many pieces of information and encouragement.

Fergal Holmes, Nigel McGuiness, Derek Palmer and Máire Iremonger for their participation in the production of the book trailer, 'A Frustrated Angel'. Find it on YouTube.

Andrew Brown of Design for Writers, for the cover design; Jane Adams, of The Literary Consultancy for her sensible editorial advice; and David Heap for checking that my spelling and grammar are up to scratch.

Many other friends who put up with me in their different ways while I was writing this book. They have promised enjoy it; I hope they do!

Coming soon: "Revisited Sins"

If you have enjoyed "Despite the Angels", you will want to look out for its sister novel, which will be published in 2014.
Here is a short preview:

Revisited Sins, Prologue

I need your help. Well, actually, anybody's help, so if you know anyone who is good at solving problems, please rope them in. I'm beginning to feel desperate. Of course I should be able to sort this out this on my own, I've had all the training, and plenty of time to think about it, but maybe that is the problem. Too much time and too much involvement. I care such a lot, you see.

I love Gina, and I don't want to see her make a mess of this, and at the moment she is poised to make one huge cock-up. So huge it will ruin this life for her completely, and it might have worse repercussions than that, which would really piss me off. She is letting emotion run away with her over something that should be nothing. But that is the way with humanity, making mountains out of molehills and storms in tea-cups all the time. Of course, she doesn't have all the information. She would be calmer if she did, but I can't tell her.

So I'm telling you. It's not a mystery, you don't have to work out 'whodunnit'. I'll give you all the facts, and at the end, you give me your opinion. Okay?

Now, my Gina. I think of her as Ayolo, of course, because that's what we call her here on what fanciful humans call the 'other side'. As though this wasn't the real place, and all those earth lives just learning opportunities. Ayolo has been friends with Halla ever since they were both put into the same group as infant souls, and both of them are living lives in Dublin now. Halla is called Alan this time around, and Gina and he are married. Because Ayolo and Halla have been together for millennia, I know Alan pretty well too, and really care what happens to him. Usually his guide and I make a good team, but at this stage we're both stumped.

I think it's time for you to meet Ayolo and Halla. I mean Gina and Alan. I need to take you back about five weeks, - no, let's go back six, to before Clive came. To an ordinary average evening.....